# THEIR ESCAPE BECAME
# A ROLLER COASTER RIDE

As the pilot put the plane through a series of maneuvers that just managed to prevent their pursuers from opening fire, Hanae huddled against Sam. He felt her shaking and smelled the sweat of her fear. She gripped him tighter. He looked down to see her staring out the windows into the darkness.

"What is it?"

"I don't know," she replied. "I thought I saw . . . There! There it is again."

At first all he saw was darkness and the lights of the metroplex. Then Sam saw the creature breathe a short burst of flame. The backflash shone on the beast, highlighting its scaly snout and ivory dagger teeth. Sam could deny it no longer—that was a Dragon in the skies of Seattle. . . .

# SHADOWRUN: NEVER DEAL
# WITH A DRAGON

D1440083

### Exploring New Realms
### in Science Fiction/Fantasy Adventure

*Titles already published or in preparation:*

## The Day It Rained Forever by Ray Bradbury

Myth-maker extraordinaire Ray Bradbury has created in his writing a world of uncanny beauty and fear. In this collection of twenty-three classic stories there are the gentle Martians of *Dark They Were and Golden-Eyed*, the killers of *The Town Where No One Got Off*, the sweet sounds of *The Day it Rained Forever* and much, much more.

## Of Time and Stars by Arthur C. Clarke

Strange new worlds stretch the imagination and the emotions as Arthur C. Clarke writes of Earth's destruction, trouble with computers, creatures from other planets, spaceflight and the future.

## The Neverending Story by Michael Ende

Bastian Balthazar Bux is nobody's idea of a hero, least of all his own. One day he steals a mysterious book and hides away to read it – only to find himself stepping through its pages into the world of Fantastica. Enchanted, perilous, dying, Fantastica is waiting for a Messiah, its faery people doomed, until Bastian appears as their Saviour ...

## Walker of Worlds Book 1: Chronicles of the King's Tramp by Tom Dehaven

Jack, a Walker, is in danger. He has learned a secret; he has earned an enemy. Jack must flee the world of Lostwithal. He must flee to Kemolo. The secret he carries could mean the end of all the worlds, not just his own. But Jack cannot violate the Order of Things, not even to preserve it. Jack, a Walker, must walk the worlds.

SECRETS OF POWER
VOLUME 1

SHADOWRUN:

# NEVER DEAL WITH A DRAGON

# ROBERT N. CHARRETTE

A ROC BOOK

ROC

Published by the Penguin Group
Penguin Books Ltd, 27 Wrights Lane, London W8 5TZ, England
Viking Penguin, a division of Penguin Books USA Inc.
375 Hudson Street, New York, New York 10014, USA
Penguin Books Australia Ltd, Ringwood, Victoria, Australia
Penguin Books Canada Ltd, 2801 John Street, Markham, Ontario, Canada L3R 1B4
Penguin Books (NZ) Ltd, 182–190 Wairau Road, Auckland 10, New Zealand

Penguin Books Ltd, Registered Offices: Harmondsworth, Middlesex, England

First published in the USA 1990
First published in Great Britain 1991
1 3 5 7 9 10 8 6 4 2

Roc is a trademark of New American Library, a division of
Penguin Books USA Inc. Shadowrun, and the distinctive Shadowrun
logo, are trademarks of the FASA Corporation,
1026 W. Van Buren, Chicago, Ill. 60507

Printed in England by Clays Ltd, St Ives plc

To Paul, for fellowship on the long and twisted path
from Hawkmoor to
the Sixth World.

## Acknowledgments

As usual, the first thanks go to Liz for the usual effort above and beyond the call. Additional thanks go to the suits and the aesthetic police at FASA for the typical job of trouble-shooting and troublemaking. We all survived it again. Thanks also to Nix Smith for the loan of Castillano. And, of course, thanks to the original shadowrunning team, without whom etc.

PROLOGUE

# Into The Shadows

# 2050

The soft roar of the surf slowly dissolved into the murmur of voices and the breathy huff of the air-conditioning system. The sharp salt smell mutated to the harsh tang of disinfectant. The return to the waking world brought awareness of the ache in Sam's skull. His brain felt too full, pressing against its boundaries like a helium-filled balloon under a fathom of water.

The voices stopped as he let out a groan. Whoever was out there in the world beyond his closed eyelids seemed to await another sign, some indication that he really was awake. But Sam was not yet ready to accommodate them. The light was painful enough through the thin flesh that shielded his pupils. He had not the least desire to open his eyes.

"Verner-*san*," a disembodied voice said. The tone was questioning, but held a hint of command.

He forced his eyes open, only to snap them shut again as the fluorescent stabbed for his brain. His involuntary wince and moan brought an immediate response from one of his visitors. The lights dimmed, encouraging Sam to venture a second attempt. Squinting, he surveyed his four guests.

Standing by the door, her hand still on the dimmer switch, was a woman in a white lab coat. His doctor. Her benign smile left no doubt that she was pleased with her handiwork. The other three people in the room were males. Two of the men Sam recognized at once. The third was apparently a bodyguard.

Seated at his bedside was the impressive figure of Inazo

Aneki, master of the sprawling Renraku corporate empire. The old man's presence was as surprising to Sam as the obvious concern on his lined face. Sam was no more than a minor employee of Renraku, and he had yet to make any significant contribution to the corporation. Nor had his implant operation been anything out of the ordinary, by twenty-first-century standards. It was true that the director had sponsored Sam into the company, and some said he looked on Sam with special favor. However, the old man and his supposed protégé had not been in personal contact since that brief introductory interview. All the more surprising to find Aneki-sama here in the recovery room.

Standing behind Aneki was Hohiro Sato, Vice President of Operations and the director's current executive assistant. In some ways, the dapper Sato's presence was even more astonishing. The pinch-faced official had a reputation of indifference to any subordinate's problems unless it affected the company's profits. In his infrequent encounters with Sato, Sam always came away chilled by the man's distant manner and perfunctory politeness.

Why were they here?

"We are pleased to see you awake, Verner-*san*," Sato said briskly. Belying the words, his gold-irised Zeiss eyes speared Sam with the contempt for non-Japanese that Sato rarely displayed before his superiors. If his voice held any emotion, it was certainly not pleasure. Sato was obviously not at Sam's bedside of his own volition. He was here, as formal protocol compelled, in the role of Aneki's intermediary to one of a lower social position. "We have anxiously awaited your return to the waking world."

"*Domo arigato.*" Sam's dry voice rasped out the formal thanks. His attempt to rise and bow was stifled by a head shake from the doctor and a raised hand from Aneki. "I am unworthy of your attention."

"Aneki-*sama* is the best judge of that, Verner-*san*. The doctor assures him that your datajack implant operation was routine and totally successful, but he wished to see for himself."

At the mention of his new addition, Sam reached up to touch the bandages. His head did not register the touch, but his fingers could feel the hard lump on his right temple. He knew from the pre-operation interview what it was: a chromium steel jack designed to accept a standard computer-interface plug. The addition of the datajack was intended to increase his efficiency in handling computer files and accessing data. Sam would have preferred to continue operating through a terminal keyboard, but the corporation had mandated a datajack for someone of his position and rank. Sam had, of course, agreed.

"I guess I'll be ready to get back to work soon," he mused aloud.

"A week or so of rest would be advisable, Verner-*san*," the doctor said softly. "Limited-access familiarization at first."

"Sound advice," Sato cut in. "Renraku has too much invested to permit an ill-timed return to a normal schedule. But all will work out for the best. You would have little time to resume your researches, with all the details of your move."

Move? Sam didn't understand. He wasn't planning a move.

Ignoring Sam's questioning look, Sato barely missed a beat. "It is perhaps regrettable that you cannot return immediately to work, but the timing is fortunate. Your transfer to the arcology project in Seattle—"

"Transfer?"

Sato's face soured briefly at Sam's interruption.

"Indeed, this is so. I hasten to assure you that Aneki-*sama* does not intend it as a demotion. He continues to hold you in the highest esteem. Nevertheless, he believes that your particular talents will best serve the corporation in Seattle.

"The company has taken the liberty of transferring your apartment lease. All your goods, save those you will need for the rest of your hospital stay and for the trip, have been packed for shipment." Sato nodded as though being reminded by a secretary. "And your dog has already begun the journey. She seemed in excellent health and should pass easily through the local quarantine kennels.

"As an expression of Aneki-*sama*'s regret at the suddenness of the transfer, Renraku Corporation will absorb all travel and relocation expenses. Your tickets for the JSA suborbital flight to North America are waiting with your personal effects. You will leave as soon as the doctor certifies you sufficiently recovered."

Sam was dazed. How could this be? When he had entered

the hospital two days ago, he had been a rising star in the staff operations office of Renraku Central. What of all those rumors that Aneki was a patron of Sam's career? He had seemed assured of great things with the company. Now they were exiling him to the corporation's North American operation. Even though the transfer was to the relatively prestigious arcology project, it would take him away from the main office, the heart of the corporation, away from Tokyo, his chosen home. It was clear that he had fallen . . . no, been kicked . . . off the fast track. What had he done?

Had he offended Aneki-*sama?* A covert look at the director's face showed only sympathy and concern.

Had he crossed a rival or insulted a superior? In a rapid mental review of his recent activities and projects, he dismissed that as well. He had been courteous to all, often beyond what was expected. That was his way of trying to make up for the fact that he was not a native Japanese. In all his time in Japan, Sam had never encountered more than the ordinary distrust and dislike the natives accorded any non-Japanese. Surely, his behavior was not at fault.

Nor could his work have given cause for what Sam could only perceive as a demotion, despite Sato's denial. He routinely put in long hours, completing his assignments with thoroughness and on time.

So what had he done?

He searched Sato's face for a clue. If the man's expression hinted at anything, it was impatience and boredom. Sam suspected that Sato had no personal interest in Samuel Verner and must consider this visit an interruption of other important work.

"Perhaps the director . . .'' Sam began haltingly. "If he would be so kind as to inform me of whatever fault has occurred, I could correct it.''

"Your request is impertinent,'' Sato snapped.

Aneki looked distinctly uncomfortable, then rose from his seat before Sam or Sato could say any more. He sketched a bow to Sam and headed for the door, oblivious to Sam's own return nod, the best he could manage while lying in the bed, and the doctor's deep formal bow.

"Enjoy your rest,'' Sato said as he followed the bodyguard toward the door. He, too, ignored the doctor. As the vice-president reached the doorway, he paused and turned briefly toward Sam.

"Condolences on your recent loss."

"Loss?" Sam was more baffled than ever.

"The regrettable incident with your sister, of course."
Sato's expression was of utterly feigned innocence.

"Janice? What's happened to my sister?"

Sato turned away without another word, but not before
Sam caught the vicious smile that lit the man's face when
he thought no one could see. As Sato retreated down the
corridor, Sam's repeated questions echoed vainly after him.

Sam tried to stand, intending to follow and force an answer, but a wave of dizziness slammed him the moment one
foot touched the floor. Head spinning, he fell limply into
the arms of the doctor. Struggling with his weight, the
woman returned him to the bed and insisted that he lie quietly. He let her rearrange the bedclothes for a few minutes
before he reached out to grab her arm.

The doctor stiffened at his presumption. "You are over-
wrought, Verner-san. You must rest quietly or risk damage
to the delicate connections in your neural circuits."

"Damn the circuits! I want to know what's going on!"

"Impertinence and physical coercion are not the recommended methods of polite inquiry."

Sam knew she was right, but he ached with concern for
his sister. She was all he had left since their parents and
siblings died on that terrible July night in 2039.

He unclenched his hand and lowered it slowly. He was
shaking with the effort to control himself. "Please excuse
my improper behavior."

The doctor massaged her arm briefly and smoothed down
the sleeve of her immaculate, white lab coat. "Severe emotional states can result in uncontrolled behavior, Verner-
san. Such behavior among the wrong people or at the wrong
time could be disastrous. You do understand this?"

"Yes, doctor. I understand."

"Very well. You had a question."

"If you would be so kind?" He waited for her nod of
assent. "Doctor, do you have any idea what Sato-sama
meant about my sister?"

"Regrettably, I do."

She seemed reluctant to continue, but Sam had to know.
No matter how bad it was. "Tell me, doctor," he prodded.
"Please."

The doctor gave him a long, steady look. "Two days ago,

your sister began *kawaru.* We felt it best not to inform you before the operation.''

"Lord, no." The horror of it washed over Sam. *Kawaru* . . . the Change, as the Japanese so politely named it. Goblinization was the word that the English-speaking world used for the process that distorted and restructured an ordinary person's organs and bones into one of the metahuman subspecies known as Orks or Trolls. Occasionally, the unfortunate victim was warped into something far worse. "How can it be? She's seventeen. If she were going to change, it would have happened before. She was safe."

"Are you an expert on *kawaru,* Verner-*san?* Perhaps you should instruct the scientists at the Imperial Research Institute.'' The doctor's face was stern. ''The best of our researchers have yet to unravel the mystery of *kawaru.*''

"It's been thirty years," Sam protested.

"Not quite. But it has been long decades of frustration for those seeking the cure. We know so little even now.

"When the somatic mutation event first struck, it affected some ten percent of the world's population, but, in the chaos, few had a chance to study or understand the phenomenon. We are able to make observations now, but because *kawaru* has become less common, we have less opportunity to do so.

"We learn a little bit with each case studied, but we still grope in the dark of ignorance. There is so much variation. The best we can do is identify those who *might* change. And even that only after lengthy genetic testing."

"Testing that Janice and I never had."

"Even if you had, the results are not completely reliable. Families of ordinary background still produce children who might undergo *kawaru.*''

"Then there's no hope."

"We are still studying the biological changes in the strange new races of man that *kawaru* has unleashed upon the world. Their reproduction, and the continued occurrences of the mutation event, remain a puzzle to our best minds. How is it that some of the Changed breed true, perpetuating whatever form they have taken, while others produce children who are perfectly normal humans? Still others have offspring who appear to be normal humans, only to experience *kawaru* later in life, when they metamorphose into some *thing* else. Even the best genotyping cannot predict who will be affected or what he will become."

"It must be magic, then," Sam whispered.

One of Sam's earliest memories was of a man's face coming on the family tridscreen to talk with conviction and emotion of a new world, an Awakened World. The man said that magic and magical beings had reawakened in the world to challenge technology—not just for supremacy, but for the very survival of the Earth. The man called on people to abandon their technology, to go back to the land and live simply.

But Sam's father had never accepted the way the coming of magic had twisted the ordered scientific world beyond anything recognizable. He had raised his son in traditional ways, avoiding almost all contact with the Changed world. Even on their trips to zoos, the family had avoided the paranatural exhibits that displayed griffins, phoenixes, and other creatures once thought legendary.

"Magic?" the doctor scoffed in perfect imitation of his father's tone. "There may indeed be magic loose in the world, but only a weak-minded fool relies on it as the explanation to every mystery. Your corporate record indicates that you are no simpleton who believes magical spells are all-powerful and that mystical energies can accomplish anything. The so-called mages who infest our corporate structures have their limits. They may manipulate energies in ways that seem to contravene the physical laws we understood in the last century, but their alleged sorceries must have boundaries and will be understood in time.

"Progress has been slow. We lost so much valuable data when research facilities were destroyed in the chaos that followed the first massive outbreak of *kawaru*. How could dedicated scientists cope with the unnatural and unexpected when all order was crumbling around them, swept away in the hatred, fear, and loathing that engulfed the world as men, women, and even children were warped?

"Those days of chaos are behind us now. In time, we will understand *kawaru*, perhaps even be able to prevent or reverse it. But we will do so scientifically. The ephemera of magic offer no hope."

The doctor was voicing beliefs that Sam had grown up with, but the words had a hollow ring. He felt empty, scoured by despair at what had happened to his sister. Their

father had tried to protect his family from the twisting of
the Change, but now it was thrust upon them with a violence that tore both Sam's and Janice's lives out of joint.
Whatever perverse power fueled goblinization had taken his
own sister. How was it possible? Sam fought down a scream
of anguish.

"How is she, doctor? Will she be all right?"

The doctor touched his shoulder in a gesture of sympathy.
"It is difficult to be sure, Verner-*san*. She is undergoing a
lengthy Change. Her vital signs are strong, but the ordeal
seems far from over."

"I want to see her."

"That would be ill-advised. She is comatose and would
receive no comfort from your presence."

"I don't care. I still want to see her."

"It is not in my hands, Verner-*san*. The Imperial Genet-
ics Board permits only the attending medical teams to enter
the *Kawaru* ward. It could be dangerous should a patient
suddenly complete the Change and go berserk."

"But you could smuggle me in, couldn't you?" he
pleaded. "I could wear an orderly's gown . . . pretend to
be a medical student."

"Perhaps. But discovery would be a disaster. For you.
For me. Even for your sister. It would almost certainly result in revocation of her relocation funds, should she survive. Her adjustment to the new life she faces will be
difficult enough. And you would surely lose whatever status
you have left with your corporation."

"I don't care about myself. She'll need me."

"She will need you to be working and bringing in a salary. You can help her best by obeying your superiors. There
is nothing you can do here in the hospital."

"You don't understand . . ."

"No, Verner-*san,* you are wrong." The physician shook
her head slowly, her eyes wells of sadness. "I understand
too well."

Her image swam before his eyes as she spoke. For a moment, Sam thought it was tears for his sister that blurred his
vision, then he realized that the doctor must have directed
the bed to inject a tranquilizer.

His earlier dream of the ocean returned, and he was
dragged down by an irresistible current, down into a yawning darkness where grinning Trolls and Goblins reached for

him. Struggle as he might against it, he only continued to tumble deeper down. A new lassitude crept through his limbs and flooded toward his brain. The visions of monsters faded with his awareness, leaving only a bright circle of pain throbbing at the side of his head. Then that too faded, swallowed up in oblivion.

Darkness had covered the land for some hours when the Elf stepped out under the sky to relieve himself. The forest was full of soft sounds, its life undisturbed by the presence of the lone Elf. A slight breeze meandered among the great dark boles of the trees, tickling their leaves into a soft rustle. The same wayward air played with strands of his white hair and caressed his skin, making the Elf smile with pleasure.

Though he did not call this forest his home, as did many of his kind, he always felt its powerful lure. There was great peace among the looming wooden giants, peace even amid the nightly games of survival unfolding all around him. Sometimes he even wished to remain here, but that did not happen often. His work was important to him, and it was work he could rarely do here.

He looked up at the sky, rejoicing in the multitude of stars showing through the gaps in the clouds to shed their light on him. So many, burning through the cold of space with tantalizing promises of their hoard of universal knowledge. Someday, he promised them, we will come to you.

A slight motion caught the Elf's attention. A falling star, he thought. Changing his focus, the Elf saw it was not a falling star, but a craft moving across the heavens faster than the celestial objects themselves. Time in motion.

Time.

The thought broke his communion trance and returned him to the mundane world where seconds passed inexorably, hurrying past the now that was the forest's life. A quick check of star positions told him that the others would be already in place, waiting for him. He stepped back under the canopy and knelt by the small, low table.

He snugged the surgical steel jack into the socket at his temple and his fingers flew across the keyboard of his Fuchi 7 cyberdeck, launching him into the Matrix. His vision shifted to that dazzling electronic world of analog space where cybernetic functions took on an almost palpable reality. He ran the electron paths of cyberspace up the satellite link and down again into the Seattle Regional Telecommunications Grid. Within seconds, he was well on his way to the rendezvous with his companions inside the Renraku arcology.

The lights of the Seattle-Tacoma International Airport vanished behind the craft, only to appear again in front of it. The plane was circling. Sam briefly wondered why, but dismissed his concern, sure that the pilot would inform the passengers of any problem. His own life seemed to be circling, too, returning him to the country he had so willingly left for a scholarship to Tokyo University. Around and around he went, chasing his own tail and getting nowhere.

Three hours ago, he had gone through the latest in a week-long series of brush-offs of his efforts to learn the state of his sister's health. They wouldn't even tell him exactly where she was being treated. He had lost his temper when his Renraku escorts began to hustle him away from the telecom and along a boarding corridor to the waiting JSA spaceplane. It was only the fear that, once away from Japan, he would lose all contact with Janice that allowed him to give in to his anger. His escorts, members of the famed Red Samurai security force, had simply taken his histrionics in stride and deposited him, per their orders, on the aircraft.

Two hours later, Sam was on the ground at his destination, being greeted by a Renraku employee in a fringed synth-leather jacket, floppy pilot's cap, and pointy sequined boots. The clothing was no less outrageous than the woman's overly familiar forms of address and rude jokes. First she led Sam through the intricacies of Seattle customs and security checks, then she took him onto the field to a waiting Federated Boeing Commuter marked with the Renraku logo. The woman assured him that the tilt-wing shuttle plane would take them to the arcology in the most expeditious manner. When Sam had boarded and taken his seat in the luxurious passenger cabin, his escort vanished through the forward door to the cockpit. A few moments later, the craft lifted from the ground. Take-off was accompanied by the pilot's commentary on minor faults in the lower control's procedure.

Sam decided for the twentieth—or was it fortieth?—time

that there was little he could do at the moment. To distract himself, he turned his attention to his fellow passengers. Like him, all were bound for the Renraku arcology.

Seated at the bar was Alice Crenshaw. She had sat next to him during the trip from Japan, but had said little, which suited Sam's dark mood just fine. What Crenshaw did tell him was that she, too, was being transferred to the arcology project. She was equally unhappy about it, insulting the steward who politely inquired about the reason for her transfer.

Crenshaw had boarded the Commuter a moment after Sam, saying nothing to the others already aboard the VTOL transfer shuttle and ignoring their friendly attempts at conversation. Instead, she had busied herself almost immediately with a bourbon and water.

Chatting quietly on a broad bench seat were a couple who introduced themselves to Sam as Jiro and Betty Tanaka. He was Nisei, a second-generation Japanese born in the Americas, and she was from the California Free State. Sam envied the simple hopes and fears of the salaryman and his wife. For the young Jiro, an assignment to work as a computer specialist in the Renraku arcology would actually be a step up in his career.

The only other passenger was a Mr. Toragama. Put off by Sam's distraction and Crenshaw's disdain, he had buried himself in his middle-manager concerns, alternately tapping the keys and studying the screen of his lap computer.

Sam turned his head to gaze out the window again. The Commuter had left its holding pattern and was moving across Seattle toward the glitter of lights that marked the heart of the metroplex.

There, looming ahead was the Renraku arcology, its massive presence dwarfing the tall office buildings of the nearby central business district. Even though portions were still under construction, the arcology already enclosed a dozen city blocks. Beyond it in the distance, Sam saw the garish neon of the Aztechnology pyramid proclaiming the arrogance of the corporation's Atzlan owners.

The Commuter banked, gliding past the sloped southern face of the arcology. Diamond reflections of the aircraft's landing lights glittered from the banks of solar concentrators sheathing the surface and again from the dark waters as the plane moved out over the Sound. Though the noise was muffled by the cabin's superb sound-proofing, the vibration of the shift from horizontal to vertical flight mode permeated the cabin. The craft dropped a little altitude as it moved over the Renraku-owned docks and warehouses skirting the water-face of the arcology. The VTOL tilted in toward one of the many landing pads.

Sam could see the landing lights getting closer, but the pad seemed deserted. No official greeting party waited, not even the usual scurrying ground crew. As they neared touchdown, the aircraft gave a slight lurch before steadying itself and settling slowly to the pad.

No word came from the pilot's compartment as the passengers waited. The Tanakas pointed out sights to one another through their window overlooking the Sound. Mr. Toragama stowed away his computer to the accompaniment of tinkling ice as Crenshaw mixed herself a last drink. Unwilling to move, Sam sat staring at the still-spinning rotors. A sharp clack resounded in the cabin as the outer hatchway latch turned.

"About time," Crenshaw groused.

The hatch eased open and the gangway rattled into position. The noise level in the cabin suddenly increased as the sound of the Commuter's idling engines swept in. Smells came in, too, the tang of the ocean permeating the harsh odors of aviation fuel and heated metal and plastic.

Then all ordinariness died in a thunder of gunshots and automatic weapons fire. Crenshaw dropped her drink and started to reach into her suit jacket but stopped in midmotion as a massive figure dove through the hatch and rolled quickly to his feet. Bulky with muscle and armor, the intruder was an Ork. The cabin lights glinted off his yellowed tusks and blood-shot eyes, but the blue steel of his HK227 automatic rifle gleamed with cold perfection.

"Move and die," the Ork snarled in barely understandable English.

His words were garbled, but the yawning muzzle of his rifle spoke clearly. Crenshaw eased her hand out of her jacket, but no one else moved. Betty Tanaka began to hiccup softly, and Jiro, shivering fearfully, did nothing to comfort her.

Satisfied that he had cowed them, the Ork moved cautiously into the plane. A swift sidestep took him past the closed door of the pilot compartment. His movement made room in the doorway and two more invaders quickly filled it. The one in the fringed leather duster was a woman. The other, ragged in surplus military gear, was an Amerindian male. Sam barely had time to register all that before an eerie howling filled the air.

Frozen with unreasoning fear, Sam stared in horror at the massive shape bounding into the cabin. The huge, hound-like beast shouldered aside the Amerindian to land with a snarl at the feet of the female invader.

Yellow teeth snapped at her, catching the fringe on the left arm of her coat. She shoved that arm straight into the beast's mouth, jamming it back into the hinge of the animal's jaws. The beast backpedaled, seeking to disengage, but the woman's free hand whipped around to grasp the studded collar around its neck. The hound reared on its hind legs, lifting the woman off the floor.

Suddenly the animal arched violently as a yellow, sparking glow ran along its collar, the light revealing the Renraku logo etched in the band. Throwing itself away from its antagonist, the beast slammed against the bulkhead with a yelp of pain, then twisted and bit at itself as though trying to fend off its agony. The animal howled again, but this was not the bone-freezing sound that had paralyzed Sam and the others. Only pain and the animal's own uncomprehending fear remained. It crashed to the floor and whimpered once as it died. The stench of singed fur was overpowering.

Had the woman dispatched the beast with magic? Sam couldn't be sure, never having seen a magician in action, but he could think of no other explanation.

Hollow-eyed and panting, the woman spoke softly, almost to herself. "Damned Barghests. Why don't they ever go for the muscle first?"

Weapons sounded outside the aircraft again, filling the cabin with sudden death. The woman threw herself to the cabin floor and the man dodged back against the Commuter's bulkhead. The Renraku employees were slower to move. Betty Tanaka jerked and tumbled backward as slugs ripped into her. Jiro spun, blood spraying from his shoulder, and crashed into Toragama before the two of them pitched to the floor. Sam dropped behind his seat just as bullets chewed through the padding and light aluminum frame over his head. Crenshaw, out of the line of fire, stood still and eyed the Ork, who also remained standing, saved from the fire by a kink in the bulkhead.

The male invader made a sudden jump and snatched the hatch handle, tugging it closed. By the almost superhuman speed of the man's movement, Sam realized it had to be cyberware enhancing his reactions.

As the woman picked herself up from the floor, her duster gaped open, revealing an athletic body clad in little more than weapon belts and amulets. She cursed softly as one of her feet caught on her scabbard. Sam stared at the weapon it held. Though he had never seen one before, he guessed that this ornate and intricately decorated object had to be a magesword. For the first time in his life, he stood in the presence of a magician. The idea brought cold sweat to his brow.

This was a most dangerous gang if one of them could perform actual magic.

"Where's the pilot?" the woman demanded of the Ork.

The big ugly jerked his head toward the forward door. "Hiding up dere."

"Go get him moving. Those trigger-happy Raku goons aren't going to wait forever before bringing up the artillery to pry us out of here. We need to get off this synthetic mountain now."

The Ork gestured toward the back of the cabin with his gun. "Can't leave dem here on our ass."

"We'll watch them."

"Should geek dem now," the Ork grumbled around his tusks.

"No time to waste. Get to the pilot."

The Ork snarled, but the woman, who seemed to be the leader of the band, did not budge. Giving in, the Ork readied his weapon and threw open the door. When nothing happened, he slipped into the passageway. His bulk blocked the view, but Sam could hear the faint voice of the craft's computer as it repeated over and over, "Please signify if you wish engine shutdown."

The woman ran her gaze over the carnage left by the short burst of gunfire that had followed her into the Commuter. The stench of death hung heavily in the cabin. Betty Tanaka lay sprawled across the bench seat, her blood soaking the cushions and splattering the wall and window behind it. Sitting on the floor by her side, oblivious to his own wound,

Jiro held his dead wife's hand and wept. Mr. Toragama was a huddled, lifeless lump in the main aisle.

"No one has to get hurt. Take your seats and buckle in," the woman said quietly. When no one moved, she repeated the words in crisp Japanese.

Sam was amazed. Hadn't they already been hurt?

"And keep your hands in sight," the man added in broken Japanese. He emphasized his point with a slight shake of the Ingram machine gun in his left hand. The one he held in his right remained rock steady and aimed at Crenshaw.

"We're hosed real good," the Ork bellowed from the cockpit. "De flygirl had a window open and took a stray shot. She's ready for de meat locker."

The woman flicked a glance at the man, who nodded and moved to join the Ork. As he passed behind her, she reached under her duster and slid a short-barreled shotgun from a holster.

Sam tried to watch Crenshaw. The obvious attention the attackers were paying her suddenly lined up with the deference the Red Samurai had shown back in Tokyo. She was likely a special corporate operative, what the screamsheets liked to call a company man. He wondered if she would try something against the reduced odds. The magician looked exhausted, drained from using the powerful spell that killed the Barghest. That would surely slow her reactions enough to give the veteran Crenshaw an opening. The invader's leveled shotgun seemed to be threat enough to restrain Crenshaw, however. She complied with the orders, found a relatively gore-free seat and buckled herself in.

Sam felt betrayed. Of them all, Crenshaw should have taken the lead. She was trained to deal with thugs like these. Why hadn't she protected her fellow employees instead of folding in the face of danger? What more could *he* be expected to do? Resignedly, he pulled Jiro away from his wife's corpse and into a seat, but the man seemed not to hear Sam's attempts at soothing phrases.

Sam was buckling himself in when the Amerindian called from the cockpit. "We've got real problems, Sally. This damn thing only has rigger controls."

"Told ya we shoulda brought Rabo," the Ork whined. "He coulda skimmed us out real wiz."

"Rabo's not here," Sally snapped. "The veetole's dog-brain will never be able to get us past the patrols."

The two male invaders reentered the cabin, dragging the limp form of the pilot.

"We can use dese suits as hostages or shields," the Ork suggested with an evil grin, as he dumped the body on top of Mr. Toragama.

Sally's only reply was a look of disdain.

"What about the Elf?" the Amerindian asked. "Could he take us out by remote?"

"I don't know," she said. Taking a small black box from a pocket, she flipped up the screen and pulled out a cord, snapping it into the jack port on a bulkhead intercom panel. She tapped in a code.

"At your service," said a voice from the crackling intercom speaker. "Where are you? Your signal is quite poor."

"We're cornered in a veetole, with a handful of Raku employees. Pilot's dead and the damn ship is rigger only. Can you get into the autopilot and fly us out?"

"I wish it were otherwise, Sweet Lady, but what you ask I cannot do. I'm a decker, not a rigger. I don't have the wiring to control the aircraft.

"I do suggest that you find an alternate means of transportation. And quickly. Their deckers are starting to move now and my position becomes more precarious by the microsecond. I have been able to isolate the communication attempts by the varlets who pursue you, but I fear that central security will soon become aware of the blind spot in their coverage. Even maintaining this communications link is a danger."

"There must be something that you can do, hotshot," the Amerindian insisted.

"As you have had to abandon the planned route out, there is very little." The Elf's faint voice paused. "Perhaps one of the passengers is a rigger."

Suddenly, Sam felt the group's attention focus on him, all eyes on his datajack.

"What's your name, boy?" Sally asked.

"Samuel Verner."

"Well, Verner, are you a rigger?' the Amerindian demanded.

Should he lie? If he did, could the magician read his mind and know? Perhaps he could pretend to have trouble with the aircraft. If he could delay these brigands long enough,

Renraku security would catch them. But surely not without a fight. Two people had already died for simply being in the way. Sam shook his head slowly. "It's a datajack. I'm a researcher."

"You ever flown anything?"

"Gliders. Used to have a Mitsubishi Flutterer."

"Great," moaned the Ork. "A toy pilot. I'd rather trust de dog-brain."

From the intercom, the Elf's faint voice spoke. "Oh thou great lump of flesh, the boy might not be a rigger, but he does have some experience in flying. His input could add the necessary randomness to the autopilot's rather limited repertoire of behaviors. Even if he is no pilot, it might give you enough edge."

"That's right." It was the Amerindian who spoke up. "We might have a chance if the Elf could redirect their anti-air and send some of the patrols on the wrong vector."

Sally looked thoughtful for the briefest of moments. "Well, Dodger. Can you do that?"

The intercom crackled softly as the Elf considered the plan. "It will not be easy, given that they are on alert, but I shall endeavor to do as you wish, Fair Lady."

"Then it's time to fly," she announced. "All right, Verner. Up front."

Sam looked to his fellow Renraku employees for support, Jiro's eyes were locked on the body of his wife, and Crenshaw's face was wholly noncommittal. As for the dead, they were offering no advice. He unbuckled his seatbelt and stood.

The cockpit stank as much of blood and feces as the cabin. Trying to ignore the blood that stained the pilot couch, Sam lowered himself into it. The Amerindian slid into the co-pilot's seat.

"I am called Ghost Maker in some parts," he said. "I may not be a pilot, but I know something about this stuff. Try anything and we will find ourselves relying only on the autopilot. *Wakarimasu-ka?*

"I understand."

"Good. Jack in and get us going."

Sam slid the datacord from its nesting place in the control panel. He had never been given the limited-access familiarization exercises with the datajack that the doctor had recommended on the day after his operation. He was scared.

He had heard how a rigger melded with his machine, becoming a brain to direct the body of the vehicle. He had also heard that some couldn't handle the transition, losing their minds in communion with the soulless machine.

This machine was built strictly for rigger operation, a monument to the hubris so common among the pilots of powerful machinery. No one without a datajack could do more than request a destination and departure time from the autopilot. Hardly the way to make a fast getaway.

These brigands wanted Sam to jack in and override the decision-making functions of the autopilot. Without the special vehicle control implants that would link a pilot's cortex to the operations of the machine, he could do little more than make decisions about direction, flight altitudes, and when to take off or land. The autopilot would still do the flying. Without him in the link, though, the Commuter would communicate with Seattle air traffic control, following some controller's directives and restricting itself to well-defined flight paths and low-risk maneuvers and speeds. The invaders wanted him to make their escape easier, and they cared little what it might cost him.

Sam understood that this hookup would allow him access to only a limited selection of controls, but it still seemed a dangerous risk. Sensing the man beside him becoming impatient, however, he decided that *not* jacking in would soon become an even greater risk.

As Sam snugged the plug into the jack in his temple, pain flashed through his skull, but faded swiftly. Like an afterimage, dials and control information appeared in his mind, projected onto his optic nerve by the aircraft's computer. He could shift his head and "see" different portions of the imaginary control panel. Spotting the *help* panel, he reached out toward it, mentally "pressing" the button. The computer fed him instructions on basic aircraft operation. The machine's voice in his head was cold and alien, unlike the tones it gave through the speakers. The uncanny nature of his rapport with the Commuter unnerved him and the back of his skull began to ache.

Bullets pattered against the armored cockpit glass in a hasty rhythm seconded by the Amerindian's urgent, "Get moving!"

Sam reached out to the control yoke. Whether it was real or a computer simulation, he no longer knew. He ordered the engines to rev, and pulled back. The counter-rotating blades of the Commuter's twin engines spun faster, quickly creating enough lift for the craft to clear the pad. With the autopilot doing the real flying, Sam commanded the Commuter up into the night sky.

"Where to?" he asked Ghost Maker.

"North over the plex. For now."

Sam complied.

They had been in flight for five minutes when Sam decided that the anti-aircraft missiles he had been expecting were not coming after all. The Elf was evidently as good as his word. Calling up the radar, Sam could find nothing that looked like pursuit. He was equally surprised at the lack of challenges from the Seattle Metroplex air traffic controllers. The Elf decker must have inserted a flight plan into their computers as well, concealing the hijacked shuttle VTOL among the normal traffic.

They were passing over a suburban residential district when Ghost Maker ordered Sam to extinguish the running lights and change course to head for the Redmond Barrens, that desolate sprawl of shanty towns and abandoned buildings. The autopilot attempted to turn the lights back on, but Sam overrode it.

As they headed across the district, the lights of the apartments and homes of corporate salarymen became rarer, replaced by the garish neon and corpse-gray glow of advertising tridscreens near the edge of the Barrens. Out beyond the commercial zone, the lights were few.

Sam watched the Amerindian scan the darkness below. He wondered if his captor had augmented eyes to go along with his reflexes. Most of the adventurers and muscleboys who called themselves street samurai did. This Ghost Maker was certainly one of that breed.

"Lower," Ghost commanded.

As Sam directed the Commuter to comply, the autopilot whined, "Altitude becoming dangerously low. Do you intend a landing?"

"Shut it up."

Sam flipped the rocker switch to silence the cabin voice. "Are we landing?"

"Not yet. Head northeast."

Sam adjusted the craft's heading, telling the autopilot that landing was not imminent and that the altitude was intentional.

They flew for another ten minutes, making several more course changes, some to avoid the burnt-out shells of buildings and others to satisfy some unknown whim of Ghost Maker. When the samurai finally gave the order to land, Sam was glad to engage the Commuter's automatic landing routine. The long minutes of dodging the darkened hulks had worn him down to where, even had he been familiar with the aircraft, he would not have wished to land it manually.

"Damn it! Kill the lights," the samurai snapped as the autopilot engaged the landing lights.

Startled by the man's vehemence, Sam complied, cancelling almost as quickly the Commuter's complaints about safety and FAA regulations. The VTOL settled unevenly on a field of rubble, close by a row of boarded-up tenements. The samurai popped the jack from Sam's head and urged him out of the pilot's seat. Sam reached to cut the engines.

"Leave them."

Sam shrugged and headed for the cabin. The others had already deplaned, leaving the interior empty save for the dead.

"Why can't you just leave us alone?" he heard Jiro say.

The response came from the Ork. "Let's just call it a little insurance."

The Renraku employees were hustled into one of the derelict buildings just as the Commuter lifted off again. From the doorless entryway, Sam watched as the VTOL went straight up until well clear of the low buildings, then turned south and shifted to horizontal flight mode. The Commuter climbed away into the sky, its dark bulk eclipsing the few stars that shone through the breaks in the cloud cover. A shadow ship, crewed by ghosts.

The samurai materialized in the the doorway, silhouetted briefly before slipping inside. Once safe in the darkness, he spoke. "The veetole's on its way out to sea."

"Think it was on the ground too long?" Sally asked.

"We'll know soon enough if it was," he replied.

In the silence that followed, Sam could hear the Ork changing magazines for his HK227. The other two followed his example, then silence fell again.

It was less than a minute before the Ork complained, "We can't just haul dis lot down de street."

"Cog is sending a car."

"We're supposed to wait around? Frag it! If de badges or de Raku samurai are on our tail, we're meat sitting here."

"We can't move our guests safely without a car," Sally insisted.

"So who needs dem? We're back on our own turf. De're dead weight now." The Ork's slight emphasis on "dead" made it clear what he considered the proper way of disposing of the Renraku prisoners.

"I think you underestimate their value."

"We did de job we was paid for. And we got de disks dat Ghost grabbed. Dat's plenty. You're looking for too many extra creds."

"I have expenses to meet."

"I ain't paying your expenses with my life."

"You want to buzz now? Give me your credstick and I'll give you your cut," Sally said, holding out her hand. "Of course, you'll only get the standard one on ten for leaving before the goods are fenced."

Sam could feel the tension mount as the magician and the Ork stared into one another's eyes. Finally, the Ork looked away. He shrugged, mumbling, "Job's a job."

"Sally smiled. "Don't worry, Kham. This one's going to finish just fine."

The Ork snapped her a sullen look as if he had heard it all before, then he vanished, grumbling, into the dark interior of the building.

While they waited, Sam looked after Jiro's wound as best he could, ripping up a piece of his own shirt for a bandage. The salaryman seemed dazed by the loss of his wife and still said not a word as Sam worked over him. Having done what he could, Sam sat down cross-legged on the filthy floor, his thoughts as dark as the room.

Ghost appeared in the doorway again, startling Sam, who had not seen the Amerindian leave.

"Car's here."

Sally gestured to the door with her shotgun. "Let's go."

The car was a stretched Toyota Elite, its opacity-controlled polymer windows set to dark. The driver's window was down and a broad-faced Korean kid grinned a gap-toothed invitation. He flipped a switch and the rear door yawned wide.

The Renraku employees climbed in, taking the plush synthleather and velvet seat while Sally and the Ork settled into jumpseats facing their prisoners. Ghost Maker slipped into the front seat on the passenger side.

As soon as the doors closed, the driver babbled something in a street dialect from which Sam only made out the name Cog. Sally nodded and switched on the audio deck. The voice that came out was rich and deep.

"Your friend's call caught me just in time, Ms. Tsung. I've been unavoidably called out of town, but I am most happy to provide this small service before I leave. The driver is one of my regulars. You may rely on his discretion."

There was no more to the message, but Sally seemed satisfied with its content. At least the noises she made to the driver sounded agreeable.

The privacy panel slid up from the seat, cutting off Sam's view of the street ahead and the driver's rearview screen. The blackened windows wrapped them away from the world and held them in silence as the vehicle proceeded on its twisty path through the Barrens. Only once did something from outside impinge on them as a heavy thump struck the right rear quarter panel. Their captors remained unperturbed.

Perhaps an hour later, the car slowed and the privacy panel dropped, revealing a litter-strewn alley lit fitfully by the intermittent violet flashes of a neon sign just out of sight on the cross-street ahead.

The doors opened on both sides, but the car did not stop.

"Out," Sally ordered.

Were they being released? Sam could hardly believe it. Crenshaw was up and out the door while Sam was still struggling to extract himself from the embrace of the soft cushions. The Ork's foot helped him on his way, sending him sprawling headfirst into a noisome pile of trash. Sam emerged in time to see Sally leap gracefully from the car and five shadowy figures scramble into the vehicle. The doors snapped shut just before the Toyota cleared the alley mouth. It turned left, away from the neon sign, and was gone.

So, their captors were not releasing them, after all. In

fact, their numbers had grown. At least a dozen youths, male and female, were in the alley with them. In the flickering light, he could see that many wore fringed and beaded garments, and all wore feathers in their headbands. The smallest of the bunch sauntered up to the tall shape of the street samurai. A flash of neon threw his features into silhouette, revealing a profile as hawklike as that of the man he addressed.

"Hoi, Ghost Who Walks Inside. Welcome home."

He knew he ought to be hungry, but he couldn't feel it. The sight of the bowl of krill wafers and soycakes their captors had left the night before only turned his stomach. The water bag, however, was flattened and limp, almost empty. Water he must have, even this tepid, foul-tasting stuff.

The day had passed in a sweaty haze. Their captors had left them in a room with a single door and windows sealed with opaque rigiplastic sheets. A little light crept through where one of the panels had lost a corner. Sam's attempts to peep though were rewarded with a limited view of graffiti-covered bricks. He recognized the general pattern of the taunts and protection slogans, but found the gang's symbols unrecognizable. It was still enough to confirm his suspicions that this turf belonged to a gang of Amerindians.

Jiro moaned, awake again. The salaryman had been drifting in and out of fitful sleep for hours now. "What is happening?" he murmured groggily. "I do not understand."

Crenshaw harumphed her annoyance. "Quit your whining. It gets on my nerves."

The woman's utter lack of feeling was getting on Sam's nerves. "I suppose you don't object to what's happened."

"I've been in worse situations."

"How could it be worse?" Jiro moaned. "Betty is dead."

"You could be dead," Crenshaw retorted.

"Perhaps that would be better."

"Don't talk that way, Jiro," Sam said.

"What difference does it make?" Jiro said listlessly. "We will be killed by these . . . these . . . terrorists."

"Terrorists!" Crenshaw scoffed. "Kid, you don't know the meaning of the word. These clowns are garden-variety shadowrunners. Their best card is that street mage, but they're still petty criminals hiding from the bright lights of the corporate world and scavenging whatever pickings they can. They're human rats.''

''Even if they are not terrorists, they still hide from the law,'' Jiro said weakly. ''How can they let us go when we have seen their faces and heard their names?''

''Don't matter much,'' Crenshaw shrugged. ''The names are just street names, and the faces can be changed easily enough. These runners have no records in the databanks, so what's to trace? They'll let us go if we behave ourselves. All we've got to do is wait.''

''Wait? The only end is death,'' Jiro said in a flat voice. He lay down again and was asleep in moments. Sam wondered how the man did that. Crenshaw picked a soycake off the plate on the floor.

''You should eat, kid.''

''I'm not hungry.''

''Your loss.''

Crenshaw popped the cake into her mouth and wolfed down a few krill wafers before upending the water container and draining it. Sam was appalled at her selfishness. Suddenly he wanted to be someplace else. Any place. Just so long as he was away from the suffocating presence of his fellows.

He got to his feet and began pacing. Crenshaw watched him for a while, but soon lost interest and closed her eyes. Shortly thereafter, she began to snore.

Sam wanted to escape more than ever.

Without hope, he tried the door and was surprised to find it opened to his touch. Cautiously, he swung it wide. The outer room was as bare and dilapidated as the inner. Sally lay asleep along the inner wall. The door to the hall was open and he could see two of the gang's warriors standing guard. They were chatting quietly in a language he didn't understand.

This room had windows to the outside world. Desperate for fresh air, Sam moved to the open one, beyond which a fire escape formed an inviting balcony. He was halfway through the frame before he noticed Ghost standing on the iron grillwork, leaning against the wall.

''Wouldn't be thinking of leaving, would you?''

Sam stammered a negative response, surprised to realize

he hadn't been thinking of escape. Though he wanted to get away from his fellow Renraku employees, he had not thought of abandoning them. "I just wanted to get some air."

"You're welcome to your fill of what passes for it around here." The samurai seemed pensive as he leaned back against the wall and looked out across the sunset-painted stretch of battered tenements. Ghost said no more until Sam was beside him. "You really are a strange one."

"What do you mean?"

"Well, for one thing, you weren't lying about trying to leave."

"I couldn't run out on the others."

"*So ka,*" Ghost said with a knowing nod. "I can understand loyalty to your friends."

"They're not my friends," Sam blurted. To the samurai's raised eyebrow, he added, "We're all Renraku."

"*So ka.* The bond to the tribe is even stronger.

"My people here would never be called a tribe by those fancy ethnologists who wet their pants over the back-to-the-land dreamers out there beyond the plex. Those white-coats would call my kin a gang. But that doesn't make them any less a family, a tribe that takes care of its own.

"We're not like the Reds that live out in the Salish-Shidhe. Those dreamers can't see that life in the world these days means life in a city. Red Men have to take to the concrete the way they took to the horse, or we will pass from the land entirely.

"Since the Whites came, some of us have fought them, some have welcomed them. Didn't make much difference in the end. We lost control of the land and ended in misery, despair, and poverty. And then they threw us into the camps, where they tried to strip away our souls."

Sam could see the pain in the man's face. Ghost was too young to have been in those death camps that had been President Jarman's attempt at a final solution to the Indian problem, but he seemed to feel the anguish of the camps as his own.

"When Howling Coyote came down from the hills with his Great Ghost Dance, he sure handed the Whites a surprise. Made the Man realize that Reds weren't going to take it anymore. Broke their technology with his magic, he did.

But that was then. The Whites have magic now, too, but some of my people don't want to face it.

"The old men who led the Dance don't understand what it did for us. It didn't banish the White Man, as advertised, or the Black Man, or the Yellow Man. They're still here. And so are their cities and works—weakened maybe, and pushed back by the magic and the power of the Awakened— but far from beaten. What the Dance really did was give us breathing room. It gave us a chance to beat the others at their own game.

"It ain't going to be easy. It's going to take real warriorship, but my people are ready for that challenge. We'll show them. In the end, we will win. But to win, we have to survive, and surviving means nuyen. You ain't got the bucks, the Man don't listen. There's lots of loose creds waiting around for shadowrunners to liberate."

Ghost fell silent, seemingly exhausted by the long string of words. Sam didn't know what motivated the man to speak so, but the speech gave him hope that these were not bloody-minded thugs who would as soon kill them as look at them. He began to think it was possible he might get out of this predicament alive.

Ghost's next words startled him even more than had his confidences.

"Why am I talking to you?" the Amerindian snorted.

"I don't know. Maybe you needed someone to listen to you."

"Don't need no drek from some soft Anglo corporate," Ghost said gruffly. Giving the darkening skies a last look, he ordered Sam back inside.

The samurai's sudden mood shift left Sam again unsure of what he faced among these shadowrunners. Nothing they said was exactly as Sam understood it to be. It made sense one minute, only to become totally alien the next. They seemed to live in another world. Confused, he climbed awkwardly back into the squat.

An Elf had arrived while he had been on the balcony. He sat cross-legged in a corner, his attention on a data-reader in his lap. From the jacks on his left temple, Sam surmised that the Elf was the decker who had been riding Matrix cover on last night's shadowrun.

Sally still lay on the foam pad that was the room's only

furniture, but she was awake. She looked rested now, the hollow circles of exhaustion gone from her eyes. Ghost shouldered Sam out of the way and passed through a doorway hidden by a curtain that Sam had taken as a decorative wall hanging. The samurai returned with a tray of cold tofu and steaming soykaf, which he brought to Sally. She thanked him with a sad smile.

"I'm getting too old for this, Ghost."

It seemed an old story between them.

"Drink your soy." Ghost waited while she drained half the cup. "You haven't told us yet what you plan for the Raku."

"Avaunt, Lord Musclebrain," the Elf ordered from his corner. "The fair Lady Tsung needs her rest before pressing on with this sordid business. You street samurai are all alike—no proper sensibilities, no understanding of delicate persons or sense of timing.

"All you want to do is flex your muscles. Once you impress us with your hyped resources, you only stay long enough to grab your blood money before scurrying back to your squalid dens."

Thin, sparkling needles slid from beneath the fingernails of Ghost's right hand. Sam guessed the Elf was pushing the limits of the Amerindian's tolerance, imposing on his hospitality. Sally laid a hand on the samurai's back, out of sight of the Elf. The needles vanished.

"Can it, Dodger," she said. "Ghost's not pushing. A decision has to be made."

The Elf huffed his annoyance at the rebuff. Satisfied, Ghost walked to the window and stared out while Sally put her tray aside and sat up straighter. "So what's on the disks we pulled?"

"Quite a bit actually, Fair One." All trace of annoyance was gone from his voice, and was replaced by cool professionalism. "Production schedules. Some personnel files. A couple of patent applications. A fine swag, which would have considerable street value if the run had not terminated so noisily. As is, we shall have to wait until cooler weather before safely disposing of it."

"Meaning we lost a lot of value?"

"Of course."

"Well, at least we'll get paid for the plant."

Sam was confused. He understood that their stolen data

would be less valuable on the open market if they waited to sell it, but he had thought they were simple thieves. "What plant?"

Ghost started to say something, but closed his mouth when Sally spoke.

"We made a little donation to the cleaning supplies of the computer systems research office. An aerosol generator disguised as cleaning spray. It will dispense a little bug called Vigid along with its cleaning solvent. In a few hours, a lot of Renraku wageslaves will be going home sick. The next few days will be somewhat uncomfortable for them and most displeasing to the Renraku management, what with the inevitable schedule disruption. While they limp along, our client, Atreus Applications, gets the jump on the competition. It should allow them to hit the Matrix with a new software package a full week ahead of Renraku.

"That was the real job. Atreus wanted us to snatch some prototypes to hide the nature of the operation. We picked up the disks as a fringe benefit."

It all sounded straightforward—making allowances for the basically devious nature of shadowruns. But something nagged at Sam. Something about the delivery system of the disruptive bioagent. He ran Sally's words over in his head. Why not simply spread the agent around? The runners could have been given an antidote beforehand. Why combine it with cleaning fluid? Simply to delay implementation? A tailored time-decay capsule could do that effectively enough. Why cleaning fluid, or was that important at all? Somewhere deep in his brain a synapse fired and a memory awoke.

"Excuse me," he said tentatively, "But the solvent in the cleaning fluid. Was it acetone-based?"

"Who knows," Sally said. "What does it matter?"

Sam took a deep breath. "If it was, I don't think that the Vigid will do what you expect it to."

"Ah," sneered the Elf, "observe how the merchandise displays an extensive biotechnical knowledge. We may yet realize a handsome profit."

"I'm not a biotech," Sam said, letting his annoyance show. "I'm just a researcher. But I've got a good memory. I saw an article on Vigid once. Some researcher for the UCAS government had done an experiment. It got contaminated when an assistant spilled some acetone while cleaning glassware. The acetone interacted with the protein shell of the virus, stripping parts of it and causing the core genetic material to mutate in an isomeric form.''

"So it's a different bug," the Elf drawled.

"It's a lethal bug. That lab assistant died. In a replication test, thirty to forty percent of the analog mice exposed to the isomeric virus died."

Sally's look became grim during Sam's recitation. She placed her kaf mug on the floor in a slow and deliberate manner. "We weren't hired for wetwork."

"Certes, the fee was far too low," the Elf agreed.

"Frag the fees!" Ghost snarled, needles flashing at his fingertips. "Somebody set us up."

Sally nodded slowly. "I think we need to talk to someone about our recent employers before we go to meet them."

Sam was not sure why the runners had brought him along, but he didn't think it politic to ask. They had been rejoined by the Ork called Kham, who seemed outraged at the possibility of a set-up. He had to be dissuaded from bringing heavy weaponry along to the meeting with the fixer.

The walk to the meet-site was through a kind of place Sam had only seen on the trid. The streets were crowded, filled with rockerhaunts, gutterpunks, and chippies. Squatters held their miserable alleys and boxes against muscleboys from the gangs, and razorguys hung tough behind their moneyed charges. The hungry and the thrill-seekers mingled cheek to chromed jowl in the harsh glare of the neon and public tridscreens.

The noise and crowd swirled around them, parting and reforming as they passed. Even the hardest-looking street samurai and Ork bullyboys seemed to fade from their path without causing trouble. Maybe the mage had something to do with it, or maybe it was simply Sam's imagination.

They stopped at an abandoned storefront in a less congested area. Through the smashed window, what little Sam could see of the building's floor was as littered and stained as the sidewalk. Even from outside, the odor of stale urine and refuse was intense. No one on the street paid the least attention when the group entered the building.

Three men waited inside. All were tall and rangy. Hard muscles showed wherever their street garb exposed flesh.

All carried obvious weaponry. Street samurai, Sam guessed, but he saw none of the obvious cyberware the breed favored. Either they were so good they didn't need enhancement or else their modifications were very subtle. Either way, they had to be dangerous.

The blond one on the left had a large dog by his side, at least half-wolf in its bloodline. The beast growled softly when Sam and the runners entered. While the others exchanged opening pleasantries with the men. Sam crouched and held out his hand to the animal. Cautiously, its posture indicating suspicion, the beast advanced to sniff at his hand.

"Freya bites," one of the fixer's men warned.

"I'm sure she does," Sam returned, without taking his eyes from Freya. The animal gave the tips of Sam's fingers a tentative lick. He smiled, reaching his other hand out slowly to ruffle the fur at the side of Freya's head. "She's marvelous. Where did you get her?"

"She followed me home one night," the guard said sarcastically.

The sound of a man clearing his throat caused Sam to turn. The runners were already facing the newcomers. Two more rangy samurai flanked a bigger man. He was dark, even without the benefit of backlighting from the street. His richly tailored suit was out of place among the ruins, but he seemed completely at home. The man, obviously the fixer they had come to meet, stepped forward.

"Making new friends?"

Sam thought the raspy-voiced fixer was speaking to him, but Sally replied.

"Always. You know what a party girl I am."

If the fixer was amused, his heavily pockmarked face didn't show it. He simply turned his cold eyes on the magician.

"I'm glad you could spare the time for a meet," she said. "I'm sure I can make it worth your while, Castillano."

Castillano shrugged. "Why me? Cog's your preferred connection."

"Cog's unavailable."

The fixer's face remained expressionless. "I'm second-best," he said, making his question a statement.

Sally gave him a light laugh. "Let's just say I thought you were the best choice tonight."

"You need a specialist?"

"What we're most interested in right now is information."

"A target?"

"An employer."

Castillano rubbed his hands together meditatively. Had his face shown any interest, Sam might have thought him a merchant scenting an easy sale. The fixer opened his mouth slightly and ran the edge of his tongue along the lower lip. "That sort of information is in high demand at the moment."

The shadowrunners exchanged glances. "Something come down that we haven't heard about?"

"Maybe," Castillano responded noncommittally.

"Add it to the bill."

The fixer nodded in acceptance. "Smilin' Sam and Johnny Come Lately."

Sally cocked her head to the side, her expression slightly annoyed. "News about the firefight at the After Ours Bar is hardly a commodity. The screamsheets were full of it."

"Screamsheets don't mention the rifle."

"What rifle?" Sally asked in sudden interest.

"Arisaka KZ-977. Sniper model. Not silenced. Lone Star Security picked it up in the street in front of the building where your two acquaintances were killed."

"They don't use anything big," Ghost interjected.

"Yeah," the Ork agreed. "Johnny never did like loud noises. A real runt pup dat way."

Castillano stared at the Ork.

"What's the point, Castillano?"

"Mr. James Yoshimura died of a single shot to the head as he left the After Ours. Pair of Lone Star officers saw Yoshimura go down and heard the shot. They spotted Sam and Johnny. One of the runners panicked and shot at the cops. Cops shot back. The rifle fell. The runners died.

"Lone Star ballistics matched the gun to the lethal bullet. Trajectory puts the shooter in the vicinity of the runners. The rifle survived the drop better than Smilin' Sam."

"No other witnesses?"

"None," Castillano confirmed.

"Dirty cops," Ghost concluded. "Sam and Johnny were bagmen and cats. They didn't do wetwork."

"Maybe. The Lone Stars have clean records. Apparently incorruptible. Just quick to shoot."

"Then Sam and Johnny were set up."

Castillano shrugged.

"And you know something about it."

"I never said that. Enquiries into the matter are likely to be unhealthy."

"It seems to have been a bad week for running the shadows. We had someone twist us around too."

"Looking for a connection?"

"If it's there, we'll do something about it. If not, Sam and Johnny were big boys," Ghost declared.

"What exactly is it you want?"

"Let's start with a bioproduct called Vigid."

"Anti-riot agent. Fast-acting incapacitant with pronounced after-effects similar to a bad stomach virus. Aerosol vector. How much do you want?"

"Had more'n enough already," the Ork snarled.

"We want to know what might happen if the substance were subjected to an acetone bath."

If Castillano was surprised or curious about the request, he didn't show it. He walked across the room, avoiding the debris as though by instinct. From a countertop, he lifted what looked like a moldy pile of garbage to reveal a telecom port. He took out a pocket computer and plugged it in. After a few minutes of plying the keys, he announced, "This will take awhile. When do you want to meet?"

"Check UCAS *Chemistry Today*, December 2048," Sam said. "There's no time for you to replicate it."

The fixer entered a document search. "Wilkins and Chung?"

"That's it," Sam confirmed, nodding to the runners as well.

Castillano stroked his mustache as he studied the screen. "Looks like Vigid reacts badly to acetone. Gets very toxic."

"Do you believe me now?" Sam asked of the runners.

The Elf, silent until now, answered him. "You gave the reference, Sir Corp. The document could be a plant."

"Unlikely," Castillano said. Even Sam was startled by the fixer's uncharacteristic free offering. "He didn't get the month right."

"Let's assume the damn stuff really does mutate. Who makes it, Castillano?"

"Genomics holds the patent. Exclusive manufacturing contract for Seretech."

"Seretech!" Ghost spat.

"Fraggin' hellfire!" the Ork howled.

Sally and Dodger just looked worried.

"What does it mean?" Sam asked.

"We've had a few misunderstandings with them in the past," Sally said softly.

"Then you think they might have been behind this? That they deliberately set you up?"

"Indubitably," the Elf put in. "They must have used Atreus as a cut-out to allay our suspicions. They probably arranged for Renraku security to find out about our mission."

"But not until *after* we had placed their dirty little toy," Sally added bitterly.

"How would it help them to have you caught?"

"Dey don't like us, Mr. Suit," the Ork growled. "Dat's enough reason for anybody."

"They didn't even have to get us geeked on the way out," Ghost expanded. "Any of us that got caught wouldn't know that they had hired us, so there'd be no link to Seretech. We also didn't know what their bug would really do, so we wouldn't have said anything. A simple break-in and lift of those prototypes would have been easy enough to squirm out of. Attempted robbery and breaking and entering. Light stuff. Until people started dying. For that, we'd have been blamed, and they probably thought we'd finger Atreus and take them down with us."

Sally picked it up. "Seretech would have been in the clear and sitting on fat street. They'd have hit their rivals at Renraku and gotten us too. Any of us that the Raku samurai didn't take down would be facing mass murder charges 'cause nobody would believe we didn't know what kind of stuff we were placing. Seretech pays back two debts at one. Maybe even three, if they're got a beef with Atreus. Once again, the megacorp comes out on top."

"So what happens now?" Sam prodded.

"We take our losses and stay out of the light," Sally sighed. "Seretech's bad business."

Sam was appalled. "What about those people at Renraku? They're innocent. You can't just let them die."

"Can't we?" said Ghost.

Flushed with outrage, Sam spun to face Sally, stabbing an accusing finger. "I thought you didn't do wetwork cheap. Pretty flexible honor you've got. Things get tough, and you fold. You must enjoy being somebody's fall guys. What'll happen to your hot-shot reps when the street finds out how you let yourselves be used?"

"Stuff dat. Nobody'll know," the Ork muttered.

"*He* will!" Sam shouted, pointing at Castillano. He swung his arm about to take in the guards. "They know, too!"

"Uh, Lady Tsung," the Elf said quietly, "perhaps we could go back and pull out the cans."

"It's too late," Sally said. "They'll already have used some of it."

"You could just tell Renraku what's going on," Sam suggested.

"They wouldn't believe us. Even if they did, they'd still come looking for us, figuring we had something to do with it. They'd be right, of course, and when people start dying, it would turn into a blood feud. We're better off keeping quiet."

"Wait a minute!" Sam yelped. "Castillano, let me see your computer."

The fixer simply stared at him, keeping a proprietary hand on the keyboard.

Sally sighed. "On the tab."

Castillano handed over the keyboard.

Sam fiddled with it, cursing its slowness. He felt a featherweight touch on his shoulder. He turned to find the Elf offering a cyberdeck.

"Faster this way," Dodger said.

Sam looked at the device the Elf carried hidden beneath his coat. Save for its special function keys and carrying strap, it looked like an ordinary computer keyboard. He took it gingerly.

This would not be like plugging into the Federated Boeing Commuter. This was a real doorway to the Matrix. There would be no autopilot insulation from the terrifying glories of cyberspace.

"Jack's over here," the Elf said, pointing.

Sam slid back the cover panel and pulled out the telecom connector. With a quick switch of plugs, the Elf's cyberdeck took the place of Castillano's computer. He reached for the datacord that would connect his socket with the deck. He almost changed his mind, but found courage when he remembered the innocents in the arcology who would suffer if no one tried to help. He slipped the plug in, steeling himself against the expected pain.

It came, flashing through his brain faster than before and leaving a distant malaise in its wake. Sam focused his mind on the task at hand. Turning a blind eye to the gleaming spires and pulsing data paths that surrounded him in cyberspace, he charged forward to the massive Renraku construct. Using his company passwords, he opened a portal into the main database.

Glittering rows of stars lay in serried ranks and columns all around him. Each point of light was a datafile, its tint reflecting the filing category. Sam fed the cyberdeck the key words and executed the search function. His point of view shifted with dazzling speed along the rows. He paused briefly at each file suggested by the deck, discarding useless information as he searched.

In what seemed like only a few minutes, he found it. He copied the file and fled back to where he had entered the Matrix.

"There is a counteragent," he announced to the circle of concerned faces as he pulled the data cord from his temple.

"Where do we get it?"

"That's the problem. It's not being manufactured. It only exists in the machine."

There was silence in the room. Sam could feel the runners' resolve to right a wrong slipping away.

Castillano cleared his throat.

"Biotech I know has a lab. Full computer-assisted design facilities. I can arrange an introduction. Standard fees."

Sam's spirit soared with new hope. He looked to Sally, who stood with hands pressed together in front of her chest. The tension in her arm muscles was evident as her hands trembled slightly. For the first time, Sam noticed that the magician was missing the last joint of the little finger on her right hand. She released the tension with an explosive sigh.

"Let's do it."

* * *

"Nice of you to drop in," Crenshaw said with mock politeness as Sam entered the stuffy room. He closed the door, shutting off the gray, predawn light from the outer room. The stink of wastes from the corner was overpowering.

"I've been trying to help the company."

"By sucking up to those criminals. Trying to help yourself more like," Crenshaw grumbled. "Do you think you're any better than us? That they'll treat you any different because you fawn on them?"

"You think I was trying to cut my own deal?" Sam was incredulous.

Crenshaw gave him a grin that said it was exactly what she thought.

"Just because that's the way you operate doesn't mean everyone does. Some people *do* care about others."

"Yeah, and I'm St. Nick."

"You're wrong, Crenshaw. I'm hoping to save some lives."

"Starting with your own."

"No. Starting with some of our fellow employees at the arcology." Sam told her how Sally's group had been duped, and their decision to do something about it. "I'm going with them when they take the counteragent in."

"Trying to be a hero?"

The thought hadn't crossed Sam's mind. "They need my help."

"Heroes get dead, kid. Those clowns got in once before. They don't need you to do it."

Sam supposed she was right, but surely Renraku security would have found and closed—whatever entryway the runners had used last time. "Maybe I just want to be sure they really do it."

Crenshaw looked unconvinced. "Stow the hype, kid. Let's pretend you've convinced me of your noble heart. Sentiments are worth a fused BTL chip when the shooting starts. You aren't trained for this stuff. It's dangerous, you know."

"I don't care." Sam was surprised by the conviction in his own voice. "It has to be done."

"Crenshaw-*san* is right," Jiro whispered from the corner where he was huddled. Sam had not even realized that the salaryman was awake. "Let it go. You will jeopardize your position with the company."

"So she has infected you now, Tanaka-*san*." Sam shook his head sadly. "I'm not worried about my position with the company. They will understand that my loyalty compels me to make this effort. I have to keep the shadowrunners from misusing their time within the arcology."

Crenshaw smirked and Tanaka hung his head, listless again. Sam could see that his arguments would not affect them. It was just as well. His short cyberspace run, added to his lack of sleep, had left him exhausted. He needed rest. The run was to take place the next night and it was definitely going to be dangerous. He would have to be alert. Sam lay down where he was, stretching out on the hard boards. In moments, he was asleep.

Sam awoke to a hand on his shoulder. Red light flooded the room through the open doorway. The glow illuminated Ghost's face as he leaned close.

"Time to move, paleface."

Sam sat up groggily, shaking his head to clear it. For a moment, he was confused, but the smell soon brought it all back. A quick glance told him that he and the Amerindian were the only two people in the room.

"Where are the others?"

"We thought it best to move them to a safer place till we get back."

Sam nodded as Ghost padded silently across the room. Perhaps the man spoke true. Or perhaps the runners were holding the others hostage for his good behavior. He didn't want to believe that they had killed his fellows to be free of the need to guard them, but that possibility nagged, too. Crenshaw's cynical voice echoed in his head. Could he really trust these people?

Sam creaked his way across the old boards. In the outer room, he found Sally, Ghost, and the Ork all strapping on various bits of gear and checking their weapons.

"Where's Dodger?"

Sally gave him a smile. "Don't worry. He's in a place where he can jack into the Matrix undisturbed. He'll be riding shotgun in cyberspace, just like last time."

"Are the others with him?"

"Let's not get too inquisitive," she advised.

Having inserted a knife into his boot sheath, Ghost scooped a bundle from the floor and tossed it. Sam fumbled the catch, surprised by its weight. The black paper garment was obviously covering some bulky object. He poked at it, revealing the soft gleam of metal. Sam unwrapped it further.

"A slivergun," Ghost informed him. "Can you use it?"

Sam looked down at the evilly gleaming weapon. "No."

"Great," moaned the Ork. "He's gonna get our behinds fried, Sally."

"If he does, he goes with us," she replied. "You do understand that, Verner?"

He did. All too well. He tried saying so, but the words stuck in his throat. He nodded instead.

"And don't forget it," the Ork snarled. "I'll be keeping my eye on you."

Under that watchful eye, Sam carefully placed the pistol on the floor and pulled on the coveralls that had enshrouded it. After sealing them closed, he buckled on the belt and holster he had missed in the excitement of discovering the gun.

"Ooh, look," the Ork cooed. "A ferocious shadowrunner. I'm so frightened."

"Dump it, Kham," Sally ordered. "Verner will do all right if you ease up a bit."

She settled her weapon belt across her hips and, in a swirl of fringed duster, turned for the window. Sam started to follow, but came up short as a hand gripped his arm. He craned his neck around to find Ghost's ragged grin. A poke in his ribs directed his gaze down toward the gun the Amerindian was holding. Sam swallowed hard. He didn't want it, but if they trusted him to carry it, he probably should trust their belief that it might be necessary. He took the weapon, settling its unfamiliar weight into the holster.

The fire escape creaked and rattled under the combined weight of the shadowrunners. Sam feared that it would rip loose from the crumbling brick wall and pitch them all into the alley. To his surprise, the rickety construct was still intact when they reached the bottom.

Three motorcycles waited in the alley. Two of the bikes

were sleek Yamaha Rapiers, their chrome and plastic smooth and unmarked. The third was a heavy hog, its nameplate proclaiming it a Harley Scorpion. The machine was all motor, iron, and mysterious clamps and fastenings.

"You ride with me," the Ork grunted as he swung onto the big Scorpion.

Sam climbed up behind the odorous metahuman. There was nothing to grip but the Ork himself, a decision Sam had barely made when Kham jumped the bike forward. Sam nearly tumbled off as they rounded the corner. The petrochem roar of the Rapiers soon joined the howl of the Scorpion, and they cruised in vee-formation down the streets of the Barrens.

The ride through the streets showed Sam the same face of Seattle he had seen on their walk to meet the fixer, at least until they left the urban wasteland of the Barrens. Once into the more civilized districts, the street crowds thinned and the noise and glare diminished. Somehow the runners did not look out of place. There were still other bikers in leather and long coats. The hard-edged types that had filled the streets of the Barrens were leavened with more ordinary folks, salarymen, families, and ordinary workers out for a good time.

Seattle was a border town, isolated among the wild lands of the Salish-Shidhe Council. It was an outpost of the United Canadian-American States in the midst of a foreign land, a trading post within the world of the Pacific. As such, it could be a rough-and-tumble place, just like in the old days of the wild west, Sam decided, when a man or woman often carried the law in a holster.

Even so, the corporations frowned on anything that might seriously affect business, and so there were peace officers. Private cops and the Lone Star patrols kept the heavy weaponry from the streets and protected their masters. What people did to each other did not concern the corporations, but what they might do to corporate holdings or personnel did.

Sam found this balance of wildness and civilization strange after the ordered peace of greater Tokyo. The strangeness had a vitality that the Japanese capital, with all its culture, sophistication, and history, lacked. Maybe he was beginning to like Seattle.

The closer they came to the central business district, the more civilized the street traffic became. Electric cars and public transport became common sights as the bikers became rare in proportion to the prowl cars bearing the Lone Star logo. The numbers of folk on the street shifted more in favor of the corporate workers, but the outré element never quite disappeared. The odd and the strange hung at the outskirts of Sam's awareness in a way he had never experienced on the streets of Tokyo. He found it exhilarating.

Well into downtown Seattle, they turned onto Alaskan Way and headed south. Ahead, dwarfing the nearby buildings, loomed the arcology. Shining out from the mostly darkened north face of the structure, the cool blue of Renraku's name in English and Japanese complemented the gold glow from the company's dot-and-expanding-wavefront logo.

Once, Sam had found those symbols comforting, a sign of home. They looked gigantic and unattainable floating above Seattle. And ominous. He imagined the circle that was supposed to be the source of the communication waves as a radar dish, its arc-shaped waves as all-seeing energy seeking out those who might harm the corporation. His earlier excitement fled, banished by nervous fear. Despite the crowded street, he felt naked and exposed. The Red Samurai must surely be watching their approach.

If they were, they took no action. The runners cut out of the traffic onto a side street, dodging through alleys among the dockside warehouses. They slowed as they neared the loading docks of their destination, Kinebec Transport, but the great corrugated doors remained unmoving.

"Damned Elf missed his cue again," Kham muttered, his voice almost lost in the noise from his bike's engine. "Probably off chewing dandelions."

Ghost signaled a circle around the block, drawing an oath from the Ork. "We'll attract attention."

"No help for it," Sally shouted over the bike's noise.

On the second pass, the third of the six doors yawned open as they rounded the corner. The runners guided their bikes inside and killed the engines. The massive door rumbled down, swallowing the echoes and shielding them from the street.

Ghost led them unerringly through the darkened building to a maintenance panel. Some fast work with a multitool had the panel down, allowing them to make their way to the lower level along a ladder of rusty rungs welded to the support girder. A hundred or so meters later, he took them up another ladder. The building they entered smelled of the sea. Sam could hear the faint lap of water against pilings.

" 'Kay, paleface. We're on the number one west-face dock, just seaside of Fast Freddie's Surgery. It's your lead now."

Sam didn't know where Fast Freddie's was, but he recognized the dock designation from the maps of the arcology he had seen. He led the runners onto the street and up the dock toward the arcology. A bare thirty meters from the circumference road that ran along the walls of the structure, he indicated the gate to a construction site. Before Ghost could put his tool to work, Kham shouldered into the wire gate, snapping the thin chain and dropping the padlock to the ground.

"We're in a hurry, ain't we?" he said in defense of this lack of subtlety.

Leading them past the quiet machinery, Sam took them into the basement of the skeletal structure. A few minutes' search located what he was seeking.

"This is a tap shaft to the heat-exchanger pipes that run under the arcology. We should be able to move along it and into the arcology through an uncompleted maintenance station."

"You'd better be right, chummer. Dat don't look like a comfy squirm."

Sam hoped he was right, too. His plan to enter this way was based on a three-week-old construction schedule. That document had called for the station to be completed and secured by now. He was counting on the fact that just about everything at the arcology project was behind schedule. If the workers had been uncharacteristically efficient, they would be denied access.

The crawl proved every bit as "squirmy" as the Ork had feared. Twice the bulky metahuman got wedged trying to cross junctions without divesting himself of his equipment first.

Two sweaty hours later, they had worked their way

through the steamy tunnel to the station. Faint worklights gleamed from a barrier-free opening.

Sam wiped his brow with a grimy hand. At least now he didn't have to worry about what the runners would do to him if the way had been blocked. Per plan, they located the station's terminal. Without jacking in, Sam turned it on and entered the code that would tell Dodger they had gotten inside the arcology's boundaries.

Almost instantly, the Elf responded through the terminal's speaker.

"You are late."

Sally's headshake forestalled any assorted retorts. "Are we all set for the next phase?"

"Assuredly, my lady. The bravoes manning the check points along your route have been instructed to expect a repair party. There are temporary access cards waiting for you at the main desk on alpha level, but you will need your special talents to pick them up. Unfortunately, I don't have the necessary codes to activate them and haven't had time to make counterfeits. It really is quite a remarkable system they have here. Very sophisticated."

"Save the admiration for later, Elf," Ghost snapped. "What are we going to do about those codes?"

"No need to get testy, Sir Razorguy. I think there may be a solution. If the noble Sir Corp will enter his own code, I can copy it onto all the cards. I believe I can hide the multiple entries in the guise of a system hiccup."

The runners looked expectantly at Sam. His mouth was dry. If Renraku had deactivated his access code when he disappeared, the plan was destined for failure. At worse, it would set off alarms. Either way, he would be compromising his confidentiality agreement with the corporation. As if he hadn't already done that by leading these people here.

"Dodger?"

"Aye, Sir Corp."

"If I put in my code, can you read it, or are you blind-copying it?"

"Have you so little faith? Am I not The Dodger, wizard of the Matrix? Once it is data, it is mine to do with as I please."

No, Sam thought, I am demonstrating a remarkable amount of faith. Your feathers only seem to get ruffled when you're bluffing about how good you are. "You'll not keep a copy to use on another run?"

"Sir Corp, you wound me. Of course not. Expediency is the goad that forced me to this pass. A decker of my skill opens what he will, at will."

"Glad to hear it, Dodger," Sam answered. That probably means you *can't* do it. "I'll put it in."

While Sam entered his code into the datastation, Kham pulled Sally aside. They returned with four pairs of Renraku work coveralls and matching hardhats from the locker room. As the runners started to put them on, Sam just stood there, holding the set Sally had handed him.

"This isn't going to work, you know," he told them. "Sally and I might pass, but you two are obviously not Renraku."

"S'matter, Raku not an equal opportunity employer?" the Ork rumbled.

"Not if they can avoid it."

"Just put the stuff on, paleface. Sally'll take care of it."

With little other choice, Sam complied. "What do you mean, Sally will take care of it?" he asked, sealing the white suit over the black one they had given him.

"An illusion spell," she said. The guards will see what they expect to see."

"If you can do that, why bother with the coveralls?"

"It's easier this way. The less I have to twist to make them see what I want them to see, the easier it is to make them see it."

"If you could do this, why didn't we just walk in the front door?"

"Trid," she said. "Now be quiet for a minute and let me concentrate."

She closed her eyes and put her left hand on the hilt of her magesword where it poked through the slit pocket. Her right hand contorted through a series of gestures as she moved it slowly back and forth in front of her. Sam saw, or thought he saw, a vague glow shimmer briefly into existence, trailing the path of her mystic passes.

It was too strange. He turned away in time to catch an expression of nervousness on Ghost's face. Was something going wrong? He turned to the Ork and found Kham staring in fascination at Sally. His ugly face showed a mixture of awe and lust. The Ork's elbow gouged Sam in the chest.

"I love it when she does that," he whispered.

Sally's eyes snapped open and the spell was done. She directed them to gather tool boxes to hide their weapons. That accomplished, they boarded a shuttle cart and rode to the elevators.

The guard at alpha level received them incuriously. Handing over the passcards, he barely looked at the little group. Sam thought it just as well because Kham stuck his thumb up one nostril and waggled his fingers at the guard as he stuck out his paw to receive the card supposed to be his. Unbelievably, the guard failed to react.

As soon as they were safely inside another elevator car for the ride to higher levels, Sam leaned over and whispered in Sally's ear.

"Kham's antics were hardly the expected behavior of a workman. Why didn't the guard react?"

She chuckled softly. "I'm used to Kham. I just work extra hard on his part of the spell."

When the car sighed to a halt, they exited onto a promenade. It was mostly empty. The few late-night strollers ignored them, just as they would a legitimate work crew. The same way, Sam realized, that he had always ignored work crews. He wondered if Sally's spell was even necessary here. They soon came to another guard station, and Sam was glad of the spell's effectiveness as Kham stuck out a deep purple tongue in the direction of the woman behind the counter. She only wished them good luck in an uninterested way before returning her attention back to the trid set squawking softly from below eye level.

Three more elevators and two guard stations later, they reached the Computer Systems Research office. They passed the guard there with no more trouble than before. Once inside, a quick check with the Elf got an all-quiet signal.

"It's been too smooth," Ghost declared. He pulled his Ingrams out of the toolbox, slipping one into his belt and keeping the other ready in his hand. Kham and Sally grabbed their own guns. They seemed to trust the samurai's intuition more readily than the Elf's report on the security conditions.

"Safety first, paleface," the Amerindian said when Sam made no move to reclaim the weapon they had given him. "You won't have time to come back for it if we get hosed."

Reluctantly, Sam picked up the slivergun.

"Let's be quick," Sally said, passing out the containers of counteragent that Castillano's biotech had supplied. "Spread it around. We don't know how much and exactly where the stuff's been used. I'll clean whatever's left of Seretech's dirty toys out of the closet."

They split up.

Sam was starting to spray his third room, a large work area for the system developers, when Sally joined them.

"Got them all," she said before starting to spray the far side of the room with counteragent.

A minute later, a red-clad guard appeared. The man might have been making an unscheduled patrol, or he might have been on his way to the head. He didn't appear to be in a hurry, and that encouraged Sam. After so many successes, he was almost comfortable with the completeness of Sally's spell. He felt almost safe. With Sally in the room with him, little could go wrong. Her spell would keep them from discovery.

As the guard passed him, Sam raised the hand holding the gun and waved. The man waved back and continued on his way. The guard was halfway through the door when he stopped and turned around, his eyes going wide.

"Watch yourself, lady," the guard shouted at Sally as he reached for his weapon. "Armed infiltrator!"

"N . . . No," Sam stuttered, raising the slivergun.

The guard ignored him, clearing his holster and dropping into firing stance.

Sam's finger tightened on the trigger of the slivergun. The weapon bucked as it unleashed a steady stream of plastic flechettes. Closely grouped needles traveling at slightly subsonic speed stitched a crimson line across the guard's chest and right shoulder. He tumbled backward, bright blood spraying from his mouth, landing sprawled and still. His gun struck the floor, its metal ringing with a clear note that seemed obscenely pure in the sudden gory disarray.

Sam's own gun dropped to the floor with a harsh clatter.

The sound of Sam's shot brought Ghost and Kham running.

"Aw, drek! What happened?" the Ork barked.

"Guard must have caught a flaw in the spell," Sally answered.

Sam was dazed, seeing the last few moments over and over again. He watched the guard turn, a puzzled expression on his face. No fear. No concern. Just puzzlement. Then the brown eyes had widened, focused on the slivergun.

"He seemed to see the gun."

Sally spat a string of syllables that sounded like a curse and stamped her foot.

"He should have seen it as a tool. The intent wasn't focused right. Since the slivergun wasn't something you were used to, the intent couldn't cover it as well."

"It's done now, Sally," Ghost said in a placatory tone as he moved to check the body.

"I shot him," Sam said. He felt numb.

"Don't worry, chummer," Kham said. "De corp will never know who did it."

"But he's dead," Sam protested.

"Nope," Ghost contradicted. "But he will be—without attention. If he gets that while we're here, *we'll* be dead."

"Let's finish and go." Sally's voice was brittle.

They went back to work, leaving Sam to stare at his victim.

The fallen guard looked young, not much older than Sam. A life cut short because a magic spell hadn't done what it was supposed to do and because a foolish, scared Sam had panicked. It didn't seem right.

This guard wasn't some thrill-seeker from the streets. He wasn't even one of the faceless Red Samurai, hardened to the harsh realities of life. This was just a kid, doing his job. He had even tried to protect Sally, assuming she belonged to the company and that only Sam was the intruder. What a foolish irony.

Why had Sam taken a gun from the runners? It had seemed unlikely he'd need it. Had he needed it? Whether or not, he had used it. The result lay at his feet.

How could good intentions have led him to this?

Some infinite time later, Sam became aware that Ghost was talking to him. He blinked, realizing that he was no longer in the Computer Systems Research Center. Somehow the runners had gotten him to the car pool on sub-level F. It was supposed to be their last stop inside the arcology. The Elf was to have arranged an assignment for a vehicle to take them away.

"Come on, paleface. Listen to me," Ghost was saying.
"The Elf has put in an emergency call for the guard. They'll
take care of him. Are you satisfied?"

"Satisfied?" Sam's voice seemed distant, as if someone
else were speaking. "I need to know if he'll be all right."

"Not likely."

"You go on. I've got to go back and find out. You've done
what you needed to do for your reps. You don't need me
anymore. Go on. Leave me here."

"We ain't leaving you behind to raise de troops," Kham
growled.

"I won't," Sam protested.

"You're right," the Ork said, aiming his HK227 directly
at Sam's belly. "'Cause you're sticking with us."

Sam looked to Sally and Ghost, but their eyes were cold.
Ghost plucked away the slivergun that had somehow found
its way back into Sam's holster. Sam hung his head and let
himself be led along.

As the van they had liberated pulled onto Western Avenue, Sam heard the wailing of a siren in the sky above. He
rocked his head back and caught a glimpse of a DocWagon
sky ambulance banking around the arcology, bound for one
of the landing pads. He wondered if it was in time to do
any good.

Fragments of sensations and images touched him through
the daze into which he had retreated. A dimly lit building
and a grubby pile of white coveralls vanishing into a trash
incinerator. Flashes of shadow and light. The Ork's stink.
The howl of a siren. Wind lashing his face and the throb of
a powerful engine beneath his seat.

Abruptly, he was aware that the wind and the hammering
pulse of the engine had stopped. He was seated behind
Kham, the Scorpion's roar muted now to an idle rumble.
They were somewhere in the Barrens.

"Dis is where you get off, Verner."

Sam swung his leg over the hog to stand in the midst of
the three mounted shadowrunners. He faced Sally.

"What about the others? Will you release them now?"

It was Ghost who answered. "They've been on their own
for half an hour. Should be reaching the arcology about now
if they weren't afraid to take the Third Avenue bus through
Orktown."

"What about you, Verner?" Sally asked softly. "Going to follow them back to Renraku?"

"Of course," Sam responded automatically, "I work for the corporation."

Kham stifled a guffaw. Sally lashed him with a frown and turned her eyes on Sam. "That might be a foolish move."

"I don't think so. I am confident they'll understand."

"It's your funeral," the Ork bellowed, revving his hog and roaring away into the night.

"Good luck," Sally called as she gunned her Rapier and screamed in the same direction the Ork had taken.

"You are very loyal, paleface. I hope they deserve it." Ghost tossed Sam the slivergun. "You might need this to get home, but I suggest you find it a nice trash compactor before you meet any badges."

The Amerindian's Rapier squealed as the tires fought to grab the pavement, then it sped away, chasing the echoes of the others.

Sam was alone on the street save for a mangy mutt scrounging scraps among the garbage and rats. Laying the gun between his feet, he sat on the curb.

He stared at it for a long time before realizing he had company. The mongrel had abandoned its search to sit beside him. It, too, looked at the gun.

"Don't you know what to do, either?"

The dog whined and tried to lick Sam's face.

"I haven't got any food for you."

The animal's tail thumped the pavement, dismissing the gross oversight. Sam stood and so did the dog. It skipped down the street a few meters, then stopped.

"Shall I run the streets with you, then?"

The dog cocked its head.

"No. Not tonight. Life in the shadows doesn't seem to be for me."

Sam turned in the direction he guessed would take him back to friendlier parts of Seattle. The glow in the night sky promised that he had made the right choice, He had taken only a dozen steps when the dog trotted to his side.

"Coming with me?"

The dog yipped.

"Well, friend," Sam said, as the dog began to pace him.

"Loyalty is no easy virtue. But I suppose that doesn't frighten you. You will be true to your nature, after all."

Man and dog walked on in silence. Behind them, drops of rain began to patter down on an abandoned gun left lying in the shadows.

PART 1

# It Takes More Than a Salary, Man

# 1

2051.

Samuel Verner had never believed the stories about the Ghost in the Machine.

However bizarre the tale, there was always a reasonable explanation. Some stories were pure fantasy while others were hoaxes by wiz-kid deckers or outright lies by incompetents seeking to hide their mistakes. There was no evidence for a disembodied sentience in the Matrix.

Now, under the electronic skies of the Renraku arcology's Matrix, he began to wonder.

A persona icon had entered the datastore where Sam's own projection was at work. The core of the icon was the standard Renraku corporate decker, the chromed image of a proper salaryman. The Raku logo pulsed in blue neon on the left breast, shoulders, and back of the figure's suitcoat. The chrome reflected the swirling numbers and letters that were the datastore's visual representation. Harsh red lines striped the icon's surface like angry wounds, rude shadows of the luminous outline that surrounded the humanoid shape.

That wireframe simulacrum was a caricature of a *kabuki* clown. Any patron of that bawdy Japanese theater form would recognize this figure of pathos who inspired laughter among those spared the larger-than-life trials of the clownish victim. Sam was familiar with the image in the *kabuki*, and he was also familiar with it here in the Matrix. The hollow clown and its corporate core was the adopted persona icon of Jiro Tanaka.

But Jiro had been dead for at least three hours.

Just before beginning his work for the day, Sam had made an unauthorized access into the arcology's hospital data bank. Jiro's file was closed but not yet sealed. Within the file, the patient log recorded the cessation of Jiro's brain activity at 06:03 PST. Sam was saddened but not surprised; the young corporate decker had been sinking steadily for five days since his accidental fall from the promenade in the open mall. The two-story drop to the concrete had shattered bones and ruptured organs. The doctor's prognosis had been pessimistic, citing possible brain damage and an apparent lack of will to survive.

Yet now, Jiro's persona icon was active in the Matrix, threading its way through the mazes of data. It moved slowly, hesitantly, like a newly freed spirit adjusting to a novel form and abilities. Ghosts made little enough sense in the real world; they had no business in the analog world of the Matrix. This consensual hallucination used by computer operators to manipulate the immense dataflows at incredible computer speeds was not a real "world." It had no way to trap and hold souls.

Some of the rogue deckers infesting the datanets claimed that a decker's soul could be left trapped in the Matrix when some killer-countermeasures fried his brain. Sam had seen enough scientific documentation to know that such rumors were fantasies. The persona icon was only a placeholder, a marker that indicated where an operator's attention was focused in a computer system. It had no existence, even though another operator in the same part of the system could perceive it. The icon had no objective reality. It simply indicated where the decker was engaged, an analog for his activity among the datalines, optical chips, and computer architecture that was the Matrix. There was no place for spirits in the electronic world. Souls were the province of God, and when the body died they went on to His judgement. No machine could hold them back.

There had to be another explanation. Sam's program continued to run as he pondered the riddle. While his own icon remained stationary among the tumbling alphanumerics, nearly transparent because his cyberterminal was engaged in a "flow-through" search, the Jiro icon passed him. It gave no sign that it noted his presence, no hint of recognition. Sam felt simultaneous disappointment and relief. Even a ghost of Jiro could not have passed without acknowledgement. Whoever was using Jiro's icon was a stranger.

Sam's fingers flashed over the keys of his cyberterminal. The flow-through program disengaged and he activated the program he had named Tag Along. When the terminal brought Tag Along to active status, his icon flashed opaque, resolving into the standard Raku salaryman icon. Sam stood and placed himself behind the Jiro icon, pacing the intruder step for step and turn for turn. Occasionally, Sam's icon flickered suddenly to a new location, "teleporting" with the power of Tag Along to remain out of the Jiro icon's line-of-sight and thereby out of the operator's awareness.

The teleport was a function of the program that Sam didn't understand. He knew *why* it operated, he just didn't know *how*. But then, he was a user not a programmer. He didn't have to know. The ability had proven helpful in the those first few months after the kidnapping incident and that was enough for Sam.

The death of Jiro's wife had affected the young decker radically. His behavior had become erratic, leaving him surly and solitary where he once had been open and sociable. Renraku Corporation had reacted to the change, solicitous of its employees' welfare. When Sam reported the addition the young decker had made to his Matrix icon, the company psychiatrist agreed that monitoring was a reasonable precaution. The physician had authorized company software experts to write and emplace a custom watchdog program that would allow another decker to follow Jiro as he moved through the Matrix. Hardware modifications and custom software embedded in Jiro's cyberterminal workstation made the watcher invisible to the senses of Jiro's icon.

Sam had persuaded the psychiatrist that he was a good choice as a watcher. After all, Sam was one of the few people at the arcology who knew anything about Jiro. The doctor agreed that Sam might have a good chance of noting anomalies in Jiro's behavior, possibly picking up subtle references to past events. In fact, the doctor had agreed so readily that Sam suspected he might have done so because the plan was good therapy for Sam himself. Sam didn't care. Therapy or not, he wanted to watch over Jiro. Their experiences at the hands of the shadowrunners who had hijacked their shuttle had created a bond between them. Sam could not abandon Jiro, especially after seeing how easily his friend absorbed the nihilistic attitude of Alice Crenshaw, the other survivor of the hijacking.

The Jiro icon moved out of the datastore and deeper into the computer system, jolting Sam with a sudden shift in perspective. He was no longer accustomed to the forced movement of Tag Along. It had been months since the psychiatrist had certified Jiro as stable and thus discontinued the Tag Along authorization.

Sam fought off the disorientation, focusing on the task at hand. If this wasn't Jiro, then someone had entered the Renraku system illegally. No legitimate user could operate with someone else's persona programming; they wouldn't have the codes or know the passwords to unlock the software. Sam had a duty to the corporation to prevent misuse of the system.

He thought briefly about disengaging and alerting security, but rejected the idea because it would break his contact with the intruder. The Raku security deckers would probably find the outsider in short order, but in the meantime no one would know what he had been doing. And when they caught up with the icon, a dogfight would likely dump the intruder out of the Matrix. It would get rid of the intrusion but not the mystery behind it. Sam wanted to know who was impersonating his friend.

The icons slid down the datalines, passing by some nodes and through others. Occasionally, they passed images of red neon samurai. These guard figures were fixtures of the Renraku Matrix, the software that provided intrusion counter-measures, or what decker slang knew as ice. The guards were Matrix versions of Renraku's elite Red Samurai security forces, though the icons looked more like ancient Japanese warriors than the real guards in their neo-feudal body armor. As Sam expected, none of the samurai moved to oppose them. The passcodes embedded in their icons attested to their legitimate presence. Whoever was manipulating the Jiro icon was counting on such protective coloration.

In some of the areas through which they moved, the Matrix imagery was muddied, the sharpness of line in the constructs less than standard. At the first few nodes where the phenomena was obvious, the Jiro icon paused, seemingly interested in the effect. This was another clue that the intruder was an outsider, for every Renraku decker was familiar with the fuzzy areas that had become increasingly common along the datalines of the Raku architecture. The imagery-haze phenomena were random in duration and location, seeming not to affect computer performance. None of the deckers knew the origin of the disturbances, and their reports had drawn nothing more than a directive to continue logging all encounters with the phenomena.

The intruder spent time in several datafiles, but not once did Sam observe the stillness and flicker that he associated with downloading a file into a persona's memory. If the Jiro icon's controller was not going to steal any significant data, what was he up to? Was he simply a "joyrider," using Jiro's terminal to play around in the Matrix?

The intruder moved on.

At last the Jiro icon stood before the glittering barrier that the company deckers had tagged the Wall. The Wall was a featureless expanse of sputtering static, shades of gray contrasting starkly with the soft blue glow that suffused the Renraku architecture. This was forbidden territory, even to Raku deckers. The Jiro icon remained a long moment before the barrier as though contemplating it.

Was this the intruder's goal? An assault on the Wall? Sam disengaged the Tag Along just as the Jiro icon stepped forward, merging with the Wall and vanishing from his perception. Before Sam could enter the alert code, the icon reappeared, tumbling backward through the Wall. The clown-shape flickered, hissing and sputtering as the icon crashed into and skidded along the invisible surface that was the "floor" of the Matrix.

At the same moment, the Wall extruded a samurai that was of a piece with its parent, a menacing shape of static. The shifting surface tones blurred and disguised the detail in the samurai icon's imagery. It stepped free of the Wall, drawing a *katana* from its sash as it advanced on the Jiro icon. The sword blade crackled with lightnings as the samurai swept it up.

The Jiro icon rolled away from the first blow, leaving behind a ghostly image of itself. The samurai icon advanced on the ghost image. As the ghost struggled to rise, the samurai attacked, its *katana* slicing through the ghost's neck, neatly decapitating it. The head had barely separated from the ghost's body before both winked out of existence.

Snapping its head to the side, the samurai icon focused

on the real Jiro icon. Though the deception had bought only a fraction of a second for the intruder, it was enough for him to ready an offensive program. The interior icon held a deadly looking pistol while the *kabuki* overlay superimposed a sputtering matchlock handgun on the standard Renraku Matrix image of the attack program. Chrome salaryman and wireframe clown raised their weapons, firing as the samurai charged.

The pistol roared on autofire. The reflection matchlock, operating as its prototype never could, fired again and again. In a crazy kind of slow motion, Sam saw the bullets impact the sputtering static armor of the samurai. There was no perceptible damage.

Reaching its opponent, the samurai icon loomed over the intruder. The *katana* swept up above the armored head and poised briefly before flashing down. The sword sliced through the outline clown but failed to connect with the inner chrome shape as the Jiro icon threw itself to the side. The wireframe outer Image vanished with a pop. The samurai took another step forward, twisting its body around to convert the momentum of its swing into another strike. The blow caught the Jiro icon as it tried to stand, staggering it backward. The chrome surface of the Jiro icon blackened where the sword had touched.

As the *katana* swept up, the battered remnant of the Jiro icon lifted an arm in a futile gesture of defense. The sword whooshed down, slicing through the upraised arm and driving into the chromed breast of the icon.

The Jiro icon vanished instantly. The samurai remained poised in full extension from the deadly blow, then snapped to an *en garde* pose. Above its head, the sparkling blade hissed evilly.

Sam remained still as the gray and black samurai turned in his direction. What he had just witnessed was not a computer-moderated game, nor a training exercise, nor a trideo entertainment. Its imagery may have been virtual, but its effects had been very real. The intruder controlling the Jiro icon was now likely dead or a mindless husk, the higher functions of his brain destroyed by the deadly attack of the computer-controlled samurai. Sam feared the samurai's scrutiny as the dark eyeholes of the armored facemask swept across his position, but the guard icon merely sheathed its sword. With a contemptuous swagger, the samurai turned back to the Wall and stepped into the flickering static. The figure merged with the Wall, vanishing as though it had never been.

Alone on the plain outside the Wall, Sam considered his options. If he reported the incident to his superiors, he would have to confess to following the Jiro icon instead of reporting it immediately. It would also mean revealing that he had observed Renraku's ownership and use of illegal black ice.

Sam's head ached and his fingers were cold as they hung poised over the keyboard. He stared at the Wall, half-seeing images of destruction in the volatile surface. He could do nothing here. Instead of retracing his path to the datastore he had been researching, he jacked out.

His icon disappeared from the Matrix as his awareness returned to the cubicle where his body sat hunched over his cyberterminal. With a sigh, he pulled the plug from the datajack on his left temple. He rubbed his face with both hands, trying to banish the nagging headache that always accompanied his forays into the Matrix. Usually the rubbing replaced the dull pain with a clean tiredness, but today his head continued to throb.

Black ice.

That was what protected the Wall. Killer-countermeasures intended to wreck an intruder's equipment and quite possibly take his life. The presence of such deadly software meant that Renraku so valued whatever was behind the Wall that the corporate masters had no compunction about sending deadly electrical impulses through the lines to fry the brain of anyone who illegally accessed their system. Killer ice was illegal, but its use was never reported to the authorities because it was always directed against criminal intrusion. The corporate world of the twenty-first century relied on the old adage that dead men tell no tales. But now Sam had seen the killer ice in action, and lived to tell about it.

He would never have believed that Renraku would stoop so low, showing such callous disregard for human life. How could Aneki-*sama* allow it? Sam suspected that the shrewd old man was not aware of what his underlings were doing here in the arcology, and he believed his duty was to inform the director-*sama* of this terrible turn of events. But how to do so? He guessed that the samurai's last look meant that those behind the black ice knew Sam had witnessed their villainy. If he made an attempt to reveal what he had seen today, at the very least, they would use their power to block or alter his report. If Sam tried to go public with the information, even if only within the Renraku corporate structure, he would be making enemies. Powerful and deadly enemies.

# 2

Dirty, spiteful faces surrounded her, leering. Rough, gutter voices called her names and mocked her. The faces were laughing, split with snag-toothed grins, taunting her. She had spent her whole life trying not to be part of their world, hating its helplessness. Helplessness—what she hated even more than those faces.

They were scum. The same all over the world, the hopeless and the lost huddling in the shadows of the great metroplexes. They were street people, chippers, drudges, and bums. They were petty criminals, pimps, sleazers, and whores. Some of the scum thought they were better than the rest, malcontents who called themselves shadowrunners and played at being noble idealists. As though a fancy name could change what they were—thieves, two-bit terrorists, and parasites on the body corporate.

Sometimes the scum got the upper hand, caught someone before he or she could get out with enough skin intact for the corporate doctors to rebuild. But revenge was possible if one awaited her chance, worked for right time to strike like a tiger from ambush. That was the way a professional handled it. Sooner or later, the vermin always made a mistake and a pro would hand them their heads. At least that's what she would have done if some snivelling traitor hadn't sold her out, had her drugged, and traded her bodily integrity for his own.

In the dark, the flashes of sweaty, grunting bodies fueled her rage. Filthy, fetid room. Grimy, groping hands. A bad-toothed grin under mirror eyes. Slobbering mouths. Pain.

She hated traitors. Weak-minded perverts who sold away their company's heritage and fellows for their own gain and sold off their fellows for their own comfort. She hated the slime that let others do the dirty work they were afraid would dirty their hands. Worse than those, she hated the ones who got away with it, the ones who went crawling back to their corporate cocoon as though nothing had happened. As if they had betrayed no one.

One by one, the faces changed, their features flowing and coalescing until each face had a single set of features. A broad, dirty face with mirror eyes that belonged to a gutter animal. Street scum. A sleazer. She would never forget that face.

The leering visage splintered like a glass mask, the shards falling away to reveal another face underneath, deceptive in its ordinariness. Blond hair close-cropped in a salaryman's cut, a chromium steel datajack on the left temple. Square jaw. Straight nose. Hazel eyes. She knew that face, too. She knew it as well as her own, knew all the wrinkles and blemishes. Placid, dog-stupid, trusting, and innocent, it was a traitor's face, mocking her and her helplessness.

She hated it.

Blam!

The Ruger Super Warhawk in her right hand roared, blasting 11mm slugs into a jeering visage. No more datajack.

Blam! Blam!

No more hazel eyes. No more pearly toothed smile.

Blam! Blam! Blam!

Faces splintered under her bullets, the traitor sent to oblivion. Atonement for her shame.

No traitor. No shame. If only it were so easy to expunge him and the memories in the real world as it was to imagine his face on the range's targets.

"Nice shooting, A.C."

Crenshaw spun, acquiring target without a thought as the smartgun link fed data through the induction pad in her hand. The gun's snout homed in unerringly on the speaker's face. He blanched as she increased pressure on the trigger.

The hammer fell with a click.

She smiled at the terror on his face. Her link had told her that the gun was empty, but he didn't need to know that. Let him think she was a little wild. It wouldn't hurt her reputation. She was slower than most of the other Renraku special operatives, and her cyberware at least a generation behind. If fear would give her an edge, she'd take it. Any edge was better than none. She didn't care if the grunts thought she was crazy; the people upstairs knew she did her job. They were the ones who counted, only their opinion mattered.

"Frag it, Crenshaw! What're you doing?"

"Anybody who sneaks up on me regrets it, Saunders. Don't forget it, because next time the gun won't be empty."

Saunders stepped back, face rigid and eyes wide. Crenshaw slipped off the sound-suppressor headset and walked away from the firing line. As she passed the armorer's counter, she tossed him the gun, not bothering to see if he caught it. On her way through the door to the lockers, she grabbed a towel.

"You're frizzed! You know that, Crenshaw," Saunders called out to her back. "Totally glitched."

She could hear the forced bravado in his voice. She smiled.

# 3

A poke from Kiniru's wet nose was usually enough to wake Sam, but today the akita had to resort to planting one of her huge paws on his stomach. The sudden pressure forced all the air from Sam's lungs in an explosive burst. He sat up, gasping.

Kiniru, a canine grin on her usually somber face, sat gazing at him eagerly. A glance at the wall screen, which he always left set for a view from the outside, showed him the gray clouds hauling a threat of rain in from the Pacific. That gloom would soon banish the morning sun, making the day suitable for a funeral. He flicked the control, and the trideo set boomed to life. While Heraldo Fong's *Enquiring Eye* raked through the story of some sensational thaumaturgical murder, Sam tossed back the covers, shaking his head in wonder that the arcology programming director would broadcast such hysterical drek at this hour. As Sam swung his legs over the side of the bed, Kiniru stood and skipped back. She padded to the door and looked back expectantly.

"Hold on. I've got to get some clothes on."

Kiniru barked her impatience.

"Go talk to Inu. He knows enough to keep quiet."

Instead of obeying and joining Sam's other dog, Kiniru sat down, tail beating against the doorway. Ignoring her impatience, Sam clicked Fong off in the middle of a tirade against unlicensed magicians in order to use the screen for the room's computer. There were no messages waiting, so he started a check on his continuing inquiries concerning his sister's whereabouts and condition. The screen flickered, displaying the status of his programs as he dressed. The same as yesterday—nothing. Sam ignored the flashing symbol from the expert system monitoring his apartment's computer. He knew what it wanted, but he was not yet ready to let it send the message he had composed for Sato-*sama*. It had possibly become irrelevant; Sato was due to arrive at the arcology in a few days.

Kiniru butted his leg.

"All right. Let's go."

Inu was exactly where Sam expected, sitting calmly by the door. The brindled black and white mongrel barked its greeting and stood. As Sam palmed the door open, the dogs squeezed past him, jostling their master to the side. He watched them run down the corridor toward the open area at its end. The Level 82 park was big enough for the akita to get a good run. Because the other residents knew and liked the dogs, they never complained about them running free. Inu stopped just inside the shadows of the corridor to glance back reproachfully at Sam.

"Go on, Inu. I'm staying here."

Inu waited until Sam made a shooing motion with his hand before gamboling out into the sunlight to join Kiniru and some of the level's children in a game of chase-and-tumble. Sam wished he could be as carefree as the former stray. It was Inu that had followed him back to the arcology that night of a year ago, making a place for himself in Sam's world as though it were sheer destiny. While Kiniru was pure-bred, this creature of the streets was almost feral, yet he had settled into arcology life as though he'd been whelped there.

Sometimes Sam wondered if this were only a veneer, a canine version of his own resignation. When Sam had returned to Renraku after the kidnapping, he'd expected the

corporation to treat him as a disgrace. Instead, he and Jiro
had been sent for evaluation to certify that the kidnapping
had not unbalanced them. No accusations of wrongdoing.
In fact, not a single mention of the events. Stupefied, Sam
had gone along with official efforts to ease him back into
corporate life, expecting at any moment to be denounced
by the guard he had shot. Censure never came. It was as
though nothing had ever happened.

But that didn't mean Sam could forget. Inu was always
there to remind him. Sometimes he awoke in the night, the
guard's face frozen in his memory and the accusing voice
saying over and over, "I was Mark Claybourne. You took
my life from me." Surprised and frightened when Claybourne penetrated Sally Tsung's illusion, Sam panicked. He
had shot at the young guard, but had only intended to wound
him. It was Sam's agitation and unfamiliarity with firearms
that left Claybourne so horribly injured that modern medical
science had been hard-pressed to save the guard's life. When
the doctors were unable to restore full nerve function, Claybourne committed suicide. Claybourne may have taken his
own life, but Sam took the blame.

It was only after Sam's return to the arcology that he
discovered the identity and fate of the guard. It had not been
an easy job. Someone had sealed Claybourne's medical records as though actually trying to hide Sam's deed. Once
Sam had the information, Claybourne took up residence in
his dreams, a ghost of the mind. Unable to atone, Sam
struggled daily with the guilt, praying for forgiveness and
understanding and vowing that his hand would never harm
another innocent life.

What about the shadowrunners whose schemes had so
enmeshed him? Did they feel any remorse? Did they care
that they had made a killer out of Sam? Not likely. Like
Inu, they were almost feral, their way of life at complete
odds with Sam's corporate world. He presumed the bunch
was still out there somewhere, cooking their deals and running their shady scams. They probably didn't even remember him. He was just a suit to them, passing briefly through
their shadow lives. They were runners and he was corp, an
alien in their world.

Renraku, one of the corporations that made the world go
round, had taken care of him and his sister after their parents died. Having grown up thinking of the corporation as

both home and family, Sam's loyalty had been fierce. The events of last year, however, had left him numb with shock. Now came another severe blow to his image of the corporation he called family. What he had seen in the Matrix two days ago raised painful questions of ethics and responsibility. Questions to which he hadn't the vaguest answers. Hell, questions he didn't even want to think about. But it was becoming harder and harder to make Renraku resemble his old beliefs.

When his wake-up alarm chimed, Sam let the demands of the moment push all these disturbing thoughts into the background. Hanae would be here soon and he still hadn't eaten or showered up. He stepped back inside. He was dumping the empty packets from breakfast into the disposal slot when the door chirped. "Who's calling, please," he said into the intercom, at the same time hitting the switch to send his refuse down to the arcology's recycler.

"My, we are formal this morning. All right. Hanae Norwood, sir. Perhaps you remember me? We met at the Independence Day celebrations last year."

Sam palmed the door open to a giggling Hanae. The jet black helmet of her hair set off her bright Eurasian features, but the drab gray of her very proper suit was out of character. Though suitable for a funeral, it was a far cry from the bright colors she favored. Lifting herself onto her toes, she kissed Sam's cheek as she entered.

"This would have been much simpler if I had stayed here last night."

"I wanted to be alone."

"Don't sound so worried. I understand," she assured him as she fished through her purse. "I've got an armband for you here somewhere."

Mumbling his thanks, he took the black band she held out. It was so like her. Knowing he'd probably forget the band, she'd taken it upon herself to keep him from making a gaffe of corporate etiquette. Like a good helpmate, she understood those little details that seemed so meaningless but were worth points on the corporate ladder. Loyal, attentive, ambitious for him, and not least of all, charming and pretty, she was everything a salaryman could want in a woman. He should formalize their relationship, but something inside him held back.

Hanae followed him into the bedroom to check her

makeup while he finished dressing. The mirror was near his computer console. Too late, he realized he had not blanked it. He could see her reading the screen as he pulled on his shoes.

"You still haven't sent off your letter to Sato-*sama?*"

*Not now.* "I don't want to talk about it."

"You really should," she insisted softly.

"What's the use? If Sato remembers me at all, he remembers our last meeting at the hospital in Tokyo. He made it abundantly clear that he resented wasting time on me, even if Aneki-*sama* thought it worthwhile. Sato has no love for *gaijin* and still less for anyone who might threaten his position by siphoning off Aneki-*sama*'s attention."

She looked confused. "But you weren't a threat to him."

"Aneki-*sama* was watching my career. That's threat enough for someone like Sato."

"You're exaggerating. Sato-*sama* is a smart man. He couldn't be otherwise to become Aneki-*sama*'s special assistant. He knows that a simple researcher would never be a threat to a man of his position. You must have misinterpreted his intentions."

"Misinterpreted? He seemed pleased enough to see me exiled to the arcology. Everybody knows that the only people who have any real future with Renraku work out of the home offices in Japan. The arcology project may be important, but it's just a side show."

"Of course it's important." She seemed offended that he could think otherwise. "That's why you're here. Aneki-*sama* probably wants you to get experience you'll be needing later. It's just a stepping stone, not a punishment."

"You really don't understand, do you?" A familiar rage made Sam snap at her. "I saw Sato's face when he told me about what had happened to Janice. He enjoyed giving me the bad news."

"That's unkind."

"*He* was unkind. No, cruel. Not that he cared what happened to my sister. He was pleased at what it meant for me. Whether Janice lived or died, she had shown that the Verner bloodline is what they call tainted. As if not being Japanese weren't taint enough for someone like him. Like everything in Japan, the *kawaru* affects more than the one who is changed. A whole family can be destroyed. My sister's metahuman blood is enough to bar me from rising in the corporation.''

"But they didn't fire you," Hanae observed as though that settled the question.

"Doesn't make a lot of sense, does it? I've often wondered why. I've heard of enough others who've been sacked under similar circumstances.''

"Perhaps it was Aneki-*sama*'s influence. He was your patron and wouldn't abandon you. So you see, he probably sent you here for training.''

Her optimism never failed to cheer him, perhaps even more so when it helped him to continue believing in his old life. "Maybe he didn't abandon me. But even the head of a major multinational corporation has to bow to the immense power of social conventions in Japan. This exile to Seattle was probably the best he could do, perhaps an expression of regret for the dictates of unfortunate circumstances.''

Hanae smiled. "Aneki-*sama* is a good man.''

"Whatever the intention, Renraku is keeping me away from Janice when she needs me the most. They've blocked every attempt to see her.''

"It's hard to believe that Aneki-*sama* could allow such a thing.''

Sam's new doubts made him wonder, but another part of him still wanted to believe that Aneki was, indeed, a good man, that it was others who were corrupting Renraku.

"Someone else must be responsible,'' she concluded.

"Like Sato?''

"I don't think so," Hanae said firmly. "Aneki-*sama* would never let such nastiness so close to him.''

Again, Sam wanted to believe, but he had heard the viciousness in Sato's announcement with his own ears and who was closer to Aneki-*sama* than Sato? Sato might be the villain, or he might not. Sam had no evidence other than the man's disagreeable nature. Not knowing who to blame only made Sam angrier and more frustrated. "Whoever is responsible, I'm stuck here in Seattle, confined to the arcology 'for security reasons.' What a joke! They haven't let me near any sensitive data since I arrived. They keep me busy on trivial researches. I've done my job and been a good little researcher, but I still don't know what happened to Janice.''

"Maybe you should hire someone," she suggested.

"With what? Arcology prices are outrageous. With my lower job rating, I haven't got enough credit to hire a detective even if they would let me contact one."

"Then you should work through the corporation."

"What do you think I've been trying to do for the past year?" Sam snapped. "It hasn't done any good. Janice has become a nonperson to Renraku. I know they provided her with the usual benefits of relocation and restart money, but that's all I know. The Imperial Japanese government is scrupulous about that. They despise metahumans, but they do care about their global image as a compassionate government. Compassionate! Metahumans are the new *bunrakumin* in Japan; a new class of outcasts, doomed to misery, poverty, and the dirty jobs that the upper classes disdain. Even the *bunrakumin* look down on metahumans. That's what Janice has now."

Hanae quailed from his intensity, fright in her eyes. Having been raised entirely within the corporate environment, she still believed in the corporation and the great *zaibatsu* spirit. She was even more sheltered than Sam had been at the moment his step into the shadows showed him that all was not as it seemed. Hanae truly didn't understand what he was trying to tell her.

There was no point in pushing the issue. His own feelings were in turmoil; he didn't need to upset her further. Shrugging into his suitcoat, he said lamely, "We're late."

Hanae nodded timidly and took the hand he offered. "We can talk more later if you want."

He reminded himself that she only wanted to help. "Sure. Later."

# 4

The outer doors of the hangar opened slowly, their electric motors whining in protest at the unaccustomed work. Standing on the other side was the Dragon, its golden scales glinting gloriously in the morning light. When the doors had completely retracted, the beast furled his great, membranous wings against his body; they were too wide to permit him to pass through even this opening intended for aircraft. Dipping his neck, the Dragon lowered his wedge-shaped head enough for the great paired horns to clear the lintel.

Katherine Hart was as impressed as ever at the size of the beast. Western Dragons were the most massive of the dracoforms, lending them a greater air of power than their more slender cousins. She performed a formal bow of greeting as the great beast advanced into the shade of the hangar. The Dragon's massively muscled body moved sinuously past her without acknowledgment. He paced down the ramp into an unlit tunnel.

He was obviously in a bad mood.

The only good thing was that the Dragon's annoyance was not directed at her, she had been on time, as directed. As the closing outer doors left them enveloped in a soft darkness, she turned to follow him. Untouched by sun or artificial light, the tunnel corridor they entered was darker still. Within that blackness, a soft hissing accompanied the clanging of steam pipes. The temperature and humidity rose, and the tang of rust overlaid the antiseptic smell of the corridor as the antiquated climate control system struggled to do its job.

*Good,* Hart thought. *Maybe this will improve the old lizard's mood.* It did little for hers. She hated the clammy air that Dragons seemed to prefer, but she was willing to put up with it and its effects on her wardrobe if it made the beast at her side less irritable.

With the first step onto the flooring, she knew her hopes for an improved mood were slim. The Dragon would be annoyed by the cold, smooth tiles, disliking the uncomfortable hardness and poor traction. Why couldn't the suit in charge of the physical facilities have prepared better for the Dragon's visit? His claws were rasping gouges into the carefully polished surface. Perhaps the person responsible would take a hint from the Dragons' destruction of the flooring and replace it with something more to the beast's liking. At the very least, they could have sanded the corridor.

The beast's tail swept back and forth in an unconscious rhythm that broadcast its pique. The spines on his tail could eviscerate someone in moments. Though her position just aft of the creature's hindquarters allowed Hart to demonstrate proper deference, it placed her too close to those barbs. She hoped the big lizard wouldn't get so ticked off that he forgot she was there.

As they paced toward the faint light ahead, Hart nearly tripped in one of the half-meter furrows, but fear of the lashing tail kept her on her feet. The Dragon would no doubt be aggrieved if he accidentally killed her. After all, the services for which she had been paid had yet to be performed. Sincere or not, however, the Dragon's grief wouldn't make her any less dead.

Flashes of light probed toward them from the depths of the corridor, the cyan tones glinting a green highlight on her companion's golden scales. He belched slightly in annoyance, halting the flames before more than a wisp of smoke escaped his jaws. Hart breathed her relief aloud; if the beast unleashed a blast of fire, it would set off the building's sprinkler system. A bath from the sprinklers would really raise his anger. Hers, too. Her hair was going to need repair as it was.

Though annoyed, the Dragon showed no concern over the nature of the light. She assumed, therefore, that it was no more than a side effect of the activities at the end of the corridor or some kind of scanning beam. Either way, the Dragon appeared to deem it harmless. Or at least harmless to him, she corrected herself. No matter that he wanted her services, she could not be sure that he would warn her of any risk that affected only her. It would be just like a Dragon to haul her into danger as a test of her skills.

Nothing threatened them as they traveled the corridor to a pair of retracted containment doors. Beyond the arch, the passage was blocked by a wall of glowing green light, a magical barrier of great strength. Hart shook her head at the foolishness of the proprietors. Were they going out of their way to annoy the Dragon? They should have opened the circle as he approached, instead of making him wait. This Dragon disliked being kept waiting by those he considered inferior.

The pair stood for a long minute before the pale green glow ebbed away, crawling back from the center of the corridor like acid eating away at paper. Within the boundaries protected by the circle was an inner set of doors. These sighed open even before the magical barrier had widened enough to admit the Dragon's bulk. A Human awaited them, bowing and mumbling apology and welcome.

The man wore a pale green lab coat embroidered in stylized designs. A heavy silver disk swung from a chain around his neck as he held himself bent at the waist. Hart recognized the markings as cabalistic symbols, real ones rather than the crude protective runes worn by the superstitious. The symbols were much like those she used, but with subtle variations whose study could give her a clue to the magical orientation of this person. It was obvious from the arrangement and profusion of the markings that the wearer was a mage and member of an hermetic order. She didn't recognize the particular group, but she knew enough about Human magical orders to tell that this mage was a minor member of his organization.

"Greetings, Lord Dragon," the Human said in a louder voice. "We are honored by your presence today."

The Dragon disdained to reply.

Hart caught a flare of emotion from the beast, confirming that he was as testy as she had feared. She remained outside the archway as the Dragon continued on, sliding his great golden bulk past the man. When the Dragon's tail flicked toward her leg, she sidestepped quickly, the sharp spines missing her knee by centimeters. The mage, holding his bow, was oblivious to the danger. *Foolish, norm. Always keep your eyes on a Dragon.*

The tip of the beast's tail had barely cleared the door when Hart saw the ripple begin in the powerful tail muscles. Ivory spines arced up as the Dragon's tail swept toward the mage. The man grunted in surprise and pain as the barbs tore across his left thigh and into his belly. The impetus of the blow lifted him from his feet and slammed him aside, into the wall. He slipped to the floor, moaning.

*"Perhaps you will not be so slow the next time."*

There was no sound to the Dragon's words, but Hart knew the mage *heard* it as well as she did. Dragon speech was a trick of mind and magic, something much more than a voice, something less than telepathy. The creatures still needed to know a language before "speaking" it. Their "words" had a consistently flat intonation, but carried emotional overtones in a way that Human speech could not. The emotional content that they broadcast needed no language. The Dragon's annoyance and irritation would have communicated even to someone who spoke no English.

The beast proceeded into the chamber, heedless of the

spatters of blood that flicked from his tail spines and the wail that arose from his victim.

Hart approached the fallen mage. A brief glance was enough to tell her that his injuries were beyond her own skills. She bent and placed her hand on the screaming man's forehead. Taking advantage of the pain that shuddered through him, she overrode his will and sent him down into sleep. A small enough blessing.

Behind her, she heard running footsteps. A glance over her shoulder confirmed that the mage's co-workers were coming to his aid. One woman ripped a first aid kit from its wall receptacle and almost caromed into a white-haired fellow with the most elaborate coat Hart had yet seen among them. The woman's haste to prepare mundane aid earned her no kind thoughts from her superior, judging from the glare he gave her. Hart had to agree; it should have been perfectly obvious that the fallen mage would need more than coagulant and spray seal to save him.

Hart stepped back to let the new arrivals tend to their comrade. Noticing that her sash was stained where it had dipped into the mage's blood, she briefly considered its worth as a material component for ritual purposes and found no significant value. This mage was too stupid to ever make it necessary. She untied the knot that held the band around her hips and let the scarf flutter to the floor. *One thousand nuyen on the expenses, Old Lizard. That was real silk and a Scaratelli to boot.*

Dismissing the ruined sash from her mind, Hart surveyed the chamber, It was large, a vast womb in the belly of the earth. The ceiling was hidden, even from her eyes, in darkness and haze. Lights mounted on the exposed girders of the structure cast sharply defined cones of light onto the floor. Hart stood on the highest level, a platform with twin ramps leading down in opposite directions. She could just barely discern other platforms hugging the walls at various levels below her. The chamber formed a great bowl, each level spiraling toward the crowded floor of this carefully guarded sanctum.

In the center, a great vat made of some transparent substance sat on a platform of machines and monitors. Technicians stood in a recessed pit around the cylinder, monitoring consoles and adjusting dials. The color of their clothes was washed out by the iridescent glow emanating from the vat. They paid no attention to the motions of a dark shape that roiled the milky fluid within the receptacle.

Still watching the activity below, Hart strolled down the ramp the Dragon had taken. She caught up with the beast on one platform that offered a wide, graveled area with an unobstructed view into the theater. As she approached, he settled his bulk on the rough surface and arched his neck until his head rested on the railing around the landing's perimeter.

In the bowl below, mages and technicians bustled about, performing activities that sent mingled odors of rank organics, the ozone of technology, and the sharp scent of sorcerous workings wafting up to the visitors. *This environment should be more to his liking,* Hart decided as she watched the beast nestle into the gravel.

*"This is more satisfactory,"* the Dragon confirmed, unasked.

Hart and her employer observed without interruption until Hart noticed someone approaching. It was the master sorcerer who had arrived at the side of the wounded man just as Hart left to catch up with her employer. The mage stopped a few meters away to compose his face into a pleasant expression before stepping forward to where he thought the Dragon could see him. From where she leaned against the beast's withers, Hart felt more than heard the soft chuff that she recognized as a sign of the Dragon's amusement.

Hart knew that the beast could see that the mage stood waiting. The Dragon let him stand there for some minutes, a period sufficient to establish dominance, then inclined his head to signal his attention.

The Human smiled. "You are just in time, Lord Dragon. It's almost ready."

*"It will work as desired, Doctor Wilson?"*

"Certainly. The last two prototypes performed well within parameters. Mutability factors have all been right on prediction and there has been no decay in stability. We have no reason to believe the process is flawed."

*"Well that you should not."*

Wilson swallowed, his fear apparent to Hart. She had no doubt that the Dragon sensed it, too. He could probably smell it.

"I meant no disrespect, Lord Dragon. It's just that, as both a mage and a scientist, I expect all new processes to have some problems. It's only natural. This project has gone very smoothly under your guidance. I have no doubt that the product will meet with your satisfaction."

The Dragon flexed its wings slightly, dismissing Wilson's remarks. *"Show me."*

"As you wish, Lord Dragon." Wilson wet his lips with a pink tongue that only slightly protruded beneath his mustache. "With your indulgence, it will take a few minutes."

The Dragon remained silent. Wilson turned quickly and vanished into the darkness of a side tunnel. A moment later, he reappeared, emerging from a corridor onto the floor of the chamber to have a brief conference with a quartet of his fellows.

Hart wanted to get a closer view of the operation. Reaching into her shoulder bag, she retrieved a pair of glasses. She tapped once on the frame to adjust the setting to magnification and settled them on her head. What she saw on the screens was fascinating, though she understood very little of the abstruse hermetic formulae, much less the chemical formulae. She wished she had a copy to study at leisure.

The consoles forfeited her attention when they blanked at the first faint strains of thaumaturgic chant beginning to drift up from the group of mages gathered below. She scanned the bowl's floor. All the ordinary technicians, save one, had disappeared. That one was attaching a hose to a wheeled canister. The other end of the hose was fastened to the vat. The technician moved to a nearby panel, where she adjusted a few knobs. Bilious green swirled into the vat's fluid, commingling with the liquid until it resembled molten jade. As more and more of the green substance entered, the shape in the vat slowed its motion, ultimately becoming still. Apparently satisfied, the technician shut down her panel and vacated the floor.

As soon as she was out of sight, the mages raised their voices, strengthening the chant spell. The four who had joined their master split away in two pairs to take up station's at opposite sides of the container. Their song rose again in volume as Wilson stepped up to the tank. The paired mages split, one of each couple remaining in place while the other walked a quarter of the way around the circumference. The cardinal points occupied, they raised their chant almost to a shout before dropping it to a soft, monotonous tone.

Within the hermetic circle, Wilson executed a series of intricate hand motions. The sweeping gestures described by his arms grew ever smaller until only hands and fingers moved. Then they too stopped. A heartbeat later, Wilson stepped back. A casual gesture of his right hand brought a harness down from the obscurity of the ceiling. A flaccid spider trailing its web, the straps plunged into the once more translucent liquid to snake around the limp shape. Wilson raised his hand and the harness rose in sympathetic motion.

The figure that emerged from the tank was humanoid. Though it was naked, Hart could discern no sexual characteristics, primary or secondary. Now that it was no longer a shadow, she could see that its skin was as milky white as the fluid had been when they arrived. The flesh was soft and unlined, barely disturbed by the swell of muscles. It seemed somehow undefined.

Around the bowl, computer screens sprang to renewed life, displaying columns and rows of figures as well as formulae and diagnostic illustrations. Hart had no interest in numbers or pictures. The limp shape, at once compelling and repulsive, absorbed her whole attention. The strength of her fascination blew her usual cool professionalism away on the faint breeze from the air purifiers.

"Quite extraordinary, isn't it?"

Hart was startled. She had not registered Wilson's departure from the floor of the chamber, let alone his return to the platform.

"I've never seen anything like it."

"No one has. That is part of what makes it so valuable."

*"Direct your attention to the reaction data, Hart."*

She was annoyed at the beast's use of her name in front of the mage, but she did as she was told. Scanning the screen displaying physical data, she whistled. The specs would look good on an Olympic athlete, but no Olympian had ever excelled in so many areas. "Superlative," she concluded.

The Dragon chuffed his satisfaction.

*"Very good."*

The mage bowed in acknowledgment. His face was a carefully constructed combination of the praised servant and the acknowledged savant, but Hart could see behind the subservient mask to the relief that was the man's real emotion.

The Dragon stood, arcing its neck in a stretch that radiated satisfaction. When they had left the birthing chamber behind and the barriers both astral and mundane had been restored, the Dragon spoke. *"I believe it is time for Mr. Drake to begin Operation Turncoat."*

Hart could feel the beast's anticipation.

# 5

"We came from the dust of this planet and to the planet we return our bodies, recycling without end. Yet, while our mundane dross returns to oneness with the Earth, our spirits soar onward to answer for our stewardship. Let us consider now the works of men, especially those of our brother Jiro."

The priest stopped speaking and, after some scattered "amens", silence filled the small chapel. The room was not crowded. Besides Sam, Hanae, and the priest, only ten others were present. Jiro had not made many friends in his year at the arcology. Most of those attending were business acquaintances. Of his family, only an uncle had come.

The only flowers were a single twig of cherry, its forced-growth blossoms wilting quickly. Their scent was overwhelmed by the musty odor of the earthen floor.

Sam contemplated the pasteboard coffin. It was cheap, degradable paper in keeping with the Conservationist creed. Paper was still relatively inexpensive in the Northwest. He'd read that believers in other regions used cloth bags or didn't bother with a covering at all.

The priest rustled his cotton robes to attract the congregation's attention. "Brothers and sisters, we are still here, alive in the living world. Our brother Jiro has moved on in the never-ending cycle. We pray that he has achieved unity with the great spirit of life. Now we commit his shell, not to interment within the earth, but to a proper and glorious dispersal. What our brother was shall enrich us all."

As the priest spoke, the coffin slid back toward the chapel's inner wall, disappearing into the darkness. After it had moved, Sam could see the faint lines of the dirt that had slid into the trackway for the electric-motored platform that was carrying the coffin away. Somewhere in the darkness, attendants would remove the box and place it on a conveyor down to the recycling operation. Any usable parts would already have been sent to the storage banks. The remains would be rendered down to constituent components. Conservationists took recycling seriously.

"The family has asked me to announce a luncheon at Hsien's Natural Foods on Level 144. Those wishing to make a memorial contribution will find cards with a list of preferred organizations in the rack at the door of the chapel. You may, of course, contribute directly to the Church of the Whole Earth, Incorporated. All donations are tax-deductible. Thank you for coming."

The priest bowed, then disappeared into the darkness at the rear of the chapel. When Sam and Hanae turned to leave after a moment of deference, Sam was startled to see Alice Crenshaw standing near the door. He would never have expected the hard-nosed security woman to show up. She always made such a show of being hard-shelled.

Deciding that he wanted to talk to Crenshaw, Sam nudged Hanae in the direction of the security officer. Before they had taken two steps, however, a small, weedy man with a porcelain datajack in his right temple blocked their path. The jack and his lapel pin identified him as a Renraku decker.

"Geez, ain't it weird," the man began without preamble. "You keep finding out stuff about people even after they're dead. I didn't know Jiro was a Conservationist. Did you?"

"No," Sam replied, annoyed at the man's boldness.

"Hey man, you must of," he insisted. "You were his best buddy. Warner, ain't it?"

"Verner. I couldn't say I was his best buddy. We were friendly. Jiro didn't let anyone too close after his wife's death."

"Yeah. Thought you might have known him better than us guys down in Data." The man's eyes darted around the chamber. "You're right about him not having many friends. I would have expected more guys from the office to come, even though he was a loner. *Zaibatsu* spirit and all that. But I guess if you want to get that spirit up, it takes more than a salary, man. You know?"

"The company makes no demands with regard to religious observances here in America," Sam observed, keeping his voice carefully neutral. He thought that was the best way to make the man cease his inquisitiveness and let Sam get on with his business.

"Here in . . . oh man, that's right, you came in from Japan about the same time, didn't you?" The man didn't wait for an answer. "Guess it's real different over there. No Injuns lording it over proper educated folks. I hear they don't even take guff from the Metas. Keep them on reserves or something."

"I wouldn't know," Sam said through his teeth. His detachment had fled. "I didn't get out much."

"You ever hear about that island, Yomi, I think it is, where they ship all the Orks and Trolls?"

Sam controlled his anger. This man was obviously insensitive. Arguing with him would be worthless, and besides, Sam didn't want to make a scene in the chapel. "I was a *shaikujin*. Like a good salaryman, I never went far from Renraku property except on corporate business. The company has little to do with the so-called Awakened, so I didn't see much of them."

"Don't I know what you mean! Had a buddy who was a real good mechanic. Casey, real nice gal, even if she was a Dwarf. Got a job with Raku through EEO. Wasn't six months before her boss had her up on negligence charges. Couldn't have been true, or course. I knew Casey. Man, she took care of machines like they were her babies, but she packed it in rather than face the charges. Heard she was over at Mitsuhama. They're Japs, too, but they go a lot lighter on the Asian superiority thing, you know."

Sam could see Crenshaw stepping outside. "Look . . . ah . . ."

"Addison," the man supplied helpfully. 'Billy Addison."

"Addison-*san,* it's been a pleasure talking to you, but I really do have to get along."

Sam took Hanae's arm and tried to walk around Addison. The decker held his hand up in front of Sam's chest.

"Wait a minute, man. Look, I really wanted to ask you something. I . . . well . . . us guys down in Data were kind of wondering about something. You see, we knew you were friends with Jiro and . . . well . . ."

"Well, what?"

Addison shifted nervously. He craned his head around, looking to see if anyone was close enough to overhear. When he saw that the chapel had emptied, his face relaxed slightly. "There's . . . there's a rumor going around that Jiro was chipping when he fell."

"Chipping?" Hanae asked.

"Yeah, you know, using BTL."

Hanae put a hand to her mouth in shock. BTL stood for Better Than Life. BTL chips were supposed to be entertainment simulations that someone plugged into his head through a datajack or a special chip receptacle. They allowed one to "relive" an experience as though actually doing it himself. But the experiences were more than realistic. Unlike ordinary simsense entertainments, all BTL sensory impressions were heightened electronically, pushed into realms beyond any normal person's experience. The enhanced impressions were supposed to be unbelievably thrilling, more sensual than anything that real life had to offer. Sam didn't know if that were true, but he did know BTL was highly addictive. Users often lost themselves in the chip's world, abandoning the real world until they died of neglect or the real world intruded fatally on what they perceived.

Sam suddenly realized that a user might, lost in his false reality, stumble over a railing and fall to his death. Had Jiro? With the anniversary of Betty's death coming up, Jiro had been increasingly depressed. It was true he had done some chipping shortly after his return to Renraku, but he had stayed away from the heavy stuff. His doctor had even approved, prescribing certain chips and calling it re-entry therapy.

This put a new light on matters. Sam certainly didn't want to discuss it with Addison, nor did he want to go into the subject with Hanae around. "That's really none of our business. Besides, what difference does it make now?"

"Well, not a whole lot to Jiro. But we been thinking about the rep of the department, you know, if word got around that he was chipping, and certain parties started an investigation. You do know that *Kansayaku* Sato is coming? You know, the axman? He might . . ." As his words trailed off, the man arched his brows in a conspiratorial expression. "Well, you know. We were worried."

Worry Sam could understand, especially if someone in Addison's group needed to keep something hidden. Whatever the problem to which Addison alluded, it could not possibly be a material danger to Renraku. If it were, Addison or whoever was involved would already be running.

The mention of BTL might mean that somebody in the department had a chip habit. Lots of deckers used chips for recreation, but most knew enough to stay away from BTL. The implication that a decker was involved in the dangerous pastime could get him a black mark in his record that would affect the promotion schedule. Justifiably. No legitimate corporation wanted to trust its Matrix secrets to someone who was an addict. There were too many cases of blackmailed deckers stealing files, or crazed Matrix runners crashing systems when their delusions crossed over into the already hallucinatory reality of the Matrix. A decker who chipped would likely be canned and blackballed.

Then again, maybe the chipper had already paid the price. If Addison or one of his buddies had supplied Jiro with a chip, and if Jiro had taken his fall while under the influence, the charge would be manslaughter at the least. Sam couldn't recall any mention of BTL chips in Jiro's hospital file, but that didn't mean much. If someone had arranged for Jiro to get such a chip, that same someone might easily have been there when Jiro fell and then removed the chip before the medics arrived. Such a person would dread an investigation that might uncover his or her complicity.

Had someone in the department been running Jiro's icon when Sam encountered it in the Matrix last week? The data department would have known about Jiro's injuries, and they would have had physical access to Jiro's cyberdeck. A brain-fried decker would be impossible to hide, but a good back-up team might have been able to jack out the icon's controller before the black ice got him. Using someone else's deck was punishable by expulsion from the corporation as well as hefty fines, but that wasn't always enough to deter a dedicated hacker. But whoever had been running Jiro's icon had tampered with the Wall, which meant even harsher sanctions. If it were one of Addison's group behind Jiro's icon, they would all be subject to dismissal if their actions were discovered. They had more than enough reasons for a cover-up.

"Don't worry. Addison-*san*. I don't think there will be

any BTL investigations.'' Even as he said it, Sam also knew that there should be. Jiro *did* have a history of chip abuse, but his hospital file contained no mention of it. Just as there should have been an investigation of Jiro's accident. On the other hand, if Addison and his cronies were part of some cover-up, the decker wouldn't be here nervously asking questions. Someone else was involved, hiding something behind the official lack of interest. Crenshaw was in security. Maybe she knew something. ''We really do have to go.''

''Yeah, sure, man.'' Addison stepped back, a nervous smile flickering over his face. ''Well, thanks anyway, Warner. You're an O.K. guy.''

Sam hurried out the chapel door. Hanae, unquestioning, tried to keep pace, but after a few steps, she gave up. Sam raced ahead, anxious to catch Crenshaw. Scanning the park surrounding the chapel, he failed to spot her. Then she appeared from behind a hedge, walking along a path and almost out of sight. He ran after her.

At the sound of his footsteps, the woman looked back, but did not stop walking. Sam raised his hand and started to hail her, but she pivoted away and quickened her pace. She turned when the path branched at the statue of Chief Sealth and passed out of sight behind some trees.

Sam ran after her. His breath started to come hard. He was too fat, too out of shape for this. He skidded, trying to turn as he reached the intersection of the paths. Baffled by what he saw, he let momentum carry him into the statue. Leaning on the pedestal and puffing, he stared. The path Crenshaw had taken was empty.

There were no turnoffs that she could have reached in the time it took him to get this far. She must have left the path. She had deliberately eluded him. Why?

He wouldn't find the answer today. He had no hope of tracking her through the park. Crenshaw surely knew more than enough tricks to evade his amateurish pursuit.

She had been there when Betty Tanaka died and shared captivity with him and Jiro. Crenshaw had felt enough . . . what? affection? loyalty? curiosity? to come to Jiro's funeral. She had seen Sam and must have known he wanted to talk with her. Why had she fled?

It didn't make sense. There just weren't enough hard facts. All he had were possibilities. He was beginning to suspect that maybe he didn't want to know what was real and what was polite fiction or an outright lie. He had grown up believing that truth was important, but he was starting to suspect he wouldn't like the true story.

Someone was hiding facts connected to Jiro's death. Possibly someone within Renraku Corporation itself. Someone, perhaps an ambitious executive, was practicing deception for personal ends, twisting the corporation to suit his or her own plans for individual power.

*Listen to me. I sound like dupe of the week from Channel 23's "Confessions of a Company Man."*

Sam wanted to laugh it off, but could not. He had seen too many signs of something rotten. How much of what he had taken for granted was deception? He was still mulling over the matter when Hanae came panting up, her face flushed. Sam could tell that it was simple exertion and not anger. Concern and worry wrinkled her brow.

"Why did you run away?"

"I didn't. I saw Alice Crenshaw. I wanted to talk to her about Jiro. She knew him, too. I was trying to catch up to her, and she deliberately avoided me. She knew I wanted to talk to her, and she walked away. Just like the rest of the company, avoiding me."

"I'm not avoiding you, Sam," Hanae said softly.

It was true. She had been very good to him, always available with a soft shoulder. Why did he have doubts about his feelings for her? As always when he wanted to ease his discomfort, he embraced her. Hanae snuggled close, seeming well satisfied with the physical security of his arms. She hadn't yet noticed that he did not relax the way she did. Or if she did, perhaps she put it down to the tensions affecting him for as long as they had known one another. He certainly had complained about it enough.

"My life is a dead end here," he said, knowing it was an old line.

"Don't talk like that, Sam." Distress was evident in her voice. "Renraku is our home."

"Some home. They pen me in. I never get good assignments. They've lowered my security rating. It's a dead end."

He felt her tense up within his arms. She always said she liked him best when he was happy, that she would do anything to make him that way all the time. He wanted to believe that. Even more, he wanted to believe she could do it.

When he felt the yearning for her comfort, he wanted to fulfill her expectations, to be the man she wanted him to be.

"I could accept all that, if they would just let me contact Janice. They know what happened to her. Why won't they tell me?"

"They must have a good reason."

Sam wasn't so sure. Not anymore.

Hanae seemed not to notice his lack of response.

"When Sato-*sama* gets here, you'll see that things will change. He'll need you to get the project going, and he'll surely help you. After all, he is Aneki-*sama*'s assistant and Aneki-*sama* was your mentor. Renraku takes care of its own. All your trials will have been for a good reason. Sato-*sama* will help you."

*Like he helped in Tokyo?* "I don't think so."

"You must try, anyway."

Sam forced a smile. "All right."

# 6

Alice Crenshaw closed the door to the outer office, shutting off the protests of the security director's receptionist. The little twit should be used to her barging in on the director by now.

The director's aide, Jhoon Silla, stood halfway between the door and the director's desk, eclipsing Crenshaw's view of his master. Silla was dressed in his usual immaculate red jumpsuit, the gold Renraku logo and captain's star gleaming on his collar. His white Sam Browne belt gleamed softly in the indirect lighting of the lushly appointed office. The intense young man was rigid, stretched to the edge of action; his hand was under his holster flap and resting on the butt of his pistol.

"Very protective," she said as she advanced. "But slow. You should have been at the door before I closed it."

Tadashi Marushige sat back as she stepped around Silla. The security director folded his hands on his desk and gazed at her expressionlessly. He, too, wore the company's undress military uniform, the collar showing insignia of the exalted rank of general in the Renraku military forces. Crenshaw never knew Marushige to wear his undress uniform except to review the elite Red Samurai guards. When Marushige was in a military mood, he usually forsook his power suits for simple fatigues.

"You're early," Marushige observed as Crenshaw lowered herself into the armchair to the left of the desk.

"Useful habit."

Marushige's stare was suitably venomous.

"Feel free to continue," she offered, knowing that her insolence annoyed him.

"Quite all right," he said coldly. "I was just finishing up, anyway."

He called Silla forward with a gesture. The aide began to gather maps from the desk and shuffle them into a folder. From the far side of the desk, he produced a briefcase and slid the packet into one of its compartments. Crenshaw sat quietly, turning her head to watch as Silla crossed the room to stand the case on the floor and take up a position by the door. She noted the uniform hats and topcoats hanging behind Silla; their presence indicated that an operation outside the arcology was in the offing. Curious. She resolved to check with her sources as soon as the meeting was over.

She turned back to find Marushige waiting silently, watching her with his dark brown eyes. He said nothing. Finally, she surrendered to his patience.

"I'm not the only one running ahead of schedule today." The director's response was a nonverbal grunt that she took as a request to elaborate. "I thought you might be interested to know that your eleven A.M. meeting is moving itself up. Our friends from the Special Directorate are on their way."

"Interesting." If Marushige was surprised, he didn't show it, though Crenshaw suspected he was ignorant of the development. He had obviously been deeply involved in the planning session with his aide and would have left orders not to be disturbed. "And knowing that I would wish you to attend the meeting, you dropped what you were doing to come at once."

Crenshaw ignored the sarcasm in the director's voice. "Of course."

"Very commendable."

Praise from him, even delivered sarcastically, was unusual. Crenshaw kept her face calm, her body language unaffected by the surprise. She reached into her inner coat pocket and removed her cigarette case. Casually, she removed one of the brown-wrapped cylinders and lit it from the hot spot on the case's lining.

Marushige smiled tightly through the entire operation. When Crenshaw had exhaled her first lungful of smoke, he opened a drawer, took out a crystal ashtray, and slid it across the desk.

"In fact, your entire record here at the arcology has been commendable," he said in a soft voice. "Have you been enjoying your stay in Seattle?"

"It ain't Tokyo."

"Ay, yes. You have spent most of your long career working out of the Tokyo office."

Crenshaw didn't care for the way he said *long*. It sounded too much like a retirement speech. "We both know my record. What's the point?"

"Your *record* is the point, Crenshaw-*san*. Both your performance here and your previous experiences in Japan make you the most suitable candidate for a very special job."

*Drek! The little fragger has finally found a job that I won't be able to pass on. He's so pleased with himself that it must be a suicide run.* She took a long drag from her cigarette, letting the dry heat sear through her lung tissue to warm her body. *I didn't think he had the nerve to try that.*

"As you are no doubt aware, one of Renraku's senior officials, *Kansayaku* Hohiro Sato, will honor the Seattle arcology with a visit. He is conducting a fact-finding mission and audit for the home office. Naturally, security will be a primary concern. The *Kansayaku* will, of course, be expecting top-level attention which I, due to other pressing concerns, will not be able to supply in full measure. Therefore, it is my wish that you function as my liaison with *Kansayaku* Sato.

"You will, of course, be responsible for the *Kansayaku*'s personal safety as well."

Crenshaw felt both relief and suspicion. She surely didn't want to face an outside operation. She was too old for that nonsense, her enhancements at least a generation behind the opposition's top talent. The assignment Marushige held out had a high risk factor but was likely not a physical one.

With Renraku's resources, no enemy would be likely to take a shot at Sato. But with such a notoriously hard-to-please executive, her career would be on the line. One slip, no matter how small, in the *Kansayaku*'s sight and she could kiss a healthy retirement goodbye. "What if I don't want the . . . honor?"

"Your desires in the matter are largely irrelevant." Marushige looked down at his desk console. "You seem to have been correct about an early meeting. Two of the Special Directorate have arrived."

Tapping a key on his console, he communicated to his receptionist his decision to admit the visitors.

Vanessa Cliber announced her arrival with a bang, slamming the door out of Silla's hand and sending it crashing into an antique credenza. Her tightly bound hair was leaking from the chignon on her neck, and her face was flushed, set in an expression of grim determination. She stomped to the desk and backhanded a stack of data disks at the security director. Cassettes bounced in every direction. Most clattered to a rest on the desk's surface, but some escaped to the floor.

Crenshaw shook her head in open disbelief at Cliber's lack of restraint. This was no way to make points with a Japanese.

"Just what is the meaning of this?" she demanded. "Sherman is going to have kittens."

Marushige remained unperturbed. He stood and performed a formal welcoming bow before speaking. "Good day, Director Cliber. I do not understand your reference to President Huang, but I suspect you imply that he will be as upset as are you."

"Damn straight."

"Well, then, it will take some time to gather the disks you have so forcefully delivered, so perhaps you can tell me what it is about them that upsets you."

Marushige sat down as Silla moved a chair behind Cliber. She ignored the offered seat. "You know damn well what the problem is."

The security director shrugged. He turned his attention to the other new arrival.

"Ah, Doctor Hutten. Please excuse my poor manners. Your arrival was somewhat overshadowed. Silla, get the doctor a chair as well."

Hutten nodded his thanks before whispering something to Cliber. She gave a short jerk of a nod, then took a deep breath and sat down. Hutten followed suit as soon as Silla moved another chair from its place along the wall.

"Please excuse Vanessa, General Marushige. She's had very little sleep in the last few days. We've been having some severe problems with integration sequencers."

Marushige nodded sympathetically. "I understand perfectly, doctor. As you have arrived before your appointment, I sense that the offering of proper amenities would not be appreciated. So let us get straight to business. How may I be of service?"

Cliber snorted. "You should already know. I've sent you enough memos. We can't seem to get any action out of your people."

"Ah, yes. I assure you, director, that your memos have all crossed my desk. We of the Security Directorate are moving as quickly as possible in this matter."

"Then your staff are all fragging turtles," Cliber snapped.

"Vanessa!"

"I'm sorry, Konrad," she said apologetically to Hutten, then spent several moments visibly calming herself before continuing. "Security has not approved any of our personnel requests in the last four months. We are impossibly understaffed. We need bodies. If you can't clear the computer experts we need, at least let us have some technicians. Even researchers would help."

"Yes, indeed," Hutten agreed. "There were several promising ones among the last batch of personnel requests. We were especially interested in Schwartz, Verner, and Chu."

Crenshaw stabbed her cigarette out in the ashtray that she had placed on the arm of her chair. The force of her movement rocked the bowl from its perch. It fell to the carpet, spilling its contents into the deep pile.

"Take this Verner, for example," Cliber said curtly. "This guy worked in the Tokyo office for years. High-level, fast-track stuff in the operations staff. He even had citations from Aneki. What's it going to take to get you people to approve someone?"

"Times change, people change," Crenshaw growled.

"What is that supposed to mean?"

"Verner is classified as a security risk."

"I don't believe I saw that notation in his dossier," Hutten commented.

"He's a risk, I said." Crenshaw spat out the words. She never liked it when the soft worms in research questioned her. She expected them to know their business as they should expect her to know hers. Why wouldn't they just accept her word?

Marushige cut off Cliber's response. "We need not get caught up in specific situations. Director Cliber, Doctor Hutten, I have noted your formal complaint."

"And Sherman's."

"And President Huang's. But I am constrained in this situation. The Special Directorate's responsibility is to produce a fully sentient artificial intelligence. If this is possible, it will be a feat of world-altering significance. But we cannot let our competitors steal all our hard work."

"They couldn't catch us in years."

"So you say, director. But if their own research programs are caught on some point that we have already solved? Wouldn't a spy then be able to bring them the crucial information?"

"No one is as close as we are," Cliber insisted.

"That may be so, director. You can afford that belief. I cannot. The Security Directorate is responsible for keeping even the existence of Renraku's research into artificial intelligence from reaching our competition. Most of our own people don't even know about it. I cannot afford to let an agent into the project."

"You didn't do such a good job last week," Cliber sneered.

"Ah, you are referring to the usurpation of the Tanaka persona program."

"What else? Or have you got more security breaches covered up in your cozy hierarchy?"

Marushige's smile froze on his face. His eyes went hard, but his voice remained supple and smoothly comforting. "Of course not, director. My directorate always owns up to its mistakes. We informed you of the incident at once, did we not?"

"Sure you did. But you haven't told us anything since."

"There has been nothing worth reporting. You know better than most just how intricate our Matrix security measures must be. Most of our security deckers are working in strictly limited areas, operating without full knowledge of what they are protecting. Some report irrelevant incidents that they believe to be significant, while others are quite likely failing to report the very data we need. Our Zeta clearance operators are reasonably certain that no data was removed, but we are no closer to determining who was controlling the Tanaka program.''

"Does Verner's involvement have something to do with your assessment of him as a security risk, Crenshaw?'' Hutten asked.

"What are you talking about?''

"He was in the node when the intruder assayed our defenses.''

Crenshaw flashed a look at Marushige. The director's face was closed. If he knew, he hadn't told her. But she didn't like the implications of that at all.

"Ms. Crenshaw is handling the personnel aspects of the problem,'' Marushige asserted. "There is no solid evidence of Verner's involvement in the attempt to penetrate the AI project. I assure you that the Security Directorate is making full efforts to uncover the perpetrator.''

"As full as your efforts to clear the personnel we need?'' Cliber asked scornfully.

"This persona usurpation is an example of the difficulties we face. Surely if someone like Verner was involved in an attempt to breach the security of our computer systems, you would not wish him assigned to a position that would make it easier to steal our secrets. Would you, director?''

Cliber narrowed her eyes. "If Verner is a risk, kick him out. Otherwise, give him to us.''

"There is a risk to the project's security here, and I am responsible for security, director.''

"And I am responsible for seeing that this project makes its deadlines.''

"Then you must understand the weight of responsibility and the need to do the job right.''

"I know what you're trying to do,'' Cliber declared. "I'm going to make sure that Sato knows, too.''

"*Kansayaku* Sato will make his own observations and draw his own conclusions, director,'' Marushige responded placidly.

Cliber glared at him. "We may as well leave, Konrad. We certainly aren't getting anywhere here.''

She stood abruptly and headed for the door. Hutten rose awkwardly, a pained half-smile on his face. He sketched a bow before following his superior.

"Silla," the security director said softly, "arrange a car." As the door closed behind his aide, Marushige turned to regard her.

"You are too open about your hostility, Crenshaw. They may report what you said with regard to Verner."

She was already annoyed by his previous ploys and didn't feel like playing games with him. "Let them."

"You should be concerned," he warned. "It's your ass on the line."

"Why don't you worry about yours? If my ass gets chewed, I'll feed yours to the dogs, too. Why didn't you include Verner's computer log in the security record? You knew about him being there when the Wall was hit." Marushige stiffened, telling her that the shot had scored. He had known. She gave him a smile as she prepared to twist the knife and remind him who had the upper hand in their relationship. "You won't be able to claim your drug pump slipped on this one."

His nostrils went wide, as they always did when she brought up his not-so-secret shame. Marushige had an implanted monitor-dispenser system to keep him supplied with special psychoactive drugs, chemicals to control the imbalance in his brain that fostered violent rages. Before the implant, he had been a slave to his impulses and had almost been dismissed from the corporation. The drugs corrected the problem, but the occasional inaccuracies in the chip's calculation of dosages let Mr. Hyde crawl out. Marushige, desperate to hold his position with Renraku, did his best to cover up those lapses. His shame gave her a powerful hold over him.

"Just remember who has the monitor tape showing you abusing the late, lamented Claybourne. That kid would never have been crippled if you hadn't kicked him that way."

"He should never have gotten himself shot," Marushige said through gritted teeth.

Crenshaw chuckled and took out another cigarette. "Doesn't matter what he should have done. You shouldn't have kicked him. There're lots of ways to be a damned fool. You're the one who damaged his spinal cord."

"He was incompetent."

"That's what your superiors will say about you if they learn that you were responsible for crippling a company asset."

"Tapes can be doctored. It would be your word against mine."

"You must be getting a little hot, Marushige. We've been over this before. That tape will show up pure in any test you care to name."

"If you produce it, you will implicate yourself in the break-in. You could have stopped those shadowrunners out in the streets."

"Wasn't in my contract."

"The *Kansayaku* may not see it that way," Marushige said. "It is said that he places a premium on personal initiative."

"That's what got me where I am today. Got me back to the arcology security center. Got me a very useful trideo tape. See, I've got initiative," she said with a cold smile, "but I believe in keeping its use personal."

Marushige leaned back into his chair, making a fist with his right hand and laying his other hand over it. "You were rewarded for your silence concerning Claybourne. Despite your repulsive method of achieving the office, you have been an efficient deputy. I will only be pushed so far in this matter, Crenshaw. Be careful that you do not overstep the line."

"I'm not pushing, Marushige. You can keep the top slot as long as you want. I really don't want it. But if you try to force me out, just remember that if I go down I take you with me."

Marushige ran his thumb along the ragged scar on his left cheek. After a few moments, he said, "It would be wise for you to bury your obsession about Verner while Sato's around. The *Kansayaku* is tightly connected to Director Aneki, and Verner used to be some kind of pet of the old man. Surely neither of us needs to borrow trouble."

"Your concern is touching," Crenshaw drawled. Marushige was less concerned with her embarrassment than the possibility of Sato looking into things and discovering the security director's manipulation of the records. He would, most likely, be relieved if she managed to screw up and get canned. That way, he'd be rid of her. "I don't think you have much to worry about. Sato doesn't like Verner any more than I do."

"That is a bold assertion, and interesting, if true," Marushige commented. "How would you know such a thing?"

"Hey, I still got a few connections in the biz," Crenshaw laughed.

Marushige smiled broadly in response, but his eyes were cold and wary.

# 7

Sam was nervous. No doubt about it. His palms were wet and he wanted to find the nearest rest room. If they didn't call him in the next few minutes, he could be out and back again before it was time to go in.

Sam tried to catch the eye of the red-uniformed guard who had been his escort ever since he had stepped out of the elevator carrying him to the upper stories of the arcology. The man's stare remained as fixed straight ahead as it had since he'd taken up position across from Sam's seat on the leather couch. His stance was only slightly less fixed and rigid than his manner. It was pointless trying to communicate with him.

Reaching a decision, Sam levered himself free from the sticky embrace of the couch. Before he had straightened, the guard was by his side, face expressionless, waiting for Sam's next move. Doubtless, the samurai was as ready to be executioner as escort. Sam hoped the man wasn't too disappointed by his charge's slow walk to the receptionist's desk.

"Excuse me." He smiled politely when the woman looked up from her console. "Will it be much longer?"

Her earlier warm smile was a memory. She said nothing for a few moments, her stare and expression so harsh that all the beauty dissolved from her face. He had overstepped the bounds of expected politeness, and she intended to let him know. "Sato-*sama* will call for you when he is ready, Verner-*san*."

"But I just wanted to . . ."

"Please take a seat," she interrupted icily.

Her lack of polite forms told Sam how rude she thought

him. Rather than retreat to the clammy confines of his former seat, he gave himself a promotion based on length of wait. Crossing in front of the desk, he entered the other half of the spacious room, though he knew this was trespassing into territory reserved for those of more exalted rank. The receptionist did not react to his breach of manners, but he was sure she would record it. Let her. His minor rebellion against proper etiquette made him feel a little more in control of the situation.

This side of the reception area was no more capacious than the other, but its furnishings were more posh and it was more crowded. Two Red Samurai guards flanked the heavy wooden door to the inner office. Two more men sat on a couch that backed against that wall. One of those seemed to be dozing, but the other turned his head as Sam crossed the Persian rug. Though he couldn't see the eyes behind the implanted chrome lenses, he was sure they were studying and evaluating him.

Sam selected a chair. This time, it was one upholstered in fabric; he didn't need any help sweating. As much as he wanted to return the scrutiny of the man with the chrome lenses, Sam decided it was unwise to do so directly. Turning his head toward the glassed-in area behind the receptionist's desk, he feigned interest in the activities of the bevy of office ladies hard at work inside, occasionally letting his gaze drift over the Red Samurai with him in the waiting area.

It turned out the samurai weren't of much interest. Standard issue, they were hard, competent, no-nonsense types like his own red shadow. They would be dangerous in a fight, but they were no threat to a good employee like Sam.

The other two were different. Their lapels bore corporate pins whose expanding wavefront design was so familiar that he easily picked it out as Renraku. Despite their affiliation symbols, neither looked like Sam's idea of a typical Renraku salaryman.

With a start, Sam realized that he knew these men. Or rather, knew of them. In the week between Hohiro Sato's arrival in Seattle and the granting of this interview, Sam had used his free time to do some research. He figured the more he knew about Sato, the better he might come off in the unexpected audience. He had learned that Sato always traveled with an entourage, as was natural for a man of his stature in a multinational corporation. Besides the usual crowd of office ladies, guards, aides, and chauffeurs, several people of more obscure function were frequently part of the *Kansayaku's* traveling party.

From the pictures in the files, Sam recognized the chrome-eyed man as Kosuke Akabo, a public relations specialist. If he truly was what his job title stated, the relations he handled were not those conventionally assigned to such a functionary. He had the menace of a restrained predator, much like that of the Red Samurai guards. Akabo's well-tailored gray suit was cut from expensive material, far too costly for a typical salaryman, though the outfit mimicked the currently fashionable cut. Even to Sam's untrained eyes, it was clear that Akabo was something more than a desk jockey.

Calm but alert, Akabo made no extraneous movement, but showed none of the tense vigilance of the samurai guards. His was the composure of a man confident he would be instantly aware of any threat. As perhaps he would. His eyes had certainly been enhanced technologically; his other senses may have been as well.

Sam searched surreptitiously for telltale signs of modification, but beyond the chrome lenses, he saw no obvious cybernetic additions. That did not shake his conviction that the man in the gray suit was more highly modified than a street samurai whose reputation depended as much on visible chrome as fighting prowess. Akabo was a warrior, protection for his master. Sam was sure of it.

The other had to be Harry Masamba, because only one black man had been on the list of those associated with Sato. The dossier named Masamba as a time-management specialist, but his profession was as obvious from his indecorous attitude as from the symbol-laden slouch hat that covered the upper part of his face. No respectable salaryman would sleep in the office of his boss. Masamba was a mage. Perhaps it was because his talents were as rare as they were valuable that he could take liberties in his personal behavior.

Sam considered the presence of the magician. He had been raised to believe most of their kind charlatans, trading on the beliefs of the credulous. Unlike his father, however, Sam had grown up in what people like Masamba called the Sixth World. There was too much evidence to deny that magic really existed. Still, he didn't trust its practitioners.

Not everyone felt that way. The corporate world had embraced magic and magicians, not so much for profit as for protection. Magicians were too rare and unreliable to work on assembly lines, but they offered unparalleled capabilities in industrial espionage. And where there was magic on the offense, magic was needed on the defense, making mages a common feature of corporate security. Almost all multinational corporate heads had wizards on their personal staffs for protection. Lesser officials had to make do with the company wage mages, for a person able to manipulate magical forces was too rare a resource to be squandered lightly. That Sato had a mage of his own was a sign of his power.

Power was something Sato had a lot of in Renraku Corporation. He held the title of *Kansayaku,* but was much more than a mere auditor of financial records. He audited people as well, pruning the dead wood and nonconformists from the Renraku tree. His reputation as a hatchetman was fearsome. Now he had come to Seattle, where the arcology project was chronically behind schedule.

Sato's appointment to the arcology didn't worry Sam personally. Sam had not been involved in any significant tasks that might link him to the delays, and having been banished from staff operations when banished from Japan, he had no contacts with the management who would have to take responsibility for those delays. Even if they and their staffs were removed, he was likely to remain, checking files and crossreferencing data.

But the response to his letter requesting permission to meet with his sister was worrying. He could not see any reason why Sato would want to talk to him personally. Hadn't the *Kansayaku* shown nothing but contempt for Sam when they had last met? A reversal of attitude seemed unwarranted, despite Hanae's belief that such a happy turnabout was just what Sam could expect from the meeting. Sam had been seeing too much behind the surface lately; he held little faith in her optimism.

The receptionist called his name, cutting off any further speculation. Whether Sato wanted to help or reprimand him, lack of promptness would not improve Sam's position. He stood and straightened his jacket, then marched forward under the cold chrome stare of Akabo. Behind him, his red shadow did not move.

The inner office made the outer seem furnished in castoffs. The entrance swept away from the door in vaulted magnificence. Beyond the masterpiece-bedecked walls of the entryway, the room opened out into a broad space many times the size of the office Sam shared with a dozen co-workers. Impressive as the furnishings were, the long outer wall diminished them. The direct view of the Seattle skyline offered by the floor-to-ceiling windows was vaguely disturbing after Sam's long isolation within the arcology.

Midway between the entry and the window, a desk stood isolated from the rest of the chamber, elevated on a dais of some dark, close-grained wood. A well-groomed and carefully attired man sat in a suede-covered chair behind the chrome-legged marble slab.

Sato.

He stood as Sam entered the main portion of the chamber and stepped off the platform and came around in front of the desk.

"*Konichiwa*, Verner-*san*."

"*Ojama shimasu*, Sato-*sama*," Sam returned with a formal bow. He thought it wise to be extremely polite.

"Please have a seat," Sato offered, extending a hand toward an alcove by the window.

Sam selected a chair that placed his back to the vista. It was a relief that etiquette required him to allow his host the scenic view. He did not want to be distracted.

Sato seated himself with a comment about the current league standings of the Sonics that made it painfully obvious that the *Kansayaku* knew nothing about basketball. Sam played along, knowing that the small talk was only a preliminary. It was merely polite noise to allow the participants in the conversation to gauge each other's mood.

A woman brought a tray with tea and sweet cakes. Only as she began pouring the tea did Sam realize that Alice Crenshaw was doing the serving. Crenshaw grinned at him, and Sam suddenly felt cold.

"Ms. Crenshaw has been filling me in on your activities since you arrived in Seattle," Sato confided, dropping the faltering pleasantries. "Most interesting."

Sam didn't know what to say. How could he? He had no idea what Crenshaw had told Sato. Anything he said could easily get him into trouble.

"Nothing to say?" Sato's smile reminded Sam of the sharks in the Level 2 public aquarium. "I should think that you would want to make some comment. A reason for what you have done, perhaps?''

Sam cleared his throat. Sato had still not given him a clue to the nature of this test. ''I have always held Renraku first in my thoughts. I do not believe that I have ever performed a disloyal action.''

''That is a rote response, Verner-*san*,'' Sato observed. ''This is not morning assembly, so I do not need to hear you repeat the *shakun*. I assure you that I know the corporate articles by heart.''

''I meant no disrespect, *Kansayaku*.''

''Then I shall take no offense.'' Sato placed his tea cup on the tray. ''Yet.''

Sam returned his cup as well. The procelain clattered slightly as it met the lacquered surface. Sato's next words were so soft that Sam almost didn't hear them.

''You are dissatisfied with your job?''

''I serve the corporation, *Kansayaku*,'' Sam stated strongly. ''I do my best at whatever task is set before me.''

''Yes. So it seems. There have been no complaints about your performance.'' Sato tapped the arm of his chair. Sam thought that he detected a slight hint of disappointment. ''But you are dissatisfied.''

''I am distressed at being kept in the dark about the fate of my sister.''

''I am informed that she has been relocated safely. Renraku always fulfills its obligations in that regard. You were advised of this through official channels.''

Sam recalled the two-line entry in his electronic mail. ''I believe that the corporation has done what it considers its duty. But I don't understand. Why can't I contact her?''

''What are you talking about?''

''I have repeatedly requested communications links with my sister. They have been denied. I have not even been given the postal code of the relocation center.''

''That seems unusual.''

''I thought so too, but I have been reluctant to bring my concerns to the Contract Court arbitration board.''

''My comp,'' Sato ordered peremptorily.

Crenshaw brought it, setting it on the table and unrolling the screen before turning it on and sliding it before Sato. He spent a minute tapping on the keyboard.

''There is no record of these requests in the files.''

"How can that be possible?" Sam asked incredulously.

"Indeed," Sato agreed smoothly. "How?"

Sam scented danger. Sato had just told him that there was no official record of Sam's attempts to contact Janice. Any complaint about the corporation's inhumane response would not be supported by the Renraku Corporation's correspondence database. He was being coerced into letting the whole issue drop. Never. He would never give up his sister. She was all the family he had left.

Sato confirmed Sam's suspicions by saying, "Now you have come to me and, in a private conference, asked after your sister. I have told you that she was well cared for by the Renraku staff during her traumatic experience. She received all the consideration to which she was entitled under the law. You will receive regular reports and may undertake to send correspondence through the personnel office. There is no further need to trouble your superiors over this issue."

"I understand," Sam lied.

He really didn't understand at all, but one thing was becoming clear. For whatever reason, he was deliberately being cut off from his sister, and somehow Sato was involved.

"I am glad that we understand each other, Verner-*san.*" Sato stood, his sudden motion leaving Sam to scramble upright. "You may return to your duties."

Sam bowed to Sato's back. "I apologize for having taken so much of your valuable time, *Kansayaku.*"

Having been dismissed, Sam had no choice but to leave. As he walked past the last painting in the entryway, he risked an impolite look over his shoulder. Sato had returned to his desk, absorbed already in something on the console screen. Crenshaw was standing by the edge of the dais, watching Sam with a grin of satisfaction plastered to her face. She seemed pleased. What had he done to earn her enmity?

His guard was waiting to escort him to the elevators. During the ride down to the lower levels, Sam reviewed the meeting. He felt sure there were levels of meaning that he had missed. Try as he might, he couldn't figure out the whys of the situation.

Hanae was waiting for him in the Level 200 lobby. She stood quietly beyond the barrier while a samurai from the guard station adjusted the screamer attached to Sam's wrist. It would alert security if he strayed from those portions of the arcology that had been deemed suitable for one of his position and security rating. He was forbidden from entering the upper reaches until summoned again. As soon as he passed through the detector arch, Hanae, her face full of expectation, rushed up to him.

"How did it go?"

He did not want to disappoint her, but he had nothing to fulfill her hopes. "I am told that there will be periodic reports on Janice's welfare. I may write letters to her as well, but I am not to complain any further. At least, I wasn't forbidden to pray for her."

She searched his face. "You don't really believe that the company will follow through, do you?"

Sam said nothing. If Hanae had read enough in his face and stance to ask the question, she already knew the answer. She reached out to touch his cheek, then she threw her arms around him in a fierce hug. Her warmth felt good.

"I think you should talk to someone," she suggested tentatively.

"I don't need a shrink."

She laughed nervously. "No, that's not what I meant. I think you should talk to someone I met down in the public mall."

"Hanae, I'm really not in the mood for small talk with a stranger." He had never found her friends of more than passing interest, and he just wanted to be alone.

"You don't have to do it now. Besides, I'd have to arrange a time, anyway."

While the knowledge that an immediate meeting wasn't in the offing was a relief, her comment raised his suspicions. "Who is this person?"

Hanae nervously glanced around. "I'd rather not say her name here. She's a . . . talent scout."

"I'm not going on trid."

"No. Not that kind. She's corporate."

This was an interesting development. Talent scouts looked for dissatisfied employees who might be willing to switch corporations. Hanae was concerned enough to talk to a headhunter. Such an involvement was totally out of character for her; she was a loyal company person. He realized that he, too, was acting out of character. Here he was actually considering the possibility.

# 8

The mall was vibrant, full of sound, light, and life. After the ordered corridors of the private sectors of the arcology, Sam found that the sights, sounds, and smells of the public sections took some getting used to. The blare of the public trid screens was the worst of all, touting the latest products between reports of the latest corporate war or Urban Brawl game. He usually avoided coming to the extravaganza that rambled over the first five levels of the arcology, preferring the company malls and shops scattered throughout the living levels. There he was less reminded that he was denied travel outside the Renraku corporate world without a Renraku corporate escort.

It wasn't the crowds that bothered him. He found the people of Seattle intriguing and the mix of types exhilarating. Tourists included Asians, tribals from the surrounding Salish-Shidhe Council, corporates from all the local multinationals, UCAS citizens ranging from rich to street people, and even the occasional Elf, Dwarf, or group of Orks moved elbow to elbow with one another in the thoroughfares. Before long, Sam's discomfort faded as he relaxed and let himself become part of the crowd. Being in a group always seemed to comfort Sam, but of late that feeling had been rare.

Upon first arriving at the arcology, he had made some forays into the metroplex of the outside world, but those trips soon became an exercise in isolation and frustration. Sam's chaperones had made enjoyment impossible. People on the street were leery of approaching anyone with a Renraku guard escort, and the guards themselves were rarely good for conversation. After the first few weeks, he had given up on his outings, content to learn more about Seattle and its people from the Matrix, the trid, and travelogues.

Hanae was walking by his side wearing wraparound chrome sunglasses, an affectation in the filtered sunlight of the mall. Her hair was arranged differently, her blouse was new, and though he recognized her jeans, he knew that she rarely wore them. She was really getting into her role as an intriguer. He hoped her obvious ill-ease would not attract the attention of any of the strolling Raku guards.

He had done nothing to disguise his identity. What would be the point as long as he wore the screamer on his right wrist? Any guard who cared to check in with the central security databanks would have his identity in a second. All they really had to rely on for privacy was the guards' indifference to their "shopping trip."

Hanae had lobbied for a week to get him to accept a meeting with her mysterious new friend. Believing that any contact, however tentative, with an outside recruiter would be an irrevocable step, Sam had stalled. She had broken down his arguments one by one, and he had finally given in. Now, two days later, she had dragged him to the mall to meet the recruiter.

Spray washed over them as the ventilation system sent a stray breeze in their direction. The dampness was a reminder that the waterfall was real and not just a dazzling example of special effects holography. The water cascaded from an opening concealed on the third level. The rushing torrent tumbled along huge quartz boulders from Madagascar, the rocks framed in lush tropical greenery that enhanced their translucent shine. The slope of the waterfall lessened near the first level, gentling the flow before it reached the lagoon park where Sam and Hanae walked. Tropical birds and insects flitted past, restrained from leaving the park area by their own inclinations as well as a subtle ultrasonic barrier at the park's edge.

Sam caught a glimpse of what he thought was a large-eyed monkey in one tree. The creature's swaying movements soon convinced him otherwise. It stopped on one limb and turned its gaze in his direction. Its eyes were huge, dark, and liquid. The eyes caught and held his attention with their compelling stare. After a moment, Sam realized he was no longer looking into those eyes. The animal was gone. He searched the trees but could find no sign of it. When he told Hanae about it, she laughed. "A ghost lemur. They say there are several of them in the park, but I've never seen one. They're magical, you know."

How could he not know? The creature had vanished before his eyes. He shuddered with distaste. Every time magic had touched his life, it had been something awful.

Hanae led him away from the place he had seen the mysterious animal. They strolled over the bridge that spanned the lagoon tank and onto the walkway along the surface of the coral reef environment. The peace of the park was reasserting itself when Hanae abruptly grabbed his arm and started dragging him along the path. Ahead of them was the entrance to the Coral Cafe, a popular restaurant whose sublevel seating offered a window onto the submerged coral reef.

"Over here," Hanae insisted. "That's her."

The woman Hanae pointed out was stunning. From her platinum hair to her gold-studded black leather boots, she was a vision from the next issue of *Mode Moderne*. Her clothes were cutting-edge, but they were only a setting for the jewel of the woman herself. She was tall and slim and moved with sensual grace.

A gold Renraku ID flashed on the flaring collar of her long, flowing vest, but Sam didn't believe for a moment that it was legitimate. As they approached, she brushed back the long fall of hair that hung over her right shoulder. For a fleeting instant, the motion revealed a delicately pointed ear.

Sam had not expected an Elf. Elves were the Metahumans most common in the corporations, but that still made them rare and few were in positions of responsibility.

It all made sense now. Her slimness and height, the delicacy of her features—all characteristic of that branch of metahumanity known as Elves. He wondered how old she was. Once an Elf reached early maturity, he or she showed few visible signs of aging, so she might actually be only about twenty, as she appeared. On the other hand, she might have been one of the first babies from the Year of Chaos, which would make her about forty years old.

Doctors around the world had invoked Unexplained Genetic Expression Syndrome to account for the births of strange children to ordinary parents. But UGE was just a name for something that they didn't understand. When it became clear that the children were growing up to look so much like the Elves of fairy tales, the scientists clung to their ugly name for the beautiful children. The new generation weren't fairies, of course, but that didn't stop the popular press from applying mythical names to them. Those names stuck, but the children dubbed Elves and Dwarfs were still people, new and sudden subspecies of *homo sapiens* to be sure, but Humans still. Some people didn't believe that, denying that Metahumans of any kind were people. It was an attitude Sam never understood. Even with all his father's railing against the "claptrap of this Sixth World magic nonsense," the elder Verner had acknowledged Metahumans as "biologically sound expressions of genes." Sam had never found pointed ears and white hair to be any more non-Human than black or red skin.

All such thoughts fled as the woman turned to face them and Hanae performed the introductions.

"Sam, this is Katherine Roe. She's the one I wanted you to meet."

"*Telegit thelemsa,*" he greeted her.

"*Siselle. Thelemsa-ha.*" She laughed lightly. "Your pronunciation is excellent, Sam, but, please, let's speak English. You wouldn't want to embarrass me in public, would you?"

"How so?"

"Other than those who grew up in an enclave, very few Elves actually speak the language. We are all children of our culture, after all."

"I only meant to be friendly," Sam muttered apologetically. "It's about all the Sperethiel I know."

"And I chided you for it. Now see, you *have* embarrassed me." Roe's face flashed her chagrin momentarily. Then the smile returned. "How do you come to know any Sperethiel?"

"Oh, Sam knows lots of things, Katherine. He's one of the corporation's best researchers."

Sam felt his face flush at Hanae's enthusiasm. To Roe's raised eyebrow, he said, "I'm told that I have a rather good memory."

"Certainly an asset for a researcher," Roe agreed.

"An asset for anyone," Hanae asserted. "I'm sure you two will have a lot to talk about, so I'm going to get some shopping done. Two o'clock in front of Lordstrung's?" she asked.

He nodded and she kissed him on the cheek and left. Roe conducted him inside the Coral Cafe, where she had a table waiting. She did not take long getting to the point.

"I may be able to help you out."

"What exactly do you mean?"

"Caution is certainly advisable, Sam. You don't know me, but I know quite a bit about you." Her face was earnest as she reached out to lay a hand on his arm. "I'm going to have to tell you things in trust, but you seem to be the kind of man who knows how to keep a secret."

She waited for his response. Sam hesitated. Her concern and sincerity seemed to be more than mere show. Still, he felt the need for wariness. "I can't promise discretion without knowing what you're talking about."

Sam read relief and satisfaction in her smile.

"That's the answer of a man who takes his word seriously," she said. "All right. If you think anything I say will compromise you, then go tell your bosses. But what will they think of someone who consorts with a villain like me?"

The lightness of her tone did nothing to lessen Sam's sudden concern. If his association with Roe were known, there would be repercussions. All his nebulous fears about official sanction would become definite reality. "They would not take it well at all."

"*I'm* not going to tell them. Why should you?" When he said nothing to that, she continued. "I'll leave out all the names. That should ease your fears about having to report anything. Besides, this sort of thing happens all the time. Don't you ever watch "Confessions of a Company Man?" "

"I watch very little trid. I especially avoid fiction."

"Fiction?" she exclaimed quietly. " 'Confessions' is all true. They tell you so at the beginning of each episode."

"If it's real, why don't any of the corporations mentioned ever appear on the world stock exchanges?"

"Why, you're right. You've shattered my illusions," Roe declared with mock seriousness.

"Somehow I doubt that." She was trying to set him at ease and Sam was beginning to like her.

She smiled, dismissing her frivolity, but then her expression quickly became sober. "Seriously, though, my associate, Mr. Drake, and I are already arranging for an extraction. It would be little additional trouble to take you out at the same time."

"I don't know your principals. How do I know I want to work for them?"

"You don't have to."

"I'm supposed to believe that you and this Mr. Drake are doing this out of the goodness of your hearts?" Sam asked skeptically.

"Of course not," Roe smiled confidently. "We've got an angle just like everybody else. Our principals are paying the freight for the extraction. If we add you to it without telling them, you're out for free. Then Mr. Drake and I work with you to get a corporate placement in another city, say, San Francisco. Once we arrange a nice new home for you, we get a finder's fee from the corporation you join. It's practically free credit."

"I won't compromise Renraku," Sam said.

"You won't have to. We'll put it into the hiring contract. It'll make the sale go a little harder, but it's not impossible. You may have to settle for a slight drop in your standard of living."

Sam suddenly realized that he had made his decision and was in the process of implementing it. The future was opening up. "If I can get on with my life, it'll be worth it."

"Then we have a deal?"

"Not so fast. I want to meet this Mr. Drake."

She hesitated, but Sam thought that it was just for effect. "Sure. I'll set up a meet for as soon as you can get away."

"I thought Hanae told you that I can't leave the arcology without a guard." He tapped the continuous plastic band that encircled his wrist. Fine wires and flat chips could be discerned through the translucent surface of the screamer. "This will alert security should I trespass beyond the boundaries encoded in its memory. It cannot be removed without setting off an alarm, and the Renraku Security Directorate controls the 'off' switch. Your Mr. Drake will have to come here."

"No good," she said with a slight shake of her head. "The big guy can't come in. You'll have to wait until you're out to meet him."

From the hardening of her manner, Sam sensed the matter was not negotiable. "That's not reassuring."

"Do you want out or not?"

He did. He had walked too far down this path to turn back now. He just wasn't sure that this was the best way. "Let me think about it."

"Don't think too long." she warned. "I've got a schedule to meet."

# 9

*"Is it time?"*

*"No."*

*"But I'm getting hungry."* Petulance accompanied the statement.

*"Soon, Tessien."*

Rainbow plumes rustled, colorless in Hart's night vision as she watched the serpent settle its coils. With its wings folded against its sides and the great fanged head tucked under the left pinion, it soon resembled nothing more than an uneven pile of feathers. It was hardly camouflage. In the lane between warehouses of United Oil's docking facility on Puget Sound, such a pile was even more out of place than a dracoform.

For all its uncharacteristic impatience, Tessien was a dracoform, one of a variety of creatures that laid claim to the powers of legendary Dragons. It—Hart was unsure of the beast's gender—was of a type known as a feathered serpent, the most common of the greater dracoforms in the western hemisphere. Stretched out, it would measure ten meters of feather-scaled muscle, and its wingspan matched its length. Tessien was a dangerous beast, and had been her partner for four years of shadow business.

She almost trusted it.

A soft beep from the box in her jacket pocket alerted her that someone had broken one of the sensor beams she had placed earlier that evening. A second beep of a different tone told her the vector on which the target was moving. She slipped her hand into her pocket to silence the receiver. Its sound could betray them before they sprang the ambush. Any additional information the sensor could give wasn't worth that.

She glanced at the mirror she had propped across the lane to give her a view toward the main warehouse. Four figures were running away from the building, headed toward Hart and Tessien's position. From their silhouettes, she judged them to be shadowrunners. Three men and a woman. A faint jingling came from the leader as amulets and talismans swayed and clashed on his chest, marking him either as a mage or a very superstitious fellow.

The faint sounds were drowned out as a group of United Oil security men poured from the warehouse. The slap of their boots pounding on the concrete covered the noise made by the fleeing intruders, but that rhythmic sound was soon overwhelmed by the screeches of the brace of cockatrices they loosed on their prey.

Cockatrices were an avian paraspecies favored for security work because the animal's touch could shock its prey's nervous system into collapse, paralyzing an intruder for easy arrest by the paranimal's handler. Of course, the handler must pull the cockatrice away before it dined on the helpless victim, but the multinationals didn't worry much about a few trespassers unavoidably mauled or killed. It made for less trespassers. These paranimals were eager, flapping their stubby wings and pumping their long legs as they devoured the ground separating them from the shadowrunners.

The lead cockatrice closed with the trailing runner. It leaped for its prey, going high to swing its long, scaled tail at the man. One touch would paralyze him, leaving him helpless as its claws ripped into him. The runner dodged left, away from the tail as it swung forward and missed him.

Hart pegged the runner as a razorguy, one of those cybernetically enhanced punks who liked to call themselves street samurai and always seemed to be working as muscle for a shadowrunning team. It usually took a jacked-up nervous system to react so quickly and evade attacks so easily.

Steel glinted in the moonlight as a blade extended from the man's forearm, confirming Hart's guess. The samurai twisted as he moved, slicing his weapon into the animal's flesh. It squalled and crashed to the ground.

The second beast engaged another runner, who desperately blocked its attacks with a boxy object that Hart recognized as a cyberdeck. Hell of a way to treat expensive technology.

Before the cockatrice could pierce the desperate runner's guard, the samurai cancelled its options. He ripped several bursts of full automatic fire into the creature before raking his aim back to his first opponent and gutting it as it started to rise.

Hart noted that the samurai had not hit his partner as the muzzle of his weapon swung past. Smartgun link, she surmised.

"That one's fast, Tessien," Hart observed as she pointed out the street samurai. "Take him first."

*"Too much metal. He won't taste good."*

"You won't get the others if the razorguy slices you. I'll cover the mage while you're doing that. With the artillery and armor down, the infantry will be easy meat."

*"True."* Anticipation. *"You have a discerning eye for tactics, little one."*

She slid a hand under the ruff of feathers and scratched at the joint of Tessien's head and neck. "You really know how to flatter a girl, my friend. Now go get 'em."

Tessien broadcast its eagerness as it rose into the air with a rustle, then a roar, to challenge the runners. They skidded to a stop, motionless for a second before recovering and launching their own attack as though having planned for such a contingency. They probably had, she realized. It was common knowledge that United Oil's head of security in Seattle was the Western Dragon Haesslich.

Hart felt the power gather around the mage. The runners were relying on his spells for their first strike against the dracoform. Just as she had expected.

Lavender flames streamed from the mage's outstretched hands, lighting the sky as they washed across the feathered serpent. Hart caught a glimpse of UniOil security diving for cover behind the runners.

Tessien's coils arched straight for a second and Hart saw the mage begin to smile. The grin faded as his spell fractured and his flames flickered and died, leaving the serpent unharmed. The Dragon soared higher. Emboldened by how little she had needed to bolster Tessien's magic defense, Hart stepped out to confront the mage.

"Having trouble?"

His eyes narrowed and he nodded as though he understood what had happened. He reached toward one of his amulets.

She pumped three slugs from her Atchison riot gun into his belly. He flew backward, spraying blood, entrails, and shreds of ineffective flak vest.

The sour stench that filled the air was swirled away by super-heated air as Tessien unleashed its flaming breath on

the street samurai. Flesh cooked as the water in the man's tissue boiled. He collapsed to the concrete, a pile of charred bones, fused steel, and melted plastic.

Tessien circled the suddenly timid survivors as Hart called for their surrender.

"Drop your weapons and you won't be hurt."

A metallic clatter was her answer.

Tessien swooped behind her to settle. Its head arched up on a serpentine neck into a protective overwatch position as the United Oil security guards emerged from hiding and rushed to surround them. Nervous guards watched Tessien and Hart more closely than the shadowrunners. All around the circle, fingers rested on triggers.

"Who are you," demanded their leader.

Hart read his name tag. Major Fuhito. *So ka,* Haesslich's second-in-command. "We're your backup, Major."

"I wasn't informed of any special operatives on this case. I think you are opportunistic trespassers. I also think you're in a lot of trouble."

Wings thundered in the night, Dragon wings. Hart glanced up to see a familiar shape. She relaxed. There would be no problems with over-eager trigger fingers now.

*"What is the problem?"* the Western Dragon bellowed as he landed.

Fuhito bowed to the Dragon. "Haesslich-*sama,* we caught these two shadowrunners in conflict with the team that invaded the facility. They claim to be some kind of support for my team, but there were no specifications for back-up in the orders you left. They are probably just desperate runners who have turned on their own kind to save their own necks. The scum."

*"Fuhito, you make me wonder why I keep you on the payroll. Send your men back and take the real trespassers with you."*

"Then the serpent and the woman *are* working for you," Fuhito said stiffly.

*"Of course. I knew about the runners who invaded us tonight. I also knew that they were quite accomplished for their breed, and that they might slip through your fingers. They had to be stopped, and I couldn't be sure I'd be available to do the job myself."*

"You could have told me."

Contempt emanated from the Dragon.

"I obey your orders, Haesslich-*sama.*" Fuhito bowed, crisply and quickly. He then turned and stopped at the decker who was smirking at him. He slapped the woman, knocking her to the pavement. "You are a trespasser and a criminal. I think that you will find that you have little cause for amusement."

"Yours is just too big for me," the woman mumbled through a bloody lip. "You're gonna be in real drek with your corp bosses, Mr. Tin Plate. I'll file a brutality suit."

"You forfeited your rights when you entered United Oil territory," Fuhito sneered. He slammed his boot into her head, and she sagged unconscious. Her partner's sudden lunge was arrested by a pair of bulky guards. "Take them both to the interrogation facilities."

As the guards left, Haesslich sniffed at the corpses. *Admirable efficiency, Hart.*"

"You'll get the bill. This kind of stuff wasn't in the contract."

"*Add a surcharge,*" Haesslich suggested, amusement tinging his words. "*United Oil will pay.*"

"Done," Hart agreed. She had intended to do that anyway; her contract was very specific about compensation for "additional services."

The Dragon settled onto his haunches. "*Now, what about the operation you were hired for? Everything is arranged?*"

"Looks that way. The pigeon is still waffling, but I'm sure he'll fall our way."

"*He'd better. I do not want this schedule disrupted.*" Determination barely masked the promise of violence in the beast's statement.

Tessien hissed, but Hart reached out swiftly to touch it. This was no time for a fight.

"All of our work is satisfaction guaranteed," she assured Haesslich

# 10

Sam fretted, toying with his food. The lunchtime crowd at Garrelsen's Mall Cafe was its usual boisterous self. Even though his table was against the wall and away from the passersby outside the roping, their noise added to the clamor. Periodically, his waitress stopped by to ask after the quality of the meal, trying to hurry him along to clear the way for another paying customer. He paid no attention to all the bustle.

Roe was late.

Had she abandoned him? Been caught by Renraku security? Were the Red Samurai moving into position to arrest him for conspiracy to break his employment contract? Or was it all a test by Roe to see how nervous he was?

It really didn't matter. He was committed to this course now. If Roe didn't show, he would have to figure his own way out of the arcology. That would be hard, but staying was harder. It had become all too clear that he would never get his answers about Janice while he was under Renraku's thumb, and he could no longer sit idle.

If he was caught . . . well, that would solve his problem, too.

He had left few loose ends, putting in extra hours that almost cleared away his work load. No one would be able to accuse Samuel Verner of shirking his responsibilities, no matter how trivial. The dogs were a problem because they could hardly be part of the extraction. They wouldn't survive in the arcology without an owner, but Ms. Haramoto in Corridor B seemed fond of them and had agreed readily to care for them if Sam had to take a business trip. Since this "business trip" would likely never end, he hoped she would come to love them as much as he had. He had never been much for possessions, so not much problem there.

That left Hanae. Sweet, comfortable Hanae. Despite the lack he felt in their relationship, he couldn't abandon her. She had helped set him on this course, and he had felt better these last few days than he had for a long time. He felt good to be doing something instead of waiting for someone else to do it for him. She was part of that change and he owed her for it. It might not be the best basis for a relationship, but better ones had started from worse reasons. He would take care of her.

Sure he would. Here he was thinking about taking Hanae out of the corporate cocoon that had protected her all her life, and he wasn't sure he could take care of himself. The events in which he'd gotten involved the day he arrived in

Seattle showed him how different was the world away from the corporation. Life could get violent, even deadly. Hanae was probably less ready for that world than he was, but he was sure she would refuse to be parted from him.

The waitress appeared again, but before she could begin her nudging, Roe appeared behind her and slid into the seat opposite Sam. Roe snapped a quick order for a house salad and carrot juice and shooed the flustered girl away.

"Sorry I'm late. Had a little transportation problem. The Red Rovers and the Ancients were having a little get-together on Western Avenue. Typical gang nonsense. How have things been going with you? Made a decision?" The flush of her obvious hurry faded quickly and her normal pallor returned along with the usual smooth pace of her speech.

"I've been doing a lot of thinking."

"Glad to hear it, Sam. More stuffy corporate types should do that."

Did she mean that he was a stuffy corporate type? He hoped not. He didn't think of himself that way, and it disturbed him slightly that she might. He reminded himself that it was Roe's skills and connections that he wanted, not her good opinion. Getting out of Renraku was the most important thing right now.

"I would like to go ahead with the extraction."

"Shush on the E word," Roe warned with a sly, conspiratorial smile. "Even a public place like this has long ears."

Her levity annoyed him, but Sam knew she was right. He should have used some roundabout phrasing that could mean something entirely innocent. The circumlocutions of her business were even more obtuse than corporate slang. But he wanted to stay straightforward and on-track until everything was settled. He was not yet done with business. "Hanae has to go, too."

Roe's warm smile vanished instantly. "That makes it a little tougher."

He swallowed. This was it, time for his gamble. "She goes, or I don't."

Roe's eyes searched his. He felt the intensity of her bronze eyes and fought to keep his face immobile, hoping to mask his worry that she would call off the deal. She must have been satisfied by his resolution.

"You're lucky I'm a soft touch, chummer. Now listen up.
Here's the plan."

# 11

Sam turned away from the wall screen and looked around
the room again. This apartment had been his home for just
over a year, but only a few knick-knacks, some bare spots
on the carpeting from the dogs, and a handmade bowl from
Hanae said anything about the man who had lived there.
The rest was company issue, down to the pictures on the
walls.

He would leave behind his clothes, too, for a suitcase
would be too suspicious. He would have to make do with
what was on his back and whatever Roe promised to provide
once they had escaped. His scrapbooks lay on the table by
the sofa, their pages strewn over the surface. He had spent
most of the night culling them, choosing the few photos
most important to him. He had narrowed it down to a couple dozen choice items, a miniature history of his family.
He and Janice in Kyoto, her graduation from Tokyo University and his from Columbia, several snapshots from the last
family outing before he and Janice were orphaned, his father in his old U.S. Navy uniform, his mother hosting one
of her regular card parties, scattered selections from his
childhood, the wedding pictures of his parents and grand-
parents, and finally an old tintype of Thaddeus Samuel Hel-
mut Verner, the first of the family to come to the Americas.
They would be his lifeline to the past, memories too precious to give up.

He looked at the bookshelf. There were few volumes
among the objects and small electronics. He had never been
a real book-lover like his sister or his father. The feel of a
hard copy didn't seem to be important. To him, it was always the content that mattered, not the form. The only book
he wanted was his Bible. Unfortunately, like a suitcase, it
would cause suspicion.

He would not be without its comfort, though. A chip copy
was safely snugged into the case in his pocket. Keeping the

computerized Bible company were a few other reading chips. Most were references, but he had also taken a copy of his father's diary and a record of his correspondence. On a whim, he had included the instruction manual for his unfinished flight simulation course. He also had the four gray chips.

Those chips held the persona programs from his cyberterminal. To take them was, technically, a theft, but the programs had been tailored for him and they would be destroyed before someone else took over his terminal. It was actually cheaper to burn a new set for the new man or woman. The chips contained no data, and he was sure his new employer would supply fresh persona chips suited to their own systems. Taking these was symbolic. His Matrix presence would leave along with his physical body.

Maybe that was why he had decided to take the flight manual. Perhaps it was a symbolic statement of his flight from psychological bondage. Or maybe it had to do with the flight he took with those shadowrunners a year ago. He was about to embark on another dangerous experience whose outcome he could not entirely predict.

He checked his watch.

"Almost time," he called to Hanae, who was still puttering in the bathroom.

"Just a minute."

He hoped it wasn't one of her fifteen-minute "minutes." He paced, unconsciously following the track Kiniru used when waiting for Sam to take her for a walk.

Hanae emerged a few minutes later, dressed far more sensibly than Sam had feared. Though she wore a loose, flowing dress, the material was sturdy and the cut unrestrictive. She had a bulging satchel slung over one shoulder.

"Isn't that bag a little large for a trip to a club?"

"It is big," she said hesitantly, "but it should be all right. It's part of the latest look. Lots of leather, beads, and fringe."

"I hope it's not too heavy. We'll have to cross the club's landing pad to the aircraft in a hurry."

"If they cancel out the signal on the screamer, we should be able to stroll out to the plane. After all, people leave that way all the time."

"Not in DocWagon aerial ambulances."

She shrugged. "If it's too heavy, you'll help me. We'll be fine."

He prayed that they would. He didn't want anything to slow them down now that the time had come.

Despite Sam's misgivings, they reached the Club Quarter on Level 6 without incident. No one seemed interested in a couple out for a night on the arcology. The halls of the quarter were already crowded, though it was still early. Music of all kinds bled from the sound-insulated clubs to blend into a puddle of unintelligible sound. The revelers didn't seem to care. Many danced in the halls, moving to music in their heads. Some danced to their imaginations; others wore chipsticks in skull-mounted jacks or carried simsense players that fed the music to their brains.

It wasn't too difficult to find Rumplestiltskin's. Roe wasn't there yet, but hundreds of other hopefuls were already queued up in the vain hope of entry into the fashionable club.

"I had no idea," Hanae said when she saw the line.

"I wonder if Roe did."

"If she did, it must be part of the plan." The quaver in Hanae's voice didn't match her confident words.

"I guess we get in line."

Ten minutes later, Hanae took Sam's arm and pulled herself close. "Maybe she's already inside. Maybe she left without us."

"Don't worry," Sam assured her, hiding his own growing doubt. "She'll keep her part of the deal."

Thirty minutes later, they were still in line. The club doorway had come into view and they caught their first sight of the doorman. Like many clubs, Rumplestiltskin's employed a Troll to handle the lines of hopefuls. Too well-dressed to be called a bouncer, his size and demeanor left no doubt that he could fulfill that function. Almost three meters of muscle and thick hide was more than enough to intimidate all but the rowdiest partyboy. They were still ten meters from the front of the line when Roe suddenly appeared.

"This will never do," she said. Taking each one by the arm, she led them directly up to the doorman. She twirled a shiny credstick in her right hand. The four dark bands on the end of the cylinder marked it as certified for at least one hundred nuyen. She tossed it to the man. "My friends here are late for their table."

She turned back to them. "Giacomo will take care of you, so there's no worry. Everything's wiz, but I've got to make a call to check up on the other member of our party. See you in about half an hour. Have fun."

Sam watched her walk back along the line to converse with a quartet of scruffy men and women. Even at this distance, he could tell that the biggest was an Ork. Her tusks were capped with silver and glinted coldly in the hallway lights. She carried a large case with a casual ease born of enormous strength.

Roe's companions were surely shadowrunners, her team for the extraction. They had a hard, used look about them. Maybe even overused, Sam thought. He had little experience in these matters, but he had expected Roe to show up with a team that was more . . . more what? Imposing? Dangerous? At ease in the Club Quarter? More like Tsung and her runners? It didn't help his state of mind to wonder about their competence.

Roe and the runners walked toward the head of the line for a block, then turned into a corridor that took them away from Rumplestiltskin's. They passed Sam and Hanae, and getting a closer look only fueled Sam's fears. As Roe's team moved in and out of the hall's pools of illumination, the play of light and shadow focused Sam's attention on the person in the middle of the group. That one maintained a steady, if oddly gaited, walk while the others shifted around. They seemed to be running interference, keeping the crowd from jostling the dark-clothed figure.

The person's long overcoat effectively concealed gender along with almost everything else. All Sam could glimpse was a pallid face showing between the turned-up collar and the slouch hat. The skin looked soft and unlined as a baby's. The eyes were hidden behind some kind of heavy goggles. The face turned briefly, and Sam had the distinct impression he was the object of that stare. Then the face was gone, masked by the crowd. No look of recognition, antipathy, concern, or any other emotion marred the sexless smoothness. Whoever that person was, Sam found the appearance of the dark-coated albino unsettling.

"Sam, you're staring," Hanae whispered. Louder, she

said, "Come on, darling. This nice Mr. Giacomo has found our reservation."

"Thought I saw someone I knew," he mumbled as he allowed himself to be led into the club.

# 12

The pickup had taken less time than she had expected. Mr. Target—she found it easiest to think of him that way—had been waiting in the quiet little bar, as arranged. Her tardiness must have made him think she wouldn't come and he had begun drinking. He had gotten a good start. When she arrived, his face was already flushed, making the silver metal of the datajack in his temple stand out starkly.

Between his relief that she had not forsaken him and his nervousness about their rendezvous, it was easy to persuade him to a few more rounds. The more alcohol a target had in his system, the less likely he would notice any anomalies in the world around him. She had only toyed with her own drink, waiting for the chance to suggest that they go on up to the executive suite. It was child's play overcoming his propriety and natural caution. So many brains cells, she thought, so easily overruled by hormones and the animal need for comfort.

"Hope I don't have this much trouble with you, Kathy," he said with a leer as he tried a second time to get his credstick into the slot. His corporate rank would open the door as soon as the maglock read the ID encoded on his stick. But he had to get it into the hole first.

"Here. Let me." She kissed the hand from which she took the credstick, then smoothly slotted the stick home. "I can usually put things where they belong."

As the door slid open, she skipped past him. Trailing her scarf along his shoulder, she gave him an inviting smile as she backed into the chamber. She had every confidence that Jenny was monitoring the room and would have the ground team squared away in their hiding places.

Mr. Target followed her in. He was a bit unsteady, as though he'd overextended himself. Not too hard for someone so out of shape. Though not particularly overweight, he was soft from easy corporate life. She doubted he had seen much of the world outside the arcology, which was just as well. His deskbound focus made him more open to her advances.

After two steps, he stopped and turned back to the door. She tensed, ready to drag him back, but relaxed to see him reaching for the control panel. He grinned like a child as he turned from punching numbers into the keypad.

"Wouldn't want to get interrupted. I have my reputation to consider."

"No," she purred. "We most certainly don't want to be interrupted."

Playing her part, she bounced deeper into the room and looked around with wide eyes.

"Wow," she exclaimed, trying to force into her voice all the awe she had felt upon first seeing the chamber. "This place is wiz. Totally ritz."

The street slang was inadequate to describe the room's opulence. From the scattered furs of extinct and endangered species and rare paranormal animals strewn over the redwood flooring, to the masterpieces of art on the walls and carefully highlighted on pedestals, to the cutting-edge trid screens with their vistas of ocean and forest that filled the walls, it was furnished with only the most rare and precious items. A construct of chrome frames and alternating clear and black lacquer panels offered all the standard small electronic entertainments, from simsense headsets and trid screens to cases of dreamchips and illegal wire ports. The spread of expensive liquors, herbs, and exotic delicacies was extensive. The central piece of furniture was an enormous bed shimmering with the silken sheen of its sheets. It was more than sybaritic. It was unconscionably decadent.

"Renraku takes good care of its important people." He tossed his coat over a leather-upholstered Louis XV chair in a gesture of casual possessiveness. "We've got several of these little hideaways on this level. They are convenient for private meetings with special guests."

"Being here certainly does make me feel special."

She detected a flicker of doubt on his face. He had complained to her that people liked him only for what he could do for them. This was no time to make him feel defensive. "But I always feel special when I'm with you."

That made him smile. He still had that look of awkward nervousness, but he was no longer suspicious. Once again the hopeful suitor, he squared his shoulders with determination to impress his chosen lady. In another time and place, she might have found his naiveté charming.

"Attention, computer," he said. The command was spoken with familiarity, but the next words were less assured. "We'd like some music. *Bolero*, I think. Do it."

As the opening chords filled the room, he stepped close and began to paw her inexpertly. He was awkward and focused on his own needs, hardly surprising in a man so wrapped up in his work that he had little time for people. She slid deftly from his embrace, but left him a caress as a promise. "Whoa. Slow down. This is our first time, and I want it to be special. I need to use the powder room."

"I like you fine the way you are." Frustration and want filled his voice.

"You won't like it if I pee all over you. My bladder's a tad bit too full. I don't want any distractions."

His fastidiousness forced a grimace onto his face. It didn't last long, as the booze-fueled lust reasserted itself. "Go on then. I'll be ready."

He was unbuttoning his shirt before she entered the bathroom. She palmed the doorpad and caught the panel as soon as it slid open enough for her to squeeze through. She threw him a promissory kiss and closed the door behind her before tapping the light switch. The room was enormous, bigger than the apartment she maintained in Bellevue, but she paid no attention to the lustrous marble and gleaming metal. She only had eyes for the body that lay on the floor, naked save for a single datajack. The androgynous form lay pale and hairless on the tiles, obscene as a slug on a dinner plate. It didn't look like the predator it was designed to be.

Hart knelt and satisfied herself that it was still breathing. The whole operation would be a loss if the thing had an abreaction to the drugs in its system. The ground team had dosed it with the stuff to activate it. Something in that compound was also supposed to keep it anesthetized until she administered a stimulant, but she was wary of such a bastardized creation of science and magic. She had seen the stats on the thing and wasn't sure that she trusted Wilson's assurances that its activation would follow a strict timetable. Living things rarely performed as precisely as machines.

The last thing she needed was for it to awaken before it could be focused on its target, leaving it to fixate on her instead.

She stood up and began stripping off her dress. It was far too expensive to risk in any rough play. The necklaces and dangling jewelry came off, too, following the rest into a black satchel waiting on the vanity. Clad only in her underclothes and boots, she addressed the microphones she knew were listening to the room.

"Jenny?"

"Yes, boss." Jenny's voice came instantly from the bathroom's sound system speaker.

"Are you all set?" Hart took a black case from the satchel, opened it, and laid it on the vanity.

"Aces on this end, boss. The Matrix is clear. When you showed up in the corridor, I took control of the local locks and started feeding security a static image. Both your suite and next door look empty to the guys on the monitor consoles. They don't know we're here."

"How are our hirelings doing?" She removed a syringe from the bag and affixed the injector cartridge.

"Pretty good. Kurt's just gotten the bird in the air. Chin Lee is waiting on the go signal, but your locals aren't showing much discipline next door. Greta's into the booze and Sloan's auditioning chips."

"Damned amateurs." Hart popped the needle's protector cap into the case. "Adjust the room's inventory to cover what they take and stay on the mikes. I want you listening. If this blows up, tell Tessien to wait at least a week before it goes after Drake."

"Will do, boss."

Hart turned to kneel again at the side of the pale figure. It barely quivered as she stabbed the needle into its jugular vein, then emptied the amber fluid into the thing's bloodstream. Rising, she swiftly replaced the syringe in its case and returned the case to the satchel. As she tapped the switch to plunge the bathroom into darkness, she said aloud, "Open the door in ten seconds, Jenny."

"Roger," came the disembodied voice. Hart shivered, but it was more than the chill of half-nakedness. Even Jenny's familiar voice had an eerie quality now that she was alone in the dark with the thing. She wished there had been time to don the uniform in the satchel, but any delay risked

Mr. Target getting suspicious. She stepped into the shower stall and slid the panel shut. She sat on the tub's edge and leaned against the cool tiles. Out of sight, out of mind, Wilson had said. She hoped he was right.

As Hart began a breathing routine that would calm her and make her presence negligible to ordinary senses, she heard a scrabbling in the darkness. Drek! The thing was awake, but the doorway to its intended victim wasn't open yet! Either the drug had cancelled the effect of the soporific too fast, or its metabolism was faster than Wilson thought. Either way, she was in trouble unless the bathroom door opened soon.

As if on cue, the door buzzed softly. The panel slid open a crack, then jammed. The creature tensed. Jenny's curse was a burst of static on the room's speaker. The pallid hunter ignored the sound and remained rigidly alert.

The light that spilled through the crack was not enough to illuminate the entire bathroom, but it was enough for Hart's eyes to discern the crouched shape in the center. The body still lacked muscular definition, but there was no mistaking it for anything but a predator now. Its nostrils distended as it swung its head back and forth. The arcs shortened until it was staring at the shower stall. Its lips curled back, revealing a ridge of undifferentiated ivory. Its eyes seemed to glow with a lambent green light as it took a tentative step toward her hiding place.

"Kathy?"

The hunter's body froze while its head whipped around at Mr. Target's voice. For a moment nothing happened. Then, apparently deciding that Hart's nearer presence marked a more assured victim than some distant voice, it refocused its attention on the shower stall and took another step forward.

She considered her options. If she tried a spell, the thing would be on her before she could finish. Her gun was still in the satchel and the thing was between her and the vanity. The only weapon she had was the knife in her right boot. She slid her hand down and closed it on the familiar hilt. Fifteen centimeters of steel weren't going to be much against this thing, but she had to try. If she could wound it and make it back off, that might win her enough time to get off a spell. Or at least buy her a chance to reach her gun and settle it.

The plan would go to hell, but all that seemed far away at the moment.

The thing pressed its wan hand against the translucent plastic of the stall's sliding panel. Hart tensed, readying her knife thrust. She hadn't dared shift her body, so she was ill-positioned for a sure strike. The only advantage she had was that the thing seemed somewhat unsure of her presence. If it were more certain, it would be moving faster. Even with surprise on her side, Hart knew she would get only one chance. It was far too quick for her.

The panel bulged slightly as the creature put pressure on it. The soft flesh of its hand spread flat against the plastic. Slowly the panel began to slide.

"Kathy, are you trying to play hard to get?"

Hart was blinded momentarily by the flood of light. She heard the creature's snarl and the thump as it hit Mr. Target and tumbled both of them into the main room. She was out of the stall and fumbling for her gun before her eyes adjusted fully. As she found it, the screaming started.

She stepped into the room in time to see Mr. Target pull away from the thing. Blood speckled his arm where its hand had held him. The panicked corporate flung a gray pelt at his attacker. It crouched in an easy dodge and uncoiled in a leap onto him. The two of them crashed to the floor. After a short struggle, the thing managed to grab Mr. Target's head with both of its hands. It got to its knees, then stood, forcing the man to rise with it. His fists pummeled it, but it showed no reaction.

The creature's skin began to suffuse with pink, and dark stubble appeared on its naked scalp. Bulges rippled under its skin surface like moles burrowing in soft ground. It convulsed once, then its skin tautened as muscles defined themselves where smooth flesh had been a moment before.

Its fingers shifted their grip, leaving red pock marks on the man's skin wherever they had been. Its thumbs forced his mouth open as the creature extended its startlingly long red tongue. It placed its lips gently on the man's in an obscene parody of a kiss.

He struggled harder.

Thin, translucent tendrils exuded from the thing's body. They waved, blind worms groping in the light. Wherever they touched the man's body, they stuck and burrowed into his flesh. The strands soon tinted pink, then red. The man screamed as if his soul were being sucked from his body.

For all Hart knew, it was. Overcome by the horror, she stumbled back against the wall. As soon as her back touched the smooth surface, her legs gave out, and she slumped to the floor. Stupefied, she stared at the two figures standing locked in malignant embrace.

When the screams stopped, the creature released his victim, who fell backward onto the bed, ripping free from the tendrils that had bound him to it. Those soft, fleshy vessels fell flaccid and were reabsorbed into the thing's body. It caressed itself, running newly wrinkled hands over its body. It spun on one foot and flung itself backward onto the bed.

Hart stared at the two figures sprawled across the bed. The mirror above them reflected two faces and two bodies. There was little to distinguish them. One wore jockey shorts and dark blue socks. The other, flushed with health, was naked. Wilson's creation had lived up to its billing. It had become a living copy of the man she had led here.

Doppelganger.

That was the name Wilson had given it. A creature that could take on the identity of another. Having seen it perform, she knew that her earlier fear of it was more than justified. She hoped fervently never to become prey to it or any other like it.

She forced herself up, using the wall as a brace. Overriding her knees' desire to buckle, she warily approached the bed. The doppelganger didn't move.

The sexless thing was neuter no longer, but emphatically male. Its skin was flushed with blood and its chest rose and fell with its panting. It languidly watched her with half-closed eyes. She stripped the man of his shorts and socks. Not wanting to get close to the doppelganger, she balled up the garments and tossed them.

Its hand flickered up to snatch them out of the air. The somnolent predator sniffed the clothes before letting them fall to its side. It grinned back at her, the ivory ridges behind the lips now differentiated into teeth that she was sure would match its victim's dental pattern. The stolen face was distorted with a look that was pure perversion.

"Why don't you stay awhile?" it rasped, sounding like the man might have a sore throat.

"You know the schedule." At least she hoped it did. The

chip emplaced within its datajack was supposed to feed it instructions once the change triggered it.

It just leered at her.

Her skin crawled with disgust. She turned away to hide her reaction. Hart felt its eyes on her as she walked slowly to the bathroom. The sensation was unpleasant, wholly unlike the feeling she had felt the last time she had taken that path. She was glad to slip into the coveralls that were in the satchel. Feeling less exposed, she picked up the satchel and re-entered the bedroom.

"All right, Jenny," She was surprised to hear how steady was her voice. "Let's get on with it."

The ocean on the far wall flickered and went out. The door it had concealed opened, and her ground team emerged from the adjoining suite. They all wore their DocWagon uniforms. Sloan and Black Dog were picture-perfect DocWagon paramedics, though Greta looked particularly silly in her nurse's outfit. But then Ork women looked silly in whatever they wore.

Now that she was no longer alone with the doppelganger, more of her confidence returned. "Jenny, where's the air?"

"Kurt's got the veetole hanging behind the Mitsuhama building." The tremor in Jenny's voice told Hart that her decker had seen at least some of the process and was equally affected by the sight. They would have to talk later. Right now, they had the important business of getting out, which Hart was very eager to do.

Greta and Black Dog went right to work putting the man on the collapsible gurney that came out of the Ork's case. Sloan stood to one side, glancing back and forth between the doppelganger and its victim.

"Pretty good make-up job," he said to the thing in the bed. "Hardly tell you is an albino."

"I have some special advantages," it replied casually. Already its voice sounded more like its victim's normal tones.

Sloan chuckled. "Yeah, I bet. Hope you pull it off, chummer."

"Come on, Sloan. Give the others a hand," Hart snapped. She ignored his scowl and addressed Jenny. "Any traffic in the area?"

"A few private blips, but Lone Star patrols are all elsewhere. All 'Wagons down or already got passengers."

"Put out the call. Kurt can move as soon as he gets it. Full sirens. He's on a mission of mercy, after all." Hart smiled grimly as she watched them strap the man's limp body onto the gurney. Operation Turncoat had just passed a major milestone.

With Sloan's help, she bound her hair quickly and snugged it beneath a soft green cap. After fastening the front of her uniform, she shrugged the strap of the satchel over her shoulder. She, of course, was the doctor.

"All set."

"Yuh," Greta replied as she slid the last tongue into the last buckle. "Baby's ready for his ride."

"Jenny, lock up here as soon as we're out. Then you're riding cover for us." Hart checked the trideo feed that Jenny had set up to ensure that the hall outside was empty. "All right. Let's roll."

# 13

Some kind of turmoil was brewing in the back of the main room. The flash of pale green uniforms amid the varicolored finery of the club's clientele gave him a moment's warning of what to expect before the crowd was split by a bellowing Ork nurse. She was using her size to cut a path for the gurney that followed her. Two attendants wheeled the cart and its passenger under the direction of a woman in a DocWagon physician's coverall. Between the oxygen mask and the blankets swathing the patient, Sam had no clue to the person's identity or condition.

The doctor was a different matter. A cloth mask obscured most of her face, but her bronze eyes told him what he needed to know. She winked at him.

"That's them, Hanae. Time to go."

With most of the crowd gathering around to see the impromptu show, he and Hanae had little trouble slipping into the mostly vacated area near the doorway to the landing pad. Through the glass, Sam could see a Federated Boeing Commuter with DocWagon markings come in for a landing.

The tilt-wing's great rotors kicked up dust as the VTOL craft settled dead center on the landing circle.

The medical team cleared the crowd and dashed for the doors. Sam pulled one open to ease their way. The Ork shouldered the other open and the gurney slid through. The runners raced across the pad, leaving Sam and Hanae at the door. Roe was the first on board, guiding the cart through the hatchway.

Sam and Hanae ran for the plane.

The throaty roar of the craft's engines could not drown the high-pitched whine as the screamer on Sam's wrist went off. Floodlights winked on, filling the pad with light. Through the glare, Sam looked for Roe in the VTOL, but she had disappeared.

Inside the club, red-uniformed guards were struggling to get through the crowd around the door. Along the strings of pads, armored Renraku security men pelted toward the club's landing pad.

The leading guards called for them to halt. Hanae did so, almost instinctively obedient. Sam shoved her back in motion. There was no stopping now.

They reached the aircraft just as the first squad reached the edge of the landing pad. The sound from the Commuter changed its pitch as the engines increased power for takeoff. Hanae scrambled up, but her bag caught on the edge of the hatch. Sam ripped the strap from her shoulder and let the satchel tumble to the concrete. Hanae started to grab for it, but Sam gave her a hard push forward. She fell in a heap inside the passenger compartment, and he leaped in after her. Behind them, Hanae's mementoes spilled out across the landing pad, scattered and lost to the night by the wash of the aircraft's props.

"This is your last warning," boomed the amplified voice of the helmeted guard captain. "Shut down your motors."

The female Ork swung into the hatchway. The Ares Predator looked almost small in her huge fist. "Frag off!"

Her gun boomed, sending guards scattering in all directions. One sprawled flat on his back.

The guards returned fire. Their automatic weapons spattered gel slugs across the hull of the VTOL. One had swapped the standard duty magazine for another that carried lethal ammunition. His slugs chipped at the aircraft's hull, stitching a path that ended at the Ork. She grunted with the impact, but remained standing in the hatchway.

"Gotta do better than that to take old Greta down, you bloody breeders."

One guard took her at her word, placing his shot between her eyes. She tumbled from the plane as it lifted from the pavement. Wind howled through the open hatchway as the VTOL headed up and away from the arcology.

"What went wrong?" Sam shouted to Roe.

She shrugged. "My decker wasn't as good as he thought. Sorry."

Sam reached out and grabbed the knife hilt he saw protruding from Roe's boot. She watched quietly as he slid the blade under the band on his wrist. With a grunt and a twist, he sliced through the tough plastic. He threw the band across the compartment, where it caught in the slipstream and whisked out the door. Sam tossed the knife to Roe, who caught its hilt.

"Thanks," he said, turning to comfort Hanae, whose closed eyes leaked tears.

Roe slipped the knife back into its sheath. "Black Dog, get that hatch closed."

The man she addressed rose and tugged the panel across the opening. As he latched it, the noise level dropped dramatically. The other runner took advantage to lean across to Roe.

"What about Greta?"

"What about her, Sloan?" Roe stripped off the doctor's cap and shook out her hair. "She knew the odds."

"She was one tough lady. Real wiz in a fight," Sloan eulogized. "Gonna miss her."

"Enough to pass up the extra share you get?" Black Dog asked.

Sloan sent him an evil look. "I'll take the share, but I'll miss her."

"Till you're into your next chip," Black Dog muttered.

"You shuddup."

"Take more than you to do it, chiphead."

Sloan reached under his tunic. The gun he pulled was small and black, but Roe kicked it out of his hand.

"Save it, you two. When this run is over, you can tear each other's throats out. Until then, you work for me. We're all pals and it's business as usual. Got it?"

"Yuh. Just business," Black Dog agreed with a grin. Sloan nodded sullenly.

They flew on without further conversation until the Commuter tilted suddenly. Hanae was thrown from her own seat into Sam's lap and Sloan crashed to the deck. The others barely managed to keep their seats and the gurney tugged at its moorings, threatening to slip them.

"What're you fragging doing up fragging there, Kurt?" Black Dog howled.

"Company on our tail," came the shrill reply from the cockpit. "Raku hot air."

"How bad?" Roe asked tensely.

"Computer pegs it as a hopper jet. A little less maneuverable than we are, but more than enough firepower to burn our tail. They're offering to do just that if we don't put down right away."

"Drek!" Sloan exclaimed as he scrambled back to his seat. "Roe, we gonna get fried. This crate can't go up against anything with armor or guns."

"On ice, Sloan," Roe ordered. "Kurt, keep close to the buildings. They won't shoot if it risks hitting one of their corporate bedmates' towers. And turn off the radio. You don't need them distracting you."

"Gotcha," he shouted back as he banked the VTOL. "I'll head for the Mitshuhama Tower. Hellfire, those nuts might take down the Raku ship on general principles."

"Sure," Black Dog moaned. "So they can haul us in themselves."

"No plan's perfect," Roe observed. "Do it, Kurt."

The flight became a roller coaster ride as Kurt took the Commuter through a series of maneuvers not intended by the craft's designers. Through it all, he always managed to keep some valuable piece of real estate between them and their pursuers, preventing the latter from opening fire. The people clinging to stanchions and seats in the passenger compartment could do nothing but rely on the pilot. Sam prayed, but he knew that their luck, or their fuel, would run out sooner or later.

Hanae huddled against Sam, clinging to him rather than her seat. He felt her shaking and smelled the sweat of her fear. Suddenly she gripped him tighter. He looked down to see her staring out the window into the darkness.

"What is it?"

"I don't know," she replied. 'I thought I saw . . . There! There it is again."

At first all he saw was darkness and the lights of the metroplex. Then he saw the shadowy, serpentine shape briefly eclipsing the neon demon shapes adorning the Aztechnology pyramid. Sam didn't want to credit his eyes.

The winged form flashed through the lights of the Commuter and cut back behind it. As the VTOL banked again, Sam saw the creature breathe a short burst of flame. The backflash shone on the beast, highlighting its rainbow feathers, scaly snout, and ivory dagger teeth. He could deny his eyes no longer. That was a Dragon in the skies of Seattle.

The beast was not much longer than the aircraft, but the breadth of its wings made it seem much larger. But then any Dragon was too large. Was it here to destroy them? Renraku used black ice against computer intruders. Did it unleash Dragons against those who ran from the company?

Sam watched in fascination as the Dragon cut around the Commuter and rushed toward their pursuers. The Renraku pilot reacted instantly, skittering his jet sideways in a burst of directed thrust before banking up and away.

"They're running," Kurt screeched triumphantly from the cockpit. "Something spooked them."

"A Dragon," Sam said in a voice suddenly hoarse. He looked directly at Roe.

"Tessien," she said. "We work together."

Sam waited for her to say more, but she merely stood up and made her way forward to the cockpit. He leaned his head back and closed his eyes.

*Lord, you send strange salvations.*

Once again, Sam was flying off into the Seattle night, involved in somebody else's plots. The first time was bad enough, but now there was a Dragon involved. What else had Roe neglected to tell them? What had he and Hanae gotten into?

PART 2

# It's a Different World

# 14

All night long they were shunted from place to place in an assortment of vehicles. Roe told him that all the shuffling was supposed to throw off any pursuit, but Sam realized it was also to confuse him and Hanae so that they could never expose any facilities or people that were part of the runners' network. Despite it all, Sam knew they were somewhere in the Redmond Barrens. He could smell the infamous "Tacoma aroma." Not even the best shadowrunner trick could hide that.

The Redmond Barrens was not a nice place. Covering most of the old city of Tacoma, the Redmond District was officially part of the Seattle metroplex, but it was a slum mostly neglected by the government. That was even more true for Lone Star Security Services, who held the police contract for the plex. From what Sam had glimpsed during the transfers between vehicles, some parts of the district looked as though they had been through a war. The rest looked like the war was still going on.

The building where the van finally stopped was an old automobile sales facility, full of hollow echoes and old grease. The vehicle sat in a repair bay. When the bleary-eyed passengers rolled up the back door to debark, they found the feathered serpent coiled and waiting for them.

Hanae shrank back at the sight, gripping Sam as though he could protect her should the beast attack. Even the hardened runners seemed reluctant to exit the van near the serpent. Shouldering past them all, Roe walked up to the beast and ruffled the feathered mane at the back of its head.

To Sam's amazement, he felt a hint of the dracoform's pleasure from Roe's caress. In some uncanny fashion, it was broadcasting its emotional state. He wondered if the others were feeling it too, then decided they must be. Everyone in the group had visibly relaxed. Even Hanae looked less tense. It was as though the Dragon had reassured them that it meant no harm.

"Hey, Roe," Chin Lee called out. "This mean we gonna be here for a while?"

"Till dark anyway. Make yourself at home," she answered without looking at them. "Sack if you want to."

Sloan and Black Dog jostled past Sam and Hanae. Digging into a pile of sleeping pads heaped among some crates near the van, each appropriated a prize and dragged it to a separate corner. The rivalry that had flared occasionally during the ride continued as the two men watched each other warily through sleepy eyes. Kurt, who had spent the night in a variety of driving seats, never left the vehicle. He simply put his head back against the rest and started snoring.

"Well, I'm hungry, " Chin Lee announced to no one in particular. Ever since emerging from the Commuter's cockpit with Kurt, the Ork had been stuffing things into his mouth—krill wafers, soycakes, and a seemingly endless supply of Krak-L-Snaps. Now he rummaged around in a crate next to the one that had yielded the sleeping pads until he found a zip-heat package meal. Pulling the tab, he tossed it on a nearby oil drum to heat and rummaged some more. By the time his meal was hot, he had restocked the satchel at his side and tossed a half-dozen more meal packs on the drum. He opened his packet, breaking out the eating utensil on his way back to the vehicle. Flopping down on the van's tail, he stirred the contents of the packet and began shoveling the gooey mess into his mouth.

"You two help yerselfs," he mumbled around a mouthful.

Hanae looked a little green, but Sam thanked the Ork. He led Hanae around to the side of the van, careful to stay between her and the dracoform. The runners were ignoring them, though Sam felt sure someone would get plenty interested if they attempted to leave.

After settling Hanae in a relatively clean spot between the boxes, he fetched a pad and blanket from those the other runners had rejected. He made another trip to gather a pair

of the least awful-looking food packs and a six-pack of Fizzygoo; the jugged water looked even less drinkable than the
Fizzygoo. As expected, Hanae wouldn't even look at the
stuff, but she would be hungry later. He lay down next to
her and held her until she fell into a fitful, exhausted sleep.

Sam was tired, too, but sleep was fugitive, vanishing from
his grasp as had his former dreams of a happy corporate
life. Carefully disengaging from Hanae, he sat up. He wasn't
really hungry, but had nothing better to do, so he set a meal
pack to heating. As he leaned back to wait, Roe appeared
at the outer edge of their crate-walled sanctuary.

"Better get some sleep, chummer."

"Too much to think about."

"Oh, ho. Tough work, thinking."

"Sometimes," he agreed. Roe seemed relaxed, though
as exhausted as the rest of them. Perhaps her tiredness would
lower her guard enough to let slip some clue to what he had
gotten Hanae into. "I've been thinking about that fellow in
the van."

Roe gave a tired chuckle. "Kurt sleeps like that all the
time. He'll be fine when it's time to roll."

Was she deliberately misunderstanding him? "Not him.
The Renraku executive whose name no one seems to know."

"Names can be dangerous," she warned. "I thought you
understood that."

"I do understand. I'm not asking because you've made it
clear you don't want me to know." Sam didn't have to pretend concern. "I'm just worried about him. He's been unconscious all night."

"And it looks like he'll stay that way a while longer."
She reached out and snagged one of the ration packs. With
a deft flick of the wrist, she opened it and snapped the
eating tool free of the cover. "Don't get the wrong idea,
Sam. We're not sedating him or subjecting him to mind-
control drugs or anything like that. It's a side effect.

"Simulating an illness was a good way to get him out of
the arcology, and he agreed. He came up with the idea for
his own ailment, and even got the drug that would fake it.
From his med file, we knew that the injection might induce
a temporary catatonia, so we brought along what we needed
to make sure he'd come out all right. He was very anxious
to leave and thought it was a reasonable risk.

"Paid off, too. His vital signs are stable, so don't you

worry. Trust us," she cajoled, offering the tray from which she'd been eating. *"He* trusts us."

Sam took the offered food, but said nothing. They traded the packet back and forth until it was all gone, then he opened a Fizzygoo for her. She accepted it with a look of distaste, then lifted it in a toast and downed half the container.

"What happened to the albino?"

She eyed him for a moment, but he couldn't read her expression. She shrugged. "Got sloppy and got caught while we were getting your compatriot out."

"His loss just a part of the marginal costs of business, like Greta?"

Roe carefully placed the Fizzygoo packet on top of one of the crates before speaking. "Look, Sam. We all know the risks when we take on a job like this. Renraku is in the big leagues. They play rough. We runners live on the edge, betting our lives that our skills, knowledge, and luck are enough to keep our butts from being boiled. Sometimes we lose."

"Why didn't you do something to recover her? Why did you leave her behind?"

Roe closed her eyes and hung her head. "Didn't you see? She was head-shot. Medicine's real good these days and magic can do quite a bit, too, if the mage knows the right spells. But she didn't have a hope in hell."

Sam shook his head in disbelief at her callousness. "Don't you feel any loyalty to her? To the others?"

"As much as they feel for me."

"In other words, none."

She looked away, then said softly, "They're getting paid."

"Just like you."

"No credit, no fun in this world," she said with a laugh.

Sam didn't hear much joy in that laugh. "Then you're only in this for money."

"Why not? Pays better than doing it for free."

Sam's disappointment surprised him. He should have expected no more from her.

The feathered serpent unfurled its wings, arching its neck upward in a sudden burst of motion. The ebony talons of one hind paw scraped gouges in the cement floor as it sent waves of resentment tinged with something else. Sam thought the emotion felt a little like fear. Roe was up in a flash, searching the darkened end of the building toward which the serpent gazed.

At the far end of the bay, one of the great doors rumbled upward. A black limousine purred into the building, its polished paintwork, chrome, and dark windows reflecting the dinginess of the surroundings as it rolled to a stop. Protective guards snapped automatically into place over the tires.

The rear door opened, and after a moment, a man emerged. Lean and dark, he moved with elegant grace. His clothes, too, were impeccably tailored, showing neither wrinkle nor spot. Scanning the chamber once, he strode purposefully toward the van.

Roe met him halfway, and the two talked quietly for a few minutes. Sam couldn't hear much, but he did make out Greta's name. The man seemed pleased. He spoke briefly again, and Roe responded, once gesturing toward Sam and Hanae. Within moments, she was escorting the visitor in their direction. Sam stood as they approached, stepping away from Hanae so not to be disturb her.

"Sam, this is your benefactor, Mr. Drake."

"Pleased to meet you, sir." Sam offered his hand.

Drake ignored it as he looked Sam up and down. "Ms. Roe has told me of the modification to the plan. I trust you understand your position."

Sam was confused by the reference to a modification. "Excuse me?"

"Ms. Roe's arrangement with you was done without my knowledge. I would never have approved."

Sam didn't know whether to be startled or apologetic.

"But I am not heartless, Mr. Verner. And I know this kind of business requires a certain flexibility. You and your lady friend may take advantage of our guest's transportation arrangements so long as you do not endanger his reaching his destination. I will impose no additional costs or obligations on you beyond requiring that you swear not to interfere with Ms. Roe's execution of her contract with me. Is this satisfactory?"

What could Sam say? Roe doing her job for Drake only helped him and Hanae. "Yes."

"Very well then. Both you and Ms. Roe must understand that, from this point on, you are her responsibility."

Sam nodded.

Drake smiled his satisfaction. "Since we understand each other, Mr. Verner, I wish you and your lady friend a pleasant journey."

With that, Drake returned to his car and was gone again in less than a minute. Roe had drifted back to the feathered serpent. Reluctant to go near the beast, Sam refrained from confronting her about why she had pretended that Drake was part of the offer to extract him from Renraku. Had she wanted to increase her status in his eyes? Or was it just a petty lie, indicating that he couldn't trust anything she said? He didn't understand what would motivate such behavior, but the increasing suspicion that he was surrounded by duplicity made Sam uncomfortable and very, very nervous.

Shadowrunners were dangerous. Living outside the law, they had little respect for it. If he got in their way, it was doubtful they would search for a legal solution. The other runners he had met, Tsung's people, had seemed to have a code. Rough and selfish perhaps, but still a standard of behavior. Roe's crew seemed less . . . finicky.

And Drake, their master, was as hard as any of them. But that wasn't really surprising. He was likely a shark in the corporate world. Drake's easy expectation that everyone around him would jump at his call told Sam that his toughness was no facade. The dark man showed greater confidence in his own power than even *Kansayaku* Sato. The man obviously had control over his runners, which was saying a lot. Sam may not have seen it all, but he'd seen enough to know that nerve and grit were almost sacred among those who dwelt in the shadows of the corporate world.

Drake had warned him not to interfere with Roe. Did he think that Sam and Hanae's presence might jeopardize his carefully laid plans? If so, why was he willing to settle for the pittance that would be his share of the finder's fee for Sam? Wouldn't he want an increased return from an increased risk? Drake would expect something in return for his generosity. Sam didn't like not knowing what Drake's game was, but he hadn't dared question the man's offer.

Other things about the deal bothered him even more. No matter what story Roe gave him, Sam thought it likely that Mr. Drake's "guest," the unconscious man in the truck, was leaving Renraku involuntarily, the victim of a kidnapping. For their own reasons, the runners did not want Sam or Hanae to know that. The two of them would probably be safe as long as they never questioned the story. Perhaps the runners wanted someone to attest that the extraction had been voluntary rather than hostile.

He and Hanae would have to go along, with no questions asked. These runners had shown no reluctance to use their weapons.

The prospect of that sort of violence was frightening enough, but people's violence didn't hold the elemental terror of the Dragon. Sam knew too many documented cases of dracoforms making meals of people. The thought of Hanae's tender body being chewed to a bloody pulp in the serpent's toothy jaws nearly brought his meal back up.

All he could do now was keep his word to Drake. Interfering with the extraction would only put Hanae in more danger. He would keep his eyes and ears open, and they would escape the runners, soon as he could find a way. Delivery of Drake's guest was the runners' primary concern; they wouldn't bother to chase him and Hanae down. At least, he hoped they wouldn't.

Sam moved back to the niche where Hanae slept, assured that he would protect her. How could he betray that trust? He had to see her to safety if he could.

He sat down where he could see her face in the predawn light filtering into the building. She looked so peaceful. He leaned his head back against a crate; it was hours before sleep finally came.

# 15

Crenshaw stood by the door for a few minutes, watching the activity in the room. Most of the work stations were occupied. A quick glance at the duty board showed that the personnel belonging to the empty slots were out on assignment. Everyone was busy, or at least busy looking that way. Marushige presided over the room from his operations desk. She took the dark circles under his eyes as confirmation that the security chief had been up all night watching events develop on the situation screens that filled one wall.

Despite her personal interest in the case, she had slept.

Let others do the groundwork and the backchecking. This one was not going to be a hot pursuit. She didn't care much for the chase anymore, but she intended to be in on the kill.

She crossed the room to the ops desk, avoiding several collisions with scurrying staff. She would normally have resented that they didn't watch where they were going. When she had worked in such a room years ago, *she* had always been aware of what was going on around her. But today was different. She felt good, knowing that she had been vindicated.

"Told you he was a problem," she said, coming up to Marushige.

He glanced at her, letting his mouth quirk up in an expression of annoyance. "Yes, you did. Do you feel that you have accomplished something?"

"If you had listened to me, this all could have been avoided."

"Is that what you've told Sato?"

"I haven't told Sato anything."

"How considerate," Marushige snapped.

Crenshaw ignored the sarcasm. She was really feeling expansive today. "He does want a full report, though. He seems concerned that your lack of security will reflect on him. He doesn't like that sort of thing."

"So speaks the great Lord Sato's new mouth. I'll make a report when I receive a request through channels. He'll have to get in line behind President Huang."

"The president has forsaken his computers and taken an interest in this? How fascinating."

Marushige shot her a sour look. "Look, Crenshaw. I don't need this right now. Huang's interest is purely routine, just like this extraction. Verner was only a minor researcher and the woman was only an office lady. They are no loss to Renraku."

Crenshaw chuckled. "All of this interest on your part is hardly routine."

"As you said, Sato doesn't like security problems of any kind."

Crenshaw knew that Marushige was aware of Sato's power. Hadn't he assigned her to the *Kansayaku,* hoping that she would screw up in front of him? Sato's presence was a two-edged sword. Marushige's own performance was in the spotlight now. He desperately wanted to keep his job, and Crenshaw was in a position to slant the *Kansayaku's* opinion. Sato's displeasure would be enough to get Marushige sacked, which the security chief knew as well as she did. All he wanted to do was to tie up the loose ends and put this problem to rest. But there were too many connected with Verner's extraction.

"The Dragon that scared off our pursuit craft suggests some real muscle behind this run," Crenshaw said.

Marushige grunted noncommittally as he tried to read a report just handed him by an aide.

"Verner must have lifted something important."

The security chief slapped the flimsy down. "Don't you have something better to do?"

"Just trying to understand what has happened, general," she responded with false innocence. *"Kansayaku* Sato might ask me some questions. I would hate to have to tell him that the arcology security chief doesn't know what happened or why."

"I'll bet you would."

"I've told you before that I don't want your job." She was used to his disbelief on that point. "But I do want to see that thief Verner get what's coming to him."

"We've found no indication that he left with anything other than himself and his lady friend. Nothing reported missing from any of the labs and no Matrix security breaches. With his limited access, the likelihood that he carried off any significant data is extremely low."

"Maybe his benefactors thought his connection with Aneki would be worth something." She brayed a laugh. "They'll be disappointed."

"Yes, well, it won't be the first time someone lost an investment in a speculation."

True enough, she thought. But she was still convinced that Verner was involved in something more than a simple escape. He had shown himself too stupidly loyal to Renraku, too obsessed with his goblinized sister. Getting Sato to tell Verner that he could write letters to her should have kept him in the arcology. The wimp wouldn't have run out. There was another angle to this operation, and she was going to find it.

"What about the guy on the gurney?" she asked.

"What about him? No other personnel are reported missing, so he's not one of ours. We have several reports of some Rumplestiltskin's customer getting sick just before the DocWagon aerial ambulance got there. That guy vanished only a few minutes before the runners came through with their gurney.''

''So you think he was the patient?''

''Our rooftop cameras recorded the extraction, and the sick man matches the physical description of the body on the gurney. Seventy percent certainty.''

''But not one hundred.''

''One cannot expect much better from only verbal descriptions and trideo surveillance of a masked and shrouded person.''

''That's true.'' So Verner wasn't selling someone else out. Still, there had to be more. ''Pity about the Ork dying. She might have told us something.''

Marushige gave a predatory smile.

''Oh, but she did,'' he said, waving the report he had been trying to read.

''This identifies her as Greta Wilmark, a freelance runner. Her regular associates include Harry Sloan, Black Dog Sullivan, Kurt Leighton, and another Ork, Chin Lee. Sloan and Sullivan make an eighty percent match with the two paramedics on the landing pad, and analysis of the ambulance's flight pattern suggests strongly that Leighton was the rigger in the pilot's seat.

''That accounts for all of Wilmark's regular team except for Lee, but runner teams are notoriously mutable. The female ''doctor'' was probably a substitute for Lee. All in all, it looks like a small-time operation.''

''Except for the Dragon,'' Crenshaw insisted.

''That may have been an unrelated occurrence,'' Marushige said with a shrug. ''Our pilot did not stay around long enough to establish a link between the runners' escape and the dracoform's presence. It seems unlikely that such small-potatoes runners could have arranged such backup. As soon as the report is prepared, we'll close out the case.''

Crenshaw frowned. Marushige might be satisfied that he had all the answers he needed, but she was not. Even if everything was as simple as Marushige thought, she wanted Verner to be caught and punished.

''What are you planning to do about Verner?''

''Unless something new turns up, nothing. The costs of

hunting down such petty fugitives are high. Past experience indicates that such an investment isn't worth the yield.''

Her eyes narrowed. ''Sato won't like you doing nothing.''

''You mean *you* don't like it.'' He recovered his composure as she lost her own. ''Sato is a businessman. When he sees the reports and the cost estimates for any retaliatory operations, he will agree with me.''

Crenshaw's day had gone sour. This should have been the opportunity to take down Verner for good, and legally, at that. Instead, it had twisted around. Marushige was going to let him get away.

Well, there had to be something she could do about it, and she would find it.

# 16

''She's stopping,'' Kurt announced.

''About time,'' griped Sloan.

''Whuzamatter? Your bottom sore from the ride?'' Black Dog asked.

''At least I got something down there to be inconvenienced.''

''You're looking for trouble, Sloan.''

''You wanna give it to me?''

''Dump it, you guys,'' Kurt ordered, without bothering to look at them.

Sloan and Black Dog had been sniping at one another ever since they'd left the hideout, stopping only long enough to get through the border check station. Sam was relieved when they did, sure that their bickering would draw unwanted attention from the guards. Roe had assured him their travel passes through the Salish-Shidhe Council lands would pass inspection, but Sam was nervous the whole time the tribal representative examined them. The SSC cop apparently thought the group looked harmless enough because he didn't give any of them a second look.

Before they left the metroplex, the runners had traded their panel van for two Chrysler-Nissan Caravaners. They ushered Sam and Hanae into one, while Roe and Chin Lee loaded their guest into the other. Once past the checkpoint, the two vehicles drove south separately, meeting occasionally at rendezvous points along what used to be Interstate 5. Only half an hour ago, they had linked up in the middle of nowhere and struck out cross-country. The vehicles were traveling without lights. Roe, being an Elf, could see quite well by moonlight. Kurt, the rigger, had to rely on the vehicle's sensors feeding information to him through his link with the Caravaner. The ride was bumpy, but not as bad as Sam expected. Caravaners were built for this sort of thing.

When Kurt stopped their vehicle and popped the door, the fugitive moonlight revealed Roe standing beside her Caravaner. Its drab green paint and simulated wood paneling blended well with the surrounding trees and bushes.

"Something wrong?" Kurt asked as Roe approached.

She shook her head. "Tessien is supposed to meet us here. Let's break for a while and rest. This cross-country driving is tough."

"Get a rig," Kurt suggested, tapping his datajack.

"Sure will. As soon as a car is the only thing I want to talk to." Roe laughed lightly. "All right, chummers. Bail out and stretch your legs. Soon as he changes bottles on our guest, Chin Lee will be setting up the stove. We'll grab some food before we move on."

The runners responded quickly. Kurt enlisted Sloan to help him pull a pair of lanterns out of the back, and Black Dog trotted off to the bushes to take care of some personal business. Sam and Hanae were left standing with Roe.

"Katherine."

"Yes, Hanae."

"Where are we?"

"Near the Tir Tairngire border."

"Are we going into Elfland?" Hanae eyes went wide with wonder.

Tir Tairngire encompassed the old U.S. state of Oregon and a bit more. The territory had been awarded to a powerful coalition of the Awakened in return for the help they had given the Native American Nations in their struggle to regain the land. It was not long before Tir Tairngire split off from the Sovereign Tribal Council that ruled NAN, declaring their independence. No one knew much about what went on within Tir Tairngire, for the Elves who conducted its business guarded its privacy. The only fact they broadcast was that much of the land had been returned to its natural state. Tir's official policy encouraged all other nations to do the same, offering Elven magic to aid such efforts.

"Straight across the Tir is the shortest route to San Francisco."

Sam cleared his throat. "It's obvious you plan a surreptitious passage. I've always heard that the border is closed and well-patrolled."

"Yuh, the suit's right. They got Dragons and Griffins and stuff. And them fragging paladins. Nobody said we were gonna have to mix it with them paladins." Sloan's voice was angry, but Sam detected fear. The runner softened his tone. "I heard that if they catch you trying to run the border, they steal your mind."

"You got no worries, Sloan. The paladins won't be able to find yours," Black Dog cracked as he returned.

"Sloan's got a point," Sam insisted, forestalling the runner's return slur. "The Tir Tairngire border patrol is famous for its efficiency. Just about every week, there's a story about someone getting dumped on the highway after trying to get in."

"That's why we have to do it quietly, off the roads, and away from the regular patrols," Roe said. "I'm going to send Tessien ahead to do recon. When it comes back with the all-clear, we'll move out and the Dragon will fly air cover. There should be no problems."

"I'm sure you will get us through, Katherine," Hanae announced.

The runners did not seem so easily convinced. Sam didn't think the plan any too practical, either, but further discussion was cut off by the arrival of the feathered serpent.

The rush of air from the dracoform's wings kicked the dried leaves up into the air. Chin Lee cursed as the camp stove's flame blew out. Once on the ground, the beast lowered itself onto its hind limbs and furled its wings before coiling tightly in on itself.

While Roe strolled over to the creature and began a quiet conversation, the other runners found a sudden interest in Chin Lee's efforts. Sam noticed that the stove happened to be about as far away from the Dragon as one could get without leaving the clearing. He and Hanae quickly joined the latter group.

A few minutes later, the feathered serpent stretched out its body and, with a leap and a beating of wings, took to the air and sped out of sight over the treetops. Roe stopped at her Caravaner to check on the passenger before joining the others.

Meanwhile, Chin Lee's stew was ready. The Ork had scrounged up some wild herbs that gave even the soyburger and reconstituted tubers some taste. After eating, they all settled down. Hanae nestled quietly within the span of Sam's arm. Even Black Dog and Sloan were relaxed, talking about some old shadowrun rather than harassing one another. Chin Lee set a pot of water on the stove and started a card game with Kurt. In the saffron glow of the lanterns, all seemed peaceful.

Above them, the cloud cover grew steadily as the moon slipped lower. The surrounding forest hummed with the soft sounds of wildlife going on with its own business, barely disturbed by their presence. Once, Sam thought he heard a wolf howl. He couldn't be sure, though, never having actually heard a wolf before.

Whatever it was, Hanae heard it too.

"I don't like it out here," she complained.

"Why don't you try to get some sleep?" He knew how she felt. All the open space, the lack of walls, the rawness of the air. The forest just didn't have the comforting, protective safety of the arcology.

"That's a good idea," Roe seconded. "It looks like Tessien won't be back for a while yet. Once we get moving again, none of us will get any sleep."

"I don't want to sleep out here," Hanae said. "It's too open. Too strange."

"You can sack in the van," Kurt said, indicating the Caravaner with his head. "There're pads and blankets in the back."

The peace of the forest was making them all solicitous.

Some time after he and Hanae had settled down in the van, Sam came awake. A check of his watch showed that a little over an hour had passed. Hanae slept peacefully. Careful not to disturb her, he eased his way out of the Caravaner. The night was quiet except for the sounds of the camp. In the stillness, he could hear the soft talk of the runners. Sloan and Black Dog were exchanging insults again.

Movement near the other vehicle caught his attention. The

tall, feminine shape he saw could only have been Roe. She slipped a rucksack onto her back, then pulled a shotgun out of a locker and slung it over her left shoulder. Without a word to the others, she walked around the Caravaner into the darkness.

Curious, Sam followed.

He spotted her again, crouched by the edge of the trees, and walked up to her side. She surprised him by grabbing his arm and pulling him down. Saying nothing, she held a finger to his lips.

Sam's scalp prickled. He didn't know much about the natural world, but earlier there had been so many sounds. The wind in the leaves. The buzzing and clicking that he was sure were insect noises. The soft scratchings in the undergrowth. That had all stopped now, yet he could see the leaves of the trees still moving against the clouds. They should be rustling and bringing the moist smell of the forest with them. But there was nothing.

Something was very wrong.

"Roe," he whispered. "What is it?"

"I don't know."

He scanned along the treeline. Dark boles shone slightly in the light of the lanterns and the camp stove's flame. Leaves that he knew were green glittered with an evil blackness.

A glint of light caught his attention. He squinted in that direction. After a moment, he thought he made out a figure standing several meters into the trees. It was tall and thin . . . like an Elf.

He tapped Roe's shoulder and pointed. She looked in the direction he indicated and cursed softly. She began to search through her pockets.

The breeze rose suddenly, kicking up dead leaves as the Dragon had done. The soft brown detritus rustled as it skittered away.

Then that small sound was swallowed by the heavy thwopping racket of rotor blades. Sam looked up as a dark shape swept over the trees. A second and third rushed in its wake. They were followed by still more.

"Yellowjackets," Roe breathed as she rose.

Sam stood, too. He knew Yellowjackets from seeing them on tridcasts of corporate settlement wars. They were small, fast, one-man helicopters that carried more than enough armament to take on a light armored vehicle.

Sam discovered that the Yellowjackets also mounted searchlights when shafts of light began to stab down from the craft as they swept over the camp. Sam counted six bright beams cutting across the open ground.

He and Roe were outside the area illuminated by the lights, for the moment undiscovered. She held something out to him.

"Take it," she said, stepping away.

He grabbed it reflexively with both hands. Looking down, he saw it was her shotgun. As though it were red hot, he opened his hands in horror and let it fall to the ground. No more guns, he had sworn. He expected Roe to say something, but she had already vanished into the darkness.

The weaving lights had spaced themselves into a circle that bathed most of the clearing in harsh glare.

"By the authority of the High Prince of Tir Tairngire, I order you to surrender without resistance. Do so immediately and you will not be harmed."

For a moment, no one moved.

Sloan broke the tableau by sprinting for the Caravaners. As he ran, he screeched, "You ain't taking my mind."

"Remain where you are," the disembodied voice boomed. "This is your last warning."

Sloan ignored it. He pulled an automatic rifle from under the seat and spun on his heels. Locking the stock under his elbow, he triggered the weapon, ripping a burst at the chopper with the loudspeaker. Sloan's rifle stuttered in a piping tone, piercing the steady thump that came from the whirling blades of the surrounding aircraft. Higher-pitched whines shrieked as the weapon's slugs tore at the craft's fuselage until, in a shattering of glass and a shower of sparks, the lead chopper's searchlight winked out.

"Mother, he got me," the mechanical voice said. Sam was sure the voice did not intend for those on the ground to hear. After a moment, it spoke again as though in reply to a question. "They've drawn blood, Bran. They can damn well drink it. All units, lights out. Fire at will."

The clearing plunged into darkness as the hovering choppers extinguished their lights as one. Before the after-images had faded, red tongues of fire erupted in place of the lamps. Heavy slugs tore gouts of earth in lines across the camp.

Kurt, racing for cover against the other van, was thrown to the ground when one copter's fire caught him. A second craft's machine guns sought his downed form, slicing through him and leaving him dismembered on the bloody ground.

Sloan opened up again, firing wildly into the night. Tracer rounds from his gun flared orange in the darkness. He shouted incoherently as he fired. The Elves responded forcefully. Fire illumined one of the Yellowjackets briefly, turning it into an alien insect god of destruction as it launched an air-to-ground rocket.

Time seemed to freeze for Sam. He saw, or imagined he saw, the slim, deadly shape leave the launch tube. As the rocket cleared the tube's mouth, its fins extended, snapping into place to control its flight. The missile roared toward the van beside which Sloan shouted and raved. Hanae had been sleeping inside that van.

At that instant, Sam saw her face appear at the door. She was bleary-eyed and her hair tousled, looking disoriented by the turmoil and destruction. Just as Sam started to shout a warning, the missile struck.

Thunder split the night.

The Caravaner bucked under the impact and roared into an instant inferno as the warhead detonated. Sloan was lifted into the air and flung away, arms flailing.

Sam ran forward, but then tripped and fell sprawling. He looked back to see what had made him fall. In the flickering light, he saw Sloan's face, rigid with hate and fear. The runner's hair was half-burned away on one side. His body was nowhere in sight.

Sam scrambled to his feet and staggered once more toward the burning van. Its roof began to sag from the heat, and noxious smoke poured from the pyre. The interior of the van was incandescent with the heat of the conflagration. A sudden spout of flames drove him back. A large hand closed powerfully on his arm. Sam tried once to tug free before turning to see Chin Lee's tusked face.

"You can't help her now," the Ork yelled over the roar of the fire and the thunder of the circling helicopters. "Come on, head for the trees. The fragging Yellowjackets can't follow us there."

The Ork released him and sprinted for the shelter of the

forest. Sam gave the van another look. Chin Lee was right. He could no nothing for Hanae now.

He was alive and she was not, but Sam would make some-one pay for that. As they ran for the trees, the second van exploded in a ball of flame that climbed into the sky. Fleet-ingly, he saw the silhouette of Black Dog scrambling away in the other direction while the angry Yellowjackets buzzed over the clearing, filling it with fire and lead.

Chin Lee was well ahead, just passing the first tree when a slim shape rose up to meet him. The Ork started to swing his assault gun around, but the figure stepped close, brush-ing the muzzle up and away. A black-clad foot snaked out and the Ork crashed to the forest floor.

The fires revealed the attacker as an Elf. He stood over the stunned runner, panting slightly. Then he casually lifted one hand and sighted down his extended forefinger at the Ork. Arcane energy sparked from his fingertip.

Chin Lee screamed and clutched his arm. The Ork's hand came away slimed with goo. He yowled louder as the goo spread across his chest and up his neck. The cries died in a bubbling wheeze as his face turned to mush and slumped away from his softening torso.

"A fitting end to such an abomination," the Elf mage pronounced.

Sam had not stopped running, his legs pumping, though his eyes were locked on the horror before him. His mind was so numbed by the terrifying display of magic that he didn't realize he was heading straight for the Elf until it was too late. He barreled into the mage and they both went sprawling.

He pushed himself away, kicking at the other to untangle their legs. This Elf had just turned a living person into a puddle of slime. Sam had no doubt that he would gladly hand him the same fate.

The Elf had gathered his wits and was trying to stand. Seeing a fallen branch, Sam grabbed for it. Swinging as he scrambled to his feet, he struck the Elf in the head. The rotten wood of the branch shattered on impact. Fragments and surprised insects exploded in a cloud, sending the Elf staggering back, more confused and startled than hurt.

Sam turned and ran.

"Go ahead and rabbit, renegade. You're meat for the

hunter.'' The mage began a spell chant. He spoke it loudly, obviously intending Sam to hear.

Sam risked a glance over his shoulder. The Elf had raised his hands above his head, a flickering nimbus of ruddy light forming into a sphere around them. The killer mage was readying a spell. Fear lent speed to Sam's pistoning legs.

Then he felt a strange surge inside. Somehow he knew the spell had been completed. Heat scalded his back as the trees around him washed in flame. The hot air seared his lungs and he fell, burning.

# 17

The Mitsubishi Nightsky gleamed elegantly in the setting sun. The limousine's sable bodywork drank the light to form deep, distant reflections in contrast to the immediate glitter and shine of the chromed highlights. The rear door gaped to offer access to the cool, dark interior, a counterpoint to the oppressive heat of the day.

A woman and a man walked down the steps of the Jarman Building. Their manner and total indifference to the pedestrians passing between their corporate sanctuary and the luxury vehicle at the curb marked them as the likely owners of the Nightsky.

She wore a conservative suit of the most exquisite tailoring and materials. From the sparkling silver heels that gave a fine shape to her bared legs to the platinum chain glittering within her dramatic coiffure, she moved and breathed corporate success.

He wore a dark three-piecer and moved so smoothly that the suit hardly seemed to crease as he walked. The dark hair that framed his long-boned face might have emphasized the grimness of his saturnine features, but his obvious pleasure in the woman's company rendered him strikingly handsome. He was a dark counterpoint to her sparkle, but in every way a match to her corporate royalty.

Their expressions were relaxed as they laughed quietly at some private joke. Their eyes were only for one another and they seemed to be anticipating an evening of pleasure.

Hart slipped from the crowd to stand in front of the man. It was going to be *her* pleasure to ruin the start of that evening.

"Hello, Mr. Drake. Surprised to see me?" Drake pulled up. The woman shot him a glance that told Hart she had no idea what was going on. *Not good, chica. You should know your bedmate better than that.* "Well, Mr. Drake?"

"You are exceptionally resourceful, Ms. Hart. Why should I be surprised?"

Hart shrugged off his smooth reply. "I guess I'll just have to be satisfied making Ms. Mirin nervous."

The woman shifted her searching look to Hart, who carefully ignored the penetrating appraisal. Hart and the woman had never met, but the Elf knew Mirin would not care how Hart knew her name. She would rather be wondering what else Hart knew about her. Let her. As long as Mirin was confused, her uncertainty would restrain her.

"Young woman . . ."

"Arcstore it, Ms. Mirin," Hart said, earning a sharp, angry look for her interruption. "I am not here for conversation with you. So keep out of it. I also suggest that you not initiate any suspicious gestures. It could cost you your life. I have friends in high places." In reply to Mirin's scornful smirk, Hart added, "One of those friends has a high-powered rifle trained on your head. That person is an excellent marksman. And well aware of your capabilities."

"Is he fast enough?" Mirin said contemptuously.

Drake placed a hand on his companion's arm. "Let's humor Ms. Hart, Nadia. To the best of my knowledge, she is a woman of her word and scrupulous in reporting her arrangements. There is no need for violence at this time.

"Ms. Hart, perhaps you would care to step inside where there are fewer ears?"

Hart smiled, too, aware that fewer ears meant fewer eyes if he really did want to start trouble. "I think not."

"On the stairs, then. Away from the mob. Just you and I."

Mirin seemed ready to object, but Drake forestalled her with a slight shake of the head. For Hart, he had nothing but smiles. "Would it be satisfactory for Nadia to wait in the car? I am hardly likely to offer you violence on this public street, in plain sight of all these people."

That was what she was counting on. "She can go. As

long as she cooperates, she will be safe. My friend has explosive bullets and a convenient angle to place them into your limo.''

"I don't like threats, Ms. Hart," Mirin stated softly. There was clear menace in her tone.

"And I don't like having to make them. You aren't involved in this yet. We'll all be happier if it stays that way."

"It's all right, Nadia. Ms. Hart and I have had a simple misunderstanding. There will be no trouble."

Mirin's expression made it clear that she already thought there was trouble.

"Go on. I'll be along in a moment."

Mirin acquiesced. Hart started up the steps without waiting for Drake. She stopped halfway up and turned. The sun had slipped out of sight, and the shadows had crept down to where she stood. She shivered, more from nervous anticipation than from the cool breeze that skirted the darkened face of the Jarman Building.

"Now, what is this really about?" Drake asked as he joined Hart. The light tone he had used in Mirin's presence vanished, replaced by a businessman's poker face.

"I think you were trying to avoid completing our contract."

"Why would I do that?"

"I don't really care about your reasons, though I've got a pretty good idea what they were." Drake said nothing; he merely favored her with an inquisitive look. He was cool. Too cool to be innocent, she decided. "I was still there when the Tir Tairngire border patrol hit. They used a mage to cover the sound of their Yellowjackets. There was a full squadron; more than enough for a few second-rate shadowrunners and a couple of runaway corporates. They were looking for trouble and expecting to find it. When Sloan panicked and opened fire on them, the patrol blasted us with everything they had. Pure devastation. I could have been killed with the rest."

As expected, Drake's expression changed to one of concern, but he showed no surprise. "Perhaps you should talk to Tessien about that. Creatures of its kind have a reputation for untrustworthiness."

"I did talk to Tessien. It said that you met it in Portland, saying that plans had been changed and I was headed back for Seattle.''

"You must decide who you will trust, Ms. Hart."

"I already have," she said, locking eyes with him.

"I see," he said coolly. "I will have a compensatory bonus added to your account."

"That will patch some of the larger holes in our agreement."

"Do you require additional patches?"

"That's not my style, Mr. Drake. I'm a pro. I can keep my mouth shut without special incentives."

"See that you keep silent on our association."

"Look," she said hotly, "you had your shot and you missed it. That was business and I understand. Now I'm telling you that you don't need to silence me. I won't talk because I've got my professional pride. And the same professionalism lets me ignore what you tried to do. Let's call it even."

"As you wish, Ms. Hart, we shall let the past lie." His smile showed his gleaming, perfect teeth. "But let us not part in anger. You have impressed me with your fire and integrity. I wish to continue to retain your services. Say, 25,000 nuyen per month. Call it a retainer."

"I told you that I don't take hush money. You want my services, you pay the usual rates."

"You are a most unusual woman, Ms. Hart. I begin to believe that you will hold to your self-imposed standards of conduct. Now, are we on working terms again?"

She held out her personal comp to him. He smiled in assurance that he had regained the upper hand as he slotted his credstick and made the funds transfer. To demonstrate her trust, Hart ran a confirmation of the transfer as soon as he returned the comp.

"Your money's good."

"Good as gold, Ms. Hart."

"Better," she said hefting her comp before slipping it back into her bag. "Gold's too heavy."

As she stared down the stairs, Drake's hand shot out to grasp her arm in a painful grip. He fixed her with a stern look. "You are *sure* that there is no evidence at the site of our Renraku switch."

She dropped her gaze from his eyes to his hand, waiting until he released her before answering. "The van with our other guest was rigged to explode, per your orders. If there is anything left, they'll probably assume that it was just one more runner.''

Drake's toothy smile returned. ''And none of the dupes who were supplying the cover for our operation survived? A wounded captive could say too much.''

''Last I saw of the man, the Tir mage had fireballed him. The woman went up when the patrol torched a van. The others are all history as well.''

''A satisfactory solution. From your report, that Renraku salaryman seemed rather too perceptive in his questions. Had he remained alive, he might have intrigued the wrong people with his tales. It is far better that all witnesses be dead.''

*All but me*, Hart thought. *But I'm still on the payroll, right? Safe enough as long as I have some value or until you get what you're after.*

''I will allow no one to compromise the plan,'' was the last thing Drake said.

# 18

Sam was surprised to find himself alive.

The flames had flared all around him, igniting the trees and his clothes. He had passed out from the pain and must have fallen, tumbling down an unseen bank into the sluggish stream where he now lay half-submerged. The water must have put out the flames. He was scratched and bruised from his tumble and scorched from the fire, but alive.

He could not have been unconscious long. He heard a voice that must belong to the Elven mage that had burned him. The Elf was probably so sure of his powers that he hadn't bothered to check on Sam. Sam strained to make out the words.

''I've downed the tusker and one norm, Grian.''

''Roger,'' came a reply fuzzed with the static hiss of a radio transmission. ''Both vehicles burning. We've got three probable kills, but the clearing's in flames and we can't land there to confirm.''

''Want me to do a ground sweep?''

"Negative. You know the procedure, Rory. Nobody goes into an unsecured zone without backup. Besides, you've been pumping a lot of power."

"Null perspiration, Grian. I'm fresh enough. These gutter scum weren't as tough as the briefing indicated. I won't have any problems."

"One more time, Rory. Head back to the rendezvous point. I'm bringing the flight down there. We link up, then we all go in together."

"Don't you think I can handle them? I am a noble class sorcerer."

"That's not the point, Rory. They already winged me. I don't want anymore casualties. Meet us when we land."

"Understood," the mage said finally, but his next words were mumbled, obviously not intended for the other Elves to hear. Sam couldn't make them out either, but the tone was surly enough to guess the meaning.

Sam was suddenly terrified that the Elf might want proof of his kill. He began to pray that the mage would just leave, preferring to let others confirm his prowess. The night grew quiet as the helicopters moved out, their fading sound leaving the forest to its own noises. Once more the leaves rustled in the wind, but the animals, frightened by the noise and flames, were silent. Sam decided to follow their example. It was time for him, too, to be very still.

He waited.

Tense minutes passed and he tired of shivering in the water. He moved his arm, careful to avoid splashing or dripping water as he raised it before his face. The screen of his watch was dark. He tried the reset button, and the light feature activated only long enough to show him that the screen was misted on the inside. Useless. He flipped the toggle to release the catch, only to have the band snap in his hand, Reaching back to toss it away in disgust, he remembered that he was trying to be quiet. He slipped his hand underwater and let the broken timepiece sink to the streambed.

He waited some more, then dared to crawl back up the slope, his passage accompanied by the cracking and snapping of twigs and branches. Each sound increased his fear that he had not waited long enough for the mage to leave. When he finally poked his head above the bank, the mage was nowhere in sight.

The two Caravaners still burned, but the grass fires had

mostly died. Kurt and Black Dog lay sprawled in death, along with pieces of Sloan. Hanae was incinerating in one of the vans. Of Roe there was no sign. Between him and the devastation in the clearing lay the pool of slime that had been Chin Lee.

He was alone.

In the distance, Sam heard the howling again. This time another, different howl seemed to reply. The sound made him realize how alone he was, lost in a forest somewhere within Tir Tairngire, a nation that had demonstrated its hostility to him. The forest would be home to many paraspecies that wouldn't mind making a meal of him. Thoughts of Griffins and Basilisks raced across his mind. And Dragons. Sloan had said that the Elves used Dragons as border guards. His recent close encounter with the feathered serpent made him realize that such a beast could swallow him in a single gulp.

Chin Lee's assault gun lay nearby, lost and forgotten when the Ork got hit by the Elf's spell. Sam stared at it. Its metal parts were dark, looking cold even though faint reflections of flames danced on its surface. The ergonomically designed plastic stock and grips hinted at a seductive ease of use. Its sleek metal parts spoke of deadly efficiency. The assault gun was a weapon designed to kill people, yet Sam had vowed never again to touch such a thing.

The wolf howled once more.

He remembered the Barghest that had attacked Sally Tsung. He would never forget its terrifying howl and slavering jaws. The beast's baying had frozen him and the others where they stood. The wolf's howl did not have that power, but it was chilling nonetheless. Sam had no magic to destroy a beast as Tsung had done.

What could kill people could also kill animals. He walked over and picked up the weapon. The weight surprised him, for Chin Lee had waved it around so easily. At least it had a strap, which he slung over his shoulder as the Ork had done. He would carry the weapon in case of attack by some ravening paranimal. But he wouldn't to use it against people. That he promised himself.

Sam looked again at the clearing. If he stayed to bury his former companions, the Elves would return and catch him. Choosing his direction blindly, he turned his back on the scene and began to walk. He wondered how far he would get before the Elves came back.

Sam started to run as soon as he heard the first rustling in the undergrowth. He hadn't seen anything, but neither had he waited around to look. Now he couldn't hear anything over the sounds of his own passage. The assault gun bounced against his shoulder and back, bruising the skin even through his tough coverall. Already he was winded, panting hard for every breath. He should have gone running more often with his dogs, or otherwise exercised to keep himself in better trim. Now he was running for his life and paying for his indolence. He wanted to stop, to breathe, to rest, but did not dare. They were behind him somewhere. They wouldn't rest, so he couldn't.

A root snagged at his feet, forcing him into a sideways lurch. The assault gun dragged at him, pulling him off balance. He staggered and crashed into the bole of one of the forest giants. The tree was unimpressed and he caromed off, losing his balance totally. He toppled over backward to land painfully, the gun's magazine and stock digging into him even before his head rocked back to rap against the barrel. Dazed, he rolled over and tried to stand. Nausea swelled in his stomach and his head pounded. His vision narrowed and he fell heavily. The gun's barrel wedged against a root, and he sagged over the weapon like a limp sack as his vision dimmed.

*Lord, not now,* he prayed. *They'll get me.*

His body had no strength. It was weak, exhausted. But he could not rest until he was safe. He needed to know if the Elves were tracking him.

Sam tried to get up but the world spun, then went dark. The next thing he knew he was rushing back along the path he had just taken. Here and there some twisted tree or rock outcropping looked familiar, but he saw no signs of his pursuers. Had he lost them? Was all his running in vain?

His questions were answered as he looked out onto the clearing where the Elves had killed Hanae and the runners. He watched from the edge of the trees, the leaves shadowing his position and the bushes screening him. The scene had an unreal quality, a dreamlike distance as though it were continually receding at his approach. Everything was gilded with a faint, silvery light, yet the moon was cloud-hidden at the moment. A band of Elves roamed amid the ruins of two strangely insubstantial Caravaners, one of them still burning. All but one of the Elves wore uniforms bearing badges whose symbols spoke of protection and guardianship. Sam surmised that they were Tir Tairngire border guards. The Elf not in uniform stood apart from the searchers. Dressed in jeans and a flannel shirt, he seemed to radiate power. He was familiar somehow, and Sam concluded that this must be the Elven mage that the radio voice had named Rory. Other than these seven Elves, Sam detected no other living persons in the area.

"What's the story, Grian?" the mage asked the tall Elf who approached him.

"One deader in the burned-out van. Bran says the skeleton looks to be female and there are indications that it's the renegade from Renraku. Aidan scraped a couple bones out of the other van, so it looks like we got the second woman, too. The three in the open all match the runner descriptions, and the Ork you got accounts for all the males except the Renraku guy."

"Got him, too," Rory assured him.

"We'll see about that soon." Grian shook his head. "Too bad about the high-tech stuff in the van. Ehran would like to have seen it."

"You sure it's beyond salvation?"

"Couldn't be in worse shape if a Dragon sat on it."

Rory clapped him on the shoulder. "Well, at least we got a full count on our uninvited guests. Makes it a profitable evening."

"Don't spend it before you get it, Rory. We don't have a full count until we get a confirmation on your second kill."

"Then let's get it. The guy went down over here."

Rory led his companion toward the spot where Sam crouched spying. He feared that the Elves would discover him and cry the alarm, but they seemed not to see where he hid. They stopped near where the sorcerer's spell had overwhelmed Sam. Though they had come closer to Sam's hiding place, their voices were no clearer. A trick of sound the forest was playing on his weakened condition.

"No body, Rory," Grian observed to the accompaniment of Rory's curses. Then he raised his voice. "Bran, get over here! We need a tracker. Our cocksure sorcerer went and missed."

Grian skidded his way down the slope while Rory, more fastidious, followed him carefully. Both Elves moved with a languid, slow-motion grace. Bran arrived in time to find Grian bending over to pluck something from the streambed. At first, Sam couldn't tell what sort of device the Elf was holding. Then he recognized the broken strap and realized it was his discarded watch.

"He went down here, all right."

Rory reached out from where he stood on the bank and snatched the watch from Grian. "See. Good and charred. If he walked away from here, he didn't get far."

Grian ignored him. "Take a look around, Bran. See if you can find us a trail."

Bran nodded and headed upstream. In a quarter of an hour, he was back. He spent several more minutes studying the stream bed near where Sam had fallen. The others watched him, Grian standing patient and confident, Rory pacing back and forth at the edge of the stream.

"Don't think you'll have to worry," Bran announced.

"Why?"

"Found some hoof prints on a mud flat upstream. Looks like a single horse; riderless, I think. No signs of entry or exit from the stream for almost half a kilometer. No normal horse would take that kind of path at night."

"Water Horse, then?" Grian hypothesized.

"Looks like." Bran nodded and pointed out signs as he spoke. "Stopped about there, where our boy fell in. Stood for a while, then took off downstream like a bat out of hell. Should have reached the Columbia by now. Looks like our boy is breathing water."

"Nothing more to do here, then," Grian concluded.

Rory blocked him as he attempted to climb the slope. "What about confirmation?"

"If he took a ride on a Water Horse, there isn't going to be any body."

"Then we'll get credit for the kill?"

"More than likely."

"So I guess there is nothing more to be done here," Rory said cheerily.

Sam saw the sour look Grian gave the sorcerer as Rory started up the slope.

"All right, mark it and we're done. We'll let the regular patrol clean up in the morning."

There were murmurs of approval from the Elves as they left off what they were doing and joined their leader. Bran tapped buttons on a shiny object he took from his backpack before dropping it near the burned-out van. While he was doing that, Rory spent some time staring at the marks his magic had made on the forest. He looked troubled, as though he couldn't remember something that was important to him. When Grian called his name, the sorcerer shrugged and slowly turned away to follow the others. Sam watched the last Elf leave the clearing to follow his companions back to their transportation. They were heading well away from the direction that he had run. He was safe.

Exhaustion swept over Sam. He left the clearing, turning his eyes from the death and destruction again. He had no awareness of the walk to the tree that had felled him, but suddenly he was there again.

Something nagged at him, a sense of being watched. He stretched his senses, pushing back the fatigue that dragged at him, dulling his perceptions. The woods were still peaceful. He caught a glimpse of shadowy shapes loping between the trees.

Dark beasts, canine and at least as big as wolves.

Then they were gone.

Strain as he might, he lost them among the trees. Were they coming closer? He didn't know and almost didn't care. He had pushed himself beyond his limits. His head drooped; he was tired beyond comprehension. Lord, he was tired.

Once more, he felt the pain of the assault gun grinding into his back. All the aches of overused muscles and the small pains of scrapes and cuts swelled. It was deep in the third period of sudden-death overtime and he was an Ice Brawl puck. If the beasts were coming to get him, they could have him. He already felt dead.

Intermittent puffs of hot air beat on the left side of his face and he smelled the fetid stink of a carnivore's breath. Cautiously, he turned his head and opened his eyes. Two slanting, golden-green eyes stared into his.

# 19

Marushige was right. Sato considered it uneconomical to undertake a hunt for Verner and his doxy. Crenshaw's lobbying for just such action had almost cost her all the good will she had been building up with the *Kansayaku*. The only good thing was that Sato had not directly forbidden her to look into the matter. Not that such a prohibition would have stopped her, despite the devastating consequences that disobeying could bring down. Crenshaw figured she had always been able to look after her own interests, arranging for any devastating consequences to fall on someone else, preferably an enemy.

Still, her private investigation had not yielded much. Her network in Seattle was minute compared to the web of contacts and informants she had maintained in the Orient. What little word trickled in all came back negative. It was as though Verner had vanished from the face of the earth. Such cheap-hire runners couldn't be that good. There had to be a connection with some high-rolling player in this shadow game. All she had to do was find it.

To do that, she needed time, time the *Kansayaku* wasn't letting her have. Whenever she wasn't acting as his bodyguard, he kept her running his errands. As though Akabo and Masamba weren't enough mundane and magical muscle. As though he were trying to keep her from getting out and doing some of her own spadework.

That, she realized, was an angle she had overlooked. Might Sato be involved somehow? She didn't see what he had to gain, but he certainly had enough clout to make a person vanish. A hidden interest in Verner would explain why Sato had gone along so easily with her suggestion about offering the wimp contact with his sister.

If she could just finish her little chore quickly enough, she could get in a call to a certain Tokyo fixer who might know something.

Impatiently, Crenshaw looked through the double panes of Xylan that separated her from the clean room where the

AI team was conducting an experiment. Among the anonymous green-coated figures, the tall form of Vanessa Cliber stood out easily. After a few moments, Crenshaw identified the other team leaders among the capped and masked workers.

The strands of black hair escaping from a loosely tied cap and the constant bustle were characteristic of Sherman Huang, president of Renraku America and head of the operation. No one else would dare to be so casual about the room's cleanliness restrictions while at the same time being so passionately involved in the process.

The other leader demonstrated a precision of movement and an economy of motion that Crenshaw admired. She had noted it two days ago while observing Konrad Hutten working in the data center. For a man whose specialty was abstruse microtronic engineering, he had a physical grace that Crenshaw found attractive. When this current business was wrapped up, she just might try to find out if he was equally attractive away from his work. She wondered if he liked aggressive women.

As she watched, the test seemed to conclude. The workers relaxed visibly and all the bustling stopped. Three figures left their associated knots of green coats and headed for the airlock door of the clean room. Only the team leaders would be free to leave before all systems were verified as secure. Crenshaw felt a smug satisfaction at having pegged all three correctly.

Huang was the first through the outer door. He had already stripped away his cap and mask and was trying to stuff them into a pocket. His mind, as usual, was on other things, and the objects fell to the floor.

". . . for a whole hour. It's not like she didn't know there were going to be late nights on this project."

"Even wives don't like being stood up, Sherman," Cliber said.

"It was just a little dinner party. Nobody important was there." Huang shrugged. "She'll get over it. She always does."

"Perhaps if you took some time off," Hutten suggested.

"Time?" Huang was clearly affronted. "That's exactly the issue. Everybody wants my time. I don't have enough for the project now that it's reached this crucial stage. If they'd just leave us alone." His eyes fixed on something only he could see and the muscles around them relaxed from their habitual squint. "Just a little more time and we'll show them."

He reached down and spun a monitor to face him.

"Hah! Just what I thought. Take a look at this."

The other two peered over his shoulder. Cliber uttered a meditative "hmm." Hutten said nothing but reached past Huang to tap keys on the console.

"Good thought, Konrad." Huang nodded in approval. "That configuration should maximize throughput in the beta cycle."

"An obvious extrapolation from the modulator parameters," Hutten observed.

In her business, Crenshaw was sometimes pleased and relieved to be treated as part of the furniture. The lack of attention could even be a valuable asset. This was not one of those times. Deciding that the green coats were going to ignore her until she intruded on their attention, she stepped up and spoke.

"President Huang?"

All three looked at her in unison. Cliber's face immediately settled into its habitual glare of contempt. The other two wore expressions of mild curiosity.

"Yes?"

"Alice Crenshaw, sir. Security division."

Huang's brown furrowed, but Crenshaw noted his fugitive flash of concern. Like a child caught looking at dirty pictures.

"There's no problem, sir. I'm on assignment with *Kansayaku* Sato. He sent me to convey his apologies and regrets that your dinner meeting must be postponed by half an hour."

"Is that tonight?" Huang asked absently.

"Seven-thirty," Hutten offered. "Now eight."

"Well, I guess we'll be there. With all the bells and whistles." Huang laughed nervously.

Crenshaw groaned inwardly. They had invented the term nerd for this man. She gave him a polite smile "The *Kansayaku* is looking forward to meeting your team leaders this evening."

Cliber flashed her companions an anticipatory grin. "I'm looking forward to it, too. I've got a few things I'd like to drop into Mr. Kansa-whatever's ears." She turned on Crenshaw. "He's sure enough taken his time getting around to us. The grapevine's been buzzing about how he's in such an all-fired hurry to get the project moving. How come he's waited so long to talk to us?"

"The corporation has a lot more interests than your AI project, Doctor Cliber. *Kansayaku* Sato must concern himself with them all. He has been looking around, getting a feel for the operation here in Seattle. He has told me that he thought it best not to disturb your important work on the project more than necessary."

"No more than—," Cliber sputtered. "The personnel changes he ordered were hardly necessary. And they were very disturbing."

"As I said, doctor, no more than necessary."

"What does he know about what is necessary? You people are all alike. You have no idea of what we are doing here, but you still think that you can shove people in and out, make schedule changes at whim, and I don't know what all else. Then you expect us to dump results in your laps on order."

"Calm yourself, doctor."

"Calm myself." Cliber's face was flushed. "I haven't gotten started yet."

"I suggest you reevaluate your attitude in light of the *Kansayaku*'s mandate," Crenshaw stated coldly. "He might find your attitude nonproductive."

"Nonproductive!" Cliber tugged her cap from her head, loosing her honey-blonde hair from the pins that had bound it up.She slammed the green cap to the floor. "Sherman!"

Huang looked up confusedly from the monitor he had gone back to studying. "Hmmm?"

Crenshaw spoke before Cliber could launch her tirade. "I was just suggesting to Doctor Cliber that she place some curbs on her . . . enthusiasm. Cooperation with *Kansayaku* Sato is the fastest way to get your project moving."

Huang blinked, looking from his clearly incensed colleague to the calm security officer and back again. "Vanessa, I'm afraid Ms.Crenshaw is right. You do let your temper get the better of you occasionally and we must be careful around Mr. Sato. If he's satisfied with what he finds and no one antagonizes him, he'll go away and we can all get back to our work. You know how close we are." He gave Cliber a weak smile that seemed to calm her a little.

Then he mumbled, "I do hate all this bureaucratic non-sense."

"Hardly nonsense, President Huang." Crenshaw chided. Cliber snorted, but Crenshaw continued. "But I understand how professionals like your team may find it bothersome to abide by the necessary formalities of operating in a business-like manner. *Kansayaku* Sato is only looking out for Ren-raku's interests. He wishes all departments to work at peak efficiency."

"Then why hasn't he approved our requests for more help?"

"As a matter of fact, he has." Crenshaw produced a chip carrier from her jacket pocket and tossed it on the desk. "These are the files and transfer orders for twelve of your requested personnel. I'm sure you will want to express your thanks to the *Kansayaku* at dinner tonight. Until then."

Enjoying the stunned looks on Huang's and Cliber's faces, Crenshaw turned and strode for the door. On her way, she noticed that Hutten had seated himself at a cyberterminal and continued to work through all the uproar. A realistic and professional attitude. She liked that in a man.

# 20

Sam awoke as his muscles locked into a brief spasm. After a moment of startled disorientation, he lay back, confused. He was indoors and in a bed whose soft quilt lay heavily on his naked skin. The room was dark, lit only fitfully by indirect glow from what seemed to be a fire in the next room. He was surrounded by a vaguely familiar scent at once comforting and strange.

He couldn't remember how he had come to be here. Last he knew he had been in the forest, running for his life from the Tir Tairngire border guards. And there had been a pair of wolves.

The memory was confused, one thing blending into another.

Images of the place where Hanae had died dominated his memories. Flash-lit shards from the attack, tranquil images of the scene as they had bedded down with the shadowrunners, washed-out visions of Elves wandering among the destruction. It all dissolved into whirling impressions of the dark forest and his haunted run through the dark.

Sam remembered falling and hitting his head. A cautious exploratory hand confirmed that memory. He had a very large bump on the back of his head, but he felt curiously little discomfort on touching it. In fact, none of the scrapes and bruises from his run bothered him. They were still there, though, evidence that the nightmare in the forest had been real. His mysterious benefactors must have given him something for the pain.

Faces came to mind. One was a haughty and disdainful male, the other a concerned but faintly confused female. Both were long and thin with slightly slanted eyes. Their ears had just the hint of a point. They could almost be the faces of Elves, but they weren't, they couldn't be. It was Elves that had tried to kill him. Why would they save him? It didn't make sense. He couldn't remember clearly, but Sam was sure that hands belonging to those faces had helped him from the forest, seen to his wounds, and installed him in this bed.

Not knowing where he was or who were his benefactors made him nervous. His state of undress only exaggerated the feeling of exposure. As he sat up to look around the room, a steely glint in one corner caught his eye. Chin Lee's assault rifle leaned against the wall. Whoever had brought him here felt comfortable enough to leave him armed. Or had they?

He crept from the bed and checked the weapon as he had seen the Ork do. It was still loaded. They did trust him. Surely, then, he was not a captive of the Tir Tairngire border guards.

On a stool beside the gun was a pile of clothes. They were not his, but must have been left with the intent that he wear them. He soon found that they fit. He was pulling on the boots that had been tucked under the stool when he heard the soft murmur of voices in the next room. Lacing the footgear quickly, he moved to the doorway to listen.

The door opened onto a large chamber that ran past the bedroom. The speakers were out of his line of sight, somewhere off to his right. Distance and the muffling effect of the curtains and wall hangings made their words impossible for him to quite make out. The tones and cadences were familiar, however. He had heard these speakers before. He knew it had not been in surroundings as luxurious as this well-appointed hideaway, but he could not place them. Curious, he stepped out into the light to get a look.

Three men looked over, startled at the sight of Sam. Two of them were seated and one stood by the large windows that faced onto the forest. The standing man was totally unfamiliar, but the two men in conversation were not.

One man was seated almost full-faced toward Sam, and he stopped speaking in mid-sentence. Sam had only spoken with this man once, but the man's pock-marked skin and heavy, almost continuous brows were fixed in his memory. It was Castillano, the enigmatic denizen of the Seattle underworld whom Sam had met during his misadventure with Tsung's shadowrunners.

The other sat not quite in profile. Sam could see his pointed Elven ears and the capped studs of a datajack and a pair of chipjacks on his depilated left temple. Even before the Elf turned, the white shock of hair and familiar black leathers told Sam that it was Dodger, Tsung's decker.

Another man entered from a side room along the same wall that held Sam's room. No name came to mind, but Sam recognized him as the male from his recent memories. A wolf trotted at the man's side. The animal seemed quite at home and unconcerned that its claws clacked on wood rather than scraping on the loam of the forest floor. It noticed Sam in the doorway and padded over. He bent to meet the animal on its own level, recognizing her, too.

"Freya?"

The wolf tossed her head at the sound of her name and licked his face.

"She bites," said the unnamed man with the familiar face.

"It's all right. She won't bite me."

As if she understood his words, Freya pulled away from his hands and nipped at them before submitting again to his petting. The others in the room watched without a word. When Sam at last looked up, he met their eyes. Castillano's stare was grim, but Dodger's eyes lit with pleasure. The others were indifferent.

"Sir Corp," Dodger said. "I am glad to see you awake and refreshed from your slumber. We feared that you had taken serious harm. Come sit by the fire and tell us the tale of how you wandered so far from your home.''

Sam gave Freya a last pat and strolled over, taking a vacant chair. The wolf followed behind and curled up near his feet, back to the fire. He looked down at her, trying to buy time. He wasn't sure what to say. These people had presumably saved his life, so he owed them something. But he had no idea of where he stood.

''Whyever were you running aimlessly through the forest?'' Dodger prompted.

''I left Renraku. Now they're trying to kill me.''

''What?''

''The border patrol. They called me a renegade.''

''You are still muddled from your ordeal and present your explanation poorly, Sir Corp. You were never a member of the patrol so you could not be a renegade.''

''No. The corporation.''

Dodger laughed in disbelief. ''Corporations do not levy the death sentence on simple runaways.'Tis a penalty far too harsh. And to chase you here into the Tir . . . it is unbelievable.''

Castillano tapped his hands on the arm of his chair. ''What else you into?''

''Nothing,'' Sam said, bewildered by the question.

''A lie. Too much fuss.''

''Indeed, a great fuss has been raised and your tale makes no accounting for it. There must be more involved. Sir Corp, you had best tell us who is out to kill you.''

Sam shook his head. ''I don't really know.''

''Mayhaps you best take the tale of how you come to be so far from home and tell it whole.''

Sam nodded. It might be best to get it straight. Telling these people might make it easier for him to settle it in his own mind. Haltingly at first, he began with the growing dissatisfaction with Renraku and the frustrated desire to trace his sister that led to his decision to leave the arcology and the corporation behind. He recounted the extraction and its disastrous end, but omitted the names of all participants save Hanae. ''So you see,'' he concluded, ''I really don't know what is going on. But I'm not so far from home; I don't *have* a home anymore.''

''A most lamentable tale,'' Dodger said sympathetically.

''Smoke and fog,'' Castillano judged.

The Elf gave the man a look of annoyance. "Methinks your verdict harsh. Is it your intent to speak ill of your guest?"

Castillano shrugged.

Dodger turned to Sam. "I have had reliable word from friends in the shadows of Portland. They tell the tale of a Renraku reward for the capture or elimination, preferably the latter, of a pair of renegade employees who stole some valuable company technical secrets."

"I don't know what you're talking about." Sam protested.

" 'Tis said that these renegades were extracted by a handful of shadowrunners and driven south. They were alleged to be planning on illegally crossing the Tir Tairngire border." The Elf paused for a moment. " 'Tis but a tiny step to match the descriptions of these renegades to you and your ladyfriend."

"That doesn't make any sense. We didn't take anything but personal property." Sam shook his head perplexedly. "Maybe the other guy took something."

"Other guy?" Castillano queried.

"Sir Corp, you made no mention of another."

"Well, there was another employee being extracted at the same time," Sam said.

"Shadows say only you and the woman."

"Well, there was another guy, and he must have taken something. The Elves said there was high-tech stuff in the van he was in. He's dead now, too."

"Elves?" Castillano's tone clearly indicated that he expected an elaboration.

Sam explained what he had seen and heard of the border patrol. Castillano's face remained impassive, but Dodger looked thoughtful.

" 'Twould seem that the Dragon's words to the Tir Tairngire authorities were taken to heart."

"A Dragon?" Sam asked, suddenly suspicious. "What kind of Dragon?"

Dodger shrugged. "Whatever the form, they are all trouble. Do you know, Castillano?"

"Feathered serpent. Young."

"Tessien." Sam felt sure of it.

"You have knowledge of this beast?"

"I'm afraid so, if it's the same one." How many could there be? "It was supposed to be Roe's partner."

Dodger sat back at the mention of her name and even Castillano blinked. Sam didn't know what to make of their reactions, but he was sure he wasn't going to like the explanation.

"Roe?"

"Yes. The woman who arranged the extraction. Do you know her?"

Dodger and Castillano exchanged glances. The fixer nodded slightly, but it was Dodger who spoke. "There is someone with a bit of reputation in the shadows. Was your Ms. Roe an Elf with platinum hair and an expensive wardrobe?"

"She would fit that description," Sam confirmed.

"Roe, of course, is not her real name," Dodger said. Looking worried, he leaned back in his chair. "This shadow person of whom I spoke—there are rumors that she has partnered with a Dragon in some of her most recent escapades. That dracoform is whispered to be known as Tessien. I think, Sir Corp, that there cannot be two Elves partnered with dracoforms named Tessien. Very likely, you lady Elf is the notorious runner better known as Hart."

"Don't want any trouble with Hart. Suit, you got to go."

"We need not be hasty, Lord C. 'Twould seem that the border guards believe your guest to be dead. Hart and her employer will have the same information. No one will come looking."

Castillano shook his head. "Unnecessary risk."

"Verily, you worry too much, Lord C. Your enterprise will remain undisturbed."

"What are you doing here?" Sam asked innocently.

"Need to learn manners, Suit."

"Sorry. I thought you were a fixer. Isn't that a city thing?"

"So?"

Dodger spoke up, his light tone an apology for the fixer's gruff reticence. "Lord C. is engaged in a noble and charitable service, Sir Corp. He arranges for those who have an abundance of small, valuable items to dispose of their excess to those who have a dearth of such, but have difficulties dealing with certain arbitrary political boundaries."

"You talk too much, Elf."

"Come, come, Gracious Host. I believe that our friend

here is stalwart and trustworthy. He shan't reveal any of your secrets, for it would be most disloyal to betray his host's trust and Sir Corp places a very high value on loyalty.''

"Too many mouths; too much talk." Castillano rubbed at the palm of his left hand. "Don't want extra trouble."

"I don't want to give it to you," Sam assured him. "I won't say anything. But I need your help. I need to get back to the metroplex.''

"Got a plan?"

"I guess I'll go back to Renraku. This whole thing is so crazy. I don't see any other way to straighten it out."

"Got a lot to learn."

"I've got to do something. From what you've said, someone, either Roe, I mean Hart, or whoever is behind her, deliberately set me up to be killed. That same someone let me drag an innocent woman into their plot. It's my fault that Hanae was killed, and I've got to do something to set that right. They're murderers and I'm going to see that they pay for it.''

"Very noble."

"Scoff not at this man, Lord C. He has been wronged and his heart cries out for revenge. Surely you understand revenge?''

"I understand business." Castillano rubbed his palms together. "This is bad for it."

"I'll pay you," Sam offered desperately.

"What?" Castillano asked tonelessly. "Got no credit, no money, no gold. Only a pile of old pictures and a few chips.''

"You can have the chips. The persona programs are worth something.''

"Too hot. They're tagged."

"Sir Corp offers all he has, Castillano. Surely that is worth something.''

"Appealing to my Human nature, Elf?"

Dodger smiled humorlessly. "Call it what you will. If you do not help, I shall. Suddenly I find more merit in his desires than in the lure of your offer.''

"Your loss, Elf." Castillano stood. "Got some credit coming. Be in your account.''

"Your honor is intact, Lord C."

"Just have the kid leave the clean chips before you leave."

Castillano signed to his men and they all headed for one of the other rooms. Freya gave Sam a look that he interpreted as sympathetic before heaving herself up from before the fire and padding after them. Sam thought he heard the Elf add softly, "Though your mercy lags."

Just before vanishing into the next room, Castillano threw a parting shot over his shoulder. "Keep the Bible, kid. You'll need it."

# 21

"Eighth Street Mission," proclaimed the sign.

The faded and chipped letters had seen better days, as had the battered and scarred brick building they named. All the lower windows were sealed with opaque construction plastic behind the rusted, bent, and now obviously useless bars that once protected them. Grafitti in sufficient layers to suggest generations of down-Sprawl artists made a riotous skirt around the sedate centenarian structure. One symbol on the wall along the stairs to the main entrance was bold, as though set apart from the other scribblings. Sam had never seen the thistle in a ring design, but he guessed that the emblem proclaimed the building under the protection of the local street gang.

The mission was of a piece with its surroundings. Though much of Portland had been rebuilt, this section was still mostly pre-Awakening. It was only one of the slums that clung to the edges of the revitalized center where neo-Elven architecture, with its graceful curves, eccentric designs, and environmentally integrated architecture, dominated a sky-line that would have seemed alien to men of the previous century. Even to Sam, the Elven-style buildings seemed un-comfortably different from either the clean-lined edifices or the retrofitted make-dos of the great urban Sprawls. The shapes and outlines chosen by the Elven architects seemed to proclaim the glories of the Sixth World and to revel in the restoration of magic on Earth. Sam had been relieved when he and Dodger finally crossed into the older parts of Portland and the Elven spires were hidden from view. Despite having grown up in safe corporate enclaves, the littered streets and gloomy Sprawl made him feel more at home.

Dodger led the way up the steps to the mission and into the large room that took up more than half the entry level. The open door and dirty windows let in barely enough of the mid-morning light to alleviate the darkness. Scattered bulbs burned feebly in a pathetic attempt to compensate, while the stench of despairing and broken humanity was strong. Inheritors of the miasma were scattered about the chamber, many slumped or curled in fitful sleep. Some sat silently on the room's mismatched, battered furniture while others chattered in a steady stream, whether or not anyone was listening. The aged and the ageless in their filth partook of the mission's charity alongside dissipated youth and ragged homeless. The mission's occupants were a dirty and smelly lot, but only those obviously in the last stages of chip addiction looked malnourished. Moving solicitously among these refugees from the streets was a broad man in a dark suit. His shirtfront shone with the stark white of a Roman collar, marking him as a priest.

"Father Lawrence."

The priest turned at the sound of his name. His face was wide, in keeping with his frame. His forehead was marred by a large wart, but overall his features were pleasant if somewhat coarse. In the dim light, he seemed to have a faint gray pallor. Only when he smiled did Sam see the enlarged lower canines that revealed the priest as an Ork. A mild expression of the Ork gene complex, perhaps, but definite.

"Dodger," the priest exclaimed with evident pleasure as he recognized the Elf. "I didn't know you were in town."

"Verily, Father, that is good news. For if you did not know, then no one did."

The priest laughed heartily. "You overrate me as usual. Still, I shall have to speak to a few people."

"Not too harshly, I trust."

"No. No. But one must always be aware of the way the wind blows. *Respar sallah tishay a imar makkanagee-ha.* Eh?"

Dodger cocked his head and gave the priest an admonitory look. "Few of your patrons speak Sperethiel. What have you been up to?"

"God's work, as always." Father Lawrence said, waving his hand to encompass the mission.

"God still allows you leeway to deal with criminals, then?"

"Criminals, citizens, nobles, even paladins and shadowrunners are His children." Though his words were pedantic, the priest's voice held firm and honest conviction. "It is to the sinner that we must open our hearts, for where is the merit in loving those who stand high in His favor while spurning those who need aid? God ever favors just causes."

"As is this man's, Father. We come as suppliants in need of a bed and rest. You can call my friend"—Dodger paused for a thoughtful moment, then his face lit mischievously as inspiration struck—"Twist."

The priest looked Sam over, his eyes taking in the details of Sam's attitude and appearance and evaluating them in an instant. Whatever conclusions he reached were concealed behind his ready grin. Father Lawrence reached out and shook Sam's hand vigorously. "Welcome to the mission, Twist. Any friend of Dodger has a place here."

"Thank you."

"Are you a Christian?"

"Yes." Sam felt compelled to add, "But I'm not Catholic, Father."

"That can be remedied with good will and faith, but you won't find me pushy about it. All who observe the rules and peace of this house are welcome here. The good Lord provides as He will. Of course, He understands that we each give according to our ability."

Responding to Father Lawrence's expectant look, Dodger said, "Alas, Father, our current enterprise partakes more of just desserts than just distribution."

"I have never had cause to fault your generosity, Dodger. I will trust in an eventual donation, while praying for your success." If their welcome was less, the priest showed no sign of it. "You know your way around, Dodger, and there are those here who need my attention more immediately. I'll trust you to take care of yourself and your friend."

Dodger led Sam through the room and into the kitchen where two pots were beginning to bubble, overlaying the scent of antiseptic and the pervasive animal-pen smell with the fresh odor of soup. They took a creaking stairway down into the basement. By the time they reached the bottom, musty dampness had wrested control of Sam's olfactory perceptions.

Weaving a path through dusty, mildewed piles of Lord knew what, Dodger moved unerringly in the darkness. Only by staying close enough to catch the faint gleam of the Elf's studded leathers could Sam be assured of not losing his guide. When Dodger stopped, Sam nearly walked into him. A moment later, he felt a whuff of fresh air as the Elf led him forward into a deeper darkness. A slight scraping noise heralded the end of the basement's odiferous confines as the chamber's concealed door closed behind them.

Soft red light burst forth. In its glow, Sam could see Dodger leave the switch he had thrown and cross the room to toss himself down on a bed that creaked in protest at his weight.

"Make yourself comfortable."

Sam looked around. There was not much more than a counter and a couple of cabinets besides the bed that the Elf had commandeered. In one dim corner, he spotted an old folding chair. He retrieved the rickety chair and sat down on it backward, folding his arms across the back rest. "What now?"

"That, Sir Corp, depends upon you. I have gotten you to a safe place to rest, to think, and perhaps to plan. Have you decided on a plan?"

"Not exactly. But I have thought about what you said about going back. I think you're right; it wouldn't be very bright. At least until I know more."

"So you are not going to be *makkanagee* after all?"

"Not be what?"

"*Makkanagee*. Willfully or maliciously stupid."

Sam shook his head ruefully. "I've been stupid enough, but it certainly wasn't deliberate."

Dodger raised an eyebrow but said nothing. Sam didn't know what to say to that and so they sat silently for a while. He knew that the Elf was right. He needed a plan if he were to do anything effective, but first he had to know who his enemy or enemies were.

"If I can get into the Renraku Matrix, I think I can find some answers."

"How do you propose to do that?"

"I've still got those persona chips that Castillano wouldn't take. If I can get to a cyberterminal, I can deck into the mainframe.''

"They will have changed the access codes.''

"I think I know a way around that. Jiro once showed me a back door he said had been put in by one of the system designers. If I can get into the Matrix, I can get into the Raku system.''

"And how many people know about it?''

"Jiro said the decker who told him was the only one because the designer had died in a plane crash.''

"Oh. A decker secret passed only to a chosen disciple. Then only several hundred computer jockeys know about it, including all of Raku's roving Matrix sentries. Ah, well. Even if it were a way in, your chips are tagged.''

"Castillano said that. What does it mean?''

"My, you really are innocent of the ways of the Matrix in spite of your jack. A tag is a complex set of instructions encoded into a chip. It makes any instructions executed through that chip leave an identifiable mark on whatever programs they touch. If you use those chips as they stand, you will leave very large, identifiable footprints everywhere you go in the Matrix.''

"Then it's hopeless.''

"Nay, I said not that. But you must be aware of the dangers you face before trying to deck without authorization into a system as dangerous as Renraku's. As to the tags, I can strip them from your chips if you but give them into my care.''

"Permanently.''

Dodger laughed. "I have no need for your chips, as my own are far superior. What call has a master of the Matrix for some neophyte's persona programs?''

Sam was excited. "Then you will help me get into the Raku system?''

"If your back door is good, yes. But to assay it now would be folly, for you have no experience in such endeavors and would be iced before you passed the access node. Running a mainframe undercover is a bit trickier than doing your salaryman duties, Sir Corp. You'll need practice.''

"How do I start?''

"Ghost spoke truly of you. You do have courage.'' Dodger heaved himself off the bed and opened one of the cabinets. He took down a keyboard and cleared the power cords so that he could lay it down on the counter. He held out the datacord to Sam. "Here is an Allegiance Beta. As a cyberdeck it is antiquated, but it should perform adequately for a beginner like you, especially while you are under the guidance of a master. I'll give you the Matrix address code to a safe system. You can try running against it for a while and see what you can get out. The system is not very complicated, but it's got ice."

Sam, who had started to reach for the datacord, pulled his hand back at the mention of IC.

"Nothing dangerous," Dodger assured him. "But it will get you some experience. While you're doing that, I'll work on your chips."

Sam handed over his persona chips before snugging the plug from the Allegiance cyberdeck into his datajack. He watched as Dodger unpacked his own deck, a much more sophisticated model, and a microtronics tool kit from his backpack. The Elf had his work well under way before Sam had steeled himself to power up the Allegiance.

Several frustrating but increasingly successful bouts later, he jacked out. His head throbbed, but he was elated. He had finally managed to strip some information out of one of the system's datastores. Dodger had been right. There was a lot more to unauthorized decking than he had imagined. He massaged his temples and stretched.

"You have had some success?"

"Got a datafile."

"Very good for a first try, Sir Corp." The Elf's face showed concern. "But you should not have been taxed that badly."

"Don't worry about it. I always get headaches when I access the Matrix."

"Do you? How strange."

# 22

"Remember, you aren't really ready for this, so try not to get separated."

"I know and I will." The chromed head bobbed in agreement, mimicking the action of its controller. There was no real reason for the icon to do so. No program had been executed, no command given. The motion was an artifact of the consensual hallucination that allowed the Human mind to function in the alien space of the Matrix. "I appreciate this, Dodger."

"Your words will be proven true only if you perform as an astute and attentive student." Dodger winced inwardly. The professor would have laughed to hear him utter those words. Though his mentor had used a somewhat different phrasing, the intent was the same. Had the old Elf felt the same emotions that tugged at Dodger now? Fear that his student's nascent skill would be insufficient warred with the need to see him stand on his own. There was a very significant chance that Sam would fail disastrously on this run. And the blame would be Dodger's for not demanding that one last drill, driving home a procedure until it was reflex. Or it might be his failure to describe some seemingly obvious trick of the trade that would lead Sam to make a mistake and pay with his life or his sanity. If there were more time, Dodger could train him better, but time, even for an Elf, could be a more implacable foe than even the blackest of ice. There was no more time. Sam, ready or not, would wait no longer.

Anxious over his student's capabilities, Dodger could not let him face the Matrix alone. Not against the powerful, and almost certainly hostile, Renraku System. Even without the IC, Sam would be a fast meal for the rawest Raku deckhound roving the system. Without Dodger's experience, Samuel Verner, neophyte decker of the shadows, was likely to get his brain fried.

Dodger led the way. Their path ran through the fiber lines to the antennae hidden on the upper floor of the mission, then by microwave uplink to a satellite nexus. They shunted through the regional telecom grid connections and were beamed down into Seattle. They zapped through the local telecom grid to hover in an exchange junction box on Wharf Ten. The business system they had invaded was a minor client of the Renraku Corporation. The arcology Matrix was only a single, well-guarded step away.

They did not experience their journey as such. To their Matrix-bound perceptions, they simply stepped out and away from their home systems and seconds later stood at the foot

of an enormous pyramidal icon. Its deep, nonreflective black
was marked with a disk of glowing blue that regularly pulsed
out an expanding ring of bright neon. The wave grew until
it met the edge of the construct and another wave was unleashed. The first continued to expand, vanishing when the
planar surface could no longer contain it, leaving arc seg-
ments to grow until gobbled themselves by the more distant
edges of the construct's surface.

"Bring up the masking utilities," Dodger instructed.

He keyed his own, knowing without needing to see that
his normal icon, a small ebon child with a glittering silver
cloak, had been overlain with a simulation of the standard
Renraku corporate decker icon. Sam's Matrix imagery, having originally been one of those icons, underwent a less
visible shift. The facial features blurred and smoothed as
replicated corporate symbols and identification markings
shimmered into existence.

The badges borne by Sam's icon were faintly smudged,
darkened as though slightly burned. With more time,
Dodger could have done better, but he had to settle for un-
registered duplicates of Renraku access authorizations that
were imperfect. Though not foolproof, their disguises
should withstand casual scrutiny by ordinary anti-intruder
programming.

" 'Tis time to see if your back door really opens our way
into the castle."

"Dodger, I don't think I should let you see the code."

" 'Tis a place whose secret paths I have trodden before."

"But you got in by yourself then. I wasn't opening the
door. I . . . well, it just doesn't seem right that I should.
Even now. What if we're mistaken and Renraku has nothing
to do with the killings? It would be wrong for me to give
away this secret."

"Do as your conscience bids, Sir Corp."

"I just wanted you to understand."

"Shall we get on with it?"

"All right."

Sam's icon moved ahead. They floated upward until they
hovered at one edge of the pyramid, about a third of the
way to the apex. Sam placed his hand at the point where an
arc racing along the edge had revealed a slight discolora-
tion. Just before the next wave hit that point, Sam's icon
swung between Dodger's and the point of contact with the

pyramid. As the wave passed, the faint glimmer of an outline appeared in the surface of the Renraku construct.

Dodger opened his eyes. Usually there was nothing to watch while decking. His gaze drifted to where his companion's fingers tapped codewords into the Allegiance cyberdeck. Dodger's fingers tapped an identical sequence on his own Fairlight deck. When Sam's fingers ceased their frantic motion, Dodger's hit one more key and the sequence was locked into storage on his deck.

*Part of the price,* he thought. The passgate was too valuable a piece of data to be denied him by Sam's scruples. He refocused his full attention on the Matrix.

They entered the Renraku complex into a backwater slave module that was overseer for a bank of elevators. Such a node should not have allowed access to the system but it was, after all, a back door. The appearance was that of a small guardroom. Its smooth walls flashed infrequently with light as the elevators went about their business. A samurai dozed in one corner of the imaginary room, his neon armor dull. Because the elevators only connected a small spread of floors in areas of minimum security, the guardian ice would normally be activated only in an alert.

The run suddenly looked a lot more feasible. If Renraku had really been in an uproar over a major tech theft, the entire system would be on alert. Even here, the guard would be awake to watch the physical elevators and to report intruders to security. Such a monitor assignment was usually considered superfluous in such an unimportant node, but the presence of guardian ice was an indication of the thoroughness of the Renraku Matrix. At least that was the most reasonable conclusion if one assumed that Matrix security didn't know about the back door. Dodger didn't think such ignorance likely. He certainly wouldn't want to bet his brain on it.

Though the guard was asleep and everything seemed peaceful, it might still be a trap. If their own programs weren't successfully hiding their identities, the countermeasure programming might be sophisticated enough to present a pacific image until the intruding deckers could be drawn so deep into the system that escape was impossible. Corporate deckers could already be jacking in to hunt them down, or a tracer might be back-tracking their signal to detect their physical location prior to targeting a strike team.

Dodger hadn't survived years as a shadowrunning decker without caution. But he had some experience with this particular corporate Matrix and he found nothing to indicate that all was not as it seemed. Somewhat assured, he signaled Sam to press on.

Sam leading, they left the elevator control node and stepped out onto the ethereal pathways that connected the components fo the internal Matrix. In the infinite darkness, subsystems glowed like distant stars of arcane geometry, while pulses of data blazed comet-like across those subjective heavens. Before and behind them, their own path faded away, leaving them walking an insubstantial flare of light that came from nowhere and went to nowhere, until they reached the next node.

During the transit, Dodger noticed that Sam's icon limped. His brow furrowed as he tried to understand the phenomenon. He had seen nothing in the persona programming that indicated such a visual interpretation for the construct. Once the run was over, he would have to re-inspect the chips.

As the limping chrome mannikin led him through node after node, Dodger's confidence grew. He began to feel assured that there really was no alert. They had only encountered one roving corporate decker and Dodger's programs has masked them from him. If an alert were in progress, they wouldn't have gone three nodes without bumping into some deckhound. This might be an easy run after all.

Finally, they reached Sam's goal, a datastore for medical files on non-Human assets. When first told of it, Dodger had questioned the worth of such data to their quest. Would not personnel files, though harder to penetrate, be more useful in identifying whether the feathered serpent worked for Renraku? Sam had assured him that Renraku would classify a Dragon, even a sentient one, as an asset rather than an employee. The distinction was foolishness to Dodger, but then he wasn't Japanese like Renraku's directors. Orientals sometimes had different ideas about how the world worked. He'd seen enough of such skewed attitudes from Sally Tsung, and she was only half Oriental.

The walls of the datastore were aswirl with alphanumeric characters. Symbols flashed different colors and danced at varying speeds, the pattern complex and ever-shifting. The image represented the code systems locking the data away from unauthorized access. Sam's icon stood transfixed. "I think you'd better handle this. I might trip an alarm."

"Technomancy of the simplest sort. Keep watch."

Dodger's icon dropped its mask and an ebon hand flourished a matte gold case. Slim fingers snapped open the lid and delicately removed a tool. Kneeling before the flickering wall of alphanumerics as though before a lock, Dodger inserted the slim instrument into the flow. After a few minute adjustments, he selected another tool, slipping it into the flow to use with the first. A careful twist of the wrist and the symbols slowed, their color pulses becoming longer. Another twist, and they slowed further and further, until they froze.

"Which file, Sir Corp?"

"I need to scan them."

Sam's icon stepped to the wall and placed a hand on the seemingly solid light. The chromed head bowed as if in deep concentration and file names flickered briefly as a fairy fire fled across them. After a minute, the glow steadied and highlighted one of them. "That one."

The ebon boy nodded and adjusted the angles of his tools. The wall moved again, sequences rippling past until the chosen code lay under the position of his hands. He returned the tools to their case and it vanished under his cloak.

Dodger extended his hand into the wall. It disappeared into the light as if cut off at the wrist. After a moment, he withdrew it. He held a fat green book. Dodger flipped quickly through the pages. "No serpents."

Sam sighed.

Dodger tossed the book back through the wall and tapped twice on the glowing file code. The alphanumerics of the wall resumed their manic rush, but their clarity was reduced.

"Dodger, I think we'd better get out of here."

"What is it?"

"I don't know. I just think that we might be pushing our luck if we stay."

Dodger's suspicions were roused by Sam's sudden concern, an indication that he was withholding information. He reactivated his masking program. "Very well, but I'll lead. We shall move faster that way."

They did, indeed, move faster, retracing their route toward the exit, until Dodger pulled up suddenly. He gazed in shock at the walls of the node they had just entered. Vertical slabs of mirror reflected their icons to infinity. It was uncanny, unprecedented. What made it worse was that Dodger's reflection showed the jet outline of a boy crouched under a shimmering cloak and the markings of Sam's chromed mannikin were dark pittings in the smooth surface. Dodger felt uneasy. He had never encountered anything like this node in all his years of running the Matrix.

Fingers flew across the keyboard, improvising programs to analyze the nature of the hardware in which their programs were operating.

Somewhere in the depths of the mirrors, Dodger saw something move. It was distant and furtive. There was nothing in the apparent chamber to account for the fleeting glimmer.

Analysis programs received abort signals and new instructions were entered at a frantic pace: Cut and Run, Stand by for Execution.

He reached across the room, battling Sam's hands away from their poised position above the Allegiance cyberdeck. He keyed in the run code and punched "Execute".

The chromed mannikins in distant reflections winked out. The vanishing images continued through closer and closer planes of reflection at an ever-accelerating pace. The last images vanished, and with a pop, Sam's icon dematerialized from the node.

Dodger was alone with what moved in the mirrors.

How he knew he wasn't sure, but he was certain that it was coming closer.

His finger stabbed the "Execute" key.

His own reflections began the fugue of vanishing. The presence reacted, moving closer as well, racing the disappearing Dodgers. Its masking chrome dropped, the ebon boy raced around the room as though moving the icon itself might give his reflections the speed they needed to escape the presence. He felt the other nearing, but dared not look back. It was almost upon him as the last reflection vanished.

Pop.

He was panting and bathed in sweat, but he was safely back in the real world. He jerked the datacord from his jack. Sam was looking at him, bewildered. He didn't know enough to be scared.

"What was that?"

"I don't know. I've never seen anything like it before. In fact, from everything I do know, it was impossible."

"But you got us out, anyway." Sam pulled out his jack and tossed it on the counter. "I guess it doesn't matter what it was. We got what I wanted, and now that we're out safely, they can't trace us."

"So it would seem."

"The headache is worth it. I'm sure now that Renraku didn't order the killings. If the feathered serpent had been working for them, its medical data would have been in that file."

"They could have hired it for the occasion."

Sam shook his head. "I don't think so. Not if they wanted to stay legal."

"Pray tell, why not? The contract courts would have let them invoke a termination clause on Hanae and yourself. The villains who rule there rarely check too deeply into whether said employee was really sufficiently valuable to warrant such a clause. Renraku could easily create the fiction that you were both important enough."

Sam looked discomforted by the idea that his former corporation might do such a thing. "No. They wouldn't do that. Even if they did, wouldn't the Dragon have to be part of the corporation? Everyone knows that the courts are scrupulous about proper form during the invocation and execution of such clauses. The law states that any actions taken against the renegade must be taken by bona fide corporate officers."

"The beast could have been a bounty hunter."

"The law also says that bounties must be set and registered in court. You yourself found out that there was none."

"Alas, Sir Corp. The legal record does not always match reality."

"I won't believe there was an unrecorded bounty," Sam said, shaking his head vigorously. "Renraku wouldn't dare risk the sanctions for disregarding the regulations, especially since I didn't take anything. The cost would be far too high."

"You seem well-informed on the law concerning these matters."

"Let's say that I recently had a sudden awakening of interest in the legal status of corporate runaways. I thought the knowledge might have a bearing on my future."

"As it has." Dodger shifted his chair back and stood. Placing a hand on Sam's shoulder, he said, "With this run against Renraku, you have stepped fully into the shadows. You are now divorced from the corporations. I strip thee of the name Corp and formally dub thee Twist."

"Thanks, I think." Sam looked taken aback. "I guess we did O.K., huh? At least I no longer have to worry that Renraku is after me and I don't feel guilty that the other guy took something out, making me an accessory to his theft. Like you said before we decked, if there had been a theft, the whole system would have been on alert."

"Be not so sure that it wasn't."

Sam frowned, then offered a tentative smile. "Why not? I used to work there. Remember? There was no alert."

"Then you can tell me what those mirrors were all about."

"No, but I can tell that there were some glitches in the system. Stuff like the fuzziness in the medical datastore. You know, resolution problems. The mirrors were probably some kind of diagnostic subroutine."

Dodger didn't buy it, but there was no point in saying so. The phenomenon was obviously well beyond Sam's appreciation as a decker. Sam also didn't appreciate Dodger's concern.

"Whatever was going on there won't matter. I don't think we'll have to go back. What we learned tells me that the murderers are somewhere outside Renraku. That's where we'll have to do the rest of our looking."

"First," Dodger said firmly, "we get some sleep. You may take the first shift in the bed, Sir Twist, for I have some thinking to do."

Actually, he had some worrying to do. Not just about the puzzle of the mirrors or the riddle of the murderers. Sam's reaction to the Matrix wasn't normal. Dodger had gotten a look at his datajack when he was checking Sam out on the Allegiance. The port cover had the maker's signature: Soriyama. That name proclaimed it as one of the most expensive pieces of tech Dodger had ever seen. No street doc or hack corporate implanter had done that job. It had been put in by the best, a real cutting-edge cybertechie and there should have been a flawless man-machine interface. Sam's headaches were anomalous, strange enough even without the limping icon. Could the two be connected?

There was more to Samuel Verner than met the eye, cyber or otherwise.

# 23

"Sherman, take a look at this!"

Cliber's shout brought Huang running to stare at her console screen. His eyes widened with excitement.

"Signal conductivity and virtual memory increases simultaneous with multi-tasking crashes," Huang muttered. "Where were the crashes?"

Cliber touched a key and highlighted the locales on the architecture construct.

"Hmmm. Intrusions in progress?"

"None on report. I'll run a check," said Cliber, even as she applied herself to the keyboard.

Hutten crowded in to view the display.

"What do you make of it, Konrad?"

The systems engineer looked perplexed. "OMDRs operating beyond spec. A full three banks of 77206 chips at maximum capacity, but the Haas biochip's barely above maintenance cycle activity." He shook his head. "I don't know. It doesn't match any of the expected parameters."

"Exactly." Huang beamed. His infectious grin spread to the other two. "We'll need to confirm it."

"I'll start a full diagnostic." Hutten returned to his own station and jacked in.

From her position at the door of the research lab, Crenshaw watched and heard all. The technical details meant nothing to her, but the excitement of the researchers communicated quite a bit. She had picked a lucky time to pass through the lab on her daily observation tour. If something significant had happened, she would report it to Sato immediately. Perhaps she could claim that her intervention had motivated the laggard team, thereby improving her standing with the *Kansayaku*.

"A breakthrough, doctors?"

Huang and Cliber looked up, seeming stunned by her presence. "No," Huang said tentatively, in accompaniment to Cliber's head shake. More forcefully, he added, "Just a glitch. A hardware problem in one of the nodes."

Crenshaw nodded and said nothing. Their suddenly sober faces told her that they were lying, that they obviously wished she were not present. She decided to accept their explanation until she knew not only what had really happened but just how to use the information to her own advantage.

# 24

Sam awoke to find Dodger seated at the foot of the bed, staring at him. The Elf's eyes were bloodshot and the unkempt appearance of his clothes was the result of extended wear more than an artful fashion sense. He had obviously been awake for a long time, which meant that Sam had been sleeping a long time.

"You were supposed to wake me."

The Elf shrugged. "You needed the sleep."

That had been true enough, but Sam felt rested now. "How long?"

"All night and most of the day."

"What about you?"

"I needed the time."

"You needed the sleep. You look like you've ridden a nightmare. I thought you Elves were supposed to be bundles of energy, day after day."

"Guess I'm not old enough," Dodger said flatly.

The Elf's mood was too serious for Sam's feeble jocularity to shake it. Dodger had even abandoned the archaic speaking patterns that he favored. Sam had only noticed that before when the Elf was seriously stressed or deep in technical details.

"Has something gone wrong?"

Dodger shook his head. "I want you to see a certain person."

"Why? What's happened?"

"I think he can be of help."

"Dodger, you're not answering my questions."

The Elf tilted his head back, eyes staring vacantly at the ceiling. He sighed. "I do not have any answers. Only questions."

"What are you talking about?"

"You."

Sam was already confused and now the Elf was making him more so. "You're giving me a headache."

"Your headaches are part of the issue." Dodger leaned forward and stared directly into Sam's eyes. "The pain and disorientation you feel when decking are not normal. Your implant is the best. The cyberware you've been using is flawless. Your thought processes are ordered and logical. In short, you have all the makings of a superb Matrix dancer, but for some reason, your icon limps. I suspect the answer lies within your psyche, but I am not qualified to deal with that. You need help with this problem, and I know someone who might be willing.

"You have set yourself a daunting task. Your enemies are ruthless, as you have already seen. To succeed, you must be able to rely without question on your own abilities. Therefore, you cannot afford to be less than perfect in mind."

Did Dodger think he was crazy? Unhinged by his trials? "So you want me to see some friend of yours. He's a doctor?"

"Among other things."

"Another shadow." Sam rubbed at the itchy stubble that was beginning to sprout on his chin. "You urge me to rely on myself while shoving me at strangers and suggesting that I put my head in their hands."

"Enemies may come unbidden, but you must search for allies."

"Platitudes, Dodger? What are you hiding behind them?"

Dodger said nothing for a moment, his Elven face still and suddenly alien. "I think you should see this person."

Sam considered the Elf's statement. Once more Dodger was avoiding a direct answer. He was surely hiding something. Whatever was behind Dodger's mysterious manner, Sam sensed what he wanted to believe was a genuine concern. It might be mere wishful thinking, but, adrift in a sea of shadows, he needed such an anchor. Platitudes or not, it was true he needed allies. Could he afford to offend this one? "If I agree, what's in it for your friend? And why are you, a shadowrunner, helping a corporate refugee? I've got a lot of questions, but I haven't any credit.''

"We are not all as mercenary as Lady Tsung.'' A slight hint of humor had crept in behind the stern mask, as though grimness were no longer necessary. Had Dodger divined that Sam had capitulated to his suggestion?

"But aren't you part of her gang? I thought she was your boss.''

'' 'Tis true that the fair lady and I have worked together, but I am an independent operator. I have my own interests.''

Of course he did. No one who lived the shadow life ever seemed to be pursuing anything but his own interests. "And what are those interests here?''

"You are most persistent, Sir Corp. 'Tis a sterling quality . . . sometimes.''

"I thought you changed my name, Dodger. And comments on the virtues, or vice, if you prefer, of my persistence won't distract me.''

"Very well then, Sir Twist.'' Dodger said, with a slight bow of his head. "Shall we say then that this circumstance offers me a way to discharge an old obligation to another?

"Your acceptance benefits others as well. The person whom I would have you meet will find your case of interest, and for him, that will likely be reward enough. You yourself gain. With this trip, you get out of the city and move onward to your goal. All this whilst your humble servant reduces an onerous burden.

"Everyone wins,'' Dodger concluded, smiling.

"And the alternative?''

"Dost not bear thinking about.''

"What choice do I have?''

"Always your own choice, of course.''

The Elf's grin was beguiling, mischievous but friendly. Sam shook his head in bemusement and laughed. Once more events were tugging him forward, but this time the direction was positive. He would be going forward of his own will, toward his own goals. That was more control over his life than he'd had in a long time.

Despite Dodger's flip comment, Sam had thought about the alternatives. Otherwise, a choice would be no choice. Though it was true that his need was forcing him toward it, he was armoring himself with his trust in Dodger's sincerity and good will. If Dodger's friend could make it easier to deck, then it would be easier for Sam to track down the murderers and bring them to justice. New as he was to sha- dowrunning, Sam knew that one did not throw away an advantage, however slim. Dealing with Dodger's friend was a gamble, but it was a gamble that he would accept of his own free will. He stood up.

"Let's go."

# 25

Their destination proved to be a private compound at the western edge of the Portland city limits. From the gate, Sam could see that the estate's enclosure extended out past the city's barrier walls, expanding the owner's turf beyond the city's boundary. How far he could not tell; the mansion and groves of trees flanking it screened his view. Such a terri- tory was in violation of the Tir Tairngire ordinances requir- ing all city properties to be completely within the series of concrete, wire, and electronic fences that separated the en- clave city from the Tir proper. That the mansion's grounds existed in such blatant disregard of those laws was an indi- cation of the owner's power in the Tir.

In the far distance beyond the compound, Sam could see a few tall spires of Elven design. Those would be the pala- tial residences of the ruling powers of the Tir. He knew that past those rambling estates and their woods lay Royal Hill, the mound said to be magically created, on which sat the Tir Tairngire capitol, a magnificent complex that was the working office and home of the High Prince. The estates surrounding Royal Hill were the property of the other princes and chosen councilors. It was a very exclusive neighborhood, and Dodger's friend, with his blatantly ille- gal property, was likely a resident of high standing.

"You didn't tell me that you had these kinds of connec- tions, Dodger."

"I would prefer to term it an acquaintance rather than a connection, Sir Twist."

"Whatever. If you had told me, I would have been less reluctant to come. At least I could have dressed better."

" 'Tis unlikely that we will be treated as formal guests." Dodger led the way to the gatehouse. He pulled up short as a figure stepped from the doorway.

"What makes you think that you'll be *any* kind of guest, Alley Runner?"

The speaker was tall, even for an Elf. His close-cropped raven hair and eyebrows contrasted sharply with his pale skin and eyes of glacial blue. His business suit and accessories were all of solid, middle-manager quality, and though well-tailored, seemed out of place on him. There was something about the Elf that was at once hard-bitten and romantic. Sam pictured him in full armor, its shine scuffed and dented with hard use. Maybe it was the set of his jaw, the impasssive expression, or the warily narrowed eyes.

"Avaunt, Estios. We've no business with you."

"If you want to see the professor, you do."

Dodger looked annoyed and seemed about to launch a retort. Then he shrugged in acceptance of something inevitable. He unholstered his pistol and handed it butt-first to Estios.

Estios smiled coldly as he received the weapon. He turned and re-entered the gatehouse, leaving Sam and Dodger to follow. Once inside, he led them past the reception counter without stopping. The crisply uniformed Knight Errant security staffer never said a word as the three men paced across his domain and through an ornate arch into a back room.

The inner chamber was sparsely furnished and dimly lit. Behind a clear panel that separated the room into two halves, an Ork in a white lab coat sat at a console. Her features were lit with the gray glow of the screens she monitored, making her expression grimmer and more inhuman than it might otherwise appear. Behind her stood a Dwarf. He was broader that she, but barely topped her in height even though she was seated. He wore an elaborate amulet on a heavy chain around his neck and the lapels of his jacket were studded with arcane symbols. The Dwarf mage leaned against the wall. Like Sato's mage, he seemed to be spending his duty time dozing. Sam wondered what made magicians so indispensable that they could sleep on company time and get away with it.

In one corner of their side of the partition lay a large

white hound. It opened its eyes lazily when they entered the room but otherwise remained motionless. Sam realized with a start that it was no ordinary dog. Its faintly reflecting eyes revealed it as a paranimal and its scent was familiar, though he had only encountered one once. The beast was Barghest like the one that had attacked Tsung. As soon as he realized it was unchained, Sam retreated to the archway, fearing an attack. To his embarrassment, neither Estios nor Dodger showed any reaction to the Barghest. All they did was turn to look at him as though he were an idiot. Sam straightened out of the defensive crouch he had reflexively assumed and forced a smile. So, maybe it wasn't dangerous. How was he supposed to know? It would probably still try to tear out his throat if Estios told it to.

Estios placed Dodger's gun on a table and held out his hand. Dodger removed another, much smaller, gun from his boot and handed it over. He slipped the chain that he wore for a belt from around his waist and took a flat metal case from one pocket, passing both to the dark-haired Elf. Estios tapped hm on the right forearm.

"It is integral."

"You'll wear a disabler." It was not a question.

"I have no hostile intent. My word has always been good enough for the professor. Is it less with you?"

"There are other considerations today."

"Look," Sam interrupted, beginning to get annoyed at Dodger's treatment, "we're not here to cause trouble. I was told that our visit might be of some interest to your professor. If that's too inconvenient for you, tough. We don't need your storm trooper act. We can leave."

Estios seemed to see Sam for the first time. "A real Griffin. Will you vouch for Dodger's good behavior?"

"Sure."

"On your life?"

Sam's answer was a little slower in coming, but he surprised himself with the conviction in his voice. "Yes."

"Sir Twist is here at my insistence, Estios. He need not take your oaths."

"He already has, Alley Runner."

"I shall wear your disabler."

"No, you won't," Sam insisted. "Those things can scramble circuits permanently. It's too big a risk, Dodger, and I won't let you take it just to have a chat about my headaches.''

"Do you understand what you're doing?" Dodger asked softly.

"Sure," Sam lied.

The look in Dodger's eyes told Sam that the Elf might not really believe him, but was accepting his word. Dodger flashed him a smile that held thanks and an unexpected comradeship. "Good enough for you, Estios?"

"It'll do," he said with a shrug. He pointed to the chromium steel fitting on Sam's temple. "What kind of headware do you have?" His voice indicated that he expected Sam to give a prompt, complete, and accurate answer.

"A datajack."

Estios turned his head to the technician, who nodded. Her voice rasped through the speaker. "Consistent with the scans."

"Aren't you going to search me for weapons?"

Estios's face held just a hint of contempt. "No need. You've been scanned quite thoroughly. Let's go."

Estios led them through a door and down a corridor. He opened another door and they emerged outside. A rank of small electric carts stood arrayed against the wall. Estios waved at the first one and walked around it to climb into the driver's seat. He barely gave them time to take a seat before engaging the drive. Gravel spewed as he turned the cart onto the path leading to the mansion.

As they approached, Sam could see that it was more of a manor house than a mansion. Stone walls complete with gargoyles faced the world to protect the interior from intruders. It looked like something out of a fairy tale. Such architecture seemed only appropriate here in Tir Tairngire.

Estios pulled the cart to a stop at the foot of the steps leading to the main entrance. Without a word, he got out of the vehicle and walked up the steps. When they joined him at the top, he opened the door and ushered them into a lobby of tiled floors and half-paneled walls. Estios led them through opulent rooms furnished with antiques and fine artworks, coming finally to a large room lined with bookshelves. A blackened fireplace stood in the center of one wall, framed by ornate woodcarvings. Another whole wall consisted of windows quaintly divided into small panels. Sam suspected that they were real glass. The view of shrubbery through the windows indicated that the three of them had passed through the house to the back.

"Wait here," Estios ordered as he opened a door incorporated into the window structure. As soon as he had exited and disappeared around the hedge, Sam stepped up to the windows. He was curious to see if he could gauge how far the estate extended beyond the city limits.

All thoughts of geographical extent vanished the moment he saw the Dragon. The beast sat on its haunches, forelimbs holding its chest above the manicured lawn. Sam knew it at once for a Western Dragon, for its huge wings were unmistakable even though folded against its flank. The great head was majestically horned and longer than any of the people gathered about it. Its scales glittered gold in the sunshine.

The crowd of Humans and Metahumans arrayed around the Dragon was divided into three parties. All the normal Humans, a pair of Dwarfs, and a large, furred humanoid stood to the beast's right, spread out between it and a quad-engined VTOL whose insignia appeared to be a portrait of the Dragon's own silhouette. The rest, mostly Elves, stood in a ragged, divided semicircle in front of the Dragon. One Elven contingent was aligned behind a red-headed Elf, the other behind a blond. From the blond's gestures, he was clearly making a passionate address to the Dragon. The beast seemed unperturbed.

Estios approached the red-head's group and whispered in the leaders' ear. The Elf cast a quick glance at the house before nodding and saying something. Estios gave a curt acknowledgement and walked to the back of the clump.

*Our host, the mysterious Professor Laverty,* Sam concluded. The Elf was lanky, not as tall as Estios, but still overtopping Dodger. The curly red hair and fair skin were easily visible, but distance masked the color of his eyes. From the Elf's calm demeanor, Sam expected that they would be discerning, imperturbable eyes. Whatever their color, it would be difficult to conceal anything from those eyes. Sam hoped that Dodger was right in bringing him here.

His gaze drifted across the other group of Elves, stopping suddenly on one familiar face. After a moment of shock, he checked the others and recognized a second face. Fear jolted him and for a moment he was running through the forest, hopeless and lost. He felt hunted again.

''We can't go out there.'' The words were barely audible; his throat was too dry.

''Nervous about meeting the quality? Or is it the Dragon?''

''No, that's not it. That red-headed Elf with the cape is the guy who tried to flash-fry me in the forest. The small dark one next to him is the tracker.''

''What?'' Dodger moved to his side and stared at the figures Sam indicated. ''Frag it! That redhead is Rory Donally and the other is Bran Glendower. They're two of Ehran's paladins. That whole squad was probably his crew. You're right. We can't go out there.''

''But I thought that we got hit by the border patrol.''

''They ride the border sometimes. When they think something's in it for them or their master.''

''Ehran, you mean?''

Dodger nodded in affirmation as he stared out the window.

''Ehran? As in Ehran the Scribe?''

''You know of another?'' he replied abstractedly.

''I read his *Mankind Ascendant*. It didn't make much sense.''

Dodger turned and gave him a wry grin. ''That's the right Ehran. He is the blond Elf who looks so fond of his own argument.''

''This doesn't make sense, either. I thought he was some kind of scientific populist writer. What's he doing here?''

''From the looks of that conference, it must be council business.''

''Huh?''

''Sir Twist, your astute commentary ill becomes you. I realize that not all of Ehran's activities are common knowledge, but . . . surely, given where you are and what you see, you must have realized that, like our host, he is a member of the ruling council of Tir Tairngire.''

Sam hadn't made any such connection. Seeing the house and grounds, he had surmised that this Professor Laverty had some influence. But a member of the council! That was beyond reasonable expectations. How did Dodger come to have connections with such a person? And why did he think that Sam might be of interest to this professor? Sam's stomach lurched as it had when the elevator cable in his Mitsubishi Flutterer had snapped. There had been a yawning chasm below him and he had been nearly out of control. He hadn't panicked then. Well, not too much anyway, and had managed to fight the craft to a relatively safe landing. He'd find a way out of this disaster, too.

While Sam fought his panic, the meeting outside drew to a close. The Dragon launched itself into the air, circling while its attendants boarded their craft. The aircraft rose to join the Dragon and both flew away to the north. The two groups of Elves merged and headed for the house. Upon reaching the patio, Laverty and Ehran split from their followers and headed for the salon.

"We've got to get out of sight," Sam said. He turned to find Dodger standing by the fireplace, hand on the carved mantel. A dark space opened in the wall beside the stonework.

"In here."

Sam stared dubiously into the darkness. "It's a secret passage."

"Of course. All well-designed houses have them."

"But how did you know about it?"

" 'Tis a secret." To Sam's disgruntled expression, he added, "All well-brought-up Elves have them, too. Adds to the mystique. Now, get in here and be quiet."

The entrance to their hiding place barely closed before they heard the latch of the outer door. Then they heard the voices of the Elves as they entered the room.

". . . well enough, I think. His advisors were cowed even if your histrionics made little impression on him."

"Your observations are faulty as usual, Laverty. The worm was suitably impressed. You know that they don't display emotion as we do. It has to do with the lack of facial musculature and general structure of the skull. I must add, though, that over time I have learned to discern certain variances of reptilian physiognomy and characteristic head positions that show distinct correlations with understandable emotional states."

"Thank you for the lesson, Ehran." Laverty's voice was cold. "I have had some experience with his kind."

"One should always have a care to respect one's elders, Laverty." Ehran laughed. "I am reminded of a sage piece of wisdom I once encountered emblazoned on a wall in a burned-out alley. Lengthy for its type, but containing certain truths. It went something like, 'Watch your back, conserve ammo, and never cut a deal with a Dragon.''

"And you find that applicable to our current endeavors?"

"Let us say that I find it suggestive. I would be happy to stay and elucidate, but I have pressing matters to attend to before the others arrive. It was kind of you to host this meeting."

"It seemed the most expeditious way."

"So direct. You really must learn to be more subtle, Laverty. A bit more discretion would stand you in good stead."

"I'll try to do better, Ehran. You said something about pressing matters?"

"I did, indeed. I really must attend to them. Until later?"

Laverty's answer must have been nonverbal. Sam heard nothing more until the heavy doors that closed off the salon from the rest of the house shut with a solid thud. There was silence for a moment, then Laverty spoke. "You can come out now, Dodger."

The hiding place opened and Dodger stepped out. Sam followed him.

"Good day, professor. Estios told you we were here?"

"He mentioned no names."

"Then how did you know it was Dodger?" Sam asked. "Or that we were hiding behind your secret panel?"

"Your hiding place was obvious deduction. If you had vacated the room completely, you would have run into some of Ehran's people. That would have been a rowdy encounter, as indicated by Mr. Estios's caution in not mentioning names where they could be overheard. As no uproar occurred, I assumed that you had gone into hiding here.

"As to how I knew it was Dodger, Mr. Estios spoke of a chromed Elf calling uninvited and dragging along a Human who is a reported renegade from his corporation and presumed dead. Added to the fact that one of you knew how to hide in this room, who else would it be?

"But I'm afraid my deductive clairvoyance has not given me your name."

"Twist."

"Samuel Verner," Dodger said to Sam's surprise.

Laverty cocked his head at the name. "You won't be staying."

"You're not going to turn me in, are you, professor?" Sam's fear of exposure returned full force.

"Your apprehension by the authorities would cause a bit of discomfort to Ehran, given certain claims. Ehran's chagrin is a prospect that has some appeal, but I did not mean to imply that I intended to turn you over to anyone. I meant rather that it would be inconvenient for you to be found here. I fear that with the capabilities of my current and future guests, such a discovery would be all too likely. Thus, you cannot remain here for very long. That being the case, we should get down to whatever business brought you."

Sam looked at Dodger, who nodded. He wasn't sure he trusted this professor, but Dodger did. What did he have to lose? If the professor had wanted to betray him to those who had hunted him, it would have been easy enough. He started in on his tale, trying to suppress the thought of how easy it would still be for the professor to betray him to his enemies.

# 26

"Concentrate!"

Laverty's voice was insistent. Sam was too tired to focus on the picture of a medieval shield that Laverty wanted him to imagine. Hours of sharp questioning about his travails followed by more hours of testing, some obvious standard medical examinations and others clearly arcane. For someone who was not supposed to be staying around long, Sam had been in Laverty's company for quite a while.

"Keep the image of the shield in your head!"

Sam tried to comply, but his mental vision blurred as a sharp pain drove through his head, a spike of ice impaling his brain. He almost cried out from the hurt before rallying and driving it back. The pain receded, leaving him drenched in sweat. He slumped in the chair.

When he opened his eyes again, the Elf was staring at him, his look stern and thoughtful. Seeing Sam awake, Laverty checked a monitor screen and entered a note on a datapad. At the professor's nod, Estios stepped forward and began to detach electrodes from Sam's head.

"That is the last test."

Dodger got up from his chair against the wall and walked

over to lean against the bench that held Laverty's monitoring apparatus. "In truth, an overly long enquiry, professor. My friend is not applying for citizenship."

"You wanted to know what was wrong with him. I needed certain information to make a diagnosis. Now I have that information."

"And?" Sam and Dodger said almost in unison.

"I believe that the available data offers only one reasonable conclusion." Laverty carefully placed his datapad on the console. Then he pulled a chair around in front of it and sat down. He seemed content to draw out the moment of revelation. Just as Sam was ready to prompt him again, he spoke. "You, Samuel Verner, are a magician."

Sam blinked.

"Impossible!"

"Is it?" The professor rubbed his right index finger along his upper lip. "Your headaches are prime evidence that you cannot function normally within the hypothetical world of the Matrix. Such a limitation is almost universal in those who have strong magical talent. Had you sought counseling before, you would have learned this a year ago."

"I thought the headaches were normal, that everybody got them."

Dodger shook his head.

"Well, if I'm different, it must be something else. I've never had anything to do with magic. It must be some kind of interface problem," Sam protested. "Bad neural connections."

"Soriyama doesn't make those kind of mistakes," Dodger informed him. "The way your icon limps shows some kind of psychological interface problem. It's neither built into the software nor a glitch in the hardware."

Laverty tapped the back of his chair to get attention. "Let us put aside the issue of the Matrix for a moment," he said. "When you were attacked by Ehran's people, the sorcerer Rory Donally used what, by your description, was a fireball spell. But it did you no real harm. How might that come to be?"

Sam ran his hands through his hair. "The mage wasn't very good at his job."

Laverty smiled indulgently. "Donally may not be a full mage, but he is an accredited adept. He passed the Tir's certification competitions for noble ranking. He is a sorcerer of high skill and unusual efficiency. He would not work for Ehran if he were not good at his job.

"No, Sam. Donally's spell was ineffective because you cancelled its effects. Unconsciously, you opened a mana channel to dissipate the energies that Donally had gathered. You routed those energies back into astral space, where they dispersed harmlessly."

"Unconsciously or not, I could never do that."

"But you did. You can do it still. The last test we conducted let me watch you in action. Mr. Estios cast a spell at you while you were supposed to be concentrating on the selected image. It was a very real and a very dangerous spell. Had you not shunted the energies, we would not be having this conversation."

"You could have killed him!" Dodger rocketed erect. Estios stepped between the decker and the professor, cutting off Dodger's move toward Laverty.

"The professor knew what he was doing, Alley Runner," the big Elf sneered as he blocked Dodger's attempt to get around him.

"The lesser tests were inconclusive, Dodger. It was a risk, but I was already certain Sam had the necessary capability. I surmised that it would take a legitimate threat to trigger his latent capacity, and it did."

Sam thought the professor was pretty casual about putting someone's life on the line to test a theory, and he didn't like it one bit. But then he only had their word about the spell. All he got was a headache and he had those all the time. "Even if I did stop Estios's spell," Sam said wearily, "that doesn't make me a magician. I've read about people who can protect themselves from magic without being magicians. They're called negamages."

"Negamages don't project astrally," the professor said.

"Neither do I."

"Ah, but you do. How else did you return to that lamentable clearing where you observed Ehran's paladins?"

"I sneaked up on them," Sam said flatly.

Estios laughed heartily. "Not with you exhausted from your run, city boy. Not on those paladins."

"Didn't you say that Grian looked right at you?" Laverty asked.

Sam nodded.

"Do you know how well an Elf can see in the dark? He would not have missed you."

"He must have," Sam insisted. He was an ordered, rational person who had built himself an ordered, rational life. His father had instilled in him a deep distrust of anything to do with magic. He could never accept what they were telling him. This magic talk was too strange.

"Why do you fear the magic?" the professor asked.

"I don't." Sam heaved himself out of the chair and began to pace back and forth. "It's just that all this magic stuff is illogical. It doesn't make sense. Or it's just tricks for gullible people. It's not part of my world."

Laverty sighed. "The spell that Rory Donally used burned your clothes and the trees in the forest. The cloth and the wood were part of the real world. They really burned. If that result wasn't part of your world, then perhaps yours isn't the real one."

Sam stopped pacing and stared at the ceiling. Now *that* suggestion was the open door to madness. "I don't deny that something happens when a real magician does what he calls casting a spell. I was trained to believe in hard evidence. Yes, his spell burned something. How can I deny that? I felt the ash and smelled the smoke. But don't try to tell me it's funny hand gestures, strange words, and the power of the stars. It's got to be something else, some kind of subconscious manipulation of ultra-low-frequency electromagnetic radiation, maybe."

"First negamages and now EMR. You've been reading Peter Isaac," the professor accused.

"Once, a long time ago. My father said that if magic was scientific, Isaac was on the right track to explaining it. His *Reality of Magic* was on the public datanet and I scanned it. It made some sense, but Isaac wasn't rigorous enough if he wanted people to accept his work as science. I figured that if he was the best, then there *was* no good explanation."

"What about the work of White Eagle and Kano at Caltech? Or Ambrosius Brennan at the Massachusetts Institute of Technology and Magic? Ever read them?"

"No."

The professor gave Sam a long look. "Perhaps it is best not to be hasty about what you do not know," he said. "Magic is very real, Sam. It is much more than subconscious manipulation of energy, and at the same time, it is less. Its manipulation is both an art and a science. Magic is part of the real world. You know as well as anyone that the Awakening has brought forth a plethora of beings that traditional science cannot account for. Elves and Trolls, for example.''

''Mutational genetic expression.''

''Genetic, yes. Mutational, hardly.'' Laverty sat back. ''What about Dragons? You say one aided your escape and then betrayed you. You also saw one here today. You cannot deny their existence nor explain them away as genetic mutations. Even if you could, what about their flight? They are too large to obey the scientific laws for muscle-powered flight.

''In ages past, our planet was steeped in magic. That is how we got all those tales of fairies and dragons, monsters, and goblins. They are memories of ancient truths handed down through the years. The worldwide existence of such beliefs suggests strongly that the mana, magical energy, was once of a sufficiently high level for magical powers to work and magical beings to flourish. That time of magic has come again.''

''Didn't Ehran's book say something about cycles of time and creative power?''

''He never actually used the word *cycle,* but the implication was clear. Even if you accept the theory of cycles, what proof is there? He also implies that these cycles would be extremely long, the last ending around the time recorded history began. That's why we have no reliable written record of high levels of magic. Before that? Well, I'm afraid that mana doesn't fossilize.''

''Dragons would.''

''And perhaps they have, but a bone is pretty much a bone. Who can say whether an extinct creature was paranormal? To date, no paleontologist has described a six-limbed creature like a Dragon. Perhaps they are rare enough never to have fossilized.''

''Preservational bias?''

''Exactly. Or perhaps the Dragons dealt with their dead in a way that prevented fossilization. But these abstruse issues don't clarify the situation. Whether the mana flow is cyclical or has simply passed through a low period, the effect is the same. Here and now, magic is real. Mana has been a part of the Earth in the past, possibly for longer than man has walked the planet. It has returned in abundance to enrich our lives. Mana is as much a part of the Earth and us as we are of it. It is everywhere and in everyone.''

''And I suppose this power should only be used for good, too?''

Laverty turned his palms to the ceiling and shrugged. ''It is power. It knows neither good nor evil; those are humanity's concepts. The Earth and its mana simply *are.*''

''And it is capable of miracles? Will you tell me that magic can replace God's grace?''

''I would not presume to do so. But with skilled manipulation, some effects that might be termed miraculous are possible. Such skill only comes with years of study and training.'' The professor slid a chip case forward across the table. ''These contain some texts and practice exercises. They are elementary, but you should be able to grasp their extent.''

''I don't have years right now to stop and learn magic. Even if I could, it's the people who murdered Hanae that interest me, and that trail gets colder every day.'' Sam ignored the professor's sigh. It would be nice to gaze into a crystal ball and find the murderers. Even better to wave his hand and deliver them to justice. Presuming, of course, that Laverty was right about all this. Besides, he still had to find Janice. If magic could do miracles, let Laverty help him with that. ''Professor, are you skilled in the use of mana?''

The professor stared directly into Sam's eyes for some moments before answering. ''Some consider me so.''

''Would you use your magic to help my sister?''

''I do all I can to help the unfortunate.''

''Then you could cure her?''

The professor sat back, as though Sam's question were unexpected. His cool green eyes seemed to be assessing Sam, weighing conviction and promise. No doubt Laverty was also calculating a price.

''Many things are possible to a master of magic, but even the most powerful magician cannot change what is ordained to be.'' His tone made it clear that he wasn't promising. ''After you have completed the task you have set for yourself, speak with me again and we shall see.''

Sam took the professor's response to mean that he would do what he could for Janice. No promise of success, but Sam couldn't reasonably expect one. He had no plan for what to do once he found his sister, but now at least he had a hope. Or rather, *she* had a hope, a chance of returning to a normal life. Sam also had hope of being able to meet the professor's price, for he sensed that Laverty was a compassionate being.

It's all moot, the voice of doubt told him. You don't even know where she is.

He refused to surrender to despair. I will, Sam promised himself. First Hanae's killers, then I find Janice.

As he had told the professor, the trail was getting colder. He stepped up to the bench and took the chip case with a bow.

"Thank you," Sam said, pocketing the case. "Now, if you'll excuse me, I've got things to do."

# 27

The Elf looked completely out of place standing within the rough-hewn walls of the cabin. His suit was strictly plex wear and his shoes were beyond salvation after their meeting with the local mud. His accent was pure metroplex and his hands were soft, unmarked by any dirty work.

"I am only the messenger," he said in a cool and distant voice.

Hart bit back a retort. What was the point? Her earlier outburst hadn't affected him. He was slick, riding the smooth edge. She should have been equally so, but she hated it when a job went sour. This one had had enough problems. She lifted the gun from the table and holstered it.

It should have come as no surprise that the touted Tir border patrol had muffed it even worse than she had thought. That they should miss her was understandable. That had happened often enough. But to miss that corporate pigeon made them look like noids. It was a fluke, a bad toss of the dice. Pure good luck for that suit Verner and bad for her.

The messenger was still there. "Get out of here," she snapped, still caught up in her annoyance.

"Do you wish to make a response?"

"To your nameless principal? Get serious."

"He has the continued health of your reputation at heart."

"But won't let himself be named? I'm touched."

"His name would be quite familiar, I assure you. It would only be unwise for you to know it at this time. I was told to say that you would find his favor most useful in the future. His good will is easy to earn. All he asks in return for the information I have brought is a general outline of your plans."

"Smoke and mirrors."

"Excuse me?"

"Tell him that. Smoke and mirrors."

The messenger drew himself erect with indignation. "Very well." He turned and strode from the cabin, his expensive leather loafers squishing slightly with each step.

Got through the shine at last. A petty victory but better than nothing. Let the Elf take her answer back to his Mr. Mystery. Two could play at the confusion game.

Whoever sent the messenger could have any of a dozen reasons for passing the information to her. Mr. Mystery could be playing on just about any side in the conflict. Or he could be someone not directly involved but using the opportunity to turn things against a rival or to twist them in favor of a friend. Without more information, she could not tell. Whatever someone's reason for giving her the information, now that she had it there was no time to look into the source. The only source she could rule out was the ornery old worm that was her own contractor. Had he known of Verner's survival, he would have sent an army of goons to convey the message that she had failed in her contract.

Tessien needed to know; it had the same contract. Hart shrugged on a jacket against the cool night air. She didn't bother to lock the cabin; there was nothing to steal and no one here to steal it. She took the trail further up the mountain to the dry cave where Tessien lay coiled and dozing. The feathered serpent awoke as she entered its lair.

"Bad news, Tessien."

*"Anything that disturbs my rest is bad."* Annoyance washed through the cave.

"Well, rest time is over."

She felt the serpent's curiosity even though it *said* nothing.

"Verner, that suit we pulled out of Renraku as cover for the doppelganger plant, is still alive. The Tir border guards didn't get him, and he's popped up in San Francisco in the company of a runner called Dodger. This runner is some kind of wiz decker and the two of them are snooping around the Matrix. Sounds like their search is still mostly random, but they've got our names and will follow that up sooner or later.

"They've got Drake's name, too."

*"Does* he *know the suit is alive?"*

"Don't think so."

*"We must take care of this quickly."*

"My sentiments exactly. I hate fragging loose ends."

The serpent growled its agreement.

# 28

Sam woke to the smell of soy sauce and hot broth. He opened his eyes and turned his head. The source of the odor stood on the rickety table by the window. Dodger must have been down to the noodle shop on the corner, because two foam containers sat steaming, while a third empty one rolled back and forth in the fitful breeze from the open window. Sam was halfway through what remained of the soba when Dodger returned from a trip to the only functioning john in the semi-abandoned tenement where they had set up shop.

"Ah, Sir Twist, you are awake."

With a mouthful of noodles, Sam mumbled a garbled reply.

"No need to offer such effusive thanks for the food. Think nothing of the expense or time involved, for are we not in this run together?"

Having swallowed the last recalcitrant noodle, Sam was free to reply. "It was your turn to get the food, anyway."

Dodger's wounded look was pure mockery, but the Elf's light mood didn't quite mesh with a sudden seriousness that Sam felt. Maybe it was the mention of expenses.

"Dodger, I'm grateful that your friend the professor arranged to get us here, but won't he expect some kind of repayment."

The Elf shrugged. "The passage was no strain on his

resources. Mayhaps in the fullness of time, he will command a reckoning, mayhaps he won't. I would find it no surprise were he to rely on your own conscience to weigh the balance of benefits and services, and to repay his efforts as you see fit. He is quirky that way.''

That didn't make Sam feel any better. ''My conscience is weighing a little too heavily lately. I wish you hadn't stolen that money.''

''Operating capital, Sir Twist. Can't run without it. The funds were ill-gotten gains anyway, lost long ago to their true owners. We merely prevented some unscrupulous corporate defilers of the landscape from the profit of their crimes.''

''It's still theft.''

''Liberation.''

''Semantics.''

''Necessity,'' Dodger laughed.

Sam found himself grinning along. The Elf's mood had finally infected him, despite his misgivings about their actions. They had arrived in San Francisco with only a hundred nuyen on Dodger's credstick, ten more in corporate scrip, and another fifty in UCAS currency. The last was mostly paper and next to worthless in the Free State of California.

They had to live while they sought justice. Was it not also justice for them to subsist off criminals?

Money was a problem for them, but it was their hope as well. The world's banking was mostly electronic now and money transfers left a trail that they could follow through Matrix. The trail had already connected Hart and the serpent Tessien to Drake, the man who was pulling the mercenary runners' strings. Dodger had made no secret of his relief when Sam agreed they should concentrate on the man behind the Elf runner and Dragon. He had seemed impressed by their reputations and reluctant to tangle with them.

So they hunted Drake now, but so far he had proved to be a mystery man. They knew he was often seen with Nadia Mirin, president of Natural Vat foods. That information had come during a general data search of the news networks, and from the society section, of all places. Calling up a datapic had confirmed that the Mr. Drake who escorted Ms. Mirin was the same man Sam had met in the abandoned car lot. The connection stubbornly remained a random data point. Nothing they tried ever linked Drake to Mirin in any way other than socially. He was not connected with Natural Vat, its parent company Aztechnology, or any of the subsidiary or sibling companies that Sam and Dodger managed to check. That was unusual and intriguing. Executives of Mirin's stature usually kept their romances within the corporate family.

"Are you ready to crack those files we hooked on the last run?"

"I think so. The nap and the food have pretty much taken care of the headache." The files in question were filched copies of transaction records from Transbank. The run through the bank's security had been exhausting, with even Dodger admitting that he might not be able to crack the locks on the files and extract the data safely. By now, Sam knew that for the Elf to make such an admission meant the task at hand was extremely tricky. These files must be heavily protected.

The files turned out to be just that. It was hours before they determined that Drake had certified several credsticks through Transbank. It seemed hardly worth the effort and new headache to achieve such a dead end. A certified credstick was the electronic equivalent of cash. The money could still be traced once it reentered the financial network, but there would be no record of who had received the credstick.

" 'Twas a small hope that he would be so careless."

"Maybe if we can find some other transactions of the same monetary value as were assigned to Drake's certified sticks, we can pick up the trail by following it from wherever Transbank sends the funds. Sure, some of the matches will just be coincidence, but some might actually be the recipients of Drake's generosity. If we're lucky, some of the names attached to those transactions might mean something."

After two more days of data slogging, they had eliminated likely coincidences. That left three names. Each one connected to at least three transactions whose amounts equalled one of Drake's credsticks.

The first, Nadia Mirin, was no surprise. In her case, the amounts were the smallest, suitable as gifts to one's paramour. The second name was totally unfamiliar, but the pattern of intervening transactions was interesting. Each amount went through a series of transfers, all for the exact value of Drake's credstick. Each thread led to a sealed account in a Denver data haven. Dodger pronounced the data trail to be a record of the laundering of Hart's payments. At Sam's suggestion, they traced a similar trail from deposits made by a known client of Hart's and got the same sealed account number, confirming the Elf's supposition. The last name sat at the end of a similar, but much less well hidden, trail. The destination account was registered to A.A. Wilson.

"A. A. Wilson." Sam shook his head. "Why does that name seem familiar?"

"Familiar or not. 'Twould seem that Mr. Drake finds something about Squire Wilson worth a lot of money. But what?"

"If we knew who A. A. Wilson was, we might have a clue."

"How many people can there be with that name?"

Dodger sighed. "We don't know that it is a real name. Whether it is or not, there could be quite a few. 'Twill be another time-consuming task."

"So?"

"I thought you would say that, but it would help if we could narrow things down."

Sam thought about it for a minute. There really was something familiar about the name. "What if Wilson is a Metahuman?"

" 'Twould help, if 'twere true. How have you come by that revelation?"

"I don't know. Something in the back of my mind says Metahuman when I hear the name. Maybe I read it somewhere. Something medical."

"Mayhaps Wilson is a doctor specializing in Metahuman physiology?"

"Could be." Sam shook his head in puzzlement. "It's a place to start."

The AMA files for Seattle yielded no A. A. Wilson. A check into the complete database for the UCAS did no better.

"Try the Salish-Shidhe Council," Sam suggested. "Let's not go too far afield yet."

An hour later, Dodger had something. "A. A. Wilson is licensed to practice in Salish-Shidhe. He is listed as residing in Cascade Crow lands on an extraterritorial reservation belonging to the Genomics Corporation.''

''Genomics? Run a check on medical literature. See if Wilson has published anything.''

Dodger hacked into the public datanet and pulled the files in a flash.

''Squire Wilson appears to be an accomplished man of letters. He is principal or subsidiary author of several papers.'' Title by title, Dodger began reciting the list. ''Variational Effects of Albinism . . .''

''In Metahumans. D. Nyugen, M. T. Chan, and A. A. Wilson, *Biophysiology*, 2049,'' Sam finished for him.

''Verily. How did you know that?''

''I scanned it as part of the research I was assigned in setting up the arcology's Metahuman medical library. That project was how I knew about the medical files when we did the run to see if Tessien worked for Renraku.''

''An amazing memory, Sir Twist, but it gains us little.''

''Maybe it does and maybe it doesn't.'' Another memory prodded him. ''Dodger, there was an albino with Hart's team in the arcology.''

''Coincidence?''

''What do you think?''

''I believe an investigation into Squire Wilson and Genomics is in order. But first,'' Dodger said with a grin, ''it's your turn to get the food.''

Sam acquiesced with good humor. They had a lead now, their first hope of penetrating whatever had set off the chain of events that led to Hanae's death and his own exile from corporate society. Knowing what Drake was really involved in would make a difference. They would bring him down to pay for the murders he had arranged and all his machinations with him.

The noodle shop was closed. They had worked so hard and long that night had become early morning. The only thing that would be open now was a Stuffer Shack, and Sam found one three blocks over. The selection was dismal, but he thought a couple of packets of self-warming Nutrisoy soup would at least offer some nutritional value. By the time Sam got back to their squat, Dodger was finishing a run on the public datanet. The Elf looked glum.

''What's wrong?'' Sam asked.

''Genomics. As the name might suggest, the corporation

is a cutting-edge biotechnology firm with a specialty in genetic manipulations. As such, one would also expect a cutting-edge security system. I checked with some runners who have reason to know about their ice, and it sounds like only a lengthy siege could get at their corporate architecture from the Matrix. The only way to get the information quickly is if we can get physically inside and then use a corporate machine within the intrusion shield to get the data. Even if we had the force for an assault, without a Matrix overwatch, it could be too risky."

"But an accredited cyberterminal user could take a side trip and deck into the files."

"Most likely. But that does not surmount the other difficulty. The firm is headquartered in Quebec."

"Guess I'm going to Quebec, then."

Dodger sighed. "What will you do there? You no longer exist, remember? When you were reported dead, your System Information Number was frozen. Without a SIN, you are a nonentity in the corporate world. No air travel to get there. No passport to get in. No cushy corporate job from which to subvert their data."

Sam would not let this lead escape. "You've survived for years outside the corporate structure. That means you've found some way around the problem. False identities or fake SINs. Something that gets you past checkpoints."

" 'Tis a necessity."

"Then I'll need one set up for a researcher. That's the work I did for Renraku. A busy company like Genomics will always be on the lookout for good researchers."

"An identity patched together on short notice will not withstand much scrutiny."

"It won't have to. Background checks on low-level workers can't be that thorough, even in Quebec. A day or two to get system codes. Then once inside the IC, I'll deck into Wilson's files, get what I can and leave. With what you've shown me, I shouldn't need more than a week."

*"Parlez-vous français?"*

"Good point. I'll need a language chip, too."

*"Incroyable!"* Dodger shook his head in amazement. "Pray tell, Sir Corporate Spy, how are you planning to get there? The free and proud Dominion of Quebec is almost as sensitive about its borders as the Tir."

"You're the hot shadowrunner, Dodger. You make the arrangements."

"Your faith is greater than your bankroll, Sir Mastermind."

"Then I'll have to owe somebody some favors."

"A few days ago, you were bemoaning unknown debts. Today you profess yourself eager to plunge into more."

Sam tossed their forgotten meal onto the table. He was no longer hungry. "This feels right, Dodger. I just know that Genomics is part of this mess. I'll get something there that will make sense of what has happened."

"A premonition? How mystical."

Sam grimaced. "It's nothing like that. It's just a hunch."

"Then we shall play it out."

Dodger started to get up, but Sam reached out to lay a hand on his shoulder. "No. Not we. After you make the travel arrangements, I want you out of it. I owe you enough already."

Dodger continued to stand against the pressure of Sam's hand. He stood erect and looked down at Sam, his eyes glittering with emotion. "Sir Twist, you wound me. I am not a shylock to count each penny. You will need me to do the decking."

"I'll have to manage. Genomics won't hire both of us, so there's no need for both of us to risk our necks." Dodger started to object again, but Sam cut him off. "Besides, there's another line to be traced. Drake's got enough money or backing to hire expensive mercs like Hart, while we've only got ourselves. The longer we take finding out what we need to know, the more likely Drake will squirm beyond our reach. If I go to Quebec, I'll be tied up checking out Genomics. Somebody has to keep on trying to learn some hard facts about Drake."

"Why then do you not do it? You have named him as your foe, after all."

"If Drake's not based in Seattle, he's at least working this operation from there. I can slot a chip that will let me speak French, but nothing can make me know the shadows of Seattle like you do. You're the best man for that job."

The Elf relaxed his belligerent stance, and a new light entered his eyes. "You trust me to do that work for you?"

"I trust you."

"Ah, the fierce faith of necessity."

Sam couldn't tell how much of Dodger's comment was companionable jest and how much mocking irony. He didn't care. He knew the Elf wouldn't betray him to Drake; Dodger was too committed to the underdog. Sam wanted to believe that their time together had forged a real bond and that the Elf was a friend. His own growing affection for the rogue was real enough. Before this was over, Sam knew, he was going to need all the friends he could get.

# 29

The service monitor station was cramped and smelled of old sweat, ozone, and the battling forces of mildew and disinfectant. When the aquaculture tanks it monitored had gone on line a month ago, the overwatch had transferred to the main control consoles, leaving the station virtually unused. Crenshaw jiggled the louver of the climate control vents, but the sluggish flow of air did not improve. For all its discomforts, this place offered a quiet and privacy rare anywhere in the arcology. With an active computer console, the station was useful enough to her. And Crenshaw liked it here in the dark.

The signal from the motion sensor she'd left near the elevator chimed in her ear receiver. If it was Addison, he was early. When the second sensor chimed, she was sure it was him. The corridor leading to the station would have no other traffic at this hour. The warning signals were close together; he was hurrying, moving at a quick walk.

Probably more nervous than usual.

It was his nervous tendencies that had tipped her off. She had seen his eyes when he accosted Verner at Tanaka's funeral, and she had smelled his fear when she visited his cubicle in the computer facility a week later. It was her security badge that did it, and such fear of security meant a guilty conscience. That pleased her, for Crenshaw knew she could manipulate him once she learned his secret. Addison was a slug; it hadn't taken much to find out what he was hiding.

One of Addison's cronies, a Lisa Miggs, had made unauthorized use of Jiro Tanaka's cyberdeck to take a run at the Wall. Like most deckers at Renraku, Addison and friends had no idea what lay behind the Wall. They knew any attempt to find out was a breach of security, but they tried anyway. Typical hare-brained decker stunts. Always meddling where they shouldn't. The episode hadn't resulted in anything more than a test of the AI project's defenses, but Addison didn't know that. He only knew that he and Miggs had broken rules that could get them canned. It was the man's terror of that that put him in Crenshaw's pocket.

He had become useful even though he hadn't fulfilled her hopes of linking Verner to something underhanded. At the moment, he was employed in helping her find out what the AI project team was hiding. It was a sweet irony that what he was doing for her was exactly what he feared she would expose him for doing before. But she wasn't so stupid as to send him directly up against the IC that shrouded the project and those working on it. She wanted a lever to find out what kind of breakthrough the team had made. Something that would force one of them to tell her what she wanted to know. To get that lever, she had set Addison to snooping around the Matrix for dirt. He had called her this afternoon to set up this meeting. He must have found something she could use.

The door slid open and Addison darted in, head craning to check the corridor behind him. He palmed the panel shut, then saw that the room was still dark. "Drek, she's not here."

"Wishing won't make it so, jackhead."

Addison jumped at her voice. "Drek! Don't do that, Crenshaw!"

She stepped up to him and ran her fingers under his chin. The alloy blades she wore for fingernails creased the skin but brought no blood. "You don't give orders. I do."

"Sure," he stammered. "Whatever you say."

She tapped the switch that brought the lights up. "See that you remember it. What have you got for me?"

"I'm not real sure. Let me slot it and you can decide for yourself."

He popped a chip into the console and stared expectantly at the screen, waiting for it to light up. She didn't want to wait. "Cliber?"

"Naw. The old biddy's clean as a one-room schoolmarm. She's a real ice maiden. Lives for her machines."

"Frag it. I was hoping you'd turn up something on her. It would be a pleasure to lean on the bitch."

"Better her than me," Addison muttered.

Crenshaw heard him perfectly well but decided not to let it show. "Which one then, Hutten or Huang?"

Addison flashed a brief smile, trying to hide his tension. "Maybe both. They're both hanging onto the meat. I copped a list of the use records for the playrooms on Six. Both H's are on it, and old Huang a married man, too. Wanna bet his wife don't know?" He finally got the data he wanted on the screen and stepped aside with a magician's flourish.

Ignoring his theatrics, Crenshaw stared as the data scrolled by. She frowned. "That's not much. And it's a pretty standard pattern for a salaryman. What are the details?"

"Details?" Addison echoed. "Well, um, you can see that Huang's got a regular routine."

"A mistress, then. That might give me a hook if she's pliable. Anything else?"

"Well, maybe. But I'm not sure." Addison wilted under her glare, his voice becoming unsteady. "I think I spotted an erasure in the records."

"What's the connection?"

"It was one of Huang's regular nights and there ain't no record of him paying a visit that night."

"And our president is certainly skilled enough in the Matrix to arrange his own erasures. Was Hutten there that night?"

"Naw. His visits started about a week later. Every three or four days after that, but no regular night."

"You've checked the visual records?"

"Frag it, Crenshaw. There's tight ice on those files."

"You're supposed to be an expert," she sneered. Crenshaw knew it was too much to expect him to act on his own initiative; he didn't have the guts.

"Even I can only do so much. I don't like this stuff, Crenshaw. You're messing with important people. Any one of them could get me fired. And, drek, messing with Huang. He's the fragging president."

She stared at him, letting him squirm. "Addison, you have a lot more to worry about from me. They're too busy to notice a third-rate electron jockey like you. So just do what I tell you and you won't have any trouble."

Addison backed away. "Sure, Crenshaw. Whatever you say." When he bumped into the console, he seemed to remember the program he had running. Terminating it, he popped the chip. His every motion was hesitant.

"I can see you've got something else on your mind. Spit it out." She was tired of the slug's spinelessness.

"It's that Werner guy."

"Verner."

"Yeah, him. He was terminated, wasn't he?"

"Dismissed. Two weeks ago."

"Yeah, I thought so. Well, I was checking on some of the strange stuff in the Matrix. You know, the stuff that we think is AI. There was a log of his icon in one of the nodes where the fuzz had been real strong. Just that one node, though. Real weird."

"You didn't report it?"

"Drek, no! I wasn't supposed to be there, either."

"Good."

So, Verner had sneaked back into the Renraku architecture and was sniffing around the AI project. What a fragging snake! She had known that little drekhead was trouble the minute he'd thrown in with Tsung's gang during the hijacking. But nobody would listen to her. Marushige said Verner was a nothing. Sato said that he wasn't important enough to waste resources on. Well, Verner may have fooled them, but she had the punk's passcode. From what Addison said, it was obvious he hadn't been able to take whatever he wanted when he bolted the arcology. If that slime was stupid enough to come back, she'd have his balls. To think that she'd almost started to believe he was harmless.

"I want you to forget the playroom records for now. Check out the system around that node where you found Verner's icon logged in. I want to know of anything unusual. *Anything*. You just report it to me; don't try to interpret it. Got that?"

Addison's eyes were wide and he swallowed convulsively a couple of times before nodding. The slime mold was as afraid of her as ever. But his fear was good; it meant he'd do her work.

# 30

"Never been up close to one before?"

Sam jumped. He hadn't heard the man approach, but, even at idle, the noise of the hulking panzer drowned out anything less than a shout.

The speaker was an Amerindian, but his clothing was pure Anglo. He was broad-shouldered and narrow-hipped, with the skin on his bare chest so brown from the sun that his muscles seemed carved from teak. The grime under his fingernails was at odds with the shiny rigger sockets in his palms and wrists and the jacks on his temple.

"You Twist?"

Sam nodded.

The man smiled and stuck out his hand. His grip was firm and the induction pad in his palm rasped Sam's palm as they shook. "Cog said you were green. Name's Josh Begay, late of the Dineh."

"You're Navaho? You're a long way from home."

Begay's eyes hooded and the smile faded into a hard expanse of wrinkles. "Smart boy. Stay smart and stick to polite conversation."

From the snap in the Navaho's voice, he was obviously sensitive about his origins. If Sam was going to be spending several days in company with the rigger, he'd best stay on the man's good side. The panzer should be a safe topic; most riggers were more interested in the machines they controlled than they were in people. "I've only seen tanks like this on the trid," Sam said appreciatively.

Begay relaxed a fraction, and Sam knew he had taken the right tack.

"This one's a little different from the beasts they run in the corp wars. They want flash and intimidation; it's better for the ratings. I got more need for stealth. The *Thunderbird*'s engines are baffled and she's got a lot of extra ECM. The baffling cuts the speed some, but I'll take the quiet at the cost of a little KPH. *T-bird*'s as quiet as they come."

"Quiet?" Sam shouted. The concept seemed absurd. The panzer's engine noise was deafening as it echoed off the walls of the warehouse. Even in the open, someone would hear it coming a klick away.

"It's all relative. No machine with muscle is ever gonna be sneaky silent. Still, ain't no need to run an advertisement for the next valley over. Time any dust-eater hears *T-bird* and figures out where and what she is, we've long flown past."

"I'll take your word for it."

The Navaho said nothing, just stared at him. The pressure of the deep brown eyes began to make Sam nervous. "You come highly recommended."

Still no response.

"Cog says you're one of the best running the northwest routes. He says I'm lucky you were available."

Begay hacked and spat on the ground. "Cog's a good fixer, but he's got a White tongue." When Sam looked blank, the Navaho wiggled two fingers in front of his mouth. "Forked, you know."

Sam gave the joke a nervous laugh and was relieved to see the ghost of the former smile return to Begay's face.

"Chummer, you're lucky that I'm going where you want to go. Lucky that I got room for a second hand. Lucky there ain't nobody in town who knows how to ride shotgun and who I'm willing to ride with. Lucky I ain't got time to wait around till I do find somebody." He spat again. "I like that kind of luck. It's contagious.

" 'Course luck had nothing to do with it. My being available is pure money. From what I heard, you couldn't afford it. But you got friends who can, and that's lucky, too."

"What do you mean? I thought I was working for my passage."

"Oh, you will. Cog says somebody likes you enough to boost the Tir border patrol roster and post a couple of incentives for some old friends of mine to be elsewhere when we slide the border."

"We're going through the Tir? Wouldn't it be easier to cut around it through the Ute Council?"

"Don't run Ute territory," Begay said shortly. "Don't worry, though. We'll do most of the Tir by day and, with the fix in, it's gonna be a smooth scorch. Then we blast through the Rockies where the Salish-Shidhe Council dips down and cuts the edge of Sioux territory. Then on through the Algonkian-Manitou Council till we slide into Quebec.

"Got a resupply stop up by the Dworshak Reservoir before we cross the divide. Stop again in Portage-La-Prairie after we cross the old Canadian border. Last lay-over is Hearst, just before we try the Quebec border. Once we slide the line, I dump you and you're on your own."

"You said you were already hired so you must have a cargo, too. What are we carrying?"

Begay spat. "Cog said you was a curious one. It's bad luck to ask too many questions."

"Got it." Sam smiled in what he hoped was a disarming manner. "Wouldn't want to spoil my luck."

"Cog said you was smart, too."

Sam didn't say anything to that, apparently winning Begay's approval. After a moment or two of silent evaluation, the Navaho clapped him on the shoulder. "You smart enough to learn a few things about riding shotgun on a panzer run?"

"Try me."

Begay swung up the side of the vehicle, scrambling like a rock ape across molded grips and convenient protrusions. Sam followed more slowly, the weight of his pack shifting his center of balance enough that he was cautious of some of the handholds Begay used. By the time he reached the top deck, Begay was vanishing down the hatch into the panzer. Sam tossed his pack through and followed, snagging his holster on the hatch coaming. He had to pull himself back up to free it. The holster and the Narcoject Lethe pistol it held were a parting gift from Dodger. The Elf had wanted him to take something more lethal, but Sam resisted. Having a gun at his hip was strange enough. That the weapon was his own was even stranger. Inside the panzer, Begay showed him how to strap into the gunner's couch and started a simulation program that would let Sam get the feel of the controls. Shooting the computer targets was easy. Just like a game.

Hart unfurled the hood from the collar of her black windbreaker and snugged it down with the drawstring. She hated what it would do to her hair, but the hood was a better alternative than an invisibility spell at the moment. She didn't want the distraction of maintaining the mana flow to power the spell. It was going to be two against her one, and she would need her wits about her. Verner might be a corporate softie, but the other was an experienced runner of unknown combat capabilities. Like her whole life, this would be a calculated risk. San Francisco wasn't one of her towns, and so she'd had no time to check out quality backup. Her quarry was about to leave town, and that meant she had to be quick and fast. Good thing she'd completed the transaction for her working equipment before she'd gotten the word of their location.

She made her selections from the satchel and placed them on the rooftop before caching the bag under a rusted-out air-conditioning unit. Returning to her new toys, she tucked the sheathed stiletto into her belt, under one of the supposedly decorative ornaments that were actually her custom-styled throwing stars. Then she slipped the band of the thermal goggles over the hood and glanced around the rooftop once to confirm their quality. Satisfied, she pushed the lenses up onto her forehead, where she could pull them down in a hurry. Running gloved fingers over the Beretta Model 70, she confirmed that the serial numbers had been seared out with a laser, as specified. She initiated the self-test and nodded once in satisfaction as the LEDs signaled the laser sight in full true, the sound suppressor at ninety-seven percent efficiency, the magazine full, and the trigger pressure set at a hundredth of a pound less than she had requested. The fixer who supplied this gear was reliable; she wanted to remember him in case she had future business in the city by the bay. Having checked the Beretta, she slung it over her right shoulder. The weapon would enable her to finish the business quickly and without a trace. Once she was gone, it would be just another crime of random street violence.

She sat down cross-legged on the roof and composed her mind. From that calm pool, she called out. The summons took the form of an odoriferous scent wafting on the breeze. It was not long before the first rat showed up. It snuffed the air as though slightly confused, then scampered closer. It was no bolder than many city rats she had seen, but no less bold either. It circled her once, then stopped in front of her and stood on its hind legs. The tiny forepaws patted at the air as its whiskers quivered to the motion of its overactive nose.

Her hand darted out and pinned the beast to the roof. Her

grip behind its head held it helpless despite its violent squirmings. She touched the back of its skull with the index finger of her free hand and intoned the spell of preparation.

*Aleph!*

Affirmation of attention entered her mind.

*Take this one as a body. I want you to spy below.*

Acknowledgement touched her mind, then the rat stopped twisting in her grip. She released it and it sat back on its haunches to stare at her with suddenly intelligent eyes.

"Well, what are you waiting for?"

The rat squeaked once and dashed away.

Hart closed her eyes in order to better comprehend the inflow of data from the rat's senses. Her Ally Spirit Aleph had taken control of the animal, which would let her see and hear what the rat saw and heard through her link with the Spirit. In this part of town, a rat made a very inconspicuous spy.

It took Aleph only a few minutes to guide the rat through the byways of its kind and down onto the floor of the building. The reek of oil was almost overwhelming and the dark-adapted eyes of the beast showed her what she didn't want to see. The warehouse was empty. She had arrived too late.

"Frag it!"

The panzer, with Verner in it, was gone.

*Release it, Aleph. We've got to hit the road.*

Acknowledgement from below and she was alone on the rooftop, all dressed up for a party that was already over.

# 31

As Begay had promised, the run through the Tir was easy. Except for the border crossings, they had traveled by day, which gave Sam a chance to see some of the magically restored forest. Beautiful as the land was in its natural state and vigor, the thought that powerful magics had made it so disturbed him. It was still more evidence he could not deny. As lush and cool as was the forest, Sam seemed to notice only the pools of shadow and the dark spaces under the trees, as though some danger or precarious instability hid within the leafy canopy. Or was it only his doubts?

Begay assured him that travel by day was a practical matter rather than for sightseeing purposes. Less local wildlife was active with the sun high in the sky, he said, leaving Sam to ponder what kind of animal could threaten a panzer. All Begay would tell him was to watch the target screens, which he did, though his datajack connection to the sensors brought on the usual headache. Strain, he told himself. Magic had nothing to do with it.

Once through the Tir, they traveled by night. "Sure, the IR signature's easier to spot," Begay said, "but watching an IR screen is like watching any screen. Ain't easy to do for long. People get tired and forget to watch their screens." Sam trusted his judgement. After all, Begay was the professional.

Crossing through what used to be Idaho, they had a run-in with a Salish-Shidhe helicopter, but Begay found a hiding place in the canyons along the Snake River. After that, he launched the *T-bird*'s remotely piloted ultra-light aircraft to fly overwatch so that it might spot any telltale activity. Later, while pulling the RPV back as they bivouacked for the day, the rigger's control panel blew a chip, sending the aircraft crashing out of control at the edge of the river. They lost half the night salvaging the wreck, for Begay wouldn't leave without it. "Too fragging expensive," he said.

It was near dawn when they pulled into the shanty town on the Dworshak Reservoir. Begay turned the *Thunderbird* toward a dilapidated barn where a bunch of the locals were lounging. As the panzer neared, however, they sprang up and opened the barn doors for the *T-bird*. The panzer tucked itself in and settled to rest.

From what Sam could see, the interior of the barn was at odds with the exterior; the floor was concrete and the walls some kind of solidified foam material. Benches, power tools, vehicles, boxes, and crates were scattered about in haphazard array. Overhead, a heavy-duty crane held what looked like an engine within a net of braided wires. The locals, most of them Orks, closed the outer doors and moved toward the Panzer. Sam was still trying to understand what was going on when Begay popped the driver's auxiliary hatch and crawled out.

"Fill her up."

"You want your oil checked?" asked an Ork in grimy
coveralls.

"I'll let you check the oil the day I own a well,
Thumper."

"Ya got no faith, Begay."

"Your dipstick's too short."

"Man's gotta stay in the biz."

"Got that right."

To Sam, the exchange had the ring of an old routine.
Climbing out himself, he saw the two exchanging hand-
shakes, and knew they were old buddies. Begay waved him
over.

"Twist, want you to meet Thumper Collins, best panzer
mechanic in the west."

"Second best," the Ork contradicted. "Don't believe everything the Injun tells ya, kid. Willy Stein's still working
with the Cascade boys." Collins held out a hand. "Pleased
to meet ya, Twist."

Sam took the callused hand. Collins' grip was so strong
that Sam got the impression that the Ork could crush the
bones in his hand with only a fraction of his strength; ridged
muscles made the Ork's already blocky frame more massive. Introduction over, Collins turned his attention to the
rigger.

"Real mess you got in the starboard carry slot."

"Drek, yeah. Blew a chip on recovery."

"I can patch the R-P today, but the chip . . ." Collins
shook his head, making reflections dance on his bald pate.
"Ain't got nothing like that on the shelf and ain't nobody
this far out can cut you one."

"Frag it. I need that bird." Begay spat on the floor and
stared at the star pattern the spittle made on the concrete
floor.

"Begay?" Sam waited until the Navaho looked up. "It
looked like your aircraft had manual controls."

"Yeah. Used to be a spy dropper before I put in the rigger
controls. Left them manuals in, 'cause I thought I might
want to take up flying someday."

Collins snorted. "He means it was his backup getaway."

Begay gave the Ork a snarl, but there was no real heat to
it. Sam realized the drone's use as an escape vehicle must
be an open secret, but the rigger needed to establish that it
was his secret to share.

"Begay, I used to do some small-craft piloting. My old Mitsubishi Flutterer was something like your ultra-light. I think I could fly it if you really need a recon."

"You're full of surprises, Twist. Next you'll be telling me you're a magician." Begay laughed. "You aren't a witch, are you, Twist? 'Cause if you are, you're walking from here."

Sam said nothing. The left side of his mouth twitched into a nervous half-smile. He was saved from the need to reply when Collins stepped into the silence. "If the kid was a skinwalker, Begay, he wouldn't need to ride with you in the first place."

"What would you know about it?"

The two old friends started wrangling over who knew more about magic and the ways of magicians, giving Sam the opportunity to slip away. He didn't want to get drawn into a discussion that might end up with Begay living up to his threat to leave him stranded here in the wilderness. Sam didn't think of himself as a magician, but he didn't know what Begay's standards were. Had the Navaho seen Sam scanning the chips the professor had given him? Was that what really motivated the seeming joke of a question? Feeling quite alone, Sam found a dark corner and settled in to watch Collins' crew service the panzer.

Boise belonged to the Salish-Shidhe Council, but it was different than the towns Hart knew from the coast, where the influence of the Northwest Coast tribes was strong. The flavor here was of the Plateau and Plains tribes, a lot more like the Ute Council burgs. That wasn't too surprising; Ute territory started just to the south beyond the Snake River. Still, it was the biggest settlement around and well situated for a move on the panzer while it crossed the Snake River Plains. She had picked it as a likely choke point once she'd found a street snitch who pegged the panzer's destination as Quebec. It had taken only minimal bribes for clearances and a place on the regular shuttle to put her here ahead of her quarry.

That was what she had thought on the flight here. The shadow underground wasn't very developed in Boise, but she made a few connections and learned enough to know that she had guessed wrong again. By pretending that she was looking for a panzer runner and needing to know the

itchiness of local enforcement, she had found out that all was quiet. All of the—admittedly limited—excitement was to the north where, yesterday, a Council copter had reported contact with a panzer headed north along the river. The chopper pilot had lost the panzer in the canyons. No surprise there. Any good panzer runner could ditch a general patrol.

The panzer hadn't been identified, but Hart was reasonably sure it was the one Verner was riding. Her contacts had seemed anxious to do business, even with her flimsy story, which meant that the smuggling business was slow right now. It didn't seem that many other runs were in progress and the mystery panzer was headed in the right general direction. There were other paths to Verner's destination than the one she had decided to block, but all involved a lot of heavy terrain. Verner's run to Quebec would have gone a lot faster if they had taken the track through the plains. Perhaps the suit had anticipated opposition and chosen a less obvious route. If so, he was smarter than she thought. Or else his friends were. Or maybe he was just plain lucky.

The copter report placed the panzer too far north to reasonably expect that they would double back and take the lower road through the Snake River Plains. That meant they would be crossing the Rockies, somewhere in the wilder country. There were not many cities or even towns up there, and they'd be avoiding the few that were. Unless they were planning a long detour north, the likeliest crossing would put them out in Sioux territory somewhere near Great Falls, so that became her next stop. Great Falls passed for a city, but it was surrounded by badlands, prairies, and outback, none of which were her best working environments. And that's where they would be.

She had wanted to tie this one up herself because she was mostly to blame that Verner was still running around. She should have made sure that the Elves had done the job on him in the ambush. Now she couldn't hope to nail him herself out there. Tessien was better in the wild places than she was. She wanted Verner gone before he reached civilization again.

She stopped at a public telecom, slotted a credstick, and punched a number. She waited while the connections were made and a voice on the other end repeated the last four digits of the telecom code.

"Jenny, have our skinny friend meet me at Far Side North."

"Will do, boss."

The *Thunderbird* sat hunkered to the ground, quiet for the moment as Sam watched Begay crawl around the blackened scar on the side of the vehicle. The Navaho cursed as he fussed with the soldering gun, repairing damaged circuits.

"Why couldn't it have been Pinkskins that we ran into out here? With all their trying to be more Indian than Indians, their fragging arrows wouldn't have touched the *T-bird*. No. We got to flop on some lost patrol of fragging Wildcats. Drek, but there ain't no beauty in that."

"Wildcats?"

"Sioux special forces." Begay hopped off the *T-bird* and spat. "With anti-vehicle missiles, too. Missiles! What kind of mouse-minded idiot issues a squad missiles for a trek in the mountains."

"Maybe somebody was looking for panzers?"

"I didn't tell them we were coming."

"Neither did I."

Sam handed a water bag to the rigger. Begay swigged the water and spat again, then tossed the bag back to Sam. "Pretty slick the way you forced their Hummer into the ditch. Better shooting than I would of figured you for."

Sam shrugged off the praise.

"Woulda been easier to hose the Hummer."

Sam shrugged again. He didn't want to tell Begay that he had frozen once the sights had aligned on the Sioux military vehicle. He had not been able to pull the trigger. The lighter vehicle had been able to pace the normally faster panzer across the forested slopes, but it had no protection against the panzer's cannon. The Sioux had shown great courage in chasing the panzer and it wouldn't have been right to kill them. The Wildcats were just doing their jobs; Sam and Begay were the interlopers. The panzer guns didn't load gel rounds, so he had looked for a way to make them abandon the chase. The only thing he could think to do was to block the way, and the only way he could see to do it was to drop a tree in front of them. He had been appalled at how easy it was once the stream of projectiles from the *T-bird*'s cannon buzz-sawed through the forest giant's trunk. If Begay thought that was fancy shooting, let him. He hoped the Wildcats weren't injured too severely when their Hummer had crashed.

Leaving Sam to his silence, Begay went back to complete the panzer's repairs.

Sam's head hurt from interfacing with the vehicle's targeting system. It didn't seem to matter what the technology, any interface always left him with the ache, and now a faint nausea. The latter might simply be reaction from the chase. He hoped so.

The pocket of his coveralls felt weighed down by the case of instruction chips the professor had given him. Scanning a few of them on the panzer's computer hadn't done much for his peace of mind. They made him nervous, and he hadn't even tried any of the exercises yet. The familiar hurt of machine interface was a lot more comfortable; he understood that, or thought he did. It made a lot more sense and seemed a lot more real than all of the professor's talk about magic.

"She's patched," Begay announced as the soldering gun rattled back into the tool bin.

"Good. We'll move at dark then?"

"Can't wait. Gonna have to move fast till we get out of Sioux territory. Those Wildcats will get word out and have half the Sioux military down on our heads. Only easy way through Sioux territory is to avoid being spotted, and it's too late for that." Begay scanned the landscape. "Gonna cut north. It's the shortest way out of Sioux lands. Longer overall, but healthier, because there are more places to hide. You still willing to fly the ultra-light?"

Sam looked up. It would mean interfacing with the craft's sensors. "If you think it will help."

"Eyes in the sky never hurt. When we hit the badlands, we can't afford to waste time running up a blind canyon."

"Let's go then."

They were mounted in minutes, Sam in the gunner's couch because Begay didn't want to launch the drone just yet. The *Thunderbird* howled into the twilight.

Hart sat listening to the chatter on the Sioux military radio channels. Civilian possession of a receiver able to pick up those channels was illegal within Council lands. That didn't worry her too much; her very presence in the Sioux

Council was illegal, for she had no valid entry permit. As soon as her translator told her what was happening, she smiled. This time she had guessed right. She was only hours away from the quarry and well-positioned to intercept. If she sent Tessien on the right sweep, before long they'd have Verner for good.

# 32

A sound like a dog's bark startled Sam from the reverie of flying. He had been daydreaming, reveling in the freedom he felt at the controls of the *Little Eagle*. The ultra-light was slow and sluggish compared to the sleek mono-wings he had flown in Japan, but after the claustrophobic confines of the panzer, the open sky around him was a joy. Half-dreaming he may have been, but not so far gone he couldn't tell that the noise he'd heard had come from the radio. A glance at the comm panel showed no light indicating an open channel with *Thunderbird*. The sound was a random burst of radio noise, then.

He checked the navigation screen. Seeing that he had drifted a bit from the planned course, he banked the *Eagle* into a gentle turn to correct the error. The late afternoon sky was a brilliant blue, spotted with islands of cloud. In the distance, he could see an occasional thunderstorm cell towering among its fluffier kin. Beneath him, the land stretched away in a subtle tapestry of gray and brown, with only the occasional patch of dark green.

Through gaps in the mounds of clouds, Sam found the *Thunderbird* exactly where she was supposed to be. The panzer's shadow bobbed and darted according to the vagaries of the terrain, sometimes racing ahead of the vehicle and sometimes falling behind as it negotiated the open badlands. The *T-bird* could make better speed, but it would mean traveling at a higher altitude that would invite an enemy's missiles. Lacking the stealthy profile that allowed the *Eagle* to slip unnoticed through the skies, the mass of the panzer would almost inevitably register on radar if she flew above a certain height. Stealth was important as long as they were still within the boundaries of the Sioux Council.

Thoughts of missiles became immediate as Sam noted a second shadow rippling over the ground. This one was more slender and faster-moving. Its shape seemed to flicker and change more than could be accounted for by the terrain. The puzzle resolved when he realized that the shape casting this shadow had wings, which beat as it flew. Magnification confirmed the approaching object's nature.

Sam's extremities went cold, while at the same time sweat began to bead on his forehead. The second shadow belonged to a Dragon. Watching with increasing trepidation, Sam saw the dracoform pass over a buffalo herd, apparently without noticing the animals. For their part, the bison decided that they wanted urgently to be elsewhere. If the Dragon wasn't hunting, what was it doing out here? Sam thought he knew the answer.

"*T-bird*," he called as he activated the radio link. "you've got a Dragon on intercept vector. Two o'clock relative."

"Say again. A what?"

"A Dragon."

"Roger," Begay responded calmly. The *Thunderbird* banked hard as the rigger spoke, changing its heading.

If the newcomer was headed in their direction, it would soon be obvious. Sam prayed hard, but the Dragon adjusted direction to maintain an intercept course. To Begay, he reported, "Still following."

"Roger. It'll get nasty, then. Flash me a terrain pic, then stay high and keep your eyes open. I need to know if anyone else is coming to play."

Maybe Sam was being unduly worried. Begay seemed unperturbed by the Dragon, less excited than during the brush with the Sioux Wildcats. Maybe his confidence was based on knowing what to expect. If so, Sam wanted to give him as much time as possible. He quickly keyed the instructions to the *Eagle*'s computer, sending the terrain data downlink to appear on the panzer's navigation screen. That would let Begay select the best available spot for the coming confrontation.

Begay knew his vehicle, its capabilities, and its limitations. Why shouldn't he be confident? A Dragon was a mighty beast, but it was still an animal. What kind of animal was a match for even a light panzer like the *Thunderbird*? The beast would need composite armor like the *T-bird*'s own to resist the 20mm shells of the chain gun, let alone the heavy vehicle killers that the main cannon could spew. This would be a short fight.

From his conversations with Begay, Sam knew that the rigger would try to keep the conflict as brief as possible. Not only to keep from attracting other unwanted attention, but to keep from using too many expendables that would cut into his profit margin.

The panzer lifted out of the valley and passed over a ridge into another gully that stretched toward an open space surrounded by sentinel mesas. Rushing across the clearing and banking across the lower slope of one of the boundary formations, the *Thunderbird* kicked up pebbles and dust. On the flat again, she ran back toward the gully more slowly, her turret angled toward the Dragon's approach.

The *Thunderbird*'s chain gun ripped up real estate where the Dragon had first showed its fanged head, but the beast put on a burst of speed just before it broke cover. The unscathed serpent swept in toward the panzer.

"Frag, that worm's fast," Begay commented in mild surprise as Sam watched the fiery line of tracers chase the erratically weaving shape.

The Dragon unleashed a burst of flame as it swerved past the *Thunderbird,* but the jet of fire impacted the ground in front of the panzer. Sage blackened and smoked. The Dragon seemed reluctant to stay and slug it out with the tank. Orange tracers chased it across the valley.

From his aerial perspective, Sam observed activity a few dozen meters in front of the panzer. The earth was mounding, and Sam's first thought was that concealed enemy troops were breaking cover. The notion was soon dispelled when he saw the soil moving by itself. Rocks and pebbles rolled toward a central bulge that heaved itself up, making a wall across the panzer's path. Before Sam could warn Begay, the *Thunderbird* plowed into the weird obstacle.

Deprived of the sound, Sam could only imagine the grating and pinging of the gravel on hull of the speeding panzer. He feared that the debris would clog or damage the cooling vents, a fear more than justified as metal shrapnel from the protective louvers exploded out from the sides of the *T-bird*. The panzer charged on another ten or twenty meters, but the gravel still swirled around it in an unabated storm. Fist-sized cobbles struck the vehicle, rebounded, then struck again like maddened bees defending a hive from an interloper. The slowing panzer was nearly lost to Sam's sight in the swirling haze of sand and grit.

"How in hell do you fight dirt?"

Sam didn't think that the question was meant for him. Besides, he had no idea. Then he noticed something. "The gravel cloud's only five meters tall."

"Right." The rigger's response was clipped, but Sam knew Begay had understood when the *Thunderbird* rose up on a column of superheated air, her main thrust directed straight down. Soil and rocks were kicked out and away, only to curve about and rejoin the agitated mass. At first, it seemed that the *T-bird*'s action only made things worse, for the gravel storm rose up along with the panzer. Then Sam saw that the malefic sediment was attenuating, being stretched as though it were somehow tied to the more placid earth. As the panzer reached ten meters, the surging mass fell back. Only fugitive pebbles and streams of sand cascaded from the now rapidly rising *Thunderbird*.

Then, sudden flame washed the belly of the panzer, taking the titanium compound of the already heated nozzles past its melting point. The Dragon had returned to attack from an unexpected angle. Its thrust directors warped and partially fused, the *Thunderbird* canted to port and lost height. Starboard thrust vents opened momentarily, increasing the panzer's speed to the left before they closed as the force of the laboring turbines was redirected aft. With that, the fall became a swooping dive that the rigger could control. Black smoke boiled from the *Thunderbird*'s underside, but the chain gun whirled, sending avenging slugs toward the Dragon. The beast ducked out of sight.

The *Thunderbird*'s flight was wobbly. When she plowed a furrow through a thin ridge and slumped down the far side, the panzer slewed drunkenly to a halt. Sam was impressed with Begay's skill in managing to reach a thrust balance that had kept the panzer aloft.

"Where is it? Where is it?" Begay's voice howled through the speaker.

"Are you all right?"

"Where's the fragging Dragon?"

"I don't see it. It must have gone to ground."

"Drek!"

"Are you all right?"

"Me? I'm fine. The opticals have been sandblasted till they're frosted, the cooling system's skragged, and I got no lift. I'm just fine. Where is that fragging wizworm? I want its hide!"

Sam scanned the area, spotting the Dragon as it circled around to come at the valley where the *Thunderbird* was idling. Sam reported the sighting to Begay.

"Roger."

On full magnification, Sam could see the armor shielding on the *T-bird*'s starboard weapon pod retract. If Begay was readying the surface-to-air missile that nestled there, it meant he was through fooling around. The rigger had told Sam that such smart SAMs were hard for panzer runners to come by. They were reserved only for those times when life and liberty depended on a swift kill.

The Dragon banked around a rock tower and swept in. The swiftness of its reappearance surprised Sam, but Begay was ready with a missile that rose toward the serpent on a tail of smoky fire. The beast's long, serpentine shape contorted in an attempt to evade the oncoming weapon and just barely succeeded. Huge wing feathers fluttered away, singed by the rocket's passage. The beast craned its neck around, which let it see the missile begin a curving arc to return to its target.

The Dragon's distraction was enough for Begay. The orange tracers from the chain gun kissed the serpent's side, creating a mighty explosion of feathers and blood. The beast dropped rapidly to earth behind a fold in the ground that shielded it from the rigger's searching tracers. From what Sam could see, it was far from dead. As soon as the beast hit the ground, its powerful legs unfolded from their tucked position, and it ran behind a more massive formation to launch itself into the air once more.

As the missile completed its turn and headed back, Sam was surprised to see the Dragon head straight for it. Was it mad with pain? Just when Sam thought that collision was inevitable, the beast belched forth flame to lave the oncoming missile, then twisted violently to the side. The missile burned past, once again singing the beast's feathers. Bereft of its sensors and control surfaces, the missile followed a straight track down into the earth. Its warhead detonated, sending a geyser of rock and dust skyward.

"Get it?" Begay asked.

"No."

"Frag it!"

The Dragon hadn't stopped moving, turning sharply to slip over the ridge toward the panzer again. Its maneuver was too fast for Sam to warn Begay, but the rigger had anticipated. He was firing the chain gun as the serpent cleared a domed mound. For this pass, Begay used the main cannon as well. The big gun wasn't suited for firing against an aerial target of the Dragon's maneuverability, but one shell would be enough to blow the beast into hamburger. Unfortunately, the creature wasn't giving Begay any such opportunity. Its flight was a masterful aerial ballet of twisting, sinuous flight. Avoiding the fire, it rushed in under the guns, and before the rigger could switch to the antipersonnel armaments, it swooped low over the panzer. One black-taloned claw caught the chain gun turret. The Dragon's mass and momentum tilted the panzer over, while the vehicle's own supporting thrust helped slam the *Thunderbird* into a rock face.

The Dragon beat its wings and gained altitude, fanning away the cloud of dust raised by the panzer's impact. Sam saw the *Thunderbird* half-buried under a small landslide, with a thin strand of gray smoke or steam rising out from a rent on the engine deck. The barrel of the chain gun was gone.

"Begay! Begay!"

For a moment, the only reply was hissing static. The rigger's words came in small, breathy rushes. "Get out, Twist. You get close to the worm and you're history."

"I could distract it while you shoot it."

"Don't be a fool." His voice cut off as he was wracked with coughing. "The guns are gone. You're lucky to be out there. Walk in beauty, Twist."

The serpent swept into sight again. Wings fanned forward with feathers at maximum spread for braking. The neck arched back into an S-curve, and the jaws opened wide to belch forth flame.

Sam thought Begay still safe from that sort of attack. Surely he would have heard screams if the Navaho had been exposed to the flame? Sam looked down to see the comm light cold and dead.

Below him, the flames found a ruptured seal on a fuel tank. The side of the panzer blew out, sending a fireball with an oily black smudge of a tail into the sky.

The serpent beat its wings and gained altitude. It circled lazily, drifting in and out of the smoky column. As it rose, Sam recognized its markings. This was Tessien, the feathered serpent that worked with Hart. Drake must have sent it after him. Now Drake would have to answer for yet another life.

After what the Dragon had done to the panzer, Sam had no illusions about what would happen if the *Little Eagle* tangled with it. He banked away, seeking a thermal to take him up and away from the scene of carnage.

# 33

When an hour had passed, Sam was sure that Tessien was not following him. The *Little Eagle* was still headed north and the badlands had given way to flat prairie. He was not moving in the optimal direction, but the need to conserve fuel forced this course upon him. He needed to cover ground, and the further the *Eagle* could take him, the better. Because of the craft's limited endurance, Sam took every advantage of the prevailing winds to glide as much as possible. All the while, he looked for a landing spot where alternate transportation might be available. Otherwise, he'd be walking once the *Eagle* landed. On the bright side, he was out of Sioux territory.

By now, though, he was physically drained, his head aching from interfacing with the *Little Eagle*'s sensors as he sought to evade pursuit. He wanted to rest, to stretch out somewhere and close his eyes for a while. The cramped confines of the drone offered no solace on the first count, but the autopilot would let him rest for a bit. He fed the *Little Eagle*'s computer the parameters necessary to maintain gliding flight and to take advantage of any thermals, and instructed it to signal any significant change in the prevailing winds. He didn't trust the dog brain to pick a suitable course once the wind shifted. That done, he jacked out. Even confined and cramped as he was, sleep came fast. Dreams came, too.

Sam wandered in a Stygian darkness. To either side, black walls loomed over him and stretched away into the pitchy distance. A sound tapped regularly at the edge of his awareness like a distant clock, or was it a heartbeat? He felt a cold pressure against his back, but when he turned and stretched out his hand, he found nothing. And when he tried to take a step in that direction, he could not move his foot. Turning back, he took a few steps, and stopped again. The pressure returned, and a second attempt to walk in its direction met the same result. He took another few steps in the permitted direction before trying once more. Failure, again. He shrugged and walked on the only way he could.

He continued for a ways, occasionally stumbling over unseen obstructions that evaporated just as he touched them. Resigning himself to barked shins, he pressed on while gradually noticing a dim light ahead. As he approached, the illumination resolved itself into a face. Janice? Maybe not. Hanae? He wasn't sure. He needed to know, and began to run toward the image.

But then he was brought up short and almost fell. Looking down, he saw shackles around his ankles. Each band was linked to a heavy chain of gleaming steel links that stretched away into the darkness. Bending closer, he noted a small cloth label sewn to the metal. The inscription read, "Made expressly for Samuel Verner." He laughed. It was ridiculous to find a custom clothes label on chains.

He resented the restraints and that resentment flared up into rage. Who had the right to shackle him? He bent to the chains and found no fastenings. When he pulled at them in frustration, they proved to be stiff and immovable. He beat at them with his bare fists. He needed a tool to smash them or to let him slip free of the bindings. He howled in fury.

Somewhere in the darkness around him a dog howled, too, echoing his outburst. No, the sound was too wild and lonely to be a dog. He was in the prairie; it must be a coyote. The plaintive voice was calling . . . calling. Calling him? No, that didn't seem right. Calling . . .

Thunder rolled across the sky, shocking Sam awake. A look out the cockpit told him what he didn't want to know.

The boiling storm front seemed to fill the sky to the south-west. The thunderheads were too high for him to climb over and their leaden gray front was moving too fast to outrun. He knew enough about small aircraft to know that the *Little Eagle* would not withstand the fury of storm winds.

Sam disengaged the autopilot and dipped the *Eagle*'s nose down. Reluctantly, he scanned the prairie below, looking for a landing site that would also offer him some shelter. He would be walking sooner than he'd hoped.

The *Little Eagle* dropped swiftly. Early in the descent, Sam spotted a small village, but the turns necessary to reach it would have put him into the teeth of the storm before he could bring the *Little Eagle* to earth. The grassland rushed past beneath the craft. No better opportunity appeared, and he began to regret having passed up the village. Time was running out.

His tail wind strengthened, forcing him to ease off to a shallower glide slope or else risk a dump. He thought about jacking back in; the added response-time from receiving the sensor data directly might give him an edge. The *Eagle* shuddered as the first of the storm's winds reached her, and he knew the decision had been made. He could not afford to take his hands from the control yoke now. Seconds later, the drumming of rain announced the arrival of the storm.

Sam fought the bucking *Eagle,* trying to bring her down safely before the full force of the storm hit. His ground speed increased as the winds swelled. The prairie below vanished, replaced by a landscape as dark as his nightmare.

As the *Eagle* lurched downward, strange shapes loomed up and flashed past. Even as Sam fought to retain control. he could see that most were geological formations carved from rock by wind and rain and lit by the lightning. But the storm's gathering darkness cloaked other, almost organic shapes. Hunched giants and monstrous creatures reached out of the storm to threaten him and his fragile craft. The *Eagle* twisted abruptly to the right, and Sam watched help-lessly as the winds tore off the starboard wing tip, which tumbled away. Caught in a crosswind, the *Eagle*'s nose lifted just before slamming into a rocky spire. The port wing sheared away, leaving the craft a broken plaything for the gale. The battered fuselage was torn from the sky and slammed across the rough face of a mesa. The remains of the *Little Eagle* bounced three times before settling against a rocky bluff. Sam never felt those bounces; he lost consciousness when his head slammed back on the first strike.

Warm rain roused him to an aching body. So far, he had survived the landing. Raising a hand to explore his most immediate pain, his fingers came away sticky with what the lightning showed to be blood. Did he have a concussion? Dazed, he stared at his bloody fingers as the rain sluiced them clean.

Fitful flashes lit the barren landscape. The harsh white light washed out perspective, but Sam thought that the revealed formations looked too flat. A couple of twists of his head told him that he was only seeing out of his left eye. The other was swollen shut or gummed closed with blood. That was his hope, at least. He didn't dare touch to see if the eye was still there.

Another sharp pain announced itself in his side, but that one he was willing to explore. He slit open his palm in the process of discovering that his torso had been gashed open by a ragged strut torn from *Little Eagle*'s airframe. He winced at his own touch and vomited. New agony erupted from the convulsion.

Then he was standing outside the wreck, looking at the devastation. He didn't remember crawling free, but that was just as well. It would have been a tortuous process and he was feeling enough pain. He staggered back a step, his foot slipping in the thick, slick mud. He fell.

Pain exploded in him as he slid down toward a raging thunder that was more terrifying than the storm. He fetched up on an overhang that stopped him from plunging into the crashing torrent that rushed through what had minutes— hours?—before been a dry gulch. His reprieve was momentary, for already he felt the ground shifting beneath him; his precipitous landing had weakened the overhang.

Fear drove him from his perch and sent him scrambling upward. A detached part of his mind noted the blazing pain and the blood that flowed onto the slick mud. For every three meters he gained, Sam slipped back two, but he kept on climbing. He fainted for a bit, but the hungry water below spurred him forward as soon as he regained his fogged senses.

He had almost reached the wreck again when his foot found a solid rocky surface under the mud. He leaned into it, a safe place amid the morass. Then his hands slipped and his body twisted away from the ledge. His ravaged side screamed its pain and his foot wedged against something hard, sending a new agony searing through his leg. He slipped downward, surrendering to the pain, embracing the darkness.

# 34

"Change?"

The interrogative quavered with a faded hint of the brilliant trill the sasquatch's voice must once have held. Sasquatches couldn't speak like people, but they could imitate almost any sound. Hart wondered how this one had come to associate the word with panhandling for money to buy more of the booze that stank on her breath. Most of her kind seemed unable to make the connection between the spoken word and communication. Why, Hart didn't know. Another mystery of the Sixth World, she supposed. The large, furry bipeds could communicate with sign language, though, and this one's fingers gestured in a fumbling way. Hart didn't know the language, but it was obvious the sasquatch's words were as blurred as any Human's would be when drowned in alcohol. How could any thinking being do that to itself?

"Change?" the sasquatch repeated exactly.

Just like a recording, Hart thought, or a dog barking to get a cookie. She shook her head and motioned the sasquatch away. As the furry panhandler hung her head, her hopeful, idiot smile died. She shuffled down the street to collapse outside the bar.

Hart shook her head. Disgusting.

She went back to scanning the sky for a sign of Tessien. The Dragon had finally checked in with the transmitter it wore and she had given it the final approach vector to cut off the running panzer. Tessien had been out of contact for too long. Had something happened to it?

Standing by the battered Chevrolet four-by-four she had rented in Grand Forks, Hart waited. There was no one in sight but that rummy old sasquatch. She didn't like meeting out in the open, but no building in the town had enough space to house the Dragon. This street was at least in a nearly deserted part of town. That made it better than most for her purpose. Anyone who saw the pair would be more than happy to stay out of their way or else be on shadow business of his own.

If Tessien came.

The night cooled rapidly. Just after moonrise, Hart began to contemplate crawling into the vehicle to start its heater. When a cool breeze sprang up, she almost did so. Then she caught the musty odor of feathers among the high desert scents.

The serpent landed, surprisingly quiet. Its length coiled about the Chevy and it placed its head on the hood. The truck's suspension groaned. From the reek of blood on its breath, she knew that the Dragon had fed on its way back. It exuded satisfaction.

*"It is done."*

"He's really dead this time?"

*"The machine is destroyed. There was no life within it."*

"Where did you catch them? Were there witnesses?"

*"Three hours to the northeast. It was good land, wild. There are none to talk."*

"That's wiz. No one to tattle to Mr. Drake about our little clean-up operation. If he knew Verner was running around this long, he'd pay handsomely for our hides."

*"He could do a lot more with mine than yours."*

"He'd still want them both." She pushed at the feathered tail that barred her from the Chevy's door. "Come on, let's get back to civilization."

The furry lump didn't stir until the Dragon and the Elf had passed from sight. Then she stood, occasionally repeating the call for "Change?" as she shuffled away in the opposite direction. After a dozen blocks, she turned down an alley and approached a car. It was an expensive model, totally out of place among the debris of the alley. Showing uncharacteristic awareness for a being enslaved to alcohol, she scanned the area quickly. Satisfied that no one was watching, she palmed open the car's lock and slipped inside.

The door closed, hiding her from prying eyes and ears. She stretched with a growl, working out the kinks left from her role as a drunk. She reached into the back and opened the refrigerator compartment, from which she fished a foil-wrapped package of meat. She munched on the contents while reflecting on what she had heard.

Once the hunt had gone up from the Sioux Wildcats encounter, it had become a distinct possibility that the Dragon would achieve its lethal results. Still, her master would be disappointed, and if one was to be the bearer of disappointing news, it was preferable to have proof positive. She was always very thorough and that was good, for thoroughness was a survival necessity for her kind.

How to locate the kill? The Dragon's report gave her a general vector and an estimate of distance. She would still need to cover a bit of ground. A helicopter or a tilt-wing craft would be the most suitable search vehicle, allowing her to land in tight confines if necessary. Such a craft must be fast, though, with a higher cruising speed than the Dragon's. She wanted to get there first in case Hart decided to check the site. There was also the matter of Sioux patrols. Not to mention the weather. Forecasts called for scattered thunderstorms. If the Sioux arrived before her or if one of the storms hit the area of interest, she might lose valuable evidence from which to draw her own conclusions. She picked up the telecom headset to make the arrangements.

# 35

Sun on his face finally woke Sam. He was stretched out on his back, snugged into a mold of his own body formed when the mud had dried to a hard, lumpy shell. At his first movement, a snake slithered away from the side of his body still in shadow, fleeing the formerly quiet heat source.

He tried to sit up, but the sharp pain in his side and the blaze in his skull stretched him out again. He lay gasping, trying to recall how it had come to be. Flashes of the wild ride in the storm came back, and he knew that the *Little Eagle* must have crashed, though he couldn't actually remember it. Raising his head gingerly, he looked around with his good eye. The wreck was nowhere in sight. Only sun and shadow, mesas and hoodoos, sage and rock and sand.

The back of his head felt cool and damp. Fearing bleeding, he reached painfully back to touch it. But it was only water. His soaking from the night had been preserved under his body. He realized that what was left of his clothes were damp on the underside as well. Carefully and slowly, he rolled over onto his side, but his arms gave way. Sam fell face-down into the dirt, as waves of agony and nausea wracked his body. He retched emptily, then lay panting on his side, trying to recover some strength.

The sun had already climbed high into the sky, and his movements had put him fully in its light. At first the heat and dazzling brightness felt good, chasing away the chill and easing stiffened muscles. Before long, the sun became too hot for him to lie there much longer.

Rising dizzily to his feet, Sam pointed himself in the direction he happened to face and started walking. He limped awkwardly to favor his injured ankle, but each step brought new pain from his side. He had to keep moving, though. The hotter he got, the more he perspired and the salt in his sweat stung as it ran over raw wounds. Desperately wanting water, he plodded on, his holster slapping against a bruise that matched its shape exactly.

After a time, he found a place where the sun-baked clay of last night's mud was disturbed and broken up. Pawprints in the dirt circled the spot. There were other marks as well, but the only other ones he could make out were a trail of footprints, Human footprints. He stared at them for a time, his brain in a fog. More to rouse himself than because of any plan, he decided to follow the footprints.

He had settled into a rhythm of gasps and winces when he felt a wetness running down his leg. Touching it left his fingers daubed with blood; the wound in his side had reopened. Well, he was following somebody. They would help him. He'd catch up soon.

After a time, he came to a place where the sun-baked clay that had been last night's mud was disturbed and broken up. Pawprints in the dirt circled the spot. There were other marks as well, Human footprints. He found himself staring at those prints, slowly realizing that they were his own.

*Losing it,* he thought. *Going to walk in circles 'til I drop.*

*Need to see where I am, find some way out of this maze before it's too late.*

A rocky prominence dominated the landscape in front of him. Unlike most of the others he had seen, this one seemed to have a gentle talus slope. He might be able to climb it. From the top, he'd be able to see where he was going. He stumbled toward it.

By the time he reached it, Sam had forgotten why he was headed that way. The crumbly talus made him stumble painfully but he pressed on, driven by the need to go forward. He reached the rock face. It rose tall and forbidding above him, no longer appearing an easy climb. As he tilted his head back to stare at its height, dizziness sent colors swirling across his vision. He grabbed the rock and hugged himself to it to keep from falling.

Clinging to the stone and feeling rock dust work its way into the crusted blood and mud that matted his hair and beard, he realized that the shadow in front of him was not just an unlit strip of the cliff. The darkness was a hollow in the mesa, a runoff-cut chimney. He forced himself in.

It was cooler out of the sun's searing light. The rock had worn unevenly, leaving a series of projections and ledges. Above him he could see the sky, deep blue and inviting like a pool of cool water. He needed water, so he began to climb. It was hard work, painful work, but he persevered. At one point, he grabbed what appeared to be a convenient handhold and the stone betrayed him. Screaming in agony, Sam slid down several meters in a cascade of dust and rock fragments. He lay against the rockface, winded and coughing, willing the dust to settle.

Beams of sunlight speared through the swirling motes, lending the tall hollow the air of a cathedral. Mineral flakes sparkled and flashed like fairy dust. Save for the faint noises of his own breathing, the world around him was absolutely silent. Suddenly ashamed that he had never once prayed during his recent trials, he did so now, asking first for forgiveness and only later for the strength to continue.

Some time passed before he could think of climbing again. He didn't really feel capable of anything other than pain, but he pushed himself forward anyway. He crawled again to the chimney's edge to resume his ascent, and came face to face with a Dragon. Or rather face to skull. Embedded in the sediments of the wall, the huge skull leered a toothy grin at him from its prison of time and stone. As he reached out to touch it, the rock fractured and a whole fang came away in his hand. He stared blankly at the tooth for a moment, then shrugged and slipped it into his pocket. He had better things to do than play with old bones.

He resumed his climb. If it had been hard before, it was more so now that he was even weaker. He was a few meters from the top when he realized that he had stopped perspiring. That meant something, but he couldn't remember what. He pressed on, determined to cover those last meters before he collapsed.

The heat struck him again as he crawled out onto the surface. Shakily, he stood to survey the reward for his effort. In every direction, he saw more badlands. He might have been on Mars. Distant features were blurred by heat haze shimmer, or perhaps it was his own vision that blurred. Defeated, he lowered himself slowly to the ground. Adding insult, he sat directly on a large rock. He shifted his position to the left, only to land on another rock.

Sam wobbled to his feet, determined to kick the offending stones away. But he forgot about that as he struggled to make sense out of what he saw in the narrowing tunnel of his vision. There were more rocks. They were placed in a line. No, not a line, an outline—and a man-shaped one at that. He started to walk around it, trying to confirm what didn't make sense, but his ankle, strained beyond further use from the climb, gave way. He hit the ground heavily, screaming out the torment at this latest abuse of his battered body. The sharp knives of pain cut his way into the darkness.

When he came to, Sam was staring at the sky as it darkened to evening. He was weak, almost beyond caring. He felt forsaken and would have cried, but there didn't seem to be enough water in his body. He must be near the end, because most of the pain had faded into numbness, tamed by his acceptance of its all-pervasive presence. He felt calm, detached from his body. The world around him seemed at once blurred and more sharply defined than he had ever known it.

"Is this where I die?" he asked the first star to appear in the deep blue to the east.

"That depends."

He looked around for the voice, but saw no one. He was

alone on the mesa except for a scrawny dog that looked a little bit like his abandoned Inu. But that couldn't be. There were no dogs out here in the badlands. The animal must be a coyote. In any case, it couldn't talk. He must be hallucinating.

"You're an illusion," he told the animal.

It grinned doggishly at him. "Sure of that, are you?"

Sam decided to play along with his dementia. What harm could it do? "If you're not, what's going on?"

"You are lying in a dreaming circle."

"A what?"

"A dreaming circle. You know, a place to have visions of power. The Indians who used to come here thought it was a pretty potent place. You gonna lie there all night?"

Sam rolled over to see the animal better. There was no pain, which wasn't surprising. He was in the midst of a delirium-induced fantasy. Removing the pain was the least his brain could do for him. "Just who or what are you?"

"Call me Dog. You and me, we're going to be good buddies. I've got a strong feeling about that."

"I don't believe in you. You're an impossibility."

"What's impossible? You're talking to me and I'm talking back. How can you not believe? Don't your ears work?"

"It doesn't make any sense."

Dog cocked his head in such a way as to convey a shrug. "Or dollars, either. But we're not talking price . . . yet."

This really was impossible. Sam flopped over onto his back again. "Go away. Can't you see that I'm dying?"

"Do you want to die?"

"No."

"Then I can't help you." Dog trotted a few meters away and sat down with his back to Sam.

Sam felt annoyed. How could this figment of his own imagination turn its back on him? Hadn't it been hard enough getting this close to death?

Dog looked at Sam over his shoulder. "Dying is easy. Happens all the time. It's the next part that's tricky."

"Guess I'll find out for myself soon enough. My brain's baking in this sun. It must be." Sam rolled to a sitting position and caught his knees within the sweep of his folded arms. "I'll be completely dehydrated before long."

"That's the spirit. I knew you'd come around." Dog trotted back and sat down facing Sam.

Sam stared into the animal's eyes. The soft brown orbs seemed very old, filled with an alien wisdom. Those eyes were compelling, begging trust and encouraging the sharing of his deepest concerns. "After I die, my sister will have no one to help her. And no one will find Hanae's murderers."

"You're still mixed up, using the wrong preposition." Dog shook his head. "The word you want is *unless*, not *after*."

"Words won't matter soon. I'm dying."

"Right on both counts. But I've got a word for you that will count more than anything else in your life." Dog grew as he spoke, expanding upward and outward and growing insubstantial as he did. Deep night, not the growing twilight around them, dwelt within his shape and Sam could see the stars in unbelievable numbers. The dog shape grew to encompass the sky from horizon to horizon. It lowered onto the earth and Sam was swallowed up by the shape. A word rang in his head and echoed across the landscape, soundless but loud. *Magic*.

He was afraid.

Turning, he ran. And ran. For kilometers, it seemed, certainly further than the limited surface of the small tableland should have allowed. A Dragon reared up before him, its form flickering and melting through diverse shapes. Sometimes it was covered with feathers like the serpent Tessien; at other times, it was an Eastern Dragon, a long, sinuous shape with a pair of legs instead of wings and long barbels drooping like a mustache over its toothy jaws. Mostly it was the powerful, scaly bulk of a Western Dragon. Its wings arched up over its back and shadowed him as it stood back on its hind legs and reached for him with its forepaws. It was terror and power and the unknown, and it wore the mantle of death.

An icy chill cut through Sam, making him shiver deep inside. He dodged the Dragon's grasp and darted past its lashing tail. It turned and followed.

Questions tumbled through his mind, a mind curiously detached from the racing body that somehow managed to stay ahead of the ravening beast. Had he died and gone to hell? Was he condemned to flee pursuing fiends for eternity? Could he run forever? Did he want to?

In his pocket, the fossil tooth beat the rhythm to which

his mind sped. Questions. Questions. He needed answers. He had thought he knew an answer when Dog first spoke to him. What was happening was not real, it was the dream of a dying man. He had no need to run.

As that thought came, the Dragon overtook him and its claws ripped through his body. Sam screamed and tumbled bonelessly to sprawl flat on his face. No dream had ever caused him that kind of pain. On the other hand, he seemed to be intact.

He stood, watching as the Dragon turned and started back toward him. His legs felt too weak to carry him, but he wanted to run. Had Begay felt like this when Tessien had swooped in for the kill?

Pushing back the desire to flee, Sam reached for his gun, only to find that it was not there. The Narcoject and its holster were gone. The only thing on him that approximated a weapon was the tooth. He fished it from his pocket and brandished it at the approaching Dragon.

"Come on, Wizworm. I'm not running anymore. Come and get me, if you can."

The Dragon swooped low, its jaws open wide. Flame burst forth to wash over Sam. He felt the pressure and smelled the sulfurous foulness of the Dragon's breath, but he did not burn. Nor did he smell the burning as he had when the sorcerer Rory had fireballed him in the Tir forest.

Halting its forward rush, the Dragon pulled up before him, hovering as it slowly beat its wings. It seemed to be waiting. Sam lowered the tooth.

"What's the matter?" he jeered. "Can't hurt me if I face you?"

He got his answer as the beast lashed out with a paw, digging triple furrows of agony across his chest. In reaction, Sam struck the retreating claw with the tooth. The Dragon rose in a booming thunder of wings, and wind tore at Sam, almost knocking him from his feet.

The Dragon began to circle him. With each widening pass, its shape altered, becoming less reptilian and more birdlike. By the fourth revolution, the beast had become a giant eagle, its feathers sparkling in the starlight. Lightnings crackled around the great bird as it circled overhead. It banked toward Sam, dipping its head in acknowledgement, before banking again to turn away. The bird rose higher and higher, dwindling from sight at incredible speed. Sam watched until he lost the dark shape among the stars.

The tooth was heavy in his hand, so he returned it to his pocket. As he did, he saw it was true that he stood within the dreaming circle. Had it all been only a fever dream?

"Good start."

Sam turned to find Dog sitting at his side. He sat down next to it. If it was a dream, apparently it wasn't over yet. "Start? I thought I was . . . destined, or something, to die."

Dog performed his curious canine shrug. "All mortals die, but you're done with it for a while. You've got a life to lead and things to do. You've already started down the path."

"And I suppose you'll be right there beside me."

"Let's just say we won't be strangers anymore."

"Or any less."

Dog cocked his head and stared quizzically at Sam. "Maybe you should hook up with my cousin, instead."

Sam laughed. Dog seemed to be laughing, too. He put his arm around the animal, who snuggled close, a warm and comforting presence that filled Sam's nostrils with a familiar doggy smell. Feeling more at ease than he had in more than a year, Sam settled back with his arm still around Dog and was soon fast asleep.

# 36

As soon as he showed signs of stirring, she put away her meal and bent to check his vital signs. His pulse was steady and much stronger now, and his pupils normal. He winced when she raised his eyelids; that was a good sign. He'd be awake before long. She settled down, out of his immediate line-of-sight. Awakening bandaged and under a sun shade would be disorienting enough without her furry image being the first thing he saw.

It took several minutes, but he did open his eyes, blinking them rapidly in confusion. As he started to sit up, she reached out a hand and laid it on his shoulder to force him to lie still.

"Take it easy, dear," she said in her most soothing tones. "You've had a rough time and shouldn't be moving about yet. You nearly died."

Without turning to look at her, he said, "I thought I did."

"You should have, with those wounds." She moved around where he would be able to see her. To her surprise, his eyes remained placid, his expression calm. Her size was intimidating enough, but most norms reacted to her fangs and talons as though she might eat them on the spot. She had always found that reaction amusing. This man was acting like he was in shock, though her treatment should have removed any physical reason for his detachment. She hoped his spirit hadn't fled too far to be healed; he was wanted elsewhere. "You're lucky I found you when I did. If you'd been exposed much longer, even my healing song wouldn't have helped."

"Healing song?" he asked weakly.

"Yuh, healing song. It's what we shamans do when we attend a sick or injured person. You don't think someone bounces back like you did just from some antibiotics." She raised one hand, which held a hypodermic. "Though they help. Lie still now and this will only hurt a little."

He didn't even quiver as she inserted the needle. He just lay there staring at her, his soft hazel eyes thoughtful and curious but calm as a mountain lake. He waited until she had stowed the syringe away in her bag before he spoke, his voice stronger now.

"Who . . . what are you?"

"Tactful fellow," she sniffed. "My name's Jacqueline. I'm what you would probably call a Sasquatch."

His brow furrowed. "Never heard of a white Sasquatch. Or one that could talk either."

"My, my, we are parochial. We Sasquatch were certified as a sentient species by the United Nations Advisory Council on Metahumanity in 2042. That august body did not find our inability to use Human languages to be a barrier, and our delegates still did not have even the Perkins-Athabascan sign language to rely on. Since then, some of us have taken advantage of the benefits of technology." She pulled back the mane-like fur around her head to reveal a gleaming datajack. A permanent skillsoft cap protruded and a pair of wires lay against her dark skin and burrowed through the fur in the direction of her neck. "It's a custom job. A Renraku speech synthesizer linked to a Mitsuhama expert system capable of translation between symbolic concept and verbal expression. The software has got an idiom-handling subprogram that's a bit idiosyncratic, but it does help smooth out the rough spots. Still, I think that it's much more socially acceptable to say 'Pass the vegetables' instead of 'Me food want.' Don't you agree?

"As to the fur color, do you think we're all black-furred like those yokels from the coastal forests? That would be awfully boring and hardly in keeping with reasonable expectations of adaptive biology. Up north in the Yukon where I was born, white fur is common. Useful for camouflage in the snow, I suppose."

He seemed satisfied with her answer. Several minutes passed quietly. She was content to check astrally on the progress of his healing.

"What are you doing here?"

"Taking care of you, my boy."

A flash of irritation crossed his face. "No. How did you come to be here?"

"Pretty much the same answer, really. I was looking for you." She watched his annoyance shift to suspicious concern. His emotional guard was down, lowered by her drugs and spells. Reading him was almost too easy.

"Why?" he asked.

She smiled at him, remembering not to let too many teeth show. "Let's just say it was business."

"A bounty hunter," he said acidly.

"Now, that is jumping to a nasty conclusion. As to how I came to be here, I'd rather not get into specifics."

His eyes went hard.

"Yuh, O.K.," she said in a conciliatory tone. "I'm just doing my job. Even Sasquatches have to work for a living, you know. I do what my boss tells me, and my boss, he tells me to find this guy calling himself Twist. Says he wants this guy alive and healthy. That he's got a few words he wants to put into this Twist's ears."

"Who do you work for?"

"Genomics." She smiled inwardly at the confusion that brought to his face.

"But that's . . ."

"I know, dear. How do you think we found out about you?"

"What do you want with me?"

"That is a rather complicated matter and I think I'll let my boss explain." Sam's sour look made her decide to add, "Let's just say that he is a possessive sort and that your, shall we say, enquiries brought a certain matter to his attention. Before he acted, he wished to know if you had other information he might find useful. He seemed to believe you might have, shall we say, interests coincident with his in this matter. He wants to have a chat, so he sent me to fetch you.

"I was a bit tardy in locating you in San Francisco and, by the time I had identified your, ah, residence, you had departed in Mr. Begay's panzer. How unfortunate that the feathered worm found him first. But fortune is fickle, and she let me find you before those mercenaries did. They would surely have taken you to Mr. Drake, if they didn't kill you on the spot.

"So now, once you've recovered a bit more, you and I will travel to Quebec. I'm taking you to meet my boss."

"I look forward to it," Sam said with a smile that didn't touch his eyes. "But for now, you got any water?"

She fetched a canteen and held his head up to drink. "Not too much at once," she cautioned.

He was quiet then for some time, but still quite awake. She debated giving him a sedative to make the travel easier. Finally, his eyelids began to droop as he succumbed to exhaustion.

"You going to do your healing song again?" His words were soft and slurred.

"If necessary."

"I want to be awake when you do."

"Yuh, sure."

He grunted his satisfaction with her answer, then closed his eyes and slept.

That was just as well, for he needed rest. It would be another day before it was safe to move him to the chopper. Besides, she wasn't sure she wanted him to hear her healing song.

While doing her magic, Jaq had gotten an inkling of Sam's power. His aura was strong, reacting and shifting defensively during her ministrations. But she sensed that the activity was instinctive and as yet unfocused. The discovery tickled her curiosity because neither the dossier nor the

Renraku records she had mentioned him being magically active. More curious still was that he carried a case with instruction chips designed for someone following the path of a hermetic mage. Her sensing of his potential seemed to indicate more a tendency to her own shamanic path.

Satisfied that he was deeply asleep, she gave him another shot, a tranquilizer. She didn't want him awake until they reached their destination. After making sure he was well-covered, she walked to the edge of the mesa and stared out over the badlands. She wanted to think about this.

She stripped off the bogus speech synthesizer, scratching at the itch the adhesive raised, then groomed her mane smooth. From her satchel, she took the bundle of pics that had been bound to Verner's chip case. The old photographs were stained and warped from their exposure to storm and mud, but the newer pics on their plastic film were still in good shape. The images were mostly snapshots, with a few formal portraits of varying vintages. They seemed to be ordinary family pictures, a chronicle of people and events that had been part of Verner's life. They would, of course, have to be analyzed for hidden data.

Stuffing the pics away, she took out the chip case and turned it over in her hands. It too would be analyzed, but she suspected that, as with the pics, nothing of note would be found. At least nothing hidden. Among the instructional chips there was a Bible. Most magicians, whatever their magical tradition, had little to do with organized religion.

Then there was the Narcoject, a pacifist's weapon. Not a common choice among shadowrunners, but then this one was new to the underside. He was a curious fellow, full of contradictions. Such a personality was rarely predictable or reliably controlled. Verner hardly seemed a suitable pawn for her master's game.

# 37

The note had said, "Go to the doors at the end and wait." Sam walked in the direction the nurse had pointed, the corridor empty and quiet. With its dim lighting and rough, dark cement floor, the place looked far from high-tech. He passed a few doors, most of them large enough to admit a truck, though a few were the size of his cell-like recovery room. All the doors were unmarked and the watchful cameras hanging from the ceiling in clear plastic globes discouraged him from trying to open any. His footsteps echoed off the widely spaced walls, marking a steady rhythm. If his pace was slower than usual, it was because his side was still stiff and the muscles weak from lack of use. The rough fabric of the new clothes chafed, and his leg muscles felt mushy. His ankle no longer pained him, but he had walked little in the last few days.

While he lay recovering from his ordeal, Sam's only visitors had been a doctor and a pair of nurses. He had learned little from them, for they spoke only French and seemed not to understand his English or Japanese. The only sign of Jacqueline had been a note from her bidding him to be patient and recover. Had the words not been on paper, he might have thought her a part of his strange dreams on the mesa.

The first thing he had done on awakening was to get out of bed to try the door controls. That they were inoperable distressed him, but he was too weak to attempt running away. Where would he have gone? Sam didn't even know where he was. And the only clothing in the room was a hospital gown hardly suitable for traveling.

The doctor and nurses had been efficient and solicitous, but uninformative. Their language was circumstantial evidence that he was in Quebec, but far from definitive. They hadn't even twitched when he had mentioned Quebec or Genomics, both words that would have been understandable even if all the rest were not. Had Jacqueline lied when saying she would take him to Genomics, claiming it was her employer? Wherever he was, the medical equipment in the room and the attention he received were top-notch. He had rapidly regained his strength.

Sometime during the second day, one of the nurses brought a tray with a datareader and the few belongings Sam had carried with him in the *Little Eagle*. These included the Narcoject, which had been cleaned and oiled. The ammunition had been removed. It was distressing to see how poorly his old photographs had fared, but when all this was over he would try to get them restored.

Nothing was missing from the chip case, whose contents were the only alternative to staring at the walls. He reread Bible passages that had comforted him in the past, but now he saw odd interpretations for them and caught himself wondering what Dog would think of them. Thoughts of Dog had turned to thoughts of magic and so he had begun to scan the professor's instructional chips.

Some descriptions of the astral experience awakened disturbing memories of his dream on the mesa. Cautiously, dreading success, he had tried the exercises for astral projection. His first attempt had brought on an airy feeling while the colors in the room shifted, much as the colors had done on the mesa. From the texts, he expected to be able to pass beyond the walls of the room, but he stayed right there on the bed, unable to move.

In the midst of one exercise, the doctor had entered the room. She had seemed full of a green light that, except for a dimness on her right index finger, glowed brightly through her skin. The apparition had startled Sam back to wakefulness, where he saw that her finger was bandaged. He had husbanded his strength and practiced further, but never again achieved that state while another person was in the room.

Now, as he approached the great double door that sealed the end of the corridor, he wondered if his astral perceptions had been only more hallucinations. If real, they should enable him to see what waited on the other side. What harm in another try?

He composed himself and willed the shift. The light muted and the color shift began, then everything jerked back to normal, with Sam suddenly lying on the floor. The result brought back memories of the Dwarf mage in Laverty's guardroom and Sato's magical bodyguard. Both had seemed to slumber, giving Sam the impression they were lackadaisical about their work. Now he realized they might have been working after all, using astral projection while their bodies seemed to sleep. He picked himself up, stepped to the corridor wall, and leaned against it. The exercise text hadn't warned that he would lose control of his muscles, only recommended lying down to practice. Now he knew why. Braced, he tried again.

Once the colors shifted, he forced his point of reference to the door, hesitating a moment before pressing forward. His vision blackened for a fraction of a second, and then he was perceiving the chamber beyond the doors. Or at least thinking he was.

The immediate area was an antechamber that opened onto a larger space. On the walls hung paintings of great beauty, their emotional content varying wildly. The lure of those images and the pulsing sculptures that stood beneath the paintings at first distracted him, but once his view touched on the prominent occupant, he had eyes for nothing else. Behind a transparent wall of blue and enthroned on a mound of gold, silver, and jewels, lay a Dragon.

The beast seemed made of golden crystal that sparked power with every motion. Distortions of light like tiny auroras flickered in the air about its head. The Dragon was in conversation with a tall, hairy figure that Sam recognized at once as Jacqueline, though she looked different. The Sasquatch carried a tasseled shoulder bag and an amulet of intricate design hung around her neck. At her side flashed a smaller aurora. Sam had no time to register more, because the Sasquatch bowed as though receiving orders. With the conversation over, Sam feared the Dragon would somehow see him if its attention turned his way. He dreaded discovery, for his spying would be considered impolite, at best. He knew the stakes had gone up and did not want to compromise his position with his apparent host, whatever that position might be. Besides, his new ability was an asset, all the more potent if kept secret. He retreated.

Sam was standing in the middle of the corridor when the doors swung open and an attractive woman with silver-blonde hair exited the chamber. She wore a business suit, but her necklace pendant was identical to Jacqueline's amulet.

"Ah, Monsieur Verner," she said. "You may go right in."

There was no recognition on her face, and no sign that she had noted his intrusion. He nodded and walked past her, wondering what kind of game this was.

The moment Sam crossed the threshold, his eyes were riveted on the Dragon. Its golden scales glinted brightly, seeming to reflect and merge with the sparkling wealth that made up its bed. Its long neck was arched and its chin rested on a peninsula of treasure near the edge of the mound. It appeared to be asleep.

Sam drew nearer, treading softly. Of the rippling auroras

there was no sign, but he suspected that whatever magic they represented had not gone away. The blue wall was also invisible, but he felt a tingling as he stepped past where it had stood. Looking down, he noted a strip of arcane symbols inlaid in the floor.

Nearing the Dragon, Sam became truly aware of the beast's size. Its head was longer than he was tall, and several of the teeth, jutting past the scaly lips, were longer than one of his hands. It was the first Western Dragon he had ever been near, but something about it was familiar. He put it down to general dragonishness because its odor was similar to Tessien's. He took another few steps closer, stopping when he felt the breath sighing through the Dragon's nostrils ruffling the light cloth of his trouser leg. The beast's presence was oppressive, and Sam longed to flee, to escape from the great predator. He held his ground, though his knees felt weak and his legs rubbery.

Should he speak? What does one say to a Dragon?

The eyes opened, regarding him with pools of liquid opal.

*"I am Lofwyr."*

It was as though Sam's ears heard words, but he recognized that the Dragon's *voice* was only in his head. He had not realized it before, but Tessien spoke the same way. This creature, however, was far more menacing than the feathered serpent. That worried Sam. It lay before him almost dormant, while Tessien had destroyed a panzer with flame and magic. He swallowed nervously, then hoped his voice would remain steady. "They call me Twist," he said.

*"Your they are not many, Samuel Verner."* Amusement rippled in the air. *"Though I expect their numbers will grow."*

Startled by its attitude and use of his real name, Sam forgot some of his fear. "You know who I am?"

*"Obviously."*

The dracoform had the advantage of knowledge while Sam was in the dark. How did this beast come to know about him? Emboldened by his annoyance, he asked, "What do you want with me? Why have you brought me here?"

*"You are here because I wish to help you."*

Help was the last thing Sam expected from a Dragon. "Why is that? We've never even met before today."

*"My reasons are my own. As Jacqueline informed you,*

*we have a mutual interest in the affairs of Genomics Corporation.''*

Unless the creature could read his mind, denial seemed the safest course. "I have no interest in Genomics."

*"You had a decker inquiring into its affairs and personnel.''*

"What is that to you?" Sam asked with a brashness he really didn't feel. "Are you a cop? Are you going to charge me with data theft or something?"

*"So belligerent."* The Dragon's expression remained placid. If that fixed, toothy smile could be called placid. Sam felt its disdainful tolerance. *"A. A. Wilson, an employee of Genomics, seems to be someone who interests you particularly.''*

"So?"

*"Mr. Verner, you are not a child of your kind. Leave off the games. Normally, I would take your prying less than well, but your poking about has alerted me to an injustice against me and mine.*

*"Doctor Wilson has been making unauthorized use of Genomics resources and personnel in a project of his own. Though such initiative is sometimes admirable, he has not had the good judgement to confide his successes to me. As his benefactor, I have supported him, symbolically fed and clothed him, and now he shows his gratitude by gifting another with the fruits of his labors. You are familiar with Mister Drake?''*

*All too,* Sam thought.

*"I can see that you are.''*

Sam relaxed the muscles in his face, realizing it wouldn't take a mind-reader to see his hate. "Do you want to help me bring him to justice? He has deaths to answer for."

*"Death is the only answer for death, Samuel Verner.*

*"Though you have tasted his violent villainy, he has caused little harm to me and mine as yet. Were he to do so, I would take action and openly chastise him. But a solution suited to me is not necessarily suited to you.*

*"Any direct action by me would be hard to justify in your world's courts. He has committed no crime against me. Has he stolen from me or killed any of my retainers? Until now, he has only taken advantage of a faithless person, who will face his own reckoning in the fullness of time.*

*"Whether by plan or chance, all evidence of the misuse*

*of Genomics resources leads only to Doctor Wilson. The doctor has been deceived by a lying tongue into believing that he works in his own interest. In the end, Doctor Wilson will be returned to the Earth and I will be deprived of the benefits that I sought to nurture.*

*"It is presumptuous of this plotter to believe that he may cull his feast from a herd that I have bred. And I find this schemer and his presumption . . . offensive."* Contempt hung in the air. *"I am informed that you too find this Mister Drake offensive. And that is where our mutual interest lies."*

"So you want me to do something about Drake." Sam sensed the Dragon's agreement, and suspected he knew what Lofwyr wanted him to do. "I won't kill him for you."

*"I understand. If you killed him, it would be for yourself."*

"Just what do you want?"

*"I have yet to determine the exact nature of Mister Drake's plans. I find that vexing. What I want is for you to continue your efforts against Mister Drake, to uncover his scheme, and report it to me."*

"Why not have Jacqueline do it? She seems quite good at finding things and she's already on your payroll. Why me?"

*"You are an unanticipated player."*

Player? People had suffered and died, but this creature seemed to think it was all part of some game. Did the Dragon see Humans as nothing more than pawns to be shuffled around a gameboard?

The Dragon stretched a paw and raked talons through its hoard. Sam took the motion to indicate its response to any refusals.

*"Will you do as I ask?"*

Sam feared to say no and dreaded saying yes. He needed a way out that would not anger the Dragon. "What do I get for doing your dirty work?"

*"A great deal of money and a new identity, both of which you will need to find your sister and return her to her former estate."*

"How do you know about her?"

*"Research, Samuel Verner. Surely you understand the value of good research."*

"And when it's all over, I end up working for you?"

*"If you find that congenial. I can be a generous employer, as Jacqueline will tell you."*

As long as you are a good little samurai, blind to everything but orders, Sam suspected. "And what if I kill Drake? Do you keep murderers in your employ?"

*"How you resolve your differences with Mister Drake will be your own affair. I have asked only for information. When the affair is settled and if you have not compromised yourself with the local authorities, after all is said and done, then you may contact me through the commcode you will receive on your way out.*

*"I can make your new path easier, Samuel Verner."*

The Dragon's voiceless words implied that his help would be more than merely mundane; an offer of magical instruction from a Dragon was hardly an everyday occurrence. Why did every powerful figure Sam met want to teach him magic? He didn't want to learn it. He just wanted to be himself. Couldn't they see that? "I don't need your help."

Disbelief swelled between them, then ebbed into amusement.

*"This Mister Drake who you seek to topple is not all that he seems. You will find him a formidable foe."*

"I have other resources."

The disbelief returned as the dracoform's eyelids dropped, half-closing off the fluid orbs. *"Very well. Arrangements have been made for your return to Seattle."*

"I haven't agreed to work for you."

*"You will do my work."*

The eyes closed. He had been dismissed.

PART 3

# It's Dangerous Out Here

# 38

Dr. Andrew A. Wilson sat at his desk, scanning the letter of introduction. As he waited, Sam studied his own image on the accompanying corporate identification tag. The well-trimmed blond hair and newly grown beard framed a narrow face with calm hazel eyes and a slightly bored look. He had lost weight, but that hadn't hurt him. What showed of the suit he wore was a conservative, mid-level administrator's cut. The man in the picture looked to be a good salaryman.

What didn't show were the beginnings of toughness and smarts Sam had acquired during his recent ordeal. He hoped they'd be enough to get him through this little charade in the corporate world.

As the woman he knew as Jacqueline was hustling him onto the jet that would bring him to the Genomics reservation, she had told him that the I.D. card would only last the day. While it did, he was Samiel Voss, a Genomics certified accountant on assignment to investigate the books of Doctor Wilson's staff.

"Purely routine, doctor."

Wilson nodded, but his expression was sour as he ejected the disk from his desk console. "Everything does appear to be in order, Mr. Voss. I hope the wait hasn't inconvenienced you."

"Not at all," Sam said with a bland smile. He hoped that was the right response for an accountant kept standing while a corporate superior displayed displeasure at an interruption. It would have been the correct one at Renraku, but he didn't know the subtleties of Genomics corporate protocol.

"Fine." Wilson seemed satisfied. "I'll arrange for a work station to be assigned to you."

"I believe that my orders specified that I was to work in your office, Dr. Wilson."

"That's quite out of the question."

"Your station provides the most direct access to your staff's files, sir. Then there is the matter of confidentiality. I'm sure that Vice President Fleureaux . . ."

"All right. All right. No need to disturb the vice president." Wilson held up the I.D. tag and the introduction disk. "The station's in the corner."

"Very good, sir," Sam said as he recovered his documents. He stepped over to the work station and placed his case on the floor. Straightening, he indicated the lock. "If you would be so kind?"

With bad grace, Wilson heaved himself up and joined Sam at the workstation. The research director thumbed the lock pad, and shielding it from Sam's view, typed in an access code. As the computer beeped its readiness, Wilson stepped back to allow Sam to sit, then took up a position behind his left shoulder. Hands resting lightly on the keyboard, Sam looked up at Wilson.

"Sir, need I remind you that the International Corporate Employee Rights Act of 2035 specifically states that managers may only view an employee's personal financial records after securing a form 3329-11 and furnishing proof of malfeasance, misfeasance, criminal association, or disloyalty on the part of the employee?"

"*You* are going to be looking at them."

"Dr. Wilson, I am a certified accountant. Section 35.22 of the ICER Act specifically allows for periodic reviews of data up to the green security ratings as part of a just-compensation review. Such reviews may be instituted at any time by a call from the duly elected employee compensation spokesperson or no more than once a year by management. Additionally, in certain jurisdictions, agencies of the national government may request such reviews for purposes of ascertaining that proper tax, work permit, residency, and other requirements are being met. Furthermore—"

"Enough," Wilson cut him off. "Will you be long?"

"It is a minimal check. No more than two or three hours."

Wilson pursed his lips and exhaled through distended nostrils. "Have my secretary call me when you are finished. I'll be in Lab Three."

"Very good, sir. Have a nice day."

Sam managed to hold in his laughter until the disgruntled Wilson was out of the room. He had no idea what section 35.22 of the act contained, but apparently neither did Wilson. From the way the doctor's eyes had glazed over during Sam's matter-of-fact recitation of chapter and verse, he doubted that the research director would check.

Sam didn't waste any time getting down to business. As the workstation was slightly different from those he was used to, he took a few moments to check it out. Wilson's cyberterminal had no datajack feeder cable, for which Sam was grateful. To jack in would have been risky, and now Sam didn't have to worry about making that decision.

From his case, he retrieved the cartridge that had been Jacqueline's other gift. Like the I.D. card, it had a built-in time limit. He suspected other built-in limitations as well. Slotting it, he clicked it on. It began immediately to open files for him as its unfolding programs did the work of a trained decker. As all of Wilson's financial records scrolled onto the screen, Sam recognized several from the work he and Dodger had done in their squat in San Francisco. The doctor's own records showed Drake's money. Or so Lofwyr's chip would have him believe. The Dragon could be setting him up, duplicating the information Sam had already obtained to make it look like this raid on Wilson's files confirmed the doctor's connection to Drake.

With these thoughts, Sam realized that maybe he was beginning to understand life in the shadows, but paranoia only took a person so far.

When Sam directed the chip at Wilson's data files, the screen obligingly filled with lists of documents. None were secure research files, but that was no surprise. Lofwyr's generosity did not extend to revelations about Wilson's work.

Out of curiosity, Sam accessed the research director's personnel file. Most of it was routine, showing the steady progress of Wilson's career, with only one or two reprimands for exceeding the budget on minor projects. Nothing indicated either the corp's dissatisfaction with Wilson or his work. Indeed, Sam noted that Wilson had reported several attempts to bribe him and attempts by agents of United Oil to seduce him away from Genomics for his work with gene-tailored organisms. If Wilson was working outside the corporation, it was still a secret from his bosses.

More than ever, Sam wanted to know the nature of the doctor's research. He tried again, specifying that the chip seek out research files, but all he got back were "unacceptable instructions" messages. Using some tricks that Dodger had taught him, he set up an override program on the cyberterminal and applied it to Lofwyr's chip. The sideways approach slipped the chip's overrides and placed its penetration programs at his disposal. Grinning with satisfaction, he ordered the chip to duplicate its routines onto a blank cartridge. But when he slotted it into the console, he barely managed an abort when the chip flashed "copy attempts will erase all data." He sighed; it had been worth a try. If he was to do anything with Lofwyr's powerful can opener, it would have to be today.

He sent the chip after Wilson's research files.

An hour of coaxing and prodding got him to a data cache labelled REPLICATION PATTERNING. It contained the only file of any size that read positive for the key word "albinism." The cache was enormous and locked up tight. It took Sam another hour to open it, a feat only possible with the capabilities of Lofwyr's chip.

Time was running out. He browsed through at a rapid scan, passing extensive sections of technical documentation and experimental data as well as abstruse calculations, many of which he realized were magical formulae. That was not surprising, for Wilson was a mage. But linking magic with controversial biotechnological techniques seemed innately wrong to Sam.

When he jumped ahead to FIELD TEST RESULTS, almost immediately he was appalled. Wilson's experiments involved sentient beings, and despite the clinical euphemisms, it was apparent that all the experiments had ended in the subjects' deaths. Filled with dread as much as the urgent need to know, he called up a visual record attached to ORGANISM 5: COMPLETE PATTERN REPLICATION. Five was the highest number in the series.

What he saw only deepened his fears. Wilson's Organism 5 was vaguely humanoid and its featureless skin was starkly white. As white as that of the albino with Hart's team the night of his escape from the Renraku arcology. Before his eyes, the thing approached and embraced a man strapped to a vertical surface. What he saw next filled him with horror. While he watched, the thing insinuated extrusions into the flesh of its victim, who reacted with excruciating pain. Sam was glad there was no sound on the record. Meanwhile, Organism 5's flesh twisted and molded until it was an exact copy of the man who lay limp in the restraints. Sam retched onto Wilson's floor.

Wilson, through arts arcane and scientific, had created something demonic, a changeling that could steal a person's shape. That was why the albino hadn't left with Hart. It had taken the shape of someone inside the arcology. Renraku harbored a viper that it believed to be a loyal employee. Now he knew why he and Hanae and most of Hart's team had been betrayed to the Tir Tairngire border guards. The mastermind of this plot wanted to be sure no one lived to tell any tales.

Did Drake know that Sam was still alive? If so, he would continue trying to kill him. Perhaps the fiery destruction of the panzer had made Drake's tool Tessien believe that both Sam and Begay had perished in the wreck. Jacqueline had implied as much. Lofwyr's statement that Sam was an "unanticipated player" also confirmed the notion. If Drake believed that Sam was dead, that slim advantage might allow Sam to get to Drake first.

Sam looked down at the mess he had made. He'd never be able to explain it away if he was here when Wilson returned, which could be any minute now. He had to get out, fast. He popped Lofwyr's chip, hoping that the abrupt exit might damage Wilson's precious files. While removing the evidence of his presence, he noticed a few cartridges with the Genomics proprietary seal. He tossed them into his case. Before heading for the door, he cleaned himself off as best he could. If he looked too out of place or hurried too much, he'd never get off the premises.

"Can you tell me where I might find Dr. Wilson?" he asked the secretary.

"He left in such a hurry, Mr. Voss . . . I could call around and find him for you."

"That won't be necessary. I've finished here and left a

message for the doctor in his office. It's nothing urgent. No need to disturb him.''

Sam walked down the corridor, wishing that he could run all the way to the airstrip. He felt dirty, as though he were walking through a cesspit instead of the shining white walls and spotless floors of Genomics. He wanted to be clean again. Each stop at a security station was an agony as he anticipated an alarm. None came, but he didn't relax again until long after Lofwyr's jet had lifted him into the sky.

# 39

"I'm telling you, Crenshaw, I don't like it."

"And *I'm* telling *you* to shut up."

"But it's dangerous out here," Addison whined. "I'd rather be back in my cubicle, decking against the Special Directorate. I know how to handle IC.''

The hour was still early and most of the native wildlife hadn't crawled out from whatever smelly holes they hid in during the day, but Addison crowded her as though he feared the dilapidated buildings themselves might try to bite him. She didn't like the Puyallup Barrens any better, but she knew enough not to show fear in the face of a predator. At the very least, there would be several watching from shadowed alleys or darkened, glass-toothed windows. Addison's nervousness could mark them as outsiders, targets. If that triggered an attack, his nearness could hamper her response. She could get hurt.

She backhanded him across the shoulder and widened the distance. He blinked in surprise. "Just shut up. Keep talking and it *will* get dangerous. If this deal goes sour because of you, you can try walking back to the arcology."

"All the way from here?"

"Don't worry. You probably won't make it out of Puyallup.''

He scurried to catch up.

One block up, they reached their destination, a dive named Olaf's. The sign buzzed and crackled as the letters still lit struggled to join the already dead "a." Huddled by the door were two chipheads. One mumbled a disjointed litany of the sensations swirling through her dying brain, while the other fumbled through the usual sob-story. Crenshaw hurried past, then had to pull Addison away from the grasping hands of the panhandler.

The din of what passed for music was loud even before Crenshaw opened the door. Once inside, the noise was near-deafening. But she knew why the patrons liked it that way. It kept them from hearing the retching at the next table or a fight in the booth behind. More important, no conversation could be overheard.

She adjusted her eyes and saw that, like the streets, the crowd was sparse. She'd be done with her business and long gone before the regulars started to show up for their nightly party. That was fine with her; the regulars at a place like this tended to be toughs who thought they owned the streets and expected to be treated like kings. They were excitable and arrogant, and most of them smelled bad.

Addison stumbling along in her wake, she strode past the bar toward the back room. The barkeep caught the credstick she tossed and leaned to press the stud that unlocked the door.

Once inside the small room and with the door closed, the noise level dropped. Overhead, a small fan chopped ineffectually at air already thick with the odor of crowded humanity. A harsher, more vile stench oozed from the peeling walls and battered furnishings. Crenshaw crossed the room to put her back to the wall opposite the door. Addison followed, nervously eyeing the occupants.

One of the quartet of Orks who almost filled half the room did an imitation of the decker's body language. His companions roared with laughter. Their amusement didn't touch the two norms in the other half, who sat as far from the Orks as from each other. The one nearer the door was thin, almost cadaverous, with metal gleaming from beneath his shirt sleeves and from the implanted shields over his eyes. The other had no obvious cyberware, and seemed as nervous as Addison. The two norms watched Crenshaw and waited. She waited, too, for the Orks' laughter to die down.

"Good evening. I'm Johnson, and this is my associate Mr. Smith. Mr. Smith will be providing Matrix cover and research as necessary. He will also serve as contact point should any of you wish to pass information outside of arranged meetings.''

The thin man snorted. ''Well, well. Shoulda guessed it was you was the Mr. Johnson. I'd heard you'd moved into this burg, and the ad had your style. Thought you'd clawed up the ladder, A. C. Get your ass trimmed or you just sprawling for a thrill, like the rich folks do?''

''Nice to see you, too, Ridley,'' she lied. She hadn't liked him when he worked for Mitsuhama and nothing had changed that. But like has nothing to do with it, she reminded herself. It was business and he was good in the shadows. ''New arm?''

Ridley flexed his right arm and stroked the satin-buffed foil sheath that was its skin. ''Previously owned. Yak hack tried to geek me with it, but he wasn't fast enough. I ripped it off to compensate for the trouble he put me to. Nice piece of work, so I kept it.''

''You fast enough with it?'' one of the Orks asked.

''Try me, tusker.''

The Ork snarled and sprang at his chair, drawing a wicked knife from her boot sheath. She got no further because the biggest of the four grabbed her by the collar and slammed her back into her seat.

''Keep it friendly, Sheila.''

Sheila said nothing, but her eyes promised Ridley a reckoning.

''You in charge?'' Crenshaw asked the big Ork.

''Dat's right, Mr. J. I'm Kham and my guys are de best muscle gang on dis side of Seattle.''

''Not gonna claim the whole town?'' Ridley scoffed.

''Troof in advertising,'' Kham said, which set the other Orks to hooting again.

''Quiet down,'' Crenshaw ordered. She turned to the norm who had still said nothing. ''I'm glad you could join us tonight, Mr. Markowitz.''

''Stuff the fake courtesy, Johnson. Get on with it. The sooner I'm out of here and away from this gutter, the better I like it.''

''You stuff it, Markowitz,'' Ridley said. ''I heard about you and the Clemson kidnapping. All very noble, I'm sure, but murder is murder.''

Markowitz started to speak, then merely shrugged as he

turned to Crenshaw again. "Can we get on with it, Johnson?"

Before she could reply, the door opened to let a squat figure come strutting through. Dressed in studded leathers whose pattern indicated hidden plates of armor, the Dwarf rested his hands on the grips of a matched pair of Ares Predators. One of the Orks whispered, "Greerson," and the new arrival smiled tightly. He took a step toward the speaker, who scrambled up from his seat and retreated away from the Dwarf. Greerson appropriated the vacant chair, dragged it back to the door, and sat down, leaning the seat back against the pocked wood.

"You're late," Crenshaw said.

"You down to business yet?" Greerson asked.

"Just got there."

"Then I ain't late."

Crenshaw waited a few moments to reestablish her control. "None of you are green street punks," she said slowly, "and you all know the score. We're going to have to put our differences aside until this job is done right and you're all paid off. Till then, I want teamwork."

Greerson eyed the assembled crew with a sneer. "Dump the drek, Johnson. Name the targets and delivery date. If you got enough nuyen, you'll get what you want. I don't need any help."

"Everyone here has valuable skills, Greerson. Some in areas where your own considerable ability does not reach." Crenshaw ignored the Dwarf's glare. She pulled a handful of hardcopy files from her case, and gave them to Addison to pass around. "Mr. Markowitz has already determined that the principal target has returned to Seattle within the past few days. There are pics and pertinent data from his corporate file. Don't be fooled by Verner's innocent face. He's been edging the shadows since he hit town. I don't know how big his ring is, but he's definitely got high-powered connections with access to serious muscle. That's the reason I need a team like this. The only one of his associates that we've been able to tag is a local, an Elven decker by the street name of Dodger."

"Dodger?" Kham asked.

"That's right."

"Dis run ain't against Tsung's crew, is it?"

Mention of the notorious shadowrunner triggered unpleasant memories, but Crenshaw kept them locked behind a bland expression. "Not as far as I know. The Elf works with her?"

"Sometimes."

"I suspect that the Elf is operating independently this time."

"If he ain't, me and de guys are out."

"Me, too," Ridley said. "I'm not going up against Tsung and her bunch without magical backup."

"Dump them now, Johnson," Greerson said. "They ain't got the balls for the job, so I'll take your whole budget and do it alone."

Anticipating an outburst, Crenshaw cut in, speaking loudly and quickly. "You probably could take Verner and Dodger by yourself, Greerson, but the extent of this operation is still unclear. At one point, a dracoform was involved. If it still is, Kham's crew will, I believe, provide a necessary volume of firepower. It if turns out Kham needs to withdraw because of Sally Tsung's involvement, I will accept his decision, as long as he gives me enough time to secure replacement firepower."

Kham cleared his throat, then drew himself up when he had everyone's attention. "Me and de guys ain't weed-eaters. We ain't afraid of Tsung, see. She and me, we got a working arrangement."

"I see," said Crenshaw. And she did. She saw Kham's face floating over an H&K 227 in a Renraku-owned Boeing Commuter. She saw that face next to Sally Tsung's. She remembered Kham now; he had been part of the team that had abducted and abused her. He obviously didn't recognize her. Or care, if he did. She'd make him care, but settling with Verner came first. Kham would have to wait his turn to pay for the indignities she had suffered. But if she could twist things so that Tsung's connections turned on one another, she'd be that much closer to settling the score with them, too. "But if the Elf is working alone, you have no reservations about disposing of him?"

"Naw. Never did like de smart-mouthed fairy."

"And you, Ridley?"

Ridley folded his arms. "I guess so. But if Tsung is involved . . ."

"You do not have personal objections?"

"No. But the magic . . ."

"If we determine significant magically active opposition, I shall arrange for countermeasures."

"A good wiz is a lead-filled wiz," Greerson pronounced. "Best countermeasure I know. Magical superiority through faster firepower."

"Greerson makes a good point," Crenshaw said. "Let's all keep it in mind. A magician can't cast a spell if you shoot him first."

# 40

The Elven decker's directions had been accurate, even though his description of the final destination was not. Dodger said it was an antique shop, but the sign proclaimed it a pawn shop and offered cash for credsticks and corporate vouchers. Sam did see the ornately carved cuckoo clock Dodger had said would be in one barred window. The hands were frozen at two o'clock. If this was the place, that was a sign Cog the fixer was in and open for business.

As Sam entered, he heard no chime and saw no surveillance devices, but was sure they knew he was here. Skirting several islands of junk, he made his way to the back counter where, ensconced at one end and shielded by an actual cash register machine, a wizened old man sat reading last month's *Intelligencer*.

"Excuse me, I saw the clock in the window. Is it for sale?"

Gray eyes regarded him from under busy brows and behind old-fashioned spectacles perched precariously on the tip of the man's nose. "Sold it yesterday. Didn't you see the tag?"

"I thought that I might outbid another purchaser."

"You need to talk to the owner."

"That's right. I need to talk to the owner."

The old man reached under the counter. With a loud snick, a door in the back wall popped ajar. Sam thought he also heard a softer, echoing click from the front door, the sound of a bolt sliding closed. The caution of the fixer's minion was apt. Those who dwelt in the shadows must take precautions. *Remember, you're one of them now.*

"Go on in," the man prompted. "Sit down and wait."

Sam walked through the door, seeing no other visible way into or out of the bare-walled cubicle of a room. The only piece of furniture was a steel-framed chair fitted with soft, slick cushions. When he sat down, the door closed, apparently of itself, and he heard the lock engage. Sounds from the street had filtered into the shop, but no trace disturbed the quiet of this little room. He waited patiently for five minutes, by his watch. Then he waited another ten impatiently before a voice spoke to him.

"I do not know your face. Who are you?"

Sam could not discern the source of the voice, but he was sure it was electronically processed to change its characteristics. The person behind the voice would be none other than Cog.

"Twist."

"Dodger's friend?"

"That's right."

The fixer was silent for a moment. "You're supposed to be dead."

In reply, Sam merely shrugged, sure that his disembodied questioner could see the gesture. If the fixer had heard that Sam was dead, perhaps Drake had, too.

"Do you have proof of who you say you are?"

Sam shrugged again. "Dodger said you were a good connection."

"Now I know you are lying."

"Dodger said that you'd say that."

A thin chuckle. "Perhaps you are Twist. If so, you have proven remarkably resilient. Perhaps we can do business. What can I do for you until we establish your *bona fides?*"

"I need some cash and a place to stay. And I need an identity."

"And in exchange?"

Sam pulled his trade goods from the pocket of his vest and held them up one by one. "An I.D. packet for one Edward Vinson. A credstick tagged to Samiel Voss. A pair of data chips, late of a small genetic research firm just north of here."

"The last is a recent acquisition?"

Sam smiled inwardly at the hint of interest seeping through the modulated words. "Very."

"Place them under the chair."

"I'm supposed to trust you with it?"

"Dodger said I was a good connection."

"So he did." To Cog, Sam was a stranger, possibly a corporate plant or just a hustler peddling a sharp deal. The fixer wanted to verify the material, but he offered no surety. Trust could only be built on trust, and someone had to take the first step. Sam didn't want to trust a faceless voice, but his need outweighed caution. He put the chip case and the cards on the floor and slid them under the chair. "Now what?"

He got no answer. Then realized that was his answer. Leaning to look under his seat, he saw that his goods were gone. He straightened and settled back to wait.

Lofwyr had supplied the Edward Vinson identity. In giving it up, Sam was throwing away a potentially useful resource. The fictional Vinson had a townhouse in Seattle proper, a comfortable and nondemanding Matrix research slot with Aztechnology, and a System Identification Number that would have allowed Sam easy passage through most of the metroplex. Without that SIN, Sam was barred from some of the places where he hoped to hunt Drake. But with it, Lofwyr would likely be able to monitor everything Sam did within the public Matrix, tracking his use of facilities and observing any financial transactions Sam made using the identity. Until Vinson evaporated, he could open doors, but evaporation was a good possibility after Sam had used Lofwyr's chip to access Genomics research files. He had done it even though sure the Dragon would object. To punish Sam, Lofwyr might make Edward Vinson vanish, leaving Sam high and dry at some Lone Star checkpoint or corporate security desk.

Trust and caution at war again.

The Dragon had helped Sam because he wanted something from Sam. And when Lofwyr had that, then what? A reward of money, safety, teaching, and assistance in finding his sister. Would the Dragon keep his word?

If Lofwyr were trustworthy, his offer would stand after Sam settled with Drake, whether or not he used the Vinson identity. If Lofwyr trusted him, no problem. If Lofwyr didn't trust him, the Dragon might consider Sam's sale of the identity a theft of property. Who could know what a Dragon might think?

Caution argued that he was better off making it harder for anyone, including Lofwyr, to track him. Caution suggested he was safer if his benefactors did not know his plans and actions. Caution warned him to trust no one but himself. That was why Sam had come to Cog. Caution's voice was more insistent than trust's.

Now waiting here in the quiet little room, he was having second thoughts. Lofwyr had done him no harm. Why was Sam so reluctant to trust the Dragon? Had his experiences with Tessien soured him against all of their breed? Or was he just reacting to the beast's alien nature? Sam didn't like to think he could surrender so easily to such prejudice.

He had been raised to believe that all sentient creatures had souls and that the soul was what separated them from animals. But in his interview with Lofwyr, Sam had sensed a cold ruthlessness, as though humanity were his plaything. Did Dragons believe that only their kind had souls? Or did they even believe in souls at all?

His father had taught him to judge each person individually, but the elder Verner had never met a Dragon. The United Nations recognized at least three kinds of dracoforms as intelligent beings and thereby entitled to full rights under international law, but that didn't mean Dragons thought and acted like normal Humans. Who could ever know or understand them?

A slight hiss from the hidden speaker cut off his ruminations.

"My apologies for the delay, Twist."

Sam mentally scrambled back into his street-wise attitude. "So I am who I say?"

"Let us say that I do not dispute your claim at this time and that we may do business. Your offerings seem legitimate, though Mr. Vinson is a somewhat transparent construct."

Whether or not Lofwyr were trustworthy, Sam doubted he would hand out inferior tools. "You know as well as I do that the I.D. is solid, Cog. But nothing lasts forever, right? You might want to move it along."

"I see. That does reduce its value accordingly."

"What's your offer?"

There was a slight hesitation, as though Cog were put off

by Sam's abrupt descent to the bottom line. "Have a look under your chair."

Sam's questing hand found an envelope. Opening the rough plastic seal, he pulled out a resume for one Charley Mitchner, a disability pensioner. The other sheet of paper read "2,000, nuyen" in typescript. The resume looked good to Sam. Low-profile and totally unremarkable. A Mister Nobody was just what he needed, but the cash offer was too low. "You can do better, Cog. There was more cash on the credstick."

"I have transaction expenses, Twist."

"I have expenses, too, and I need equipment."

"Well, why didn't you say so?"

In the end, Sam walked out of the pawn shop as Charley Mitchner, former packer for Natural Vat and regular relief claimant on SIN 555-405-6778-9024. A hand-held data reader and a bug scanner weighed down one pocket of his vest. In the other was a box of ammo for the Narcoject and a slip of paper with the address of his new residence, a squat in an old relocation development in western Bellevue near the Redmond Barrens. His pocket bulged with a wad of 3,330 nuyen. He dumped 50 of that on access to the public Matrix to leave a message for Dodger in the prearranged mailbox.

Dodger leaned on the fire escape railing and sighed. He didn't need cybernetic ears or even his Elven hearing to catch the rhythmic sounds and breathy gasps coming from the squat through the open window. The two inside would know that he was waiting. Ghost Who Walks Inside's auditory enhancements would have picked up Dodger mounting the ladder. The Elf suspected that the street samurai could also monitor the challenges of his tribe's sentries at either end of the alley.

The alley was typical of the Redmond Barrens—a malodorous, clogged byway set in a neighborhood of moldering urban blight. The grimy brick wall of the neighboring tenement and the refuse-strewn concrete were hardly fit for contemplation. Dodger turned his attention to the mouth of the alley, where the flickering glare of a neon sign cast mad rainbows over the three guards.

Local residents must find the trio's warpaint, feathers, and fringed synthleather garments a routine sight, for this turf belonged to the Full Moon Society. Like most of the gangs in the Barrens, they provided soldiers, protection, and what passed for law and order in this part of the corpforsaken slum. Unlike other gangs and freelancers who affected Indian fashions, the Society members actually had Indian blood. The Full Moon Society was the physical muscle of Ghost Who Walks Inside's urban tribe.

The tribe had no name as far as Dodger knew, its members a mixture of heritages, from Salish to Blackfoot to Navajo. Most were young runaways from tribal lands, lured by the big city and fast life of the Whites and Yellows. Some were plex-born and bred, their ancestors having long since abandoned the bucolic dreams of the tribals who ran the Council Lands. Only a few were old enough to remember the concentration camps of the century's early decades; and these were the source for the handful of ancient customs the tribe followed.

Ghost's people, like most tribals in North America, had lost much of their heritage. Under the guise of combatting a rebellious and dangerous terrorist element, the former U.S. government had tried to exterminate the Reds. It had condemned them to ''re-education centers'' intended to stamp out Indian culture and racial identity. The terror only ended when the leaders of tribal unification raised the rising tide of magic to smash the tyrant's grip. The power of the Great Ghost Dance had won back liberty and land, as well as creating a new order in North America.

But the tribal peoples had suffered more than physically. Much knowledge once painstakingly gathered by anthropologists and preserved by tribal historians perished in the purges. They were forced to rebuild their heritage from the memories and tales of the old folks. The urban tribes were a legacy of the loss.

The city tribes were bound by skin color and outlook rather than the traditional affiliations, and dressed in a mixture of styles drawn from traditional garb, White clothing, mistaken reconstruction, and pure whimsy. They might be the new face of the Red man, as Ghost believed, or they might be a dead end, outcasts from the autonomous tribes of the Council lands. Whatever they were, this neighborhood was their home; they had made it relatively safe for their own members and any who acknowledged their dominance.

Those three at the mouth of the alley were the muscle who ran the shadows and the spotters and scouts who blended into the bricks until their eyes seemed everywhere. They were good at what they did. They had to be. Their type was either good or dead.

As though sensing Dodger's gaze, the leader of the three turned slowly and glared up at the Elf. Dodger didn't remember the kid's name, but the hate on his face revealed how hard the street had been before the urban tribe took him in.

Wanting the respect people gave to Ghost, known throughout the plex and beyond as a near-matchless warrior, this street warrior tried to emulate him by adopting the older Indian's technocreed and cybering up. Already he wore the red-painted warrior bars on his arm as a badge of his lethal prowess in the turf wars that were the tribe's battlefields. But the perfect vision of those chrome eyes couldn't let him see that toughness and street smarts were not enough to make a leader. As long as he held to his hate, he would be a punk, blind to the wisdom that made Ghost Who Walks Inside the chief of his people.

A hand on Dodger's shoulder broke his reverie. Turning, he saw Ghost standing before him, sweaty and smelling of sex. The ragged denim cut-offs, beaded vest, and sheen of perspiration set off the muscularity of his trim build. His curled fingers hid the faint etching of induction pads on his palms, but the absence of his habitual headband exposed the four studs along Ghost's left temple. The apparent naturalness was a subtlety of style and strategy that the punk, with his chrome eyes and blatant bodyshop muscle implants, had missed.

Ghost's dark eyes sparkled, and he grinned, showing uneven teeth. "Practicing your chivalry, Elf?"

"Discretion is ever advised in affairs concerning the fairer sex, O Samurai of the Streets."

"Give her a minute."

"Certes, Sir Razorguy." It was not as though Dodger had never seen Sally naked before, but Ghost might not be aware of that fact. He waved a hand in the general direction of the sentries. "Your warriors passed me through without a word that you and Sally were occupied."

"Not their biz."

No, but they would have known. "Perhaps they thought

to gain amusement at my expense, expecting you to react violently to an intrusion.''

Ghost glanced down at his soldiers. "Hunh. Jason just might. He doesn't know me half as well as he thinks. Let's go inside."

Ghost led the way through the window, moving slowly, no doubt to block Dodger's view until the Indian was certain Sally was decent. The Elf smiled at the Indian's back and followed.

Sally Tsung sat cross-legged on the foam pad that served as a bed. The University of Seattle T-shirt clung to her body, practically transparent in its contact with her damp skin. The shirt might have been more than long enough to cover a more modest lady, but Sally's position had hiked it up over her hips to reveal dark blue panties. A lurid Dragon tattoo crawled down the length of her right arm to rest its chin on the back of the hand brushing back her blonde hair. She was disheveled and reeked as much as Ghost, but she was beautiful.

"Dodger," she said, her face lighting with a welcoming smile. "Ghost said it was you. Haven't seen you in . . . how long has it been?"

"Not long enough," Ghost offered.

Sally shot him a look of mock anger. "Too long. Been too busy to sprawl with old friends?"

" 'Tis truth, Fair One, that I have been occupied."

"And now you're loose." She rolled to her feet. "That's wiz! We heard a rumor that Concrete Dreams will show up to play at Club Penumbra tonight. It isn't true, of course, but the crowd ought to be great. Figures that you'd show in time for a big street party."

Dodger was tempted, but he had other things on his mind. " 'Tis certain to be a full flash, Lady. A pity that I shall be elsewhere."

"Biz?" Sally asked with mild curiosity.

"Does the name Samuel Verner call any memories to mind?"

"Sure. That was the kid who tipped us to the scam when Seretech tried setting us up for murder in that Renraku run last year." Sally's laugh ended in a sly smile. "No, can't recall a thing."

"I have heard from him recently," Dodger said.

"He survived going back to Raku?" Ghost asked. "He was one brave paleface to hold to his loyalty."

"Foolish, more like. If they didn't dump him, they must of froze him solid. Junior salaryman without end, or hope. Amen." Sally snatched a soy bar from the stool that served as a table. Around the mouthful she bit off, she added her evaluation, "What a dumb kid."

Dodger looked at Ghost to see how he took the remark. Ghost, who was younger than Sally, kept his expression rigidly neutral. Dodger knew this meant disagreement, but the Indian would not voice it. Some kind of Indian macho thing. Feeling uncharacteristically sorry for the samurai, Dodger said. "I believe that he is of an age with yourself, Lady Tsung."

"Let's not get personal, Dodger," she snapped.

The Elf gave her his most disarming grin. "No offense intended, Fair One. I only meant to imply that first impressions can be deceiving."

"Are you saying there's something we should know about him? Something about that Seretech run?"

"Nay. That matter is long-buried. As to what you might want to know of him, I would not presume to say. You have ever been the best judge of what you needed, or wanted, to know of anyone."

"Dodger." Sally's voice held a warning note, but still remained light. Her tone said he had piqued her interest.

"The word I bring is that he wishes to meet with those he ran with a year ago."

"Then it *is* biz!" Sally sat up, eyes widening as a new eagerness entered her face. "Has he changed his name to Johnson?"

"Not exactly?"

"Don't be coy, Dodger."

"Far better, Fair One, that he explain it all to you himself."

# 41

Crenshaw made the formal courtesy bows at the door and again as she neared his seat, but Sato's frown did not bode well. Though the chair opposite was empty, his expression told her to not take it. She placed a chip on the low table and remained standing. Sato pointed at the case and raised an eyebrow.

"The overnight report, Sato-*sama*," she said.

Sato sat quietly for several seconds, staring at the case, then turned his gaze to the Seattle skyline visible through the windows. His voice was cold. "Will I find it any more encouraging than the others inflicted on me for the last week?"

*Not likely,* she thought. He had lived up to his reputation as a hatchetman, bringing many departments of Renraku America to heel. So far he had left one untouched, though Crenshaw suspected it was the prime reason for his visit. "All construction and implementation departments record quotas met according to your revised schedule."

"I expected no less. There is nothing new from the Special Directorate, then?" He took her silence as confirmation. "That project is the crucial matter. The advancement and well-being of Renraku depends on its success."

*Advancement and well-being for you,* Crenshaw corrected inwardly. She'd used such indirection often enough herself. Words were useful; one could aim them obliquely to avoid embarrassment, or directly to distract attention. She chose her own next words carefully. "President Huang reports that the latest test results are encouraging, *Kansayaku.*"

Sato swung his head around to glare at her, the sparkling gold irises of his eyes shrunken to mere rings around his dilated pupils. For a moment, she thought he was angry, but his words allayed her fear. "Test results have been encouraging for over a year. Such lack of progress is no longer acceptable. Huang and his team must show results."

Relieved, she saw an opportunity beginning to form. "I am sure that something will break soon, *Kansayaku.*"

"Oh, yes. *Something* will." Sato's sudden, shark-toothed grin told her that he would wait no longer.

"Perhaps there is something that I can do for the *Kansayaku?*"

"Perhaps, indeed." He composed his features into a calmer, business-like expression. "I have lost patience with the plodding Huang and that shrill harpy. The Special Directorate is not so special that it can continue to drain resources. They must achieve the goals set forth in their mandate or admit failure. It is time they found some incentive."

"I understand, *Kansayaku.*"

"I knew you would, Crenshaw-*san*. We have already invested too much in chasing their dreams. Renraku lives and dies in the world of reality and a dream that cannot become real is worth no more than an American dollar."

He turned his gaze again to the skyline. Crenshaw bowed and headed for the door. As she was crossing the threshold, he spoke again.

"I expect results soon."

"*Hai, Kansayaku.*" she bowed to the back of his head as the door slid shut. Ignoring the covert stares of Sato's bodyguards and staff, she strode across the antechamber without a word. Let them wonder what he might have empowered her to do.

In reality, Sato had given her license to continue. She was already trying to find a lever with one or more members of the AI team. At the time she'd set Addison to the task, Crenshaw wasn't sure how she might use such leverage. Her only idea had been to learn something about some member of the team that she could use as blackmail for whatever they were hiding. Now she saw a better opportunity. The more she could control the flow of data on the team's progress, the better she could make herself look to Sato. With the proper timing, she could make it look as though she had motivated any successes while disassociating herself from any failures. As well as she had performed for Sato until now, this was the task that would count. If she pulled it off, she would ingratiate herself with a Renraku man powerful enough to get her what she really wanted.

Ever since she'd matched the date of tampering in the Level 6 records with Samuel Verner's departure from the arcology, she'd known that he was part of some industrial espionage aimed at the AI project. Any day now, the team she had set on his trail would bring her the damning evidence she needed. With Sato's backing, she could wrap her revenge nicely into the package.

Once she'd nailed Verner and his shadow friends, she could concentrate on what she'd sought since the Manila affair. The *Kansayaku*'s gratitude and influence would get it for her. He had the power to get her reinstated to the home office and the assurance of a quiet tenure until retirement.

Of course, with a man like Sato, nothing was certain. He would always have more than one angle on a situation and other people working toward his goals. But she had a head start. She'd be the one to succeed once she got her leverage.

Trying to get something on Cliber continued to be an exercise in frustration. Sato's growing impatience meant Crenshaw must concentrate on the more promising lines of investigation, getting Addison to hustle in his checks into Huang's and Hutten's paramours. He hadn't gotten much yet, but he might soon.

Huang was a constant fellow and regular in his habits, but his woman was false. At least her identity was. Addison was still trying to uncover the real identity. Crenshaw was sure the woman would turn out to be an agent of some outside source seeking to co-opt the president. And if not that, the tart's reasons for concealing her identity might still be enough to persuade her to become Crenshaw's agent. Using a mistress to manipulate a man was basic tradecraft.

Hutten's situation had looked less promising at first. He didn't have a steady mistress, but varied his timing and his lovers at random. An active interest in the advantages of Level 6 had seemed out of character for him, thereby raising her suspicions. With the aid of Markowitz, Addison had been able to look deep enough to justify her suspicions. Neo-playboy Konrad Hutten's ladies all had affiliations with a company called Congenial Companions. Addison was still tracing the owners through a maze of blinds and false fronts.

The prospects for leverage were looking even better now that she had authorization for her hunt. Any number of things would be easier, including speed of search. This opportunity was her best chance in years, and she wasn't going to blow it. Not even Verner's obscure designs on the project would stop her.

\* \* \*

Ghost, Dodger, and Sally came in together. Dodger smiled and actually embraced Sam, then thrust him back to inspect him carefully. He tweaked at the beard that had filled out since San Francisco.

" 'Tis most fitting, Sir Twist. You bid fair to be a knight out of a romance."

Ghost stepped up during the Elf's performance, a half-smile on his face. Sam was surprised to see the Indian's expression so friendly. "Welcome back to the shadows, pale-face," he said, gripping Sam's right forearm. Though the Indian was smaller, Sam would never match his strength without cybernetic enhancement. He'd never want to be caught on the hostile end of the Samurai's grip.

Sally hung back and watched, clearly evaluating Sam's new appearance. He wondered what she made of it. The last time they'd met, he had been a mere *suit* in her eyes, corporate born and bred. Now he wore an armor vest and serviceable street clothes of his own. His beard, he knew, made him look older.

What struck him about her was that she was unchanged, yet looked vastly different. He realized now that her magic must have so intimidated him that he'd barely noted her beauty before. How could you pay attention to full breasts and inviting curves when you knew a woman could turn a ravening Barghest into a smoking slab of meat with the touch of her hand? She'd awed and frightened him by doing just that.

Now that magic was no longer alien to Sam, he could see Sally more as a woman. Hanae had been pretty, but she hadn't the sensuality that sang from the street mage when she moved.

"Thank you for coming," he said lamely.

"Dodger got me curious. What's the brief?"

Sam gave her a weak, nervous smile. "I had hoped to explain it only once. Isn't the Ork coming?"

"Kham the Muscle-Brained was informed of the meet, Sir Twist. To ensure his arrival, I deemed it wise to let him believe we were to meet with a corporate sponsor."

"He'll get here when he gets here," Sally pronounced, making herself comfortable in the only upholstered chair in the squat. "Hope it's worth my time."

Sam was at a loss. He didn't know how to make small talk with these people and he didn't want to get started on his story. He wasn't sure he'd be able to get through telling it twice. The runners dispersed themselves around the room, apparently more comfortable with the silent waiting than he was.

Kham the Ork showed up a few minutes later. He greeted his fellow runners boisterously before noticing Sam, when the Ork's mood suddenly shifted and grew cool. Kham grunted at Sam's extended hand and took up a chair in the corner of the room. He glowered at Sam, then threw Sally a look that Sam interpreted as confusion mixed with suspicion. Still looking at Sally, the Ork asked, "So what's de story?"

Haltingly at first, Sam told the tale of his growing disenchantment with Renraku, his departure from the arcology, and all that had happened since. The telling took longer than he'd expected, with some new duplicity to outline or postulate at every twist and turn. He finished with his discovery that Drake had managed to place an impostor into the arcology under cover of Sam's and Hanae's extraction. Those were the facts. He also told them his feelings, hoping it would help persuade them his cause was right. As for his brushes with magic and death, those he spoke of more from the need to talk than because of their relevance.

Some things he did not tell. One was the nature of that impostor. He hardly believed in the doppelganger himself, and he had *seen* the evidence. How could he tell them that a magical being had been created in a scientific laboratory and been sent to infiltrate Renraku, taking the place of a loyal employee? Somehow that seemed even more insane than his nightmare conversation with Dog. If he had told them about the doppelganger, they might have dismissed him as crazy from his ordeal in the badlands. He couldn't afford their ridicule or scorn; he wanted and needed their help.

When Sam finally finished his tale, the Ork was the first to speak. "Let me get dis straight. You want us to help you burn dis Drake guy just because he's running against Renraku and a few pieces of meat got in de way and got cooked?" Kham grimaced, then flashed a look at the faces of his fellow runners. "Suitboy, you're brain-fried."

"Kham, I believe that Drake is also responsible for the other deaths that have followed me since I left Renraku. There was no price on my head. I took nothing from them and I didn't hurt them by leaving. I worked for Renraku for years, and they were my home and family. When I think of what this impostor could do to them, it worries me. I can't stand by and let Drake's plot hurt the company.''

"Den tell dem about it and let dem jump on the mole.''

"They'd never believe me even if they would listen long enough to hear me out. Besides, I can't hand them any proof or name the imposter.''

"They still own you, then," Ghost said.

"They don't," Sam shot back. "This is personal.''

"Revenge I understand.''

"It's more than that," Sam insisted. "Stopping this plot lets me repay any debt I still owe Renraku. I'll be able to call it even.''

"What about them? Will they feel as you do?''

Sam didn't know, but it didn't matter. He had to do what he thought was right. "They'll have to make their own assessment.''

"You stand like a man." Ghost folded his arms across his chest. "I will help you.''

"An abrupt decision, Sir Razorguy, considering that you have so little data about your opponent," Dodger observed. When Ghost said nothing, the Elf shrugged and turned to Sam. "To clarify, then. Your goal now is only to stop Drake's plot?''

"No. I want Drake to pay for his crimes.''

"And what about the dangerous Ms. Hart?''

"Yeah, and dat serpent. Dey been doing a pretty fair job of wasting folks. Ain't dey bad guys, too?''

Sam looked the shadowrunners over. He knew that Tessien had killed and that Hart was deeply involved in this plot that included cold-blooded murder. That didn't excuse them, but Sam knew there was only so much he could hope to accomplish. The runners seemed far too impressed by Hart and Tessien's reputations. "They're just Drake's tools. If they come to justice, so much the better, but it's Drake I want.''

Dodger shifted, his muscles relaxing. Sam took it as a sign that he had spoken well. When Sally nodded, he was sure that he had won them.

"If you can take out Drake before those two find out you aren't dead, they may not be any trouble at all. Hart's a pro. If her cred source vaporizes, she'll be elsewhere and the serpent will go with her. She knows there's no percentage in noble causes or revenge. Leastways as long as she doesn't have a bodyguard clause in her contract.''

"I hope you're right, Sally."

"Afraid of dem, Suitboy?"

"Yes."

"Very wise," Sally commented. "I don't know this Tessien, but any Dragon's trouble and one that Hart partners with ain't going to be streetmeat. Hart's a top runner. I'd rather not cross her."

"Then if Drake's the only target, you'll help?"

Sally snorted and shook her head negatively. "Listen good, my fledgling magic man. I'll help you find your path. I'll get you settled in our little half-world." She smiled invitingly. "I'll even help you forget this mess, if you think you can handle the stress."

Sam frowned. "That's not the kind of help I want."

"It's what you need," she said, at once serious and teasing.

"I want you to help me get Drake." Sam insisted.

"Verner, you're on the streets now. A body has to be practical. You want to run the shadows with us, I'll give you a chance. You've shown some possibilities. Interesting possibilities. But if you run with me, you've got to keep the most important principle in mind. Nothing for nothing. Your proposal offers no profit."

"Sally's right, Suitboy. Ain't no nuyen in dis. You wasting our time." The Ork stood abruptly and his chair clattered as it toppled. He started for the door. "Got more profitable ways ta spend *my* time."

"Kham," Sam called. The Ork ignored him, opened the door, and walked out into the darkness of the hall.

"He's free to make his own choices," Sally said softly, her words almost drowned out by the sound of Kham's steps descending the rickety stair. "Make your own choices, Verner. I can show you a wiz time tonight."

Sam felt Dodger stiffen at his side and glanced over to see the Elf watching Ghost. The Indian's face was calm and still. Whatever was going on, he'd talk to Dodger about it later. Sam wanted Sally's help, because the magic that he didn't know how to handle was second nature to her. Her skills might be just the edge he needed to get Drake. If he went with her tonight, perhaps he could convince her. He tried to keep his voice casual. "Sounds interesting."

Sally beamed. "Wiz. Corner of Harrison and Melrose at nine. Be armed and ready to party." She bounced from her chair in a swirl of fringed leather and danced out the door Kham had left open. "Scan you later, magic man."

Sam was left with Dodger and Ghost. He already knew the Elf was committed, and Ghost had said earlier that he was in. Sam wasn't sure that the three of them would be enough.

"Ghost, do you think I can persuade her to help?"

"She has her own mind, paleface."

The room felt cold, chilled by an undertone in Ghost's voice. The Indian seemed disturbed, but something in his face told Sam not to ask questions. He decided to stick to business, hoping that the chill would thaw in the heat of discussing the problems they faced. It had worked with Hanae. "Dodger, have you found out anything more about Drake?"

"Verily, he is a true mystery man. I have uncovered enough to know that he is no more a real person than any Mr. Johnson who offers one a corporate handout. His true name and nature remain shrouded, but I have learned that he uses the first name of Jarlath."

"What kind of name is that?" Sam asked.

"I don't know," Dodger admitted.

Ghost walked to the boarded-up window. Intrusive beams from the flashing neon snaked like warpaint over his features. "And you are sure that Hart and the serpent work for him?"

"They said so."

"I heard they were involved in stopping a run against United Oil's dockyard."

Sam was pleased. "Then maybe that's a place to start. If those two were there, maybe it means that Drake works for United Oil."

# 42

The sodium vapor lamps on the buildings cast a harsh, flat light. Trapped in their glare, various big and small objects sent their shadows stretching deep into the surrounding night. Light and dark made two separate worlds.

Sam crouched in the darkness, staring with trepidation at the pools of light. Once he had lived in the other world, where light represented safety. How many times had he shaken his head dolefully at the predations of the terrorists and criminals who disrupted safe, corporate life. Now he was a part of the other world, the land of shadows that survived on corporate leavings or what could be taken from the corporations' arrogant waste. Once he had been secure in his armor of scientific rationality, believing that if magic were not a sham, some obscure physical or biological principle could explain it away. Now others were telling him that he was a magician, just as did his own weird experiences. The notion still frightened him, but seemed to beckon and fascinate as well.

The allure and alarm of magic were akin to what he felt toward Sally. Last night she had shown him uses of magic he could never have imagined, and his heart raced at the sudden memory. Sally was unlike any woman he had ever known. She was as beautiful, vibrant, and exciting as she was terrifying.

What had he gotten into?

*The United Oil dockyard,* a part of his mind reminded him sardonically. *Here,* in the shadow of one of the many squat mushroom shapes that made up the tank farm. *Now,* waiting for Ghost Who Walks Inside to return from his reconnaissance. Everything was quiet and had been ever since they'd crossed the perimeter fence. Sam didn't know whether to be relieved at fully passing the outer security or worried that United Oil's security teams lay in wait for them, laughing at the foolish confidence of the intruders.

Dodger had been certain he had nullified the perimeter security. It was easy, he said when he gave them the go-ahead over a telecom on the street outside. He sounded so confident, which was all well and good for him. *He* was not going inside physically with Sam and Ghost.

Once inside, the job got tougher. United Oil's site security strategy did not emphasize an impenetrable perimeter. Instead, it concentrated security assets in the buildings themselves. Each structure had its own level of countermeasures, the extent and complexity varying according to the value of the contents of the structure and the ease with which an intruder might affect or remove those contents. Dodger was expecting difficulties in slipping past the Intrusion Countermeasures of the target building. They were counting on him to take control of the alarms, but they wouldn't know if he had succeeded until the moment they tried to enter the building. They had been unable to agree on a form of signal that would not alert United Oil security. Once inside the building, they could communicate relatively safely through the site's computer system. But by then, Ghost and Sam would have set off any still functional alarms as they crossed the building's security barrier.

Sam knew that Dodger was good at this sort of thing, but he couldn't relax. He wiped his sweaty palms against the rough fabric of his dark coveralls.

The target building stood on the other side of the vehicle park, its face no different from the other warehouses in the row. With its weathered brick, dirty glass, and rusted window screening, the only distinguishing features were the faded numerals of its building number. No sign proclaimed it as the security field office.

They expected its physical security measures to be light, but the plans they got from Cog showed an alarm at every entrance but one. That door could be opened freely at any time of day or night without sounding an alarm. The door was the connector between a fenced enclosure running the length of the building's southern side and a series of pens inside the building's walls. Those pens were the nests for the company's cockatrices, terrifying paranimals that could calcify flesh with a touch.

Sam thought about trying an astral walk to see how many cockatrices there were and to make sure they were all outside. He dreaded what might happen if any were not. Met in the narrow confines of the nesting pens, the paranimals would have all the advantages. The men would be crowding one another, the distances would be too short for effective gunfire, and the beasts were very fast.

Staring at the door, Sam stayed where he was, firmly in the grip of his mundane senses. Sally had warned him that the creatures could see astral presences and could affect his astral body as fatally as his flesh body. Maybe she had just been trying to scare him out of doing the run, but if Sally spoke true, the creatures presented an even greater menace to his astral self than to his physical being. He had learned that the astral body was somehow a reflection of a person's essence. Could a person's essence be other than his soul? If one of those things touched him during astral projection, what would happen to his soul?

Ghost was suddenly at Sam's side, almost startling a yelp from him. The Indian waited a few seconds while Sam's breathing returned to normal, then tugged on his arm.

"Let's go. The roving patrol just started their round. Won't be back here for another ten."

They moved quickly and quietly across the lot, keeping to the cover of the vehicles. They stopped downwind, several meters from the fenced area. Sam licked his lips, tasting the greasy, ashy flavor of the face-darkening makeup he wore to eliminate reflections. "Maybe you should do the shooting."

"Your gun, your run." Ghost's face was unreadable. "You shoot."

"Right." Resigned, Sam reached into the pouch at his belt and removed a magazine. Fumbling a little in the dark, he ejected the clip in his pistol and replaced it with the one from his pouch. He was careful to slip the currently unwanted clip into a pocket.

"Got the right one, Paleface?"

"Should be," Sam whispered in annoyance. If the Indian was expecting Sam to do it, he could at least have the decency to expect he'd do it right. "You're the one with the cybereyes. Couldn't you read the label?"

"Thirty-two cee-cee's of Somulin cut with ten grains of Alpha-dexoryladrin," Ghost recited. "Make sure you put the other clip back in before we run into any guards. Any Human that takes that dosage ain't going to see morning."

"I know, I know." The Indian was treating him like a child. "You want to get touched by one of those things?"

The Indian's gap-toothed, crooked smile glinted in a fugitive beam of light. "You think they're fast enough to touch a ghost?"

"I don't know. You want to find out that they can by getting stoned the hard way?"

"No," Ghost said seriously.

"Right." Sam was satisfied that he had scored a point. "I'll change magazines when we're through the pens."

Gun ready, Sam took aim at the nearest sleeping cockatrice, which looked like no more than a dark mound. The pistol bucked a little in his hand, accompanying the soft huff of the shell's compressed air propulsion. The target's feathers quivered slightly before the mound resumed its previous slight, measured motion.

"Think I got it?"

"If you'd only nicked it, it would be screaming bloody hell. Either it's sleeping or you missed completely." Ghost paused. "We'll find out once we're inside. Dart the rest."

The Narcoject Lethe huffed four more times, spitting its tranquillizer darts at four more cockatrices. Sam changed clips and fired five more rounds. Another clip change was required before he darted the final two. Each hit had as little obvious effect as the first.

"All of them?"

"Far as I can see."

"Let's go," Ghost said, leading the way.

The gate had a simple keypad lock, but it might be more than enough to delay them until the patrol showed up. Ghost attached an unscrambler to the lock. The box hummed and digits flashed across its screen. In just under two minutes, the numbers locked into a match for the combination, and the bolt snicked open. They heard a loud guffaw as one of the guards responded to a companion's joke.

With discovery marching toward them, they entered the enclosure. Sam was afraid that one or more of the beasts would leap up and charge them, but nothing moved. The pen was rank with a musty smell that vaguely reminded him of the feathered serpent Tessien, but less savory. Sam wondered if the odor was the feathers, the scales, the combination, or just the smell of magic. One by one, he gathered up his darts with a three-pronged gripper, careful not to let his skin actually touch any part of the beasts. The task should not have been difficult, but his fear, heightened by the approach of the security patrol, made him fumble-fingered. He didn't want to leave empty darts lying about the enclosure as evidence that the cockatrices' sleep had been enforced.

The last dart recovered, he joined Ghost at the passage into the nesting area. The Indian's left hand held an Ingram smartgun and his right rested against the swinging door. With a nod to Sam, he pushed it, holding it open as he listened. Ghost motioned Sam forward with his head and let Sam take the weight of the door. The Indian moved into the deep darkness of the pens.

Sam waited at the door, his starlight goggles unable to penetrate the gloom of the deeply recessed parts of the nesting area. Light from beyond silhouetted Ghost moving carefully across the area; he was heading for the transparent wall that separated the nests from the handlers' area. A rustle in the darkness made Sam shudder. At least one cockatrice was inside with them. Ghost heard it too, and swiveled to face the explosion of feathers and scaly fury that launched itself at him.

Standing in the doorway, unwilling to tangle with the beast and even more unwilling to abandon Ghost, Sam watched as the Indian dodged the first attack. The creature landed on two strong, heavily taloned legs and turned swiftly. Its beaked head searched for the man who had invaded its nest. It stalked forward, hissing and lashing its tail. Ghost circled warily, trying to keep enough room to maneuver. His second Ingram was in his other hand; he held both weapons out in front of him but didn't shoot.

The noise, Sam realized, would give them away. Sam raised his own weapon, but could not find a clear shot as the cockatrice rushed Ghost and they began a whirling dance of strike and counter. Parrying with his weapons and dodging the paranimal's attacks by sheer speed, the samurai was being forced deeper into the nest, further into the darkness and away from the clear area in the center. Sooner or later, he would falter or slip.

Knowing that hitting Ghost could be lethal, Sam fired the Lethe, but the two combatants continued their frenetic action. He had only two more shots in the clip and the guards were getting closer. Sam fired again. The cockatrice leapt high, striking out at Ghost with its tail. The samurai ducked underneath and dove back toward the open center of the chamber. The creature landed heavily, almost falling. It turned and took a step toward Ghost before collapsing in a heap to the floor.

Sam slipped fully into the pen and let the door swing down. He leaned against the wall, breathing deeply. They had come near disaster; he could see his first dart embedded in Ghost's belt.

As Sam's breathing slowed, he heard the guard patrol pass by outside. They gave no indication that they were aware of the intruders as they tramped on to the next part of their sweep. It would be another half-hour before the guards returned to the building.

Though Sam and Ghost were within the walls of the security building, they were still isolated from the rest of the structure. From their position inside the nesting area, they could see the staging area where the cockatrice handlers kept their rigid leashes, thick, insulated gloves, and control prods. A closed door promised access to the rest of the building. Their access to the handlers' area was blocked by a sealed access port, its lock unreachable though the transparent plastic. Unless Dodger had made it through the system, this was as far as they could go.

Ghost nudged Sam and pointed at a security camera turning their way. The lens rotated as it focused on them, a mechanical eye squinting to see more clearly. Were they hosed? The lock unbolted, giving him his answer. Dodger had made it through to take control of the building's security systems. Ghost waved to the camera and the ready light blinked three times in the agreed-upon signal. Before Sam registered the third blink, Ghost was halfway to the door. Sam followed, fumbling with the magazine of his Lethe.

They walked the corridor cautiously, knowing a few people were still in the building. As long as Dodger was on overwatch they would set off no alarms, but they needed to take precautions to avoid meeting any United Oil personnel. They headed for the day offices, avoiding the main monitor room, the barracks wing, and the ready room. Ghost stopped short at the open door to the reception area, then jumped swiftly across the opening and motioned for Sam to move up and peer in.

The light spilling from the doorway was not a forgotten lamp, as he had hoped. A man was working at a terminal in the reception area, effectively blocking access to the inner offices. The man's short sleeved shirt was not the severe military cut of security personnel uniforms, so he was probably just a clerk trying to score points with his boss by pulling overtime.

Ghost tapped his Ingram with his finger, pointing at Sam, then at the man. Sam shook his head. They didn't know what the man was working on; an interruption might set off an alarm, especially if he was networking interactively. Dodger wouldn't be able to filter out the reactions of anyone in communication with the clerk. Sam pointed at Ghost and the man before crossing his own wrists in front of him. Ghost nodded in understanding and stole into the room.

A reflection on the computer screen must have betrayed the Indian's approach. Before Ghost could grip the chair to pull the clerk away from the keyboard, the man turned his head. His eyes narrowed as he realized he faced an intruder and he shot a hand toward the jacket draped on the desk. Ghost cut past the chair and thwarted the man's attempt by slamming his left-hand Ingram onto the corporate's wrist. The violent action dislodged the holstered gun that had lain hidden in the folds of the garment. Pinning the man's wrist to the desk with one gun, Ghost forced the man's chin upwards with the barrel of the other Ingram.

"Bad night to work late, Mr. Suit," he said.

The man glared at him.

"You want to get hurt, make a move. Cooperate and everybody will be happy. You, me, even United Oil. After all, they won't have an expensive rug cleaning bill or employee replacement search."

The man said nothing, but he spread wide the fingers of his trapped hand and relaxed the muscles of his arm. Ghost let him straighten and back away from the desk.

Sam entered the room, closing the door before crossing to look at the terminal screen. "You've got a pretty high clearance." Sam tapped the I.D. recall and read their captive's name. "Mr. Fuhito. You will pardon us if we take advantage of your position in the system."

Fuhito found his voice. "You will not get away with this. Do you know who is director of our company's security forces?"

Ghost grinned and stepped close to Fuhito again, placing the muzzle of his right-hand Ingram smartgun level with the man's eye. "Great big Dragon by the name of Haesslich.

And we'd be very impressed if he were here. But he's not. It's just you and us, so maybe you'll think about your future and cooperate.''

"I will not compromise my employer."

"You don't have to, Mr. Fuhito.'' Sam looked into the lens of the room's security camera. "Dodger, can you slip through into this access port?''

The monitor under the camera had been displaying a peaceful view of the vehicle park, but suddenly blanked. Words formed on the darkened screen. "Nay. Locked too tight. Grab what you can from there.''

"Right.'' Sam retrieved the chair and sat down at the keyboard. Fuhito had not been jacked in, which was just as well. A manual access to the Matrix was acceptable; it was slower, but less painful than decking. If the trip out was as tense as the trip in, he would need all his wits about him. The headache he would get from jacking in would be a liability.

He was about to trash the file Fuhito had been working on when he noticed a familiar name, Andrew A. Wilson. Scanning the file with sudden interest, Sam's surprise grew as he read. The document was a plan for a hostile extraction of Wilson by special operatives of United Oil. The source of the extraction order was not listed, but Sam knew that only higher authorities could approve such actions. Those same authorities would know if Wilson was already working for United Oil's interests. And if he were, any extraction would not be hostile. If Drake was with United Oil, his arrangement with Wilson was unknown to his superiors. Was Drake a rogue, then? Or was he unconnected to United Oil, and their trip here useless?

The answer might lie in the database. Sam closed the file and ran a search for references to Drake, Hart, or Tessien. He came up empty. Fingers poised on the keys, he tried to think what to do next.

"You are searching for information on Katherine Hart," Fuhito said. He must have been able to see the screen from where he stood. Sam swiveled the chair to face him.

"That's right. We want to know who she works for, among other things. She's involved in something we want to stop. Can you help us?''

Fuhito drew himself up, obviously having made a hard decision. "I will tell you who they work for.''

"I thought you wouldn't compromise your company," Ghost said.

"I will not. The Elf bitch and her worm work for Haesslich directly. They are under his personal contract."

"By the worm, you mean Tessien?"

Fuhito nodded.

"Why are telling us this?" Sam asked.

"Hart is a worse threat to United Oil security than you two. The Dragon gives secrets to her, a money-grubbing mercenary of flickering loyalty. Her presence is an affront to our security organization, an insult to the company."

"Why don't you tell your bosses?" Sam asked. Fuhito maintained a sullen silence. Either he had done so and been ignored, or he was afraid to. "All right, then. What about Jarlath Drake?"

"I know nothing about any Jarlath Drake. Is he another of Haesslich's adventurers?"

"We ask the questions, chummer," Ghost warned.

Fuhito turned on him with sudden heat. "I must know about this Drake. You will tell me if he is a threat to United Oil security."

Ghost laughed softly, "Take it easy, Tiger. The only threat you have to worry about right now is us."

Snorting, Fuhito replied, "You are no threat. You will not leave the grounds alive."

Ghost holstered one of his guns and stepped up to Fuhito, passing an open hand across the man's face. Locks of hair drifted toward the floor. The Indian's fingertips came to rest lightly on the man's neck, marking the course of his jugular vein. Sam could see Fuhito pale and his eyes go wide with fear. Ghost's smile was tight and hard; not a tooth showed.

"Ever try to kill a ghost?"

The tableau broke as the security monitor beeped, and the words "Time, time, time," marched across the screen. Ghost stepped away from the shaking Fuhito and moved to the door. Sam stood up, took out his gun, and pointed the Lethe at the United Oil man.

"It's been enlightening, Mr. Fuhito, but it's past your bedtime." he said, pulling slowly on the trigger. The dart struck home and Fuhito jerked, his expression flickering from surprise to contempt as he slumped. Ghost caught him before he hit the floor. The two runners arranged Fuhito at the desk, draped to appear as though he had fallen asleep.

By the time they closed the door, the knowbot monitoring the length of inactivity on secure files had blanked the screen, logging Fuhito out.

As they hurried down the corridor back to the pens, Ghost whispered, "I think you've lost your invisibility. He'll spill to Haesslich in the morning."

"I disagree. I saw enough of his kind in Japan when I was with Renraku. They're loyal to the company, but also concerned about personal honor." They were into the vehicle park before Sam had a chance to say more. "Mr. Fuhito is actually Major Fuhito, Haesslich's second-in-command of security," he said. "Being caught by a couple of runners who slipped in and out of his domain without setting off a single alarm will shame him deeply. I called him mister instead of by rank, so he'd think we didn't know who he was. He may take that to mean we won't say anything about who we caught. If none of us talks, tonight never happened. His kind find it real easy to take that line.

"Fuhito must be ambitious, which is why he works late at night. He wants to move up in the world, but he wants his world orderly. Haesslich and his personal agents are a troublesome headache to him, too random and unpredictable. Such wild cards are disturbing to a man like Fuhito. He wants them gone from his world, and that's a service we might provide in a number of ways. Whether we eliminate Haesslich's agents, expose them, or simply foul up their plans, we embarrass Haesslich.

"The Major will be looking for a way to use the Dragon's embarrassment to his own advantage. If Drake is involved with Wilson and Haesslich and the big boys of United Oil know nothing about that, I think the Major may get what he's hoping for. If Haesslich's private operatives mess up a United Oil operation by compromising a lucrative acquisition like Wilson, the Dragon will not earn points with United Oil executives. With Haesslich's stock going down, Fuhito's goes up. We, working to expose Drake's operation, will do some of the Major's work for him, making it easier for him to take Haesslich's job. No, Mister Fuhito will be very quiet about his night visitors.

"At least now we know that we can hunt down Drake without worrying about getting on the wrong side of United

Oil.'' Sam looked around. "Now, how do we get out of here?''

"Null perspiration, paleface. Just follow me.''

# 43

Hart stood by the cockatrice pen. The animals seemed sluggish, but it was still early and the day overcast. She felt a bit sluggish herself and would have liked to go back to bed. It was a good day for sleeping. Business rarely allowed one to indulge slothful habits, and today business by the name of Haesslich had called her and Tessien to check security at the dockyard. He hadn't said why exactly, but he wanted things locked up. She suspected some sort of special shipment coming or going within the next few days.

Tessien arrived in its usual flurry of dust. It radiated its own irritability in response to her greeting. *Yes, indeed,* she thought, *a wonderful morning.*

Tessien was too large to enter the security building, so they'd hold the meeting out here. She wondered how long Major Fuhito's struggle to balance Japanese politeness, company honor, and personal annoyance at outsiders would keep them waiting. The dockyard was still gearing up for the day and there was not much activity. She watched the cockatrices scratch about at the ground in the enclosure.

*"They are drugged."*

"What?"

*"The* (unintelligible sense) *have had their senses artificially dulled."* Tessien broadcast its annoyance at Hart. The serpent didn't like explaining itself.

There was no reason she could think of for United Oil to drug its entire flock of guard beasts. Something had happened, and Haesslich would want to know what. If she could solve the problem before bringing it to the Dragon, she might earn a bonus. At the very least, it might put their working relationship back on a better course. She wouldn't expect real gratitude from the beast, but he might learn to appreciate her professionalism a bit more.

And it was time to be professional. Major Fuhito and a

trio of security personnel were coming down the front steps. In contrast to his crisply uniformed aides, Fuhito's clothes looked slept in. He was heavy-eyed and his movement slow. As they approached her and the serpent, she noted that the major's gait was unusual. In the tight burst of speech that passed for a whisper among dracoforms, Tessien confirmed what she had concluded.

*"He has been drugged, also."*

After the formal greeting, she took Fuhito by the arm and led him around Tessien, putting the bulk of the dracoform between them and his aides. Tessien's tail warded off their attempts to follow.

"Well, Major," she said with a smile, "would you like to tell me about it or do you want to talk to Haesslich directly?"

Fuhito blinked like an Eyekiller suddenly dragged into the light. "What are you talking about?"

"Last night's penetration, of course."

Fuhito's face froze. "How did you know about that?"

"It's my job to know about such things," she said sweetly and watched him calculate his answer. Had he not been so muzzy from whatever the intruders had used on him, he would have hidden it better.

"I have done nothing to compromise United Oil," he said.

"I haven't accused you of anything, Major. What did they want?"

His slowness in answering warned her that he was about to tell her either a lie or a half-truth.

"They were looking for Jarlath Drake."

Drake. But the Major was holding something back. A sudden awful suspicion flared. "And just who were they?"

"Two men. An Indian, enhanced, and a Caucasian with a datajack. There was also a decker whom they called Dodger."

Dodger, too. She felt her own suspicion echoed from Tessien.

"Was this Caucasian a blond with hazel eyes? Average height and build, datajack on his right temple, four small scars on his right hand, and a corporate's spare tire?"

"Yes to all but the weight. He was slim." Fuhito's voice was less slurred now and his eyes sparkled with calculation. "Your suspect has a beard?"

Not when she had last seen him. But the description and details were close enough. Too close. The trials he had been through could easily have cost him weight, and he'd had enough time to grow a natural beard. There might be other men who matched the description, but how many would come here looking for Drake? The intruder had to be Verner. This was a most unfortunate turn of events, but she had only herself to blame for not checking the dracoform's kill in person.

Verner had enjoyed two too many escapes from death. That had to be something more than good luck. Somehow Verner had gulled her. He was slicker than she had thought.

Or had Tessien lied to her? There didn't seem to be any reason for it to do so. Their four years of partnership had been more than satisfactory to both. Or so she thought. She was certain Tessien hadn't betrayed her back in the Tir, but perhaps it had lied then as well. If their partnership was no longer important to it, the serpent might be using this opportunity to get rid of her. The lack of further attempts was not a good indicator that she could still trust her back to it. Perhaps it was only waiting for a good opportunity. Though Tessian had never betrayed her before, she decided, with regret, that she could never trust the serpent's word again.

*"He must not find out,"* Tessien announced as soon as it had worked out the implications.

The serpent's thought was twin to her own. Whatever her problems with Tessien, they both had a problem named Samuel Verner. Even if he wasn't as slick as she was beginning to suspect, Verner was a loose end that could get her and Tessien aced. Loose ends had to be tied off, finally, permanently. This time she wouldn't underestimate him.

Knowing that Fuhito had observed her silence, she hid her concerns and smiled at him. "Major," she said, keeping her tone light, "we don't have to work at cross-purposes here. I won't tell Haesslich about last night if you tell me all you know about your visitors. Your embarrassing little secret will be safe."

Fuhito's smile seemed a little too predatory to be one of relief. She would have to be careful of what he told her.

# 44

It was mid-morning by the time they returned to Sam's new neighborhood. Traffic was light on the streets, but the walks were moderately crowded. Kids scurried through the pedestrians, playing games that seemed to have mutating rules. Vendors hawked from their stalls and parked vehicles. A few shops were still in the process of running back their bars before opening. Groups of locals gathered around the tardy merchants and exchanged gossip as they waited. The crowd was varied enough that an Elf, an Indian, and a Caucasian walking together did not seem out of place.

Ghost grabbed Sam's arm and pulled him under the awning of a noodle stall. Dazed with exhaustion, Sam couldn't think of a suitable complaint as Ghost and Dodger appropriated two of the stools by the counter. Not understanding, Sam took the empty stool between them.

"Trouble?" Dodger asked.

Ghost nodded. "Think so."

The cook snarled at them to order or move on. Dodger flipped him a credstick and called for three cups of ramen. As soon as the gnarled old vendor turned back to his stove, Ghost inclined his head toward the building where Sam lived.

"Across the street, there's a dog barking at a Dwarf."

Sam and Dodger looked. The yelping animal was easy to spot. Standing stiff-legged, the street mutt yapped insistently at a short figure in a patched and tattered long coat. Pedestrians gave the interaction a wide berth. Finally responding, the derelict swatted a bagged bottle ineffectually at the animal, which lunged at the threatening hand and missed. The dog barked a few more times, then fled when the gray-haired heap of rags took a few scuttling steps in its direction.

"A castoff from society, broken and homeless. You have identified a true trouble of our world, Sir False Alarm."

"The homeless don't pack state-of-the-art weaponry."

Sam and Dodger looked again, watching as the raggedy

man returned to the sheltered hollow of a tenement's front shop. Sam didn't see anything, but Dodger must have.

"Mother of us all! You are right."

"Paired Ares Predators?" Ghost asked.

"Could be. You're the expert on ironmongery, Sir Razorguy, not I. Whatever breed they were, they were a matched brace."

"How did you spot him?" Sam asked.

"I had one of mine staked on that stoop."

Sam heard the anger in Ghost's voice. "And you think that . . ."

"The Dwarf got him. My boy wouldn't have left voluntarily."

Sam snatched another look. The derelict didn't look dangerous except to one's sense of propriety. "What do you thing he's doing there?"

"Waiting for you, Sir Twist," Dodger replied.

"He and his mates probably already hit the squat," Ghost added.

"Hit the—" Sam's stomach lurched. "Sally was supposed to be there."

Ghost turned his head to stare at Sam. His eyes narrowed, as razor-sharp chromed blades flicked in and out of his fingertips. It was the lack of expression on the face of the man with whom he had shared the night's adventure that frightened Sam. The man he had trusted with his life seemed now on the verge of taking it.

Blades vanished as Ghost spun the stool and slid off, directly into the chest of Dodger. The Elf stood with his arms wide to block Ghost's movement. Dodger folded them in around the Indian before the street samurai could slip past. The Elf had been anticipating Ghost's maneuver.

"Discretion, Ghost. Charging in blindly won't help her." For a moment, the Indian seemed ready to fight Dodger, too. Then the tension went out of Ghost's muscles and Dodger loosened his hold. "We don't even know what happened."

Dodger turned Ghost around, urged him back onto the stool, and sat by his side. Leaning over the counter, the Elf spoke across Ghost. "Sam, your magic can help."

"What magic? I don't know any spells."

"Astral projection. You can scout the building and the squat. If someone hostile is out there looking for you, they won't expect that. Anyone who knows that you're a magician is friendly and would just come up and talk."

"Greerson," Ghost whispered.

"What?" Sam asked.

"Who?" Dodger echoed.

"Greerson. Bounty-hunting Dwarf. Heard he works the ambush game."

Dodger and Sam exchanged glances. "You know him?" Dodger asked.

Ghost shook his head. "Heard of him. Meanest halfer on the coast."

"Well, Sir Twist, 'twould seem your demise is no longer counted a certainty in some circles. 'Twould also seem that your reconnaissance is not a convenience but a necessity. We cannot be sure that Greerson has not learned of your associates as well. Since none of us can walk invisibly past him, we must have the next best thing. Only your astral presence can slip in and let us know if our suspicions are correct. And more important, you can ascertain whether Lady Tsung is held captive in your dwelling."

Dodger's last argument was the clincher. If Sally were a prisoner, they would need to know everything they could to rescue her. "All right. I'll give it a try."

"That's the brave knight errant."

Sam didn't feel like a knight. He felt more like an untrained page about to be suited up in armor and tossed into a battle without a sword. "I said I'd try, but I'm not very good at this stuff. Half of it seems to be hallucination and I'm not sure I can always tell which half is which."

"But you will try." To Sam's slow nod of agreement, Dodger added, "Your best is all that you can do."

Sam closed his eyes, trying to shut out the street sounds and concentrate. The noise wouldn't go away, but the passage of vehicles in the roadway began to take on a rhythm. The harder he tried, the heavier his head felt. It sank down slowly only to jerk up again, jolting him from his effort. He tried again. This time, when the jerk came, he realized that he was standing. Now both his head and his whole body felt light, open, and clear, nearly floating. He opened his eyes and looked himself over. Everything seemed normal, except that all his equipment and belongings, save for his good-luck fossil tooth, looked slightly insubstantial. The tooth was as real and solid as his flesh.

He turned to say something to Dodger and Ghost and found them paying attention to the person slumped face-down over the counter—himself. Seeing that, Sam knew that he had succeeded, more fully than ever before. This time he was aware of his presence in astral space as well as knowing that his own body lay quietly awaiting his return. It was a liberating, exhilarating, profoundly disturbing realization.

For the first time, he was viewing astrally a scene that was familiar. At least he thought it was. The world around him had gone strange; colors shifted, buildings appeared washed out, and people glowed starkly against the urban background.

Near at hand, the fires that lit Dodger and Ghost burned brightly but were scored with dark areas, the street samurai's more than Elf's. The counterman's aura was dull with a sickly green overlay that—*smelled* wasn't the right word but it was appropriate—bad.

Sam walked over to the Dwarf who had taken their attention. Approaching him, he could see the glow that overlay the tatterdemalion image and knew, he didn't know how, that the Dwarf was healthy. His aura didn't have the "smell" of the noodle vendor and there was no taint to the color that would have been present if the Dwarf was the substance-abuser he pretended. Even more than Ghost, this person's glow was blotched and crisscrossed with dark, dead places—the marks, Sam realized, of extensive cybernetic enhancements.

Sam's approach was a test of sorts to see if he really was invisible to this watcher. He stepped directly into the false derelict's line-of-sight, but there was no reaction. Satisfied, Sam turned and crossed the street.

It was a flickering whirl of glowing people and shadow machines, flittering flashes of light from unknown sources and the sudden, fleeting presence of motion at the corners of his perception. The rapidly mounting load of sensory input drove him faster across the roadway. He fled into the building, away from the bustle of life, feeling relieved to reach the untenanted vestibule. He took a moment to steady himself before proceeding.

Not knowing how to call an astral elevator, he took the stairs, stepping though the door that his hand could not touch. After a couple of flights, he realized he could not

read the signs showing each floor's number. He could see
them and feel a sense of identity, but the words were gib-
berish. He should have counted landings. He began to stick
his head through the doors at each landing, seeking the pattern of scars and debris that marked his own floor. It only
took a couple of tries.

He walked slowly to his door. Not needing the key, he
stepped through the panel. The apartment had been trashed.
Anything breakable was broken, anything tearable torn, and
anything openable opened. What little of value he had was
gone or destroyed, but of Sally there was no sign.

"She never arrived," said a voice that he recognized.

Sam turned to face the speaker. "Dog, what are you doing here?"

"Talking to you." Dog cocked his head and gave Sam a
wide canine grin.

Sam didn't find the flip answer amusing. "I know that. I
mean, *why* are you here?"

"You have a lot to learn."

*Not again.* Sam thought. Maybe he was crazy. Tired people could hallucinate, and bad food could make for bad
dreams. Maybe he had come home from the run and collapsed to sleep away his exhaustion.

He crouched in front of Dog. "I'll wake up soon. You'll
be gone and Sally will be here. This is just a paranoid nightmare."

"Close to the mark, Man. It's a dream, all right, but that
doesn't make it any less real. And paranoia is good, too.
Downright healthy, sometimes. Maybe you'd like to learn a
song."

"I've got to be dreaming." Sam stood up. "There's a
killer on my doorstep and two more hunting me wherever I
go, I'm a stalking horse for a Dragon, and my faithful astral
companion wants to teach me a lullaby."

"Well, a lullaby's good, but not what you need right now.
I was thinking of a more powerful song."

With that, Dog began to sing, and the next thing Sam
knew, Dodger was trying to force him to drink some bitter
green tea. The stuff tasted awful but he drank it, thankful
for anything that was real and substantial.

"What took you so long?" the Elf asked. "Sally doesn't
take that long to do an astral recon. We thought they might
have gotten your spirit."

"I had a conversation with . . ." Realizing how ridiculous it would sound, Sam stopped himself. "Never mind."

Ghost leaned into his face. "What did you learn?"

Suppressing a hysterical giggle, Sam formulated the words the Indian wanted to hear. "Someone trashed the place, but Sally wasn't there. And you're probably right about the Dwarf. He's hotwired and chromed to the max."

"Time to relocate," Ghost announced.

As far as they could tell, the Dwarf, intent on his surveillance, never noticed the noodle vendor's three recent customers.

Relocation meant Ghost's turf. It also meant a little food and several hours' sleep for the exhausted runners. When Sam came to, he was ravenous. There was more food product and he wolfed down some of it to quiet his stomach. Both Dodger and Ghost had been busy while he had slept. They had contacted Sally, who assured them she was fine and that no one had bothered her. Ghost's tribesman who had been watching the squat had vanished and was presumed dead. That was definitely Greerson's style, according to the word on the street confirming the Dwarf's presence in Seattle. The mix of reassuring and unsettling news was topped off by Dodger's report about a benefit dinner at Club Voyeur.

"So you think that Drake might be at this dinner tonight?" Sam said thoughtfully.

"Verily. 'Tis the sort of affair that attracts his paramour Nadia Mirin, and she has responded positively to the invitation. Therefore, I conclude that he will attend as well. If so, we might be able to get close and plant some electronics on him. A tracer or a snitch, perhaps."

"I don't care about the electronics. I want to go there. I want to see him again for myself."

"Charging in blindly wouldn't be very bright," Ghost said. "It's a fool's errand."

"Especially at the Club," Dodger said gravely. "The proprietor is notoriously unforgiving about violence in his restaurant. 'Tis no place to settle matters, save by negotiation. That is, unless one has sufficient wealth to pour soothing oil on troubled waters."

"I don't want to talk and we're not ready to fight. All I want to do is look," Sam assured them.

"I thought you wanted him to think you were dead?"

"He doesn't need to see me."

"Pray tell, Sir Twist, just what do you have in mind?"

"Look, we're not going to be ready to take him on until we get more data. I think that I can get us some if I just get a look at him. When I use astral projection, I can see things about people."

"What kind of things?" Ghost asked suspiciously.

Sam didn't know how to explain it, not really understanding it himself. "Well, people have a kind of glow to them. It's pretty distinctive, so I might be able to learn to recognize him astrally. That could help. You know, like if he's in disguise or something. Then there's cyberware; it mutes the glow, damps it down, sort of. I think I could tell how much he's been modified. That would give us an idea of what we can expect from him."

"Sounds good," Dodger said.

"I thought you didn't believe in this magic stuff," Ghost said.

"Let's just say I'm having second thoughts." He gave them a weak smile, adding silently, *or else going completely crazy*.

Sam had picked a table where he would have a good view of the one reserved for Mirin and her guest. He didn't worry about Drake spotting him because of the special virtue of Club Voyeur. Sam's table was in the Lower Hall, separated from the Upper Hall by a wall of the finest one-way Transparex. At Club Voyeur, the wealthy and powerful dined undisturbed by the lower classes, while simultaneously being on display for the edification of those same folk. Sam thought that only vanity and arrogance would make someone voluntarily take part in an event in the Upper Hall. Club Voyeur was a bastion of class consciousness, from the magnificent platinum salt cellar in the shape of an ancient sailing ship that lay embedded in the Transparex to the waiters, whose haughtiness could only be softened by a sufficient bribe. The food, of course, was superb.

Sam's plan had already taken a turn for the worse. The long-range microphone concealed in his tote bag failed to penetrate the barrier between the halls. He would hear nothing of the conversations on the other side. He was not terribly disappointed, however. They would not likely say much of significance. Besides, he was relying on his eyes tonight.

Sam was well into his entree when the objects of his attention arrived. Nadia Mirin looked even better in person than she had in the society-page pictures. Attractive as she was, her beauty couldn't keep Sam from staring at her dark-suited escort. It was Jarlath Drake, groomed and dressed to perfection, just as when Sam last saw him in a garage in the Barrens.

The moment they sat down, the maitre d' came to their table. Sam could not hear the headwaiter's words, but the apologetic stance and hand motions were clear. Indicating an alcove near the entrance, the maitre d' solicitously led Drake away while a bevy of waiters instantly descended on Mirin to keep her entertained.

Drake reappeared in one of the many nooks in the multi-level lobby. Those small spaces were intended to provide privacy, screening occupants from view. But Drake had chosen one within Sam's line-of-sight. It was a fortuitous opportunity Sam did not want to pass up. Experimentally, he directed the microphone in that direction and was gratified to pick up the words of the maitre d'.

". . . gentleman has been awaiting your arrival, sir. He said he had a message to deliver to you personally and refused to leave. We, of course . . ."

"Leave us alone," Drake said, cutting the headwaiter off.

"Of course, sir," he said with a bow.

Drake stepped deeper into the alcove and leaned against the brass rail. He looked out the window at the lights of the metroplex. He would be completely out of the sight of anyone in the lobby or the Upper Hall.

The messenger who followed him in was a big, heavily muscled man who moved with the swagger of a tough who knows that he is dangerous. His chromed eye shields, button-disk cyber-ears, and strip-cut hair were street style, in contrast to the silk suit he wore. Though cut from expensive materials, the suit was not well-tailored enough to hide the ominous bulge under the man's left armpit. Another of Drake's outside contractors, Sam concluded.

"Trouble, Mr. Drake," the man said, softly as though he feared the response.

Drake sighed and continued staring out over the city. "Speak."

The messenger was obviously disconcerted by Drake's detached attitude. He fidgeted, reluctant to begin. Must be really bad news, Sam concluded.

"It's Wilson," the man began. "Some kind of inspector showed up and spooked him. He's rabbited."

Drake turned slowly to face the messenger. "Are you trying to tell me you've lost track of the doctor?"

The man became even more nervous. His eyes shifted away from Drake's face, then back again, sliding across the stony expression and coming to rest on Drake's collar. "Well, sort of. He's real tricky, you know. He—"

The man's words broke off as Drake's hand shot out and took him by the throat. He lifted the man, rapidly purpling, off his feet. The man's hands beat against Drake's arm and his feet kicked ineffectually. Calmly, showing no strain from the exertion of holding a struggling man aloft with a single hand, Drake spoke softly to him.

"You were charged with seeing that nothing happened to the doctor until I was ready to take care of him. If you have lost him, you have failed me most profoundly."

Relaxing his grip minutely, Drake allowed the man to get a grip on the strangling arm, supporting himself enough to choke out, "It was an accident."

It was obviously the wrong thing to say. Drake's eyes narrowed and with a twist of his wrist, he snapped the man's neck. The messenger coughed once, spraying blood, then went limp. Drake dropped the corpse and stood looking at it for a moment. He raised his arm and licked stray drops of blood from the sleeve of his pristine suit.

The maitre d' returned to discover the cause of the slight commotion. He stood frozen by the sight, his aplomb shattered by the results of Drake's sudden, lethal violence. Drake brushed past him on his way back to the dining room.

"Clean that up, please. He's had an accident."

Sam knew that Drake was not a man who balked at murder, but had never imagined he would dirty his own hands. Drake was more dangerous than he had thought and was obviously equipped for mayhem. Hadn't Lofwyr said the man was more than he seemed? The murder of the messenger proved the man was obviously enhanced. Sam congratulated himself on the success of tonight's recon. But the night wasn't over; the time had come to see just how much cyberware Drake was packing. Sam might not be able to tell just what Drake's enhancement did, but knowing their extent would let the runners gauge the opposition. The more of Drake's hidden secrets they could learn, the more likely they would eventually bring him down.

Sam focused his concentration, finding the shift to astral space easier this time. He looked across the restaurant. As usual, the shifted perceptions confused him initially, and he found himself unsure of Mirin's table. Then he found her. Her aura was strong and vibrant, making her even more beautiful. When Sam turned to her companion, he was shocked to see what sat coiled upon itself at the table by her side.

Its batlike wings were folded tightly on its back, the barbed upper joint level with the the arch of its long, sinuous neck. The wedge-shaped head had wide jaws filled with sharp teeth, and a tail with equally sharp barbs twisted around the chair where it sat. It was a miniature Dragon, its image pulsing with power and straining at a glistening constraint that restricted none of its motions but seemed to contain it in some unfamiliar way. Sam's attention was drawn to one golden claw, resting on the table. One talon wore a ring carved in the shape of a man with too-familiar features, Jarlath Drake. So it was true that Drake was, indeed, far more than he seemed. He was not a man at all. Drake didn't work for Haesslich; he *was* Haesslich!

Sam, still only a novice magician and uncomfortable with power, tumbled back into his body, retreating to the mundane senses that had served him so well. Across the restaurant, a suave, dark-haired man dined undisturbed with his lady friend.

Hadn't there been enough dragons in his life already?

He didn't know what to do next, but one thing was certain. He was in far over his head.

# 45

He had seen it before, but today the sight struck Dodger as odd. The feared and renowned street samurai Ghost Maker, known to closer associates as Ghost Who Walks

Inside, was making soykaf in the pitiful strip that served as the squat's kitchen. Maybe it was something about the slight awkwardness in the Indian's movements or the way he continually cocked his head as though listening for an anticipated signal. Something was out of place. As Ghost left the counter with a mug in each hand, Dodger saw a third mug lying on its side by the pot. That was it. In the past, Ghost had only prepared the brew for Sally, leaving the Elf to take care of himself.

"Thanks," Dodger said, taking the offered mug.

Ghost lowered himself to sit cross-legged on the floor. For several minutes, they sat quietly, sipping the steaming soykaf. Then Ghost said, "Whatever else he is, he's brave." Ghost shook his head. "Wants to haul a Dragon to court for murder."

"You sound like you're not so sure anymore. You wanting to bail out?"

Ghost looked at him bleakly. "Wanting has nothing to do with it."

*That's a lie,* Dodger thought. *There is a wanting that has an awful lot to do with it.* Dodger wasn't going to be the first to say it out loud. "Sam would understand. The situation is not what it seemed when you agreed to help him take down Drake."

"And where would that leave me, Elf? I gave my word before witnesses. I don't care that a lot of punks and cheap street hoods who call themselves samurai think the latest chrome and a bad attitude are all they need. There's a lot more to it than that. The old Japanese understood the difference almost as well as my ancestors. A warrior must be a man of honor. He keeps his word and is stronger than others, especially in his heart."

"Though you may only be a samurai of the streets, Ghost Who Walks Inside, you are a man of honor and a warrior."

"Am I?"

"Even the old samurai were men first."

The Indian quietly put down his cup. One of his hand razors slid from its ecto-myelin sheath. He scraped the sparkling needle of carbide steel against the tile of the floor, leaving tiny curls of plastic in its wake.

"What about you, Elf? Why haven't you run for the trees?"

"Honor is not the exclusive property of samurai, street

or otherwise,'' Dodger said in what he hoped was a sufficiently injured tone.

''Hasn't ever been your real worry, either.''

Ghost knew him too well. He could claim he was doing it for the thrill, as he had in the past. Ghost wouldn't believe that, either. Dodger could hardly admit that he wasn't really sure of all his reasons for doing it.

Ghost unfolded his legs and rose from the floor. ''They're coming,'' he said. He moved to face the window, leaning against the wall with studied nonchalance.

Ghost was right. After a moment, laughter drifted up from the alley. Sally clambered through the window first. Though dressed in a glittery jumpsuit that was a far haul from her regular armor-lined running rig, she had her cross-belted holster and scabbard snugged across her hips. The magesword caught on the sill, but Sam reached quickly to free it. A moment later, he climbed through. When he reached for Sally, she side-stepped his arm, only letting his lips brush her cheek. Not till then did Sam realize Dodger and Ghost were in the room. He greeted them with a sheepish smile.

Dodger smiled back. Only politeness would keep things civil. Ghost ignored Sam and spoke to Sally.

''Have you come to help?''

''Help with what? Do you need help with the cooking?'' Sally asked with a bright smile.

''*He* needs help,'' Ghost snapped, indicating Sam with a jerk of his head.

''Oh, no.'' She blew Sam a kiss, then sauntered across the room to throw herself down on the sleeping pad. She leaned on one elbow and stroked the magesword in its scabbard. ''I think he's doing just fine.''

Ghost's nostrils distended. ''Hasn't he told you what he found out?''

She tossed her head to flip her braid down her back. ''What do you want me to do about it?''

Dodger watched Sam look back and forth between the two of them, baffled by the subtext of their exchange. He looked ready to speak, but Ghost's next outburst kept him from doing so.

''What you do is your own fragging business. It doesn't affect me. But if you do nothing, it will affect him. It'll probably kill him. This run ain't against no two-bit Mr. Johnson anymore.''

"What makes you think I can make any difference?'' she shouted back.

"You've got the magic he can't control yet. Drek, woman! There're Dragons in this now.''

"There were Dragons in it before.''

"We can't face Dragons without magic.''

"Missile's as good as a fireball.''

"Kham's taking your lead. You could bring him in, and then we'd have a chance.''

"Kham's acting like an adult, unlike some people. He's a big boy and can make his own choices.''

Ghost bit down on a reply and stalked toward the window. Dodger thought the Indian intended to keep on going, but then Ghost pulled up and turned. When he spoke, his tone was quieter, his voice taking on a note of appeal.

"You know the three of us don't have enough jazz to take on Haesslich. Whether or not his plant in Renraku is a rogue operation, the Dragon is still head of United Oil Security in Seattle. That'll give him a fragging lot of resources.''

"But that would expose him to his superiors,'' Sam objected, ready to talk now that the subject was unequivocally business.

"Not necessarily,'' Sally said. "He's a canny old worm. He could come up with some way to make it look like you were after UniOil assets and then justify use of the Company's forces.''

"Even without UniOil security teams, there's the other Dragon and Hart,'' Ghost pointed out.

"If they're still working for him,'' Sam said.

"Any reason to believe they're not?'' Sally asked.

"Greerson,'' he said. "If Haesslich still had Hart and Tessien, why would he send Greerson after me?''

"Nobody said he sent Greerson,'' Sally said.

"Lady Tsung, do you know something? Is there another player in the game?''

Sally shrugged. "Possible. It's also possible that Greerson was working for Haesslich all along and you just haven't run into him till now. Even if I help, even if I coax Kham and his gang to play along, you boys are facing a real mess. It's going to take a lot of muscle to put Haesslich out of business.''

"Then you will help." Ghost made his question a statement.

Without a word, Sally rolled to her feet and strode to the kitchen counter to pour herself a cup of soykaf. Then she turned, leaned back against the counter, and drank off half the cup. Cradling the mug in both hands, she stood thinking for a moment or two.

"What about Lofwyr?" she said to Sam. "He sent you down to do his dirty work. Maybe he'd lend a hand, or at least finance some of this show."

"I can ask," Sam said.

To Dodger, it sounded as though Sam wasn't really sure he could. He would try because Sally had asked him to. The Elf wondered just what Sally expected to get out of this.

"Welcome to the team, Lady Tsung."

"Not so fast, Dodger. Let's wait and see if that Quebecker wizworm is going to put his money where his maw is. I'll play if he will."

# 46

Jacqueline noted the line through which the call was coming. It was the one set aside for Verner. He must have finally discovered the nature of his opponent. While initiating the trace, she checked the calendar. Two days ahead of prediction.

She launched the simulator that would present her Karen Montejac persona on a half-second delay, just enough time for the simulator program to match the image's facial movements to her words.

"Yes, Mr. Verner," she said, opening the line.

She had to give the boy credit. He was quick to hide his surprise at being named as she came online. "I want to speak with Lofwyr," he said.

"I'm sorry, but he is unavailable at the moment. May I give him a message?"

"I want to speak to him personally," Sam insisted. "Tell him it's about our deal."

"Do you wish to cancel?"

"No." His confusion and distress were evident to her practiced eye. "Look, I just need to talk to him. Things are different than he said they'd be, and I want to talk to him about Drake."

"I see," she responded with cool secretarial efficiency. "One of our arbitrators will be in touch. Six this evening at your current location?"

"Ah, yeah. Six is fine."

"Very good, then. You will see Mr. Enterich."

"But you don't know where I am."

"Mr. Enterich already has the information, sir, and I am sure he can provide a satisfactory response to any complaint you may have. Anything else, sir?"

"No, I guess not."

"Then have a good day, Mr. Verner." She broke the connection before she burst out laughing. She did enjoy it when the marks had no idea what was going on. Controlling her mirth, she opened a line to Lofwyr. The golden-scaled head appeared on the screen, and the Dragon fixed her with a stare. "Verner has reported, Lord. He will meet Mr. Enterich on the Drake matter at six, Seattle time."

The Dragon stayed on only long enough to pronounce the result, *"Satisfactory."*

Crenshaw nodded and Ridley kicked the door. The frame splintered and a section tore away, taking the lock plate, still fiercely resisting, with it. The door swung open to reveal a room screened from the afternoon sun by heavy drapes. Illumination came from a pair of red bulbs sitting baldly in cheap floor lamps supposed to look like candle scones.

Startled, a naked fat man scrambled up from the bed. His companion, a petite Asian woman, stayed where she was, wide-eyed in surprise and just as unclothed. She had no choice; she was tied spread-eagled to the bedposts.

Crenshaw let Ridley and Markowitz precede her into the room. The detective stopped just clear of the door, but the razorguy stalked in, catching the naked man as he lunged for his clothes.

"Now, now, John," Ridley said, grabbing the man by his hair and hauling his head back. The razorguy smiled as the man sagged in his grip, yelling in pain. "You shouldn't leave before we get acquainted."

Ridley pulled the john upright again and pumped two quick punches into his abdomen. The man doubled over, choking and starting to vomit. Ridley twisted the man's hair, forcing the john to spew away from him. When the man had retched himself dry, Ridley shoved him at the door. The man stumbled toward it, arms folded over his middle.

"Want these?" Ridley taunted, holding up the man's abandoned clothes. His laughter echoed in the hall as the man fled. "Oh, yeah. A real man."

"You didn't have to do that," Markowitz said.

"Oh, no?" Ridley gave him an innocent look. "You did the dossier, Marky. You know how tough he gets. With women, anyway. Maybe he'd have tried to take us all on. I mean, he could have hurt A.C. I was just taking a little precautionary measure."

"You're sick, Ridley," Markowitz said.

"Leastways I don't have to tie them down to get a girl. What about you, Marky? Ever manage it without a few straps?"

"Dump it, you two. We're here on business." Crenshaw turned to the woman on the bed. "We came to talk to you, Candy."

Candy stretched her neck, trying to reach the strap release with her teeth, but Crenshaw slapped her cheek and pulled the release out of reach.

"Not just yet, dear."

"I got nothing to say to you." Candy's eyes burned with hate, but she held still. "You guys just cost me 500 nuyen, and if you don't buzz now, Alfie's gonna set his stompers on your tails."

"Let him try, babe." Ridley held up his forearms and cocked his wrists inward. Nine centimeters of chromium steel blade snapped out from imbedded sheaths, glistening in the red light. "I eat stompers for breakfast, then go out for a real meal."

Crenshaw sat on the edge of the bed. "You see, Candy. In his crude way, my associate has expressed a truth. We have no need to fear your friend Alfie's bullies, as we are quite capable of protecting ourselves. You, on the other hand, have no one to protect you from us. You won't need it, though, if you'll just tell us what we want to know."

Candy set her jaw and turned her head away.

''We know that you've been seeing a corporate manager by the name of Konrad Hutten.''

No reaction.

''We also know you work for Congenial Companions, who arranged your liaisons with Hutten. Who's your boss, Candy?''

''Go check the Hall of Records.''

Crenshaw nodded to Ridley. He moved to the side of the bed where Candy could see him. Crouching, he brushed a blade down her cheek. Blood welled up in the shallow furrow it made.

''Reconsider, babe, or you're going to lose something near and dear to you.''

''Sit on your spur.''

''Bad answer, babe,'' Ridley's arm flashed down, slicing his spur through the girl's wrist. Her hand fell to the floor and was spattered with the blood pumping from her wrist. She started to scream.

''Ridley!'' Markowitz leaped forward, only to be stopped short by a bloody blade whose point was less than a centimeter from his right eye.

''It's biz, chummer. You want your own taste?'' Ridley said through clenched teeth.

Crenshaw ignored them and spoke to the girl. ''You're going to bleed to death unless you tell me what I want to know. Now, who do you work for?''

''You won't let me die?'' Candy's voice quavered. She was already going into shock.

''Of course not, dear. Who do you work for?''

''Help me first,'' she pleaded.

''No, dear. You have to talk first.''

Candy began to cry, her breathing irregular and ragged. ''The Elf bitch,'' she moaned. ''Calls herself Hart.''

''Now that's a name I have heard before. You should have spoken up sooner, Candy. There was no need for you to get hurt.'' Crenshaw stood up. ''Markowitz, tie off her arm, then call a DocWagon.''

Markowitz gave Ridley one last glare and stepped around the razorguy to reach the bed. With swift motions, he freed the vacant restraining strap and applied it to Candy's arm as a tourniquet. By the time he was done, she had fainted.

''You didn't have to maim her,'' he said.

''Null the static, Marky.'' Ridley tapped the flat of one

spur against his chrome arm. ''Her kind's always got credit socked away. She can buy the tech. They can make her faster, stronger, better!''

Ridley's wild laughter made Crenshaw's stomach go sour. The man was over the edge and would have to be watched. If it came to it, she could send him against Hart. He probably couldn't take the Elf, but it would get him out of Crenshaw's hair for good.

# 47

The street corner was like a hundred others in the metroplex this time of day. Hurrying by were corporate daywagers, salarymen, and office ladies, all trying to make it home before the city's nightlife took over the streets. Or else heading that way to ready themselves to join it. Already the first wave of night breeds was out. Chippers, chemguzzlers, and jackheads were panhandling for their next fixes while rockerfans, glitzqueens, and underage wannabees hustled off to the next scene-or-be-scene. The only thing that made this corner unique was the ebony Mitsubishi Nightsky rolling slowly to a stop by the curb.

The doors on the curbside of the limousine opened. A burly Ork rolled out of one to stand stern and vigilant sentry. The gray livery she wore was tailored to enhance her already considerable presence. Through the open door, Sam could see that the driver wore a similar uniform; he was also an Ork.

The back door gaped on a cool, dark interior. A woman who he recognized as Lofwyr's secretary sat in a bucket jumpseat that backed against the partition separating the sybaritic rear compartment from the control center of the front. Across from her sat a man whose face was unfamiliar. The man, so relaxed he could only be the rightful owner of the vehicle, was slim and well-dressed. Fiftyish and distinguished, he wore his gray hair trimmed in a slightly old-fashioned cut. When he smiled, a glint of gold showed among his teeth.

"Please get in, Mr. Verner," the man said. "The sidewalk is no place to transact business."

Sam ran his fingers through his hair, a signal to Ghost that the contact had arrived. He heard the sound of the Indian's motorcycle starting, but the noise of traffic quickly swallowed the sound. Ghost was ready to follow him, for they'd anticipated the possibility. "I guess that will be all right."

Sam ducked his head and slid into the Nightsky, then sank into the luxurious leather seat. Without a touch, the door closed silently, and the view outside the window began to move. Sam had not felt the Ork return to her seat or the car begin to roll. He turned to his host. "You are Mr. . . ."

"Enterich." He held out a hand.

Sam started to extend his own, then froze, staring at the silver ring the man wore. It was sculpted in the form of a Dragon. Haesslich had worn a silver Dragon ring when appearing as Mr. Drake.

"You are admiring my ring. An exquisite piece of work, is it not? It is a family heirloom that dates, I believe, from the fourteenth century. The image is something of a pun. You see, I had rather ambitious forebears. They thought the image of a firedrake was a better insignia for an up-and-coming family than a feathered pond paddler."

"I don't get it."

"A drake, Mr. Verner." Sam must still have looked perplexed, for his host added, "The firedrake was sometimes called simply a drake. In German, Enterich means drake . . . as in a male duck."

Sam gave a nervous chuckle.

"Do you believe in destiny, Mr. Verner?"

"Never used to."

"Which implies that you do now."

Sam wasn't really sure anymore, but what was it to this fellow? "Why do you ask?"

"You seemed to react so strongly to my ring. Perhaps you might have taken my ring or name as a sign. Many people have such beliefs these days. Part of the revival of things magical, I suppose."

"No," Sam said. "I didn't take it as a sign of anything."
*Except that you might be a Dragon yourself.*

"Ah, then it's a pleasure to deal with a rational man. I'm

sure that will make everything so much easier. Now, perhaps we can discuss your complaint regarding Lofwyr?''

"Before we get down to that, will you permit me to phone my associates to let them know all is well?. They weren't expecting me to be picked up.''

"I understand, Mr. Verner. Karen, place a call for our guest.''

"Ah, I've got my own, thanks,'' Sam said, tapping his head.

Enterich seemed amused. "I see. Karen, lower the communications barrier, please. Mr. Verner will make his own call.''

Sam settled back, rocking his head forward onto his chest, the position he had seen regular head-phone users adopt. He closed his eyes as though concentrating on sending the commands to dial. Instead, he focused on breaking through to astral space.

The transition came quickly, and he opened his astral eyes to look at Mr. Enterich, who surprised Sam by still appearing as a man. When Sam turned to Karen, he saw the furry being whom he had known as Jacqueline the Sasquatch. So his vision hadn't failed, and he could still pierce illusions. As a precaution, he checked the Orks in the front seat. They were just Orks, though heavily implanted with cyberware. Abandoning his pose of making a call, he returned to the mundane. "All taken care of,'' he said.

His host's smile was warm. "Fine. Now, back to your concern about Lofwyr's dealings with you?''

"You've already expressed some of it.''

It was Enterich's turn to look puzzled. "Which is?''

"That Lofwyr knew Drake was Haesslich. You've said as much, and *I* never told you.''

"That was not intended as duplicity, Mr. Verner. Lofwyr did suggest that all was not as it seemed with Mr. Drake. Allowing you to discover that fact for yourself and to demonstrate continued determination to proceed assured the Dragon that your effort was worthy of his support.''

"Then what does he plan to do?''

"Lofwyr leaves the planning to you. His own involvement in this matter is not politic.''

"So he expects me to tackle Haesslich on my own?'' Sam was incredulous. What did a Dragon think a Human could do if the Dragon himself was afraid to get involved?

"No need for distress, Mr. Verner. I can safely say that Lofwyr does not expect you to tackle Haesslich directly or without support. When you have made your plans, contact me. If your scheme shows a reasonable chance of success, we can arrange certain resources to aid in the effort. Discreetly, of course."

"What kind of resources?"

"Supplies, equipment, and cash are the easiest to obtain, as long as your needs are within reasonable bounds. Additional, nonspecialist personnel might also be arranged. In the meantime, please accept the services of my aide Karen Montejac as a liaison and advisor."

Sam looked at the woman he knew to be a Sasquatch and a magician. Did she know that he knew? "Mind if I call you Jaq?"

"I'd find it charming," she said, smiling cheerfully.

# 48

"Jenny?"

"Right here, boss." The decker's response came from Hart's terminal.

"Any word on Candy?"

"Nothing new. She's still sedated and we haven't yet matched anybody to the descriptions of her assailants. Good thing she's got replacement coverage on her insurance policy."

"I wouldn't send any couriers to that thing without it after what it did to the first girl. Candy will be fine in a couple months."

"Hey, boss, you think they hit her because she was a courier?"

"That's been worrying me. She's the only one who's been to the arcology twice."

"She was a busy girl before you took her on," Jenny said. "Maybe it was something personal."

"Let's hope so. Keep looking."

"Affirmative."

Hart went back to studying the files Major Fuhito had

supplied on known runners. They offered slim hope, but she kept looking for any clue that would lead her to Verner through his associates. No one walked the shadows alone; but how could there be so little on the one name they had? This Dodger was almost like a shadow, but any decker as good as his file indicated would be elusive. She had just finished reading it for the tenth time when Jenny interrupted.

"Boss, I don't think the attack on Candy was personal. Alfie's got company downstairs."

"What kind of company?"

"Woman calling herself Alice Crenshaw insists on seeing you."

"Crenshaw? Renraku security?"

"How many can there be?"

"And she wants to see the owner, right?"

"Not like that, boss. She asked for you by name."

That was trouble. For Renraku's deputy security chief to drop in on the enemy for a chat was definitely not standard procedure.

"Jenny, can you still catch tonight's courier?"

"Affirmative."

"Have her tell the thing that tomorrow night's joyride is going to be an end run. Things are getting too hot."

Crenshaw followed her guide up the stairs. She was not unduly worried. Physical security on the building was not enough to keep her from getting out if Hart proved difficult or unstable. Not that she expected such a reaction. From what she had heard, this Hart was a total pro, mercenary to the core. Crenshaw was confident she'd be able to reason with the Elf.

The over-oiled hunk of Free California beefcake opened a last door and stepped inside.

"Thanks, Ralphie," she said, brushing past him.

"It's Alfie."

She ignored him, intent on forming a first-hand impression of the internationally renowned Hart. Hart was seated, but it was obvious she was tall, like most of her kind. She also had the smooth Elven skin, oval face, and delicate, foxy features that men, norm and Elf alike, fawned over. If Hart was a bit on the scrawny side, that was a popular preference, too. Crenshaw reminded herself that Hart had to have brains, too. She'd never have lasted this long in the trade.

Hart made no effort to stand or welcome her visitor. She just sat back in her chair with a look of calm expectancy. Her hands were out of sight behind the desk. Crenshaw pulled up a chrome and plastic chair in front of the desk, ignoring the stuffed armchair already there. Hart still said nothing.

Crenshaw chose her words carefully. "Before you do something we might both regret, let me say I've only come here to talk. I thought that we might be able to see eye-to-eye, one professional woman to another. I also feel obliged to tell you that my associates nearby would not take kindly to any show of violence."

"Are they loaded for Dragon?" Hart asked softly.

"Excuse me?"

"I have a feathered friend nearby who would also, as you say, not take kindly to violence."

"Ah, the serpent who helped you extract Samuel Verner from the arcology. Good. If we've got a matching of muscle, we can get down to business." Hart inclined her head, which Crenshaw took as agreement. "How is Mr. Verner?"

"I wouldn't know."

*An admirable poker face,* Crenshaw thought. "Come now, Ms. Hart. I know that you and he are working together."

"Then you know more than I do."

"Are you saying that Samuel Verner is not behind this plot to suborn a member of the Renraku Special Directorate?"

Hart frowned. "I don't like making your job any easier, Crenshaw, but Verner is someone I'd like to see out of the picture. He's been a bit of trouble for me."

Crenshaw found a falling out among the runners interesting, but not unusual. "Whether or not you admit to working with Verner, your own involvement is clear. I also know that you have turned Konrad Hutten, though we have yet to determine what hold you have on him."

"If you have found a weak link in your corporate chain, why not just cut it out?"

Crenshaw found herself enjoying the interplay. A worthy opponent was so rare. If this play was to be the one to set her up for life, such admirable opposition would make it doubly memorable. "I have my own interests, Ms. Hart. As long as I am satisfied there's been no breach of Renraku security, I can afford to wait and deal with each aspect of this situation in turn.

"At this moment, I am interested in Samuel Verner. You say you'd also like him out of your hair. Perhaps this is one time we can be allies rather than adversaries."

Hart's facial muscles tightened slightly, which Crenshaw took as a sign the Elf was considering the possibilities. She knew she was halfway home when Hart asked, "What do you suggest?"

"Since Verner is giving us both such a hard time from the shadows, perhaps we can coax him out into the light. I know he's involved in an attempt on the Special Directorate, but you say he's not part of your operation. Whatever the case, neither of us wants him to touch the project. You, because you want it for yourself; me, because it belongs to my corporation.

"If he were to believe he had a chance to get what he wanted and keep it away from you at the same time, wouldn't he take it?"

"Possibly," Hart admitted quickly. "But what do I get out of it?"

"The obvious. Your competition is eliminated."

"While you shut down my own operation from the inside."

Crenshaw smiled. "Oh, no. At least not right away. Doctor Hutten is still a vital member of the project. You will have other chances."

"While you watch his every move."

"I didn't promise things would be easy."

Hart's operation had definitely become more difficult now that someone at Renraku knew about it. The Elf guessed that Crenshaw would let both her and Verner into the arcology to contact Hutten. Hart would anticipate Crenshaw's trap, but her associate Verner would not. The Elf could throw Verner to the proverbial wolves, escaping in the confusion and trying to take Hutten with her. It was exactly what Crenshaw would do in her shoes. It wasn't a sure bet, but what other choice did Hart have? Her big problem was Crenshaw's knowledge of the operation to subvert Hutten. With security on full alert, Hart's only chance to pull off the extraction would be during the confusion around Verner's capture.

"Crenshaw, your offer stinks. But you don't leave me much choice. Verner has to go down, and quickly. There's still the question of when." Hart flicked a finger at the screen of the terminal on her desk. "Our man was to meet with . . . me tomorrow night, sort of a progress report. Since you're onto him, I suppose you'll cancel it."

Good counterthrust, Crenshaw thought. Hart was trying to rush Crenshaw's own preparations, no doubt hoping Crenshaw would miss something or leave a loose end that would unravel the Renraku trap enough to leave her room to squirm free. Well, Sato was pushing for a resolution, too. Crenshaw would be equally happy to have Verner's hide sooner rather than later. Besides, Hart might just rush herself into a mistake. "Not at all. Just what we need to draw Verner out of the shadows where we can squash him."

"Aren't you afraid our man will run?"

Crenshaw smiled to show her confidence. "The project's made too little progress," she lied. "If you pull him out now, you'll get next to nothing for all your work."

Crenshaw was certain that now Hart was guaranteed to try to pull Hutten out. If Hart believed she could catch Crenshaw off guard, the Elf would be less thorough in her preparations. Crenshaw's trap would be ready to spring, and she'd be more than ready for the Elf. Once they'd smoked Verner, Hart was next. Whether the Elf were captured or killed didn't matter to Crenshaw. Either way, Crenshaw would get the credit for exposing the traitor, eliminating the renegade, and stopping the notorious shadowrunner Hart.

"There is one small hole in your plan to be rid of Verner," Hart said. "He can't show up unless he knows about the meet."

"Null difficulty," said Crenshaw. *I could just let you tell him, dear, but then I have to keep up the show of believing you.* "That can be arranged."

Hart was relieved when the door closed behind Crenshaw. The woman was a manipulator of the first water, but her twisted proddings confirmed Hart's fears. Crenshaw knew too much, and it wasn't likely that the rest of Renraku security knew any less. Time to cut the losses. She'd pull the thing out tonight if she thought it could be done.

Now Verner had showed up again. All her efforts had failed to locate him, and here was Crenshaw offering to lure him into the open for her. The woman seemed obsessed with the fellow, unable to accept Hart's denial that she was not connected with the man. Crenshaw might even think Hart was lying to shield Verner. Well, that suited Hart fine. Let Crenshaw make all the false assumptions she pleased. That might give Hart all the slack she needed.

She knew Crenshaw would expect her to make an attempt to pull the thing out tomorrow night, though Hart wasn't sure whether the woman knew about the thing they'd planted in her precious Special Directorate. Crenshaw's force would be waiting to keep poor misled Doctor Hutten within Renraku's warm embrace while also disposing of some troublesome shadowrunners. Hart had faced and beaten more elaborate, well-laid traps than this one. In fact, Crenshaw's complicity would get her inside the security perimeter. After that, she only had to worry about herself. Renraku security would be waiting for her to grab her inside man, but she had no intention of doing so. All Hart really needed was the data.

That was now her big concern. She hoped the bitch Crenshaw was bluffing when she said the team hadn't been too successful, because Haesslich would be very unhappy if his toy had nothing to give him. The doppelganger's preliminary reports had all been optimistic, hinting at everything the Dragon hoped for. If Crenshaw was telling the truth, that thing might be playing its own game. Wilson had assured them of its complete loyalty, but he'd been wrong before. Hart remembered the terror as she hid in the shower stall with the thing lurking just beyond. It had nearly taken her instead of Hutten because Wilson had miscalculated the thing's reaction time to the drugs. Haesslich had implied that he knew something about the doppelganger that old Doc Wilson didn't, but the worm hadn't shared the secret with Hart. The Dragon only insisted that the thing would never betray *him*. So did that mean it might betray *her*?

Was it worth the risk? Haesslich had been ready to see her killed because she knew about his plan. From all she'd heard, he dealt harshly with subordinates who failed him, no matter who was at fault. Continued service to the old worm seemed to offer diminishing possibilities of coming out of this alive.

Letting Verner walk into the trap could solve a lot of problems. With the proper arrangements, she could make sure he got killed. The doppelganger, too. Not even Haesslich could blame her if Renraku security wasted his toy. Her contract to protect the Dragon's investment in this operation would be completed.

Verner aside, the doppelganger's usefulness was over. Crenshaw knew about the mole in the AI project. If Verner walked into the trap, Renraku would snap him up and keep their secrets. If Hart went in as well, she might still manage to pull the data out. Whether Hart managed to deliver the doppelganger and its data to Haesslich or whether the thing remained within the arcology after tomorrow night, this run was coming to a close.

She sat back, weighing her chances and pondering how she might survive the finale.

# 49

The gray light of predawn began to filter in through the black-out curtains over the windows of the burnt-out tenement Ghost had chosen for the strategy conference. Of them all, only Karen Montejac still looked fresh, but Sam knew it was only an illusion. He wondered if the others noticed.

"Any other ideas?" he asked.

"Yes," Sally said, rubbing her eyes. "Sleep."

"Verily, Sir Twist. 'Twould seem the best plan of a bad lot. We have been over this ground enough. Unless something new turns up, our only option is to winkle Hutten out of the arcology."

"And I still say going in and trying to drag him out is too dangerous," Ghost grumbled.

"I know, Ghost," Sam said. "I know. But there's no other way. Hutten is the evidence we need against Haesslich."

Ghost folded his arms over his chest and frowned. "You want the wizworm down, take him down. Physically. Before he gets you. Too much risk to hit the arcology."

"That's not the way I want to do it," Sam said wearily.

"This is a matter of justice, not vengeance. Haesslich isn't a no-data runner. He's chosen to live in the corporate world by taking a job as security director for United Oil. He's even got a SIN. When he took that job, he became a part of society and he's subject to society's laws. I intend to see that he pays the full penalty under that law. Under the law. Not outside it."

Ghost shrugged and turned his face away. The silence in the room grew. Sam looked to Dodger for support, but the Elf wouldn't meet his eyes. He knew better than to try Sally. He was beginning to feel abandoned when Jaq tentatively cleared her throat.

"You are aware that there may be no alternative to killing the Dragon? None of the plans we've considered offers a reasonable chance of success to safely obtain the evidence you want. Sanction may be the only means of stopping Haesslich."

Sam looked at her, imaging the fur-framed face behind the blonde mask of Karen Montejac. Did another face, that of Lofwyr, hide behind her words? Killing was a prerogative of the state. Any individual who took that right into his own hands was committing murder, and murder was a sin. Sam was not ready to add that one to the list his soul had accumulated in recent days.

*Lord, why have you made it so difficult?*

The others did not believe there was hope of bringing the Dragon to any justice other than their own rough brand. Were they so wrong? He knew what Haesslich was. He feared what he might do if left to pursue his schemes. Was Sam's own soul worth more than the unnumbered souls who would be tainted or destroyed if Haesslich were allowed to live?

He was tired to his bones. Maybe too tired. Theirs was the easier solution. Kill the Dragon and be done. But was it a moral solution?

And if it came to killing the Dragon, how could they go about it? He had seen Tessien destroy Bengay's panzer, and Tessien was smaller, presumably less powerful, than Haesslich. It would take enormous firepower. Anything that would hurt the Dragon could also kill anyone near it. If innocents died, Sam and the others would be as bad as Haesslich. It was Ghost who'd suggested killing the Dragon. He was the warrior; he understood guns and tactics. Maybe

Ghost could devise a way to get to the Dragon without involving other people.

When Sam turned to where Ghost had been standing, the spot was empty. The Indian crouched instead by the door, an Ingram in his right hand. The others in the room had shaken off their lethargy and were also tensed for action. Sam reached for his own weapon.

After listening a moment, Ghost announced, "Kham's coming."

Breathing a sigh of relief, Sam reseated his half-drawn gun. A moment later, Sam heard the scuff of feet on the wooden stairs. The door opened and a slightly out-of-breath Kham stomped in.

"You're late, Sir Tusk."

"Dodger," Sam chided. "Glad you decided to show, Kham."

"In your ear, Suitboy," the Ork snarled, walking past him to Sally. "Just turned down an invitation to a party you might be interested in. A lot of Raku types, heavy metal boys, gonna be celebrating the coming out of a certain important person."

"When?" Sally asked.

"Where?" Sam asked.

Kham threw Sam a sour look and again directed his words to Sally. "Shuttle to Sea-Tac lands at eleven. De last stop is de Raku arc where dey expect to board de guest of honor."

Dodger whistled. "The master worm calls and his puppy comes running. Alas for the plotters, Renraku security has tumbled to their scheme. They shall detain Hutten."

"Maybe," Sam said. "I've heard that the corporations sometimes wait until a runaway tries to board an outbound plane before they step in to take him back. The added embarrassment can make a renegade more tractable. If they're waiting at the airport, they may not know he's running to the Dragon. We could make the snatch there."

Kham guffawed. "Oh dem Red Raku boys is waiting at de airport all right. Lotsa dem. Don't need mega-muscle and heavy artillery for a flabby lab rat."

"If they're ready for the Dragon, we can let them have him. Let them dance with the worm. If there are any pieces left after the fireworks, then maybe you can satisfy yourself.

If Raku is loaded for Dragon, there'll be no way we can snatch Hutten at the airport," Ghost said.

"Then we'll have to get to him someplace else," Sam announced. "This is our chance. Once he's outside the arcology walls, we'll have a better chance of grabbing him because arcology security won't be in our way anymore. Kham, how exactly did you find this out?"

The Ork never had a chance to answer.

Automatic weapons fire punched through the curtains, stitching a line across the interior wall. Kham stood in the way of that deadly pattern. Collapsing across the table, he grunted in pain and surprise.

A second later, the perforated drapes bellied inward under the impact of a chromed whirlwind of an assassin. Sally was bowled over as the invader tumbled into the room. Slicing his way clear of the entangling fabric with his twin spurs, the razorguy launched himself at the Ork. Ghost fired a burst with his Ingram, but the bullets sped through empty air.

Kham stirred on the table and rolled over in time to see the razorguy coming for him. "Ridley, you crazy—"

"Eat this, tusker," Ridley screamed as he sliced down and through the Ork's upraised arm and into the meat of Kham's thigh. The Ork howled and hit the floor in a welter of blood. Ridley didn't spare his fallen foe a glance before vaulting over the table.

Sam had no doubt about the razorguy's next target; he could see his own image reflected in the mirror eyes. He fumbled for his gun, knowing that even if he managed to shoot the wildman, the drug would not take effect before Ridley butchered him.

Time seemed to move with excruciating slowness. Sam watched Ridley land and absorb the shock on flexed knees. At the same instant, Sam saw Ghost beyond him, raising his Ingram. Ridley straightened, rising up from the cover the table had provided. Sally, recovering from her collision with the razorguy's initial rush, was also rising, right into Ghost's line of fire.

Sam's hand closed on the grip of the Lethe. Ridley stepped forward, raising an arm tipped with silver death. There was a roaring in Sam's ears as he watched the bloodied blade begin its descent.

The chrome arm connected, but not with Sam. Jaq yelped

with pain as she swept the lethal limb away from Sam's head with her own arm. Ridley, knocked off balance, recoiled, turning his eyes on Sam's rescuer.

The delay was all Ghost needed. First one, then the other, of his Ingrams sent slugs crashing into the half-metal body of the razorguy. Ridley spun under the impact, but most of Ghost's bullets had missed his meat. Sparking and bleeding, Ridley turned again toward Sam, a feral snarl on his face. Ghost's next bursts sent the razorguy jerking spasmodically against the wall. He rebounded, leaving a gory smear, and collapsed to the floor.

One gun already holstered and a 25-centimeter Bowie knife replacing it in his hand, Ghost knelt by the shattered assassin.

"Tusker ain't gonna talk now." Ridley coughed blood, but he smiled. "Not bad for an Injun, wuss. Bet you can't do it to my face."

"You're in no shape to fight."

"They'll rebuild me, trog-lover, then I'll eat your heart."

"To rebuild you, they'll need a brain," Ghost said softly as he shoved his blade up under Ridley's chin, through the soft tissue and into the base of his skull. The razorguy spasmed once.

The stench of excrement swept over the sharp odor of expended propellent. The room was quiet again.

"Any more?"

"There were two in the hall," Dodger said, reslinging his Sandler machine pistol. "They have gone the way of all meat."

"Car and driver in the street," Sally said. A secondary explosion punctuated her words. "Now that it's quiet again, I'm going to take a nap." She slid down against the wall, leaned her head against the window sill, and closed her eyes.

Sam walked around the table to where Jaq was tending Kham. The Ork was a mess. Blood was everywhere. "Is he? . . ."

Jaq shook her head. "Not yet. His armor stopped the bullets. The bruises won't be bothering him much. The arm is nearly severed and the major muscles of the leg cut up pretty bad. He's going to be spending a lot of time in hospital."

"Can't you do anything?"

"I'm no miracle worker. He needs a doctor, and a good one at that."

"There goes our muscle power," Ghost said. The only sign of his recent deed was the blood covering his right hand. The knife was nowhere to be seen.

"What do you mean?" Sam asked.

"Kham's boys won't run with us if he's down. Without those extra bodies, there's no way to pull it off."

"What about your tribe?" Ghost's instant stone-face told Sam he'd said the wrong thing.

"They have no stake in this."

Ghost was right, of course. The warriors wouldn't risk their lives for someone who was not a member of their tribe. Ghost wouldn't stop Sam from asking, but the Indian's followers were unlikely to risk their lives to satisfy some Anglo's idea of justice, especially if he were ignoring the good advice of their chief.

There were, however, others who did have an interest in the matter at hand and who had no need for Ghost's approval. Help from them entailed another whole set of obligations, but Sam saw no other way to get the force he needed in time to take advantage of Hutten's departure.

"Well, Jaq," he said. "Looks like we'll need some of your people after all."

# 50

The ebon boy in the glittering cloak raced along the pulsing paths of the metroplex air traffic control computers. He ran unerringly, headed for a destination he had visited before. Up a flight of stairs and through a shining door he went, making his way among the hierarchy of subsystems and past barriers as though they weren't there. Reaching the command center at last, he dipped a hand into the data stream and left behind a command. Then he was gone, slipping out past countermeasures that never knew he was there.

The Aztechnology airport shuttle would be delayed on the Mitsuhama pad. In its place, a Federated Boeing Commuter tilt-wing shuttle with Aztechnology markings would land at Renraku Pad 23 precisely on time at 10:42 P.M.

A stop at the transmitter controller belonging to Hadley's Hacks made sure that the launch signal went out along with the regular traffic between the innocent Mr. Hadley and his roving cabbies. With that signal, Sam's plan went into motion. The snatch team was headed for their destination and he needed to be there to meet them. The ebon boy spread his cloak and launched himself into the dark sky of the Matrix, soaring toward the great black pyramid of Renraku.

He circled the construct cautiously, looking for any hint that the system was at other than normal status. Seeing nothing after three passes, he alighted near the same back door he had used during the expedition with Sam. He entered with the code he had stolen and was relieved to find the node quiet. In his excitement, he had forgotten to activate his masking program, and he did so now. Then he rested for a moment, considering the best path to the security systems monitoring Landing Pad 23.

The arcology was still being built. It stood to reason that certain security systems had to be installed during construction. Installation meant plans, and to Dodger, plans meant a map. He ran a path through the elevators' maintenance monitors, to the systems used by the installers, and back up their lines to the master plan.

Dodger slid into a subprocessor and satisfied himself that the pattern of energy pulsing in the walls was the one he sought. Fingers tapped display instructions as the ebon boy waved his hands in pseudomystical gestures. A map of the control system for security monitors glowed into existence. Another gesture, and the image scrolled and expanded, highlighting the intermediary junction between his current location and the subprocessor overseeing slaved security nodes guarding Landing Pad 23. He scanned the path and set out again, leaving his handiwork to dissolve back into nothingness.

Two nodes later, he noticed an odd translucency to the constructs. Everything appeared as though overlaid with a deep, almost mirrorlike, polish. The ebon boy halted and stared at his own reflection in the walls of the message center. The pulsing circuitry characteristic of the architecture's construct imagery seemed to be retreating, vanishing under the glare of reflective surfaces.

Turning to flee, the ebon boy came featureless face to featureless face with an ivory girl, her jet cloak sparkling with highlights as though made from inky diamond.

"For myself, there was hope of your return."

Dodger could not find words.

Fingers flew, seeking the correct program initiations to escape the node, as the ebon boy's head twisted in search of an exit. A hand slapped at the escape pad, but the mirrors only flashed brighter.

"For myself, there was desire of your company," the girl said, her voice more seductive than any Dodger had ever heard from a fleshly woman. She reached out a hand to caress his cheek. "Come."

And they were elsewhere.

The new construct was walled with myriad jet dark mirrors, each a small segment of the walls, floor, or ceiling. There was no apparent entrance or exit. The ivory girl, her slim Elven body hidden by the folds of her cloak, was almost invisible where she stood in the center of the chamber. All he could see clearly was her elegantly shaped head. Though the head had neither hair nor definite features, Dodger was unassailably convinced of its beauty and femininity. She was a cyber siren, calling to his soul, anima to his animus, a part sundered from him by flesh but now here and waiting.

If only he could move and take her in his arms.

"He's not all there, you know," a new voice said.

Dodger was suddenly aware of another persona in the construct. On the far side of the chamber stood another female figure, her outlines blurred and refracted as though encased in water ice. She looked to be wearing biker leathers, though made of chrome rather than black synthleather. Her long platinum hair hung in a sheet down one side of her face, obscuring the left lens of her golden wraparound sunglasses.

"Who are you, Maiden in Ice?"

"My friends call me Jenny. You must be the Dodger."

"Guilty, Lady Jenny. Have you any idea where we are or what she is?"

"She?"

"Our lovely hostess."

"Your interface circuitry's gone bad, Dodger. *Lovely* is

hardly the word I'd use for the most wizard hunk of beef-cake I've ever seen.''

Dodger listened to her words, staring the whole time at their hostess. This was not an ordinary manifestation of the Matrix. ''I believe my circuits are fine. Jenny, I begin to suspect that we are in the presence of history.''

''Swell. I just want to go home.''

''Home,'' a lovely contralto voice said, but Dodger suspected that Jenny heard a bass, masculine voice.

One mirror panel of the wall lit up, a brilliant white that focused into an image of Holly Brighton, international sim-sense star. ''I'm so glad you could join me tonight,'' Holly's face said before her image froze.

Another panel on the opposite wall flashed on, and an aged, flabby man stood on a bare stage backed with curtains. ''We have a really big shew for you tonight,'' he announced as the image locked into immobility.

A third panel blinked on. This time it was an intense-eyed young man in what looked like turn-of-the-century chic. He stood in some kind of conference hall and pointed at the picture recorder as he said, ''Evil, pure and simple, by way of—''

The rest of the panels flared to life, images flickering on and off with eye-searing speed. Dodger couldn't make sense of any of them until, after a few moments, they slowed. Each panel flashed its own random series of images from the arcology's security cameras and internal broadcast channels. One slowed further, picture rolling over picture, until it settled on an image of a flight deck. Another flickered to a halt on the identical scene. A third followed and a fourth until all had frozen on the same picture. Surrounding him as completely as had the mirrors were thousands of images of Landing Pad 23.

# 51

On Landing Pad 23, Crenshaw was getting a little ner-vous. It was 10:38 and still no sign of Verner, ''Addison,'' she called on her communicator, "any sign of Matrix penetration?"

There was a delay before he answered. "Don't think so. A few glitches in the system, but nothing that looks like an enemy decker. Nothing's tripped the triggers in the subprocessors around the pad."

"Contact me the minute anything shows. Crenshaw out."

Verner's team was running a deep enough game that by now they should have a decker in place on overwatch. Could Verner's decker be so good that he'd slipped standard arcology IC and Addison, too?

She stepped out onto the landing deck where she could crane her head around to check the observation deck. The wind whipped her hair across her face, but the strands did not sting her replacements as they would meat eyes. A slight adjustment reduced the glare of reflections and let her view the small group of people watching the pad from the warmth and safety of the Transparex-shielded lounge. Sato stood next to the brass rail, hands clasped behind his back. To his left were his special bodyguards, and to his right were Marushige and Silla. Crenshaw frowned at the unwanted presence of the security director. This was supposed to be *her* show.

A squad of white-uniformed ground crew scurried out of the operations control room, heading for their stations. The shuttle would be on its approach. A slight stir traveled among the passengers waiting behind the boarding barrier. Anticipation, she thought, but not that of tourists eager for vacation. Except for Hutten, every one of those people was a Renraku security agent, substituted for the real shuttle passengers at Crenshaw's orders. They had been told to expect runners before or during the shuttle landing.

And where were those runners? Crenshaw's feed from the arcology air traffic monitor reported only the Aztechnology shuttle inbound. Ground perimeter patrol was observing only normal traffic. The double squad of Red Samurai standing in reserve inside the building effectively blocked off any approach Verner's people could make from inside, assuming they had penetrated the arcology earlier.

She walked over to the group by the boarding barrier. Hutten stood near the middle. The shadowy lighting of the pad threw his features into high relief, lending them a savage cast she had never noticed before. Suitable, she thought.

He'd been acting like a bear stirred out of its den in mid-winter ever since she'd approached him that morning to say Hart was concerned that he make his meeting. Despite Crenshaw's assurances that she was part of Hart's operation, he probably feared some kind of setup. He was right, of course. But he wasn't the target tonight. His turn would come later.

"Shuttle will be here soon. You can relax."

Hutten glanced around at the others waiting on the deck and hugged his briefcase to his chest. He leaned over and whispered to Crenshaw, "Some of these others are armed. Something must be wrong."

"Don't worry. It's 2051. Anyone with a brain has a gun. Relax," she said mildly. "Here comes the shuttle."

The cabin hummed with the throb of engines as the Commuter's wing tilted up from its forward flight configuration, turning the propellers into rotors for landing. Seeing the slanted walls of the Renraku arcology gleaming outside the windows, Jacqueline felt the heady anticipation of impending action.

With the grudging approval of his fellow runners, Sam had split the group into two teams. Jaq's was arcology-bound to snatch the substitute Hutten before he boarded the shuttle. He would never reach the airport and the Renraku security ambush waiting for him and his sponsor. While she and Sam were arranging armament matters with Enterich, they had been informed that Haesslich was not going to be at the airport after all. The Dragon would leave the pickup to his agents, taking delivery of his goods at, what was to him, a safer location—a deserted section of the United Oil dockyards. Sam had expressed relief to hear the news because it meant no bystander would get hurt when he led the other team to Haesslich. It was his plan to confront the Dragon while Hart and Tessien dealt with the disappointed Renraku presence at the airport. He called it a minor justice.

She checked the clock on the bulkhead. The other team would be in their places by now. Sam's decision to split the group's effort had worried her at first, but it had resolved in a satisfactory fashion. Though Sam wouldn't be in on the snatch, she had found a way to arrange things, anyway. When all else failed, there was always the magic.

Jacqueline checked her companions' readiness. Despite Ghost's distaste for action involving the arcology, five of his tribesmen had volunteered to come along. They were calm enough, veteran street fighters who looked fierce in their warpaint. She decided they would be good brawlers, though their presence would not significantly affect the plan. Most of them were barely modified; only their leader, the one named Jason, might be a problem. She wished there'd been more time to learn the full extent of his modifications, but she preferred him to Ghost. Jason was not as bright and lacked his leader's keen awareness, but she would still have to keep an eye on him.

Tsung, too. As the only other magician in the raiding party, she was a potential problem. So far, the mage had gone along blindly, seemingly unaware that Jacqueline's Karen Montejac image was an illusion.

If Tsung got suspicious, she might probe deep enough to discern the second spell. It would spoil everything if she became aware of the other illusion Jaq would be using on the Renraku personnel. It was her master's wish that Verner be blamed for the raid on the arcology. The illusion spell that would make Jaq appear to be Sam would handle that nicely. As Sam had been all business around Karen Montejac, Tsung was satisfied her latest conquest was safe from poaching and had shown little interest in Jaq. What a delight was Human arrogance and self-centeredness. It so often made Jaq's life easier.

Once it was clear that some gutter muscle was going along, Jaq thought it politic to match their number with her own troops. She had brought only five of her own mercenaries, not counting the rigger crew who manned the aircraft. They all had corporate war experience and appropriate modifications suited to their specialties. Well-seasoned pros, they had settled quickly into a reasonable squad. Disliking subterfuge, they had balked when told to wear the synthleathers and warpaint of tribesmen, but they soon gave in, joking roughly about what people would do for money. They were good troopers. Ten professional mercs would have easily carved the standard Renraku landing pad guards even with minimal gunfire. A motley assault by ragged Sprawl Indians would be a less effective psychological shock. Jaq hoped she wouldn't lose too many expensive mercs.

"ETA one minute," the pilot announced over the cabin speaker.

Clatters and rustles filled the cabin as weapons were checked. Tsung smiled and gave Jaq a thumbs up, which she returned. Then the mage put on a headset. "Dodger," she said into the pickup. After a moment, she repeated the name. Then she was frowning. "He was supposed to be in place to lock access to the landing pad."

"Perhaps he's too busy to answer," Jaq suggested.

"I don't like it."

"Like it or not, we're committed."

The Commuter's landing lights had come on.

The landing lights speared down onto the pad, highlighting the dust kicked up by the twin rotors as the craft dropped lower. A white-suited woman walked into the cone projected by the nose light, waving glowing red direction wands. She backed up leading the VTOL craft to a more centered position on the landing circle.

Crenshaw increased her glare compensation to peer through the brightness masking the aircraft. The Aztec sun design that marked the ship as belonging to Aztechnology's shuttle service gleamed on the tail fin. The cabin door popped open as soon as the craft's wheels touched down, and a tumble of figures exited.

"Verner," she said aloud, recognizing the first person coming down the short ladder. He had taken the bait, the story she had planted with the Ork.

There were others, including one vaguely familiar woman who was not Hart. Crenshaw forgot any question about the woman's identity as she recognized several faces among the Indians pouring from the Commuter. She had no names for those faces, but she knew them well enough. One of them, the squat one with mirror eyes, was the leader of the slime who had raped her after the traitor and the others had left for their run. This was an unexpected bonus. If he survived the trap, the two of them would have a little reunion, but this time, she'd be the one with power.

"They're here," Crenshaw said into her communicator. "Take them. Take them all down."

At her side, Hutten stiffened and stared at her with wide, dark eyes.

* * *

Jaq led her mercs out of the Commuter, spreading them to establish a perimeter and cover the aircraft against a rush from any direction. To any onlookers, the raiders would look like a troop of Indians led by the mage Tsung and her new paramour, the renegade Samuel Verner. As her mercs took their places, the people waiting behind the boarding barrier reacted to the invasion, but it was not the frenzied panic of a crowd. Instead, they split into small groups, drawing weapons as they moved. It was, as Jaq had feared, a trap. The single snatch was about to become a pitched battle.

"Code Alpha," she shouted. All around her, the mercs put their counterplan into effect. Rawlins, the heavy weapons specialist, snapped down his target sight and braced his assault rifle. As the underslung grenade launcher dumped a full clip against the observation deck window, concrete and glass joined the shrapnel exploding into the deck and showering on the landing pad. A banshee wail assaulted Jaq's ears as a stray fragment caromed off the whirling rotors of the Commuter.

Jaq smiled. There would be no snipers shooting down on them from the vantage of the observation deck. To her left, another of the mercs tossed smoke grenades, sending up billowing black clouds to screen the control center. Fugitive figures in white coveralls retreated through the growing black fog. The rest of the mercs laid down a fire pattern on the so-called passengers.

Tsung ran up and crouched at her side. "What in fragging hell do you think you're doing?"

"It's a trap," Jaq said calmly. "The passengers are all security. Can't you see their armor?"

Tsung snapped a glance. "Drek!"

"Grab Hutten," Jaq ordered, pointing at the tall man standing amid the scattering bodies. "We'll cover."

Tsung waved Jason and the other Indians forward. With them in a wedge ahead of her, she followed in a crouching run.

Jaq smiled. A glorious bit of mayhem.

Crenshaw's call came almost too late. The intruders opened fire as her people started to move. A few went down in the first volley and more tumbled to the concrete when the explosions ripped open the face of the arcology.

"No!" Hutten screamed at her side. "No!"

"Get down, you fool," Crenshaw ordered, putting a hand on his shoulder to drag him down.

With unsuspected ease, he batted free of her grip. Then his other hand snaked out, crumpling her clothes and the armor underneath as his fingers closed into a secure grip. Lifting her off her feet, his eyes were wild. "Betrayer! I won't let you do this. Not now. Not now! He promised me a life of my own."

Crenshaw struggled in his grip. Bracing against his arm, she threw a break grip into his elbow. As her hand struck an unyielding surface, she felt a shock of pain. Hutten wasn't modified; his madness must have spasm-locked his muscles beyond the leverage she could apply. There was no time for this. So far the invaders had kept their fire away from them, afraid to hit their treasure, but sooner or later a marksman would take her off Hutten's hands. Even spasmed muscles couldn't work if they were sliced; she extended her hand razors and raked them down Hutten's forearm.

Blood flowed over tattered clothing, but his grip never slackened. She struck again and again, not caring if she had to turn his arm into hamburger before he let go. His sleeve shredded to rags, and she saw the damage she was doing. Then her fear of being shot escalated to horror as she realized that the wounds were closing almost as fast as she made them.

This was not a man!

Panic threatened to overwhelm her, but she fought it back. Hutten had snarled when she cut him. If that meant he could feel pain, he was not invincible. She lashed her foot into his groin, knowing that he did at least one thing like a man.

Hutten whuffed in pain and surprise. He bent at the waist, enough that Crenshaw's second kick went wide and landed on the side of his knee. The leg buckled and the two of them went down. Crenshaw rolled away and came to her feet in a crouch.

Her antagonist landed sprawled, holding his genitals. One foot supported by the curb of the waiting area. Without hesitation, she stomped down, satisfied to hear the bone break. Hutten howled.

No, not invulnerable.

The firefight raged around them. Her scan took in the smoking observation deck. That was going to be trouble.

She had to minimize her own exposure, both to the shooting and to the repercussions. She bent over the writhing Hutten.

"You've earned this, whatever you are," she said, drawing her knife from the sheath at the back of her neck. The monofilament line grafted to its cutting edge would cut through almost anything, even the polysteel cord that bound Hutten's briefcase to the locked band on his wrist. She applied the blade to his arm and smiled at his scream.

Shaking the severed hand free of the still-sealed band, she started for the end of the pad, keeping low enough that the boarding area fences provided cover. The service door that was her destination would get her back into the arcology without passing through the firefight, which had intensified with the belated arrival of the Red Samurai reserves.

Crenshaw was reaching for the door control when something slammed her from behind. She hit the concrete hard, scraping painfully across its rough surface. The case's bloodied grip slipped from her fingers and skidded along beside her to stop, teetering, on the edge of the landing pad. She rolled over, ready to deal with whatever runner had caught her, then froze.

Hutten, teeth bared, held her ankle in an iron grip. He laid his no longer bleeding stump across her shin. As he snapped her leg bone, he said, "We'll start with this."

Crenshaw didn't scream until she saw the splintered edges of bone emerge through her skin. Heedless of the pain, she scrambled back, crashing into the fence that kept her from hurtling over the edge. Her frantic motion overturned the briefcase and it slipped, taking the fall from which the rail had saved her.

Hutten moved forward faster than she thought possible, but instead of attacking her again, he leaned over the railing and wailed. She turned her head in time to see the case hit a projection at a lower level and shatter open, spreading a debris of cassettes and chips to the wind. Hutten collapsed, bent over the fence.

A little leverage was all it would take to flip him. As her hand touched his ankle, he revived and slapped her away. Crenshaw tasted blood from her split lip. He reached down, hauled her up by the hair, and slammed her against the wall, pinning one arm against the hard surface.

"That was my ticket to life," he screamed into her face. Despite her leg and his speed, she was sure she still could get away if he was blind. She flicked out the razors on her free hand and raised her arm to strike, only to feel them slice into her own palm as he squeezed her fingers into a fist. Pale, but immensely strong despite its childlike size, his new hand crushed her bones and ground them together.

He wrenched her up again and swung her out and over the abyss. In a last act of defiance, she spat into his face. He licked the mixed blood and spittle from his face with a tongue that seemed inordinately long before releasing his grip.

She fell, knowing that she would reach terminal velocity unless she hit a projection. There wouldn't be enough left to put back together. She hoped she would black out before she struck.

# 52

One wall blinked, its images of the battle on Landing Pad 23 replaced by a detail of a racing woman pursued by a limping man who moved with uncanny speed. As he closed and they struggled, a briefcase toppled over the edge of the platform. It smashed against a projection and opened, scattering circuit boards and computer chips to the wind.

Darkness assaulted Dodger's senses as his hostess's cloak billowed out of its own accord, masking her and everything else from his sight. A keening wail overwhelmed the sounds of the firefight, and over all the cacophony, he heard her voice.

"Lost. For myself, no hope. Gone. Fled. For my scattered self, gone."

His sight returned and she had vanished.

The mad kaleidoscope began again, images racing across the facets. Within seconds, the tumult faltered as individual panels went dark or flared to stark white. Groups of panels froze en masse in blocks, crosses, or stepped triangles. Each geometric portrayed a different scene, but all the panels making up one shape displayed the same image. One showed a gold-eyed man struggling to free himself from fallen debris in a smoking room scattered with bodies. Another displayed a small cubicle where an emaciated decker lay sprawled across his board, the flesh around his datajack blackened. A third, which Dodger at first took to be a re-broadcast, was a window on the Renraku air traffic monitor center where the staff was casually sitting around. In the back of the scene, Dodger could see the reaction force pilots in their ready room, drinking, eating, and playing cards. Their wall clock showed the current time. There were other scenes from around the arcology as well, and they too showed no alarm. Then the facets of the floor froze in unison, having returned to Pad 23, where the Trojan shuttle was rising into the sky.

The fireball flared into being on the Renraku arcology's left flank. Three of the undercover guards were torched to cinders and a pair of over-eager Red Samurai were blown back, smoking, to their squad's position at the building entrance.

"Good shooting, Tsung," Jaq called out.

Tsung waved back and pointed at the remaining guards on the landing field. Jaq nodded and directed her mercs to pour on the fire. Tsung needed cover to catch Hutten.

Their target had gone down in a struggle with one of the Raku guards. Jaq hadn't expected the guard to come out on top, but she had. For a while, that is. Then Hutten chased her down and threw her from the platform. Now he stood there, looking bewildered.

When Sally reached him, his initial reaction was wary. She said something to him, but with the din of combat Jaq couldn't hear. It must have been words to the effect of, "We're here to rescue you," because Hutten looked at the Commuter, nodded, and lit out toward the aircraft. Sally and the Indians beat a fighting retreat.

No time like the present, Jaq decided. She scattered powder from her pouch into the wind and began to chant. Watching the progress of Hutten and the runners, she tried to pace the spell so that the timing would be perfect.

Debris, litter, and masonry skittered across the platform like autumn leaves before the wind. Luggage rolled on wheels or tipped end over end to race dropped weapons and loose tools to the growing wall in front of the Commuter. It was a meter high when Hutten hurdled it. It had grown to two meters when Tsung, intent on the pursuit, slammed into it. Three of the Indians went down before she could lead them through the smoke clouds and around to the sheltered side.

By then, Jaq had gotten Hutten on board and recalled her four remaining mercs. She was closing the hatch when Tsung spotted her.

"Wait for us," Tsung called, racing for the aircraft.

Jaq gave the order to lift. "Sorry, Tsung. I've got a delivery to make. Have fun with the Samurai."

Tsung and the Indians made a leap for the Commuter's landing gear as the VTOL rose from the landing pad. One of the Indians, Jason, managed a grip, but a quick response from the pilot shook him free. Jaq watched the Indian land hard and lie stunned. Tsung knelt next to him, gesturing with glowing hands. Her eyes were fixed on the Commuter as it climbed.

Jaq mustered her spell defenses to protect the aircraft and the pilot, only to feel the energies slide past and strike elsewhere. Jaq spun to find Hutten sprawled on the floor of the cabin. The mercs were drawing away in disgust as his skin bubbled and flowed.

"Have fun yourself, bitch," Sally's voice said over the radio link.

Dodger found himself able to move again, but he feared that his hostess's return would change that. In a way he couldn't describe, he felt her presence still. He wanted to run, jack out while he could, but he had seen the Commuter take off and Sally and Ghost's people behind. They needed help. He had to get out of here if he was going to do anything constructive.

He turned to find Jenny disappearing into one of the panels, which went dark before he could make sense out of the image it had been presenting. So that was the way out. Reasoning that the image might relate to Matrix positioning, he stepped up to the block that held nine pictures of the deceased decker. He was company property and his equipment would be linked for fast access. It would be a good place to start. Dodger walked forward and found himself in the subprocessor controlling security for Pad 23.

He couldn't have asked for a better location.

Accessing the camera records, he clipped a copy of the battle and tagged it onto the go-code he was supposed to send when the team had gotten Hutten. He slipped it down the link to the broadcast monitor and sent it out on priority transmit. Sam would at least know what had happened. Maybe he could figure it out.

A strong believer in backups whenever possible, Dodger readied his online storage to accept a dump of the trideo record. When he tried the access again, he got an error message. A quick check showed him that the file had been deleted since he had last accessed it. Wary, he fled the node.

It was a short hop into the pad's computer system. He activated the service lift and tapped a deck monitor to view the results of his handiwork. Pressed by the advancing Red Samurai, Sally was quick to take the anonymous offer of an escape route. She and the Indians rabbited onto the descending segment of the platform. They leaped off at the first sublevel, and Dodger sent the lift back up and locked it to seal off direct pursuit.

"Sally, are you all right?" he asked over the maintenance call system.

"Dodger! Where the hell have you been?"

"No time. Take the shaft down to Pad 19. Code 7723 opens the lock. I'll arrange something."

He could hear her calling him until he cut the link, but he had to keep moving. He locked all access doors to the sublevel before heading out to the subprocessor for Pad 19's control center. A deft touch slipped in an authorization for a corporate helicopter and scrambled a pilot to fly it. He tagged the request with a Code Orange designation to keep the rigger's mouth shut as long as he thought it was a legitimate company undercover operation. The note he left about what he'd done would trigger when Sally used the code he'd given her. She'd need to know what to expect before leaving the maintenance shaft for the pad. He realized that he should have added an authorization for helicopter armament, and was about to do so when the walls of the node began to go translucent. He fled again.

He skipped down to a slave node that ran the climate control for an office suite on the mall level, hoping the low security would leave him less visible. He wanted to go back and make sure that Sally and the boys got out all right, but he was afraid to return anywhere he had been. He just didn't have enough jazz to deal with this Ghost in the Machine.

He knew he had run as far as he could when the walls started to silver. While he still could, he jacked out.

"Good luck, Sally."

# 53

Sam looked out the window of the helicopter, not really seeing the fences and buildings that surrounded him. Ghost's departure signal had come almost half an hour ago. By now he would have led his tribesmen in through the perimeter of the United Oil dockyard. Sam had been surprised at how many volunteered after Ghost told them he would do it alone. But it hadn't been too many for Enterich to supply with arms. Sam didn't know how he would have stopped any of the warriors from accompanying Ghost, but he'd have tried if armor and weapons hadn't been available. Even well-equipped, the risks were great.

Things were still quiet, which he assumed to mean that all was well. A lot more bodies were going in than when he and Ghost had made their run into the facility, but this crowd was not going to try to get inside any buildings. They should be safe enough. With Dodger running cover on the arcology part of the operation, they were relying on a decker that Enterich supplied to override the perimeter alarms. She must have been good enough; the compound where the copter sat was close enough that Sam would have heard any gunfire or alarms. The only thing left to do was wait for the signal that Sally and Jaq had succeeded in lifting Hutten from the arcology. And worry.

It wasn't the best plan, but he had been heartened when Ghost's lieutenant and four buddies had decided to do the snatch. Sam was relieved that Sally would have some backup other than Jaq's mercs. Jason's crew wouldn't have been Sam's choice, but Sam wasn't choosing. Any bodies were better than trusting totally to the good will of Lofwyr's agent.

For the fourth time in the last half hour, he checked the case on the seat next to him to see that its circuits were in working order. Dodger was to tight-beamcast a trideo rec-

ord of their snatch for Sam to display when he confronted
the Dragon. It would be his proof that Hutten was hidden
safely away, a lever for dealing with Haesslich. Everyone
was sure Haesslich would be willing to negotiate to get his
precious doppelganger back safely, but no one believed the
Dragon would accept Sam's terms. Sam wasn't so sure himself, but he saw no other course. He must try to resolve this
in a way that would leave his conscience clear. If Haesslich
wouldn't listen, then there was always Ghost's way.

The unit beeped and the telltale indicated that it had received Dodger's coded signal. That was it. The snatch had
been made. Sam secured the receiver as soon as the transmission was complete.

"Indramin," he said aloud, knowing that the rigger was
listening. The rigger wasn't aboard, because Sam didn't
want anyone else to share the risk of facing the Dragon.
Indramin would be flying the helicopter by remote rig.
"Time to go."

The craft's engines coughed to life and the rotors began
to whirl up to speed. With a surge, the ship left the ground
and Sam was on his way to confront Haesslich.

The tail Hart had put on Crenshaw had led her to Greerson, who was surprisingly easy to convince that she, too,
was working with Crenshaw. The Dwarf, in turn, led her to
Verner's rendezvous point, where they'd watched as Verner
split his teams into two groups. From the talk overheard via
Greerson's long-range pickup, she knew that one of the teams
was headed for the arcology to snatch Hutten. The fools
would walk straight into Crenshaw's trap, but maybe they'd
save Hart the headache of taking out the Crenshaw bitch.

She was glad she'd decided to pass on trying to invade
the arcology. The chances of success seemed far too low.
The chances for a Matrix penetration weren't much better.
But if Jenny couldn't slip into the arcology's Matrix and get
a copy of the AI data from the doppelganger, Haesslich's
plan would come to naught. After tonight's raid, the Hutten
thing would be locked up tight, assuming it survived. Then
Haesslich would get nothing. She didn't like to think how
the worm would take that disappointment.

Hart had been intrigued when Verner split off from Ghost
Maker and his crew. Sensing that Verner was running a
complicated plan, she argued Greerson out of smoking Ver-

ner as soon as he was alone. The Dwarf agreed to wait till they could find out what he was up to, confident he could take Verner whenever he wanted. Following Verner, they had spent almost an hour watching him sit in the darkened helicopter. When the sound of the craft's engine drifted on the breeze, Hart was confused. No one had come to join Verner and now he was leaving. Whatever his plan, it must now be in motion. Without air transportation, she and the Dwarf wouldn't be able to follow him. So if they were going to deal with him, it had to be right now. Hart wondered if she would ever know what he was up to.

"He's airborne," Greerson said, shoving the binocular goggles up onto his forehead.

Hart stared into the night, searching for the source of the rotor's sound. She finally caught the moving shadow that was the copter. It was running without lights, moving in their general direction.

"You know, Elf lady, I thought for a while there you had something. Drek, you might still, but even your long legs can't pace a helo. Old A.C. is gonna have a metacow when neither you or Verner shows up for her party, but at least I'll get the bounty on his head." Greerson stripped off the goggles and shook out his hair, then reached for the missile launcher he had prepared as soon as they had taken station. Hart forestalled the move with a touch on the Dwarf's arm.

"We've been on his tail longer. Squatter's rights."

"Whatever," the Dwarf shrugged. "Long as the suitboy don't see daylight, I get paid."

Hart activated her transceiver. "Tessien. He's in a dark helo moving south along the waterfront toward us. He's all yours."

The flight was short, barely a hedge hop, but that suited Sam fine. Less time to get cold feet. The copter swept in low over the United Oil perimeter fence and settled down softly in an open space near the wharf. There were no challenges, no alarms, no gunfire. Enterich's informants must have been right about Haesslich accepting delivery privately. It did fit the pattern of the Dragon wanting as few witnesses as possible. Even a circumstantial connection had been enough for him to order the murder of Hanae and Sam.

As soon as the craft's rotors slowed, Sam slipped into his long coat, hefted the case over one shoulder, and climbed out. Walking clear of the copter, he set his burden down and gazed around him. The area seemed deserted. Haesslich, in either Human or Dragon form, was nowhere in sight.

He waited. Behind him, the blades of the helicopter stopped turning, but the distant sound of a jet far overhead made him look up. Moving against the stars was a dark shape heading in from the Sound. As it drew nearer, he made out a long, sinuous body slung between a pair of large wings and knew it for a dracoform.

It was just offshore when Sam realized this could not be Haesslich. It was no Western Dragon, but a feathered serpent. A taloned hind limb unfolded down from its tucked position as the serpent swept toward him.

Suddenly, the serpent checked its approach and veered higher. Sam saw why as a dark shape, bulkier than the serpent, rose on great membranous wings. Even in the low light, Sam had no doubt that this second creature *was* a Western Dragon. It cut across the path of the first.

A hiss, a roar, the crash of massive bodies colliding, and they were past each other, a flurry of feathers tumbling in the wind of their passage. The serpent's flight became erratic, its wings beating irregularly. The Western Dragon banked wide and returned in a stooping dive. This time, Sam saw the talons score bloody furrows in the other's flank. The serpent screamed its agony and twisted, trying to avoid the jaws snapping at him.

As those jaws closed on the serpent's neck, the weakened beast responded by wrapping its own body around the Western Dragon. Both began to plummet from the sky. Ten meters from the ground, the Western Dragon broke free of the serpent's coils, wings beating furiously to stay in the air. The mortally wounded serpent continued its descent, then struck the concrete wharf with an earthshaking crash.

The other pounced on it, tearing with claws and ripping with jaws. *"Hart!"* the serpent cried out plaintively, just before the Western Dragon tore out its throat.

The victor raised his head, tongue slithering out to lick his muzzle clean. When a tentative pawing aroused no response from the serpent, the beast turned its back on the corpse and marched toward Sam.

"Haesslich," Sam said.

*"Good evening, manling."*

Pinned under the beast's fearsome stare, Sam began to wonder what had possessed him to attempt this. A Dragon was unpredictable, at least to Human logic. How could he expect it to yield to any pressure he might try to apply? "Why did you kill Tessien? I thought it was on your payroll."

Contempt swelled around Sam. *"It was, but I have no use for those who fail me. I have less for those who lie to me, as it did when first reporting your demise. It will, however, make a good meal."*

"It made a mistake, so you *killed* it? And now you're going to eat it?"

*"Of course. Its associate will meet a similar fate when she arrives with my delivery."*

"I won't let that happen."

*"But you can't stop it, manling."* The Dragon's amusement rolled across Sam. *"I thought you might be trouble when we first met, but such has not been the case. Your poking and prying into my business has been totally ineffectual. I need never have been concerned."*

Sam hated this arrogant beast, and wanted desperately to humble him. What Haesslich had done, what he planned to do, were wrong, but the Dragon seemed not to know it. Sam no longer had any doubts about what he must do. Tonight, the menace of Haesslich would be stopped.

"You should be concerned," he said. "I know that your operation at the arcology was set up without the approval or knowledge of your bosses at United Oil. They won't help you now. It's not in their interest to protect a murderer who uses their assets for his own purposes. Once the evidence becomes public, UniOil will be glad to see you get the full penalty under the law. Your arrogance seems to have no limit, Dragon, but people are not toys for your amusement nor will you get away with committing murder.

"I came here tonight to offer you a chance to surrender. Give yourself up to the police and stop the bloodshed. You might earn the court's mercy. But even if you don't turn yourself in voluntarily, you'll still be brought to trial."

*"Unlikely,"* Haesslich responded, his amusement growing.

Exactly the answer Sam had expected. What he hadn't anticipated was the undertone in the Dragon's emotional broadcast. *Hunger.* His knees felt weak; he hadn't thought

about being *eaten*. He felt his resolve waver, then he remembered Hanae and Begay. They were good people whose
lives had been cut short at the whim of this beast. He knew
very little about the others who had been killed that night
in the Tir, but it still added up to too many deaths at Haesslich's orders. Tonight would be the end. Sam straightened
to his full height, craning his neck to stare into the face of
the Dragon. Haesslich's fangs glittered in the moonlight.

"Are you going to kill me now?" Sam asked, with a calm
that surprised him. "I won't make much of a meal, but
you'll choke on it."

Sam felt a peculiar vibration in the Dragon's emotional
tone. He decided it must be the Dragon's laughter.

*"Your death is no longer necessary. I will have what I
want when Hart brings it to me tonight. You and your threats
have become meaningless, but your bluff amuses me."*

"You're wrong, Dragon. Your plan isn't concluded tonight, it's exposed." Sam flicked the replay switch.
"Watch."

A ghostly image of the scene at Landing Pad 23 lit up the
wall of a nearby structure. The Federated Boeing Commuter
bearing Aztechnology markings was just landing.

Hart had felt Tessien's death. Hearing it call her name
had chilled her to the bone, telling her it had never betrayed
her, that her suspicions had been misplaced. Tears stream-
ing from her eyes, she stood staring while Haesslich talked
to Verner. She listened in shocked silence as the long-range
pickup relayed every word. She shivered when Haesslich
pronounced her death sentence.

"Looks like you're out of work, chummer," Greerson
said, revealing that he had not really believed Hart's story
about working for Crenshaw. The implications of Hart's
failed duplicity seemed unimportant right now. Greerson
crouched at her feet, assembling a sniper rifle. "But I've
still got a contract on the kid. Don't suppose you'd like to
put one on the wizworm? That launcher'll do him as easy
as a helo. Once Verner's down, I'll be glad to open nego-
tiations."

Hart was not much interested in death at the moment.
"What's the point?"

"The point is business, Elf lady. Always business."

Hart stared at the wreck that had been Tessien, the only

being she had come close to trusting in the last ten years. It was dead now. It had died calling for her, but she had failed it long before that with her groundless suspicions.

Tessien was dead. Anger roared through her, swelling into a rage. Was it Verner's fault? Should she detest him for being alive while Tessien was dead? Or should she turn her fury against Haesslich for ripping out the serpent's throat? Or should she despise herself for being the one to send Tessien in to get Sam, putting the serpent in the path of the murderous Haesslich?

Verner's portable trideo unit continued flickering its story on the wall. It showed Verner, who she had trailed all night and who could not possibly have been present, leading the raiders against Landing Pad 23. Crenshaw's trap had turned a snatch-and-run into an all-out battle. Images of death and destruction cast their reflections on man and Dragon. On the wall, Crenshaw battled with the doppelganger. Hart dropped a hand to Greerson's shoulder. "I think you'd better take a look."

Greerson slipped his goggles into place just in time to see the doppelganger tossing Crenshaw from the landing platform. "Oh, frag it!" He sat down and let out an explosive sigh. "There goes the paycheck." He started to break down the sniper rifle.

"What are you doing?"

"What does it look like, Elf lady? Packing up. This job's over." He stuffed the pieces of his weapon into his carryall. "Sure you don't want to hit the Dragon? Since I'm already here, I could give you a good price."

She shook her head.

"I'll throw in a professional discount."

"I think if it's to be done, it ought to be personal."

Greerson then shook his head and scratched at his beard. "Personal is bad business, Elf lady. Can I get out the way we got in?"

She nodded, turning her gaze back to the confrontation below them. She heard the rattle of his grapnel as he shook it loose and then she forgot him completely.

Haesslich didn't like what he saw at all. If he had noticed Sam's image on the screen, the confusion of the image was swept away by the Dragon's passion. His rage swelled until it was almost a palpable thing surrounding Sam. And yet all that wrath was simply for the failure of a plan. Again the arrogance of the beast confounded Sam.

As he watched the recording, the sight of his own image was a puzzle, though unimportant at the moment. He was seeing men die. Some died trying to do good; others died trying to do their duty. Shadowrunner or corporate, they were just as dead. He watched himself double-cross and abandon Sally and the others, realizing suddenly that the Sam Verner he was seeing must be some kind of disguise for Jacqueline. What should have been a lightning snatch, leaving the Renraku guards too surprised and outgunned to react, had been twisted into the orgy of death, destruction, and betrayal. Everything connected to Haesslich's plans, his petty attempts to increase his power, wealth, and influence, ended in death. But the only thing the Dragon saw was that he had been thwarted.

Haesslich's bitterness crackled in the air. Watching the beast scream its rage, Sam knew it would not suffer him to live much longer. The Dragon could not know that Sam had been betrayed by agents of yet another Dragon, nor would it care.

The Dragon arched its neck back and bellowed, flames flickering about its teeth in promise of a firestorm to come. Sam hoped it wouldn't be quicker than the jaws. *Death for death,* Lofwyr had said, but the Dragon hadn't quite meant it this way. *Dying is easy; it's the next part that gets tricky,* Dog had said. Well, the next part was in other hands. Haesslich would reap what he was about to sow.

A song began to run through Sam's head; it was sung by the quavering voice of Dog. What a crazy time to have a song stuck in his head. Wasn't his life supposed to be flashing before his eyes? Well, he had heard that crazy people felt no pain. He began to sing along.

Haesslich tilted his head down, lips curling back from his teeth. *"It's but a minor consolation to see your mind snap with fear before your body burns."*

"Come on, wizworm," Sam shouted giddily, his words seeming to keep time with the song. "Come and get me if you can."

As the Dragon unleashed his fiery breath, Sam staggered back, the blast wreathing him in flames. Sweat poured off, to be instantly evaporated away. Beneath his feet, the asphalt softened and bubbled. Within the fire, cocooned by the spell song, he was untouched.

With the Dragon's violence as their cue, Ghost and his tribesmen opened fire from their concealed positions. Haesslich roared, more in surprise than pain, venting flame into the sky. Uncoiling his powerful hind limbs, he launched himself into the night, giant wings spread and beating the air.

The Dragon rapidly gained altitude, escaping the tracers that sought him. Then, with a sudden wing over and a bellow, he dove toward the largest group of attackers.

The sight drove some of Ghost's tribesmen to flight, but the samurai leader remained steady, standing braced against the parapet. Even his loader fled, leaving the pack of belt-fed ammunition to lie at the Ghost's feet. The light metal box leapt from its cloth carry sack and danced on the rooftop as the belt uncoiled to feed the voracious appetite of the Vindicator minigun.

The Dragon dodged and rolled to avoid the stream of tracers seeking his hide, but each maneuver only forced him to spend more time trying to reach his attackers. Ghost swiveled the gyro-mount to follow each slip and jink, always pumping more slugs into the beast, who could not completely avoid the Indian's fire. Crisscrossed with wounds, chunks torn from his flesh, Haesslich pulled up into a stall, throwing off the deadly aim of the man on the roof.

Then Haesslich rolled into another dive, again surprising Ghost, whose tracers cut the night a full twenty meters from the beast. Wounded beyond endurance, the Dragon suddenly dropped from the air like a rock, straight into the dark waters of Puget Sound. The waters closed over him and Haesslich was gone.

# 54

Sam knelt in the asphalt, the heat spreading through the komex fabric of his jumpsuit. Spread around him, the tails of his long coat were scorched and blackened. By his side, the trideo unit was a slag heap.

*Death for death,* Lofwyr had said. And the great golden Dragon's sentence had come to pass. Haesslich's death had paid for Hanae's, but that had not been what Sam had set out to do. He had wanted proper justice, but got revenge instead. Any attack on his person was the signal for Ghost and his tribesmen to open fire, springing an ambush Haesslich couldn't escape. The Dragon had brought death on himself by trying to kill Sam. *Death for death.* Sam had expected to die tonight, trading his own life so that the Dragon could be caught in one of his crimes. Wasn't it justice that a murderer be killed in an attempt at murder?

Sam was very tired, but there was no time to rest. He'd settled with Haesslich, but the people who'd laid their lives on the line to help him were not yet safe. Jaq had abandoned Sally on the arcology. If Sally had been taken alive, he'd have to find a way to free her. He wondered if Ghost had seen the replay of the fight on Landing Pad 23; it would have been a difficult angle. If he hadn't seen, he would have to be told.

Sam had to leave the UniOil grounds before anyone showed up to ask embarrassing questions. The Dragon's roars and the gunfire would have United Oil security on its way right now. He scanned the roof from which Ghost had downed the Dragon. It was empty. Ghost would be withdrawing the men to the rendezvous point; he knew better than to dawdle. All Sam had to do was board the copter and have Jaq's rigger fly him out the way he had come in. Wearily, he hauled himself to his feet and trudged to the aircraft. Once inside, he threw himself down in the seat.

"Time to go home, Indramin."

There was no response. No voice. No engine.

Out in the compound a siren began to wail.

Lights were coming on across the compound as the siren screamed mournfully. Hart looked down the alley that gave her a view of the security field office and saw heavily armed guards pouring out. In their midst, she made out the personal combat armor of Major Fuhito. The dockyard wasn't his normal turf; he only came here when he had to. The ambitious bastard must have been keeping an eye on his boss's doings and played a hunch to be here tonight. It was probably Haesslich's own order to stay clear that had tipped him off. He was obviously expecting trouble, too, for he was already armored up.

Hart watched Verner pelt out of the helo and look around for which way to go. His chummers had already melted into the night. He was on his own.

She could show him the way out, but why should she? What did she owe him? Tessien's death. Haesslich's too, by the look of things. That thought disturbed her a little. Didn't the law call a life for a life an even balance?

The guards would corner Verner if he didn't take the right path. A rat like Fuhito wouldn't treat him kindly, especially when he realized that Verner was a corporate runaway. Did she hate Verner enough to let Fuhito get him? He'd shown himself a canny and resourceful runner. Or maybe he was just a lucky one. Either way, Hart had seen enough death tonight. She didn't have the heart to watch him go down.

She ran to the edge of the roof, and saw him hug the wall and check the shadows ahead before taking the corner. Her whistle snagged his attention. His head snapped up and his hand pulled back his long coat to let him grip the handle of his gun. She held her hands in his sight, away from her body. "No hard feelings, Verner. It was just business, but the contract's over now."

He didn't answer, but seemed to relax a little.

She gave him a smile and reached down slowly to ripple the rope that dangled to the road below. "Come on, let me show you the back door."

She watched the struggle on his face as he realized he was trapped without her help. Hart could also see he didn't trust her, for which she couldn't blame him.

A hissing like mad tea kettles rose from beyond the next building. The cockatrices were out as well as the guards.

Verner dashed across the roadway and started up the rope.

Sam watched Hart walk away. Ever since he had learned her name, Sam had thought of her as a hard-hearted, mercenary killer. Hadn't she tried to kill him before? But instead of leaving him to the guards and the cockatrices, she'd saved him. To think that he'd hoped she would run afoul of the Red Samurai at the airport. For more than the sake of his own hide, Sam was strangely relieved that she hadn't met up with the Samurai.

Hart clearly had her own concerns and agenda. Had Haesslich double-crossed her the way Lofwyr had him? What were her motives? When he had questioned her, she had snapped at him, telling him to shut up.

Alone now, he looked up at the sky. Clouds had come in to cover the stars. It would rain soon.

All he needed now was . . .

Barking came from the direction Hart had taken. When Sam turned his gaze back that way, he saw a dog come loping from the darkness of an alley. The animal was scrawnier and dirtier from living and scrounging on the street, but Sam immediately recognized him as Inu. The dog must have escaped from the arcology, but after the events of this night, Sam barely paused to wonder how the animal should suddenly appear here and now.

Inu was alone, so perhaps Kiniru remained behind in the arcology. That was just as well. The akita had never learned to make her own way; she was as dependent on people as he had once been on his corporation. But Inu was a street being and would never forget it.

Sam crouched, grinning, then let the animal bowl him over with its enthusiastic greeting. After a few minutes of getting reacquainted, the two were trotting down the street again on their way to rescue the fair Lady Tsung.

Jaq watched her team mask the windows of the Commuter. In minutes, the golden sun would be replaced with the green and silver MCT of Mitsuhama Computer Technologies. Without checking the craft's registration number, no observer would be able to tell the Commuter from a legitimate member of the Mitsuhama fleet. Her team was very good at this sort of thing.

The mercs had been paid off, with a handsome tip thrown in. They had performed well enough that she would use them again in the future.

While the Commuter was being readied, a pair of laborers were building a crate to house the stabilization unit. A freight container would be a lot less conspicuous and easier to bribe past customs than an active stabilization unit holding a deceased doppelganger. When the sound of their hammers stopped abruptly, Jaq turned to find them staring at Mr. Enterich.

"That's enough for now, boys," she said, stepping up. "Coffee break."

The workers dropped their tools and vanished.

Enterich stepped onto the base of the crate from the side that was still open. He stared at the displays. "Dead?"

"Cold and stiff, courtesy of Sally Tsung."

"I was looking forward to acquiring whatever Haesslich had sent it in to get."

"Well, he didn't get it, either," she offered nervously. "We did get a set of three skillsofts that were embedded in a custom subdermal chip mount. Preliminary scans showed them to be compendiums of computer architecture parameters. No doubt they allowed the construct to simulate the real Konrad Hutten's expertise."

Enterich showed no interest.

"The chips are very well designed. They're not unique, but I'm sure I can find a market. The sale should offset some of the operation's expenses."

Enterich stared at her with cold, flat eyes. "The doppelganger was the goal of this operation. You were to bring it to me alive."

"It wasn't *my* fault. Tsung hit it with a spell when I thought she was going after the aircraft. I couldn't protect it." She hoped he wouldn't get too angry. "Maybe there's something to be learned from the corpse. The stabilization unit should hold the cells intact enough to do DNA assays. The Genomics research labs are good at that."

"Let us hope you're right," he said, leaning over to gaze into the unit.

Jaq also crowded in for a look. She frowned, realizing that something about it wasn't quite right. Then she noticed a mist on the inner surface of the viewing plates. She checked the monitors; the unit was functioning well within operational parameters. The fragging thing should have been stable, but instead the body was starting to decompose.

Enterich's fist slammed down on the unit, sending a tracery of cracks through the Transparex. Jaq backed away. Her master was very unhappy.

# 55

When Sam rejoined Ghost and his tribesmen at the rendezvous point, he found that the fair Lady Tsung didn't need rescuing after all. She was on the radio.

"Where are you?" Sam asked, not caring who heard the concern in his voice.

"Riding high," she answered with a laugh. "Dodger rented us a chopper with a very cooperative pilot. We'll be putting down near Hillary's in about twenty minutes."

"I'll see that Cog has a car waiting," Ghost cut in. "You're all well?"

"Willy, Roadrunner, and Eagle Eyes have joined their ancestors." Sally's voice was sober now. "The rest of us are still walking. Wouldn't hurt to have Cog put some med supplies in the car, though."

"They'll be waiting," Ghost assured her.

"Wiz! See everyone soon." She cut the connection.

Sam threw back his head and sighed. Sally's safety lifted his worry about having to deal with Renraku again. The trideo Dodger had boosted from the arcology's security cameras clearly showed Sam leading the raiders. He had no idea how Jaq had managed that trick, but what did it matter? As far as Renraku was concerned, it was Sam who had led the attack against Pad 23. Thanks to Jaq's betrayal, his bridges had been well and truly burned behind him.

His status as an enemy of the corporation was now guaranteed, which meant he'd have been unable to negotiate Sally's release. Freeing her would have required staging another raid and Sam thanked God it hadn't been necessary. There'd already been too much damage done and too many lives lost.

Whatever the price, Sam knew he would have paid it, though. Sally and the others were his family now; his first loyalty was to them. He had left the corporate cocoon behind forever. When he opened his eyes, Ghost was staring at him.

"How did you manage to get out of the dockyards, paleface?"

"Hart helped me. I don't know why, but she did."

"Then Haesslich must be dead."

"We both saw him go down into the Sound. I didn't see him come up. Did you?"

"We were too busy dodging UniOil heat to see much of anything beyond the way out."

Sam was concerned by Ghost's reserved tone. "Did you have trouble?"

"No."

Ghost's denial was refuted by the shouts of his tribals. Each vied with the others to recount the most hair-raising encounter of their escape, but all acknowledged that Ghost had been vital to their success. The uproar continued until Dodger showed up.

The Elf looked haggard, but was still smiling. He and Ghost gripped arms, patting each other on the shoulder. Pleasure lit their faces, but they said not a word. Then Dodger turned to Sam, gripping him by the shoulders and shaking him. Inu barked defensively until Sam shushed him.

"Sir Twist, I am pleased to see you still with us. Circumstances conspired to make a shambles of your plan, but 'twould seem that things have turned out well in the end. I prithee, though, ask me not to trespass in Renraku's Matrix ever again."

"I thought you would dare any system. What's the matter? Your skills slipping?"

" 'Tis not the loss of my prowess that I fear. 'Tis what lurks within that icy black pyramid."

"And just what is that?"

"An artificial intelligence that is beyond their control."

"What? Dodger, what are you talking about?"

Dodger told of his capture and the room of mirrors, his voice becoming hushed as he described the persona construct that echoed his own. Listening to the story of the Elf's flight and escape, Sam would probably have dismissed the tale if it had come from anyone else. It sounded like another Ghost in the Machine story.

"Are you sure it was real?" he asked.

"As real as anything is under the electron skies," Dodger confirmed gravely.

"Well, it wasn't good enough to hold the Dodger. You got out, didn't you?"

"In that, you speak true." The Elf's mood shifted away from gloom, turning to positive pleasure when Sally led the surviving raiders into the room.

Sam caught her up in a whirling embrace while Inu danced around them barking. He kissed her, delighting in the warmth of her body. She returned his kiss as though it might be the last one she'd ever receive. When they broke their embrace, the tribesmen crowded around, eager to hear her tale. While she told it, Sam looked around for Ghost, but he had vanished like his namesake.

The raiders exchanged tales of their heroism, their shouted boasts and congratulations more an expression of relief that they had lived through another run in the shadows.

"Party's on me," Sally announced suddenly.

Amid the cheers, Dodger leaned over and whispered to Sam, "The lady's victory parties are legend."

"What victory? Death is no payment for death. It just extends the cycle."

"Naetheless, Sir Twist, the sword of justice smote the guilty. The shades of Hanae, Josh Begay, and those benighted runners who worked for Hart understand the rightness of what has been done."

"And that's the victory?"

"Oh, no," the Elf laughed, dragging Sam after the departing shadowrunners. "Our victory is the only real one. We survived."

At the door of the building, Sam stopped, watching as Sally led the runners down the street in a ragged, rowdy parade. They were dirty and bloodied and had lost good friends, but they laughed. They were exuberant, elated at having defied death and won.

When several of the tribesmen started a chant, the sound echoed in his head, bringing back snatches of Dog's song. He realized that the words were a hymn to life, a celebration of possibilities. The song filled him with a joy that he had been denying. Hours ago, he had stared into the jaws of death, yet he had not been dragged down into that darkness. He had survived to return to the shadows, where life poised on a razor edge.

He understood the runners' exhilaration now. He was alive! Death and darkness hadn't claimed him today, and that was more than enough cause for celebration. He felt free. His blood raced and he could no longer hold back. Capering away from Dodger, he spun up the street in a wild dance whose steps he invented as he went along. Inu raced around him, yapping his own excitement.

"Come on, Dodger," Sam called. "It won't do to disappoint the lady."

"Nay. 'Twould never do," Dodger replied, shaking his head. With a stretch of his long legs, the Elf passed Sam and started the race to catch up with Sally.

The dog, of course, won.